VIOLETTE MALAN

THE SOLDIER KING

A Novel of Dhulyn and Parno

DAW BOOKS, INC.

DONALD A. WOLLHEIM, FOUNDER

375 Hudson Street, New York, NY 10014

ELIZABETH R. WOLLHEIM

SHEILA E. GILBERT

PUBLISHERS

www.dawbooks.com

First Printing, September 2008
1   2   3   4   5   6   7   8   9

DAW TRADEMARK REGISTERED
U.S. PAT. AND TM. OFF. AND FOREIGN COUNTRIES
—MARCA REGISTRADA
HECHO EN U.S.A.

PRINTED IN THE U.S.A.

For Paul

Acknowledgments

As always. my first thanks go to Joshua Bilmes and Sheila Gilbert, without whom Dhulyn and Parno would be practicing their *Shora* where no one else could see them. To my friend Barb Wilson-Orange who listened to the story before it reached paper; to Sue Rohland, for her enthusiasm and helpful critiques; to Grant and Jenn Musselman (and Devin) for their unfailing support; to Stephan Furster for looking after my website; to Vaso, Maria and Jovanna Angelis, for their support, and their help in keeping me decently clothed. To Tanya Huff and Fiona Patton, always for everything. I'd particularly like to thank Brian Henry, for all those useful writing workshops, and all his support since those days, not so long ago.

Megan Primeau, better known as "Megz," purchased at silent auction the right to have a character named after her. I salute you, the Queen's White Blade.

One

P ARNO LIONSMANE LOOKED OVER the battlefield that was the valley of Limona with his nose wrinkled. Every soldier became used to the smell of the dead and dying, but not even Mercenary Brothers ever got so that they liked it. From his fidgeting, it seemed to Parno that even his big gray gelding, Warhammer, battle-trained as he was, would just as soon be elsewhere.

"What happened here?" Parno asked.

"Exactly what was supposed to happen. Exactly what I Saw in my Vision." His Partner, Dhulyn Wolfshead, shrugged, making the red cloak she'd won off Cavalry Squad Leader Jedrick swing around her knees. "Against odds, the Tegrians lost and the Nisveans won. Which is why, I remind you, we signed on with the Nisveans."

"So what *happened*? Has the Blue Mage lost his power?"

Still looking out over the field sloping away from them toward the banks of the river Limona, Dhulyn shook her head, her lip curling back in her wolf's smile. "Don't be naive."

There was movement to be seen between them and the river, the living going through the pockets of the dead.

"Well, I'm not going to rob corpses, no matter what you Saw."

"There's nothing in the Common Rule against it," Dhulyn said. "I once got a very nice thumb knife off a dead man."

"Outlander."

"Town man." She gave him the smile she saved only for him.

As Mercenary Brothers, they were not obliged to pursue those who fled from the field of battle, and Dhulyn—who was, after all, Senior Brother—had decided to look over the fallen instead.

"Do you think it very likely that we will find any of your kin here?" Parno said.

"No more likely than anywhere else," she replied. "But it's easy enough to check."

That was true. Dhulyn's distinctive coloring, pale eyes, pale skin, her hair the color of old blood, would make a person easy to find among the fallen of a battlefield. If, that is, there were in fact any other survivors of the catastrophe which had wiped out the tribes when she was a child.

"But you didn't *See* any Red Horsemen here?" Parno looked sideways at his Partner. Her lips were pressed together, her eyes scanning the far edges of the valley.

"Come now, my heart," he said. "We haven't been looking, *truly* looking that is, for very long, a few moons, no more. Don't lose heart so soon. Your Sight *is* getting better," he told her. "Since you started using the vera tiles, it's not so erratic." He scratched at the stubble on his chin.

Dhulyn's head moved in short arcs from side to side. "My Mark could be more useful if I could control it completely."

Parno drummed his fingers on his thigh. Let her tell him something he didn't already know. "Let's look on the sunny side," he said. "If we meet any more Red Horsemen, and they are anything like you, it might be more than I could tolerate."

Dhulyn looked at him without moving her head. She gestured at the corpse-strewn valley before them. "My people couldn't possibly cause as much trouble as *yours*." She brought her heels in sharply, and her mare, Bloodbone, leaped away.

"In Battle," Parno called out to her back.

"In Death," answered the sign from her lifted hand.

Parno let Warhammer set his own pace as they picked their way slowly out to the eastern edge of the valley. *Not much of a battle*, he thought, looking at the preponderance of Tegriani on the ground. *Slaughter's more the word*. The Tegriani invaders must have been shocked indeed when they began to take heavy wounds, but many were veterans of the days before the Blue Mage began to work his magics on their armies, and they had been holding their own until the Nisvean reserve, which included Parno and Dhulyn, had fallen on their left flank. Then the Tegriani had broken and run, and far more of them were cut down as they fled than would have been killed had they only stood their ground.

But then, they hadn't expected to be killed. Even now, their dead faces showed surprise.

Parno reined in as Warhammer shied to the left. From the look of the corpse at the horse's feet, this section had been picked over already, though a short cloak had been left behind, evidently too torn and bloody to be worth taking. The body looked to have been a man in his early twenties, his only wound the bleeding shoulder.

Parno leaned out of his saddle, narrowing his eyes. The *bleeding* shoulder? He swung his leg over Warhammer's withers and let himself slide to the ground. Squatting, he gave the body a long hard look, and pulled a corner of the cloak over the wound—and over the corpse's face while he was at it.

"Keep that shoulder covered," he said, his voice a low murmur that wouldn't travel far. "You're still bleeding, and dead men don't bleed. Wait until the moon's set, if you can, and then go south a good few spans before you turn west." He grunted in satisfaction when the man showed no reaction whatsoever and, turning away, climbed back into the saddle.

Doing his best to appear just as relaxed as he had been before, Parno began to angle his horse toward the river's edge, away from the "corpse," toward the bright splotch of red that was Dhulyn. She was leaning so far out of the saddle that anyone other than the Red Horseman she was would have fallen off. When she straightened, and then slid off Bloodbone's back, Parno clucked his tongue, and touched his heels to Warhammer's sides.

Dhulyn Wolfshead pursed her lips and blew out her breath in a silent whistle as she scanned the ground. They said all battlefields looked the same, but any real soldier, let alone a Mercenary Brother, could tell you that it depended which side you were on, victors or defeated. That young man right there, for example, with his leather jerkin slipping off his shoulder, holding a bloody cloth to the arrow through his thigh—she'd wager her second-best sword he and she saw the dead and the dying around them entirely differently.

And he'd be watching her approach with an entirely different look on his face if she were an ally.

He looked away when she reined Bloodbone in and, still trying to hold the bloody rag to his leg, twisted around, stretching his hand for the sword that lay just out of reach to his left. Dhulyn dropped to the ground in time to kick the weapon just a little farther away.

"From the angle and distance," she said, as if they were sitting across a tavern table from one another talking about the weather. "You came off this dead horse as it fell, and dropped that Teliscan blade you can't quite reach as you hit the ground yourself." She twisted her lips to one side, propped one fist on her hip, and measured the distances again by eye before nodding and squatting down on her heels.

"Furthermore, that jerkin is too large for you, and no soldier wearing such a thing would be riding this horse, carrying that blade, or—" she poked him in the region of his collarbone where a hard corner clearly showed through the leather. "Or be carrying a book under it." She shook her head. "There's others on this field not so experienced as I, who might actually believe you were just the common soldier you're pretending to be. And they'd cut your throat for you as not worth tending. So right off, my little lordling, I'd remove that leather jerkin you've borrowed and get back into this nice tooled breastplate you've tried to hide under your horse's carcass." Dhulyn straightened and nudged the item in question a handspan closer to him with her toe. "Sorry about your horse, by the way, he looks like a fine animal."

"And *you* won't cut my throat?" Blood and dirt were ground into the creases of his fingers. His hair was black and curly, his eyes dark, and he looked to be naturally olive-skinned under his present dirt and pallor.

Dhulyn raised her left eyebrow, wondering if she should be offended . . . and then smiled. Of course. She pushed back the hood of the cloak she'd forgotten she was wearing. She'd braided some feathers into her hair, and hadn't wanted to get them wet. Now the lordling could see her green-and-blue Mercenary badge tattooed into the skin where the hair had been removed on her temples and above her ears.

"I am Dhulyn Wolfshead, called the Scholar. Schooled by Dorian the Black," she said formally.

The young man relaxed so completely Dhulyn was almost sure a tear or two leaked from his eyes. "I give you my surrender," he said, in a voice that trembled.

"And I accept it. What were you thinking?" She crouched down on her heels and took hold of the bloodied rag, pressing firmly as the young lord stripped off the leather jerkin and struggled back into the inlaid and crested breastplate. She clucked and reached out one-handed to help him with the side ties, pushing the small bound book back into its place against his breastbone. Of course such armor was never meant to be put on by oneself, let alone while lying down in one's own blood.

Not that *much* of this blood was his.

"I didn't want to be held for ransom," he said. "I thought I could get away."

The young man's head was turned away, so Dhulyn smiled her wolf's smile. "This your first campaign, is it? Thought they'd let you walk away, did you? Well let me School *you* a little, young lord. If you're not already dead, there's only three ways to leave a battlefield in this part of the world." She held up her left thumb. "Held for ransom if you're important enough," she held up a finger, "held for the slavers if you're not, and," a final finger, "throat cut if you're not whole enough to ransom or sell."

"There's a fourth way," he said, pulling his lips back in what was meant for a smile. Dhulyn softened her own grin. For all that his hands trembled, the boy had nerve, which was more than she could say for many a noble lord she'd met before.

"What have I forgotten, young lord?"

"Taken by Mercenary Brothers, who don't hold for ransom."

Dhulyn gave a short bark of laughter. "Why, how could we do that? This time next month we might be looking for work from you."

"We're not looking for work *already*, are we?"

It was a good thing she was holding on to the boy's leg; otherwise the start that he gave at hearing Parno's question would have caused him to do more than hiss as his wound moved.

"Come hold his leg while I pull the arrow out," Dhulyn said to her Partner. "It won't hurt much, young lord," she added, turning back to the boy in time to catch his grimace.

"Just one moment, my soul."

Dhulyn looked up at the hint of warning in Parno's voice. She frowned; he was lowering himself from the saddle far too stiffly for her taste. Anyone would think he was an old man.

"This isn't just some lordling you've got here," he said. "This is someone far more important."

Dhulyn looked into the boy's face and raised her eyebrows. He licked his lips, but said nothing. She turned back to Parno.

"Another of your High Noble Houses, is it?"

But her Partner was shaking his head. "Better. Or worse, depending on your view of it. Look at the crest on the saddlecloth," he said, "and right there on his breastplate for that matter. This is Lord Prince Edmir himself."

Dhulyn examined the boy again, with more interest. "*Is* he now? Then perhaps you can explain what happened here, Lord Prince Edmir? Where was the power of the Blue Mage that has kept you Tegriani undefeated these last two seasons?"

If possible, the boy became even paler under the blood and dirt. His lips moved, but his eyes rolled up before he could make a sound.

"He's fainted," Parno said.

Dhulyn shrugged. "Good. Easier to take out the arrow."

"You noticed the fletching?"

Dhulyn nodded. "A Tegrian prince, shot by a Tegrian arrow."

Parno squatted down beside her. "Never let it be said that the Mercenary life isn't interesting."

⌐⌐

Dhulyn breathed in deeply through her nose, counted to ten in the old language of the Caids and released the breath slowly, glancing around at the faces assembled in War Commander Kispeko's tent the next day. Parno, standing to her left, raised his right eyebrow and she raised her own in acknowledgment. Losing her temper would gain nothing. When she was sure her voice would be measured and even, she hooked her thumbs in her sword belt and spoke.

"By contracting with Mercenary Brothers, you accepted our Common Rule. Prisoners taken by us go free, unmolested and unransomed. These are the conditions of your contract with us, you cannot go back on it now."

"Come now, Wolfshead, surely you realize the situation has changed." The lines around War Commander Kispeko's eyes showed how little sleep he'd had the night before.

"No situation changes sufficiently for you to lose your honor by breaking your word." *No point dancing around it*, she thought.

"I wish I had the leisure to think in those terms, Mercenary."

Kispeko's voice was colder than it had been a moment before, and his left hand—his sword hand—had tightened into a fist where it lay on maps covering the top of his campaign table. The other people in the command tent, Nisveans for the most part—a few, like the war commander himself, from Noble Houses—all reacted to her words in their own way. Many of the soldiers, even the higher ranks, grimaced, carefully avoiding anyone's eye; but there were a few, among them Squad Leader Jedrick, the one whose cloak she was wearing, whose expressions bordered on smiles of triumph.

"This is no ordinary soldier," Kispeko continued. "Not even a member of a Noble House, such as we might ransom out of hand. This is the heir to the throne of Tegrian."

Dhulyn closed her lips on all the things she *might* have said. She knew that tone, and there was no argument the man would find convincing. "I ask you one final time, Lord Kispeko, to abide by the terms of our contract."

"Wolfshead, I cannot. You must see that I cannot." Kispeko's hand relaxed, but his face was still set firmly. "This is Tegrian we are talking about, and we all know that behind any Tegrian force stands the Blue Mage."

Dhulyn nodded, conscious of the chill that passed through the tent at the war commander's words. "Not behind yesterday's force, surely?" she said. "You cannot claim that there were any magics protecting the prince's troops."

Kispeko shrugged. "Possibly the Lord Prince was acting without the knowledge of his mother the queen, or of the Blue Mage. In any case, in Prince Edmir, I have a bargaining chip that will keep Nisvea safe from invasion—at the very least, a way to turn the Blue Mage's ambitions in another direction."

"No one has succeeded in bargaining with the Blue Mage," Dhulyn pointed out. "He has no interest in treaties and allies."

"But our circumstances are different from any who have tried to treat with the Mage before. Your very presence, for which we thank the Caids, has contributed to this." Kispeko leaned toward her, his eyes fixed intently on hers. "We reorganized our troops as you suggested, holding half our cavalry in reserve, and through this good advice and counsel we have won a battle against the Tegriani—the first such victory since the Blue Mage married their queen." As if he had heard the rising pitch of his voice, Kispeko fell silent and straightened.

"And now," he continued in a milder tone, "not only have we bested his troops, but we have Queen Kedneara's own son and heir."

"Perhaps if Dhulyn Wolfshead had a country of her own, she would not speak so lightly." The voice was quiet, but taut as a bowstring. Dhulyn did not turn her head; she knew who had spoken. She wore his cloak.

"Mercenary Brothers have fought, and killed, to defend the countries of others. As my Brother the Lionsmane and I did yesterday."

"And we were glad to have you," the war commander's sharp tone brought Dhulyn's eyes back to his face. "And we will recompense you in the manner agreed upon. But I will have the prince. With him, I can stop the Blue Mage, and that, let me tell you, Mercenary, supersedes your Common Rule, or my own honor, for that matter."

Dhulyn nodded. There had only been the slimmest of chances that this could have gone any other way. "As Cavalry Leader Jedrick has pointed out, we Mercenaries have only our Common Rule, and our honor." Dhulyn drew her sword and held it, point straight up, and directed her words to the patterned blade. "I am Dhulyn Wolfshead, called the Scholar. I was Schooled by Dorian of the River, the Black Traveler. I have fought at the sea battle of Sadron, at Arcosa in Imrion, and at Bhexyllia in the West. I withdraw my service, and that of my Partner Parno Lionsmane, from the Nisvean force following the battle of Limona."

She sheathed her sword. "You are Oathbreakers, War Commander. No Mercenary Brother will ever fight again at Nisvea's call."

Kispeko's lips thinned until they almost disappeared before he spoke. "So be it."

Dhulyn turned without salute or reverence and left the command tent.

Parno fell into step behind her as they made their way across the camp to where their own much smaller and much plainer tent was set up on the southern verge. He watched the muscle jump next to her mouth and judged it was safe to speak.

"Do you think, one of these days, we might actually get paid for a job?"

"We were paid in Berdana." Dhulyn's voice was quiet, but tight, as if she spoke through her teeth.

"Very well then. Would being paid for two jobs in a row be too much to ask?"

She stopped and faced him, the small scar on her upper lip turning her expression into a snarl. "Blooded, inglera-spawning House lordling—spit on our contract, will he? *Blooded* amateurs."

Parno knew the final remark wasn't aimed at him, but he grimaced just the same.

"What about the Tegriani? What if what Kispeko says about saving his country is true?"

Dhulyn's face was stiff. "Do *you* believe it?"

It took Parno only a moment to consider everything they knew of the Blue Mage. "No, my soul. No. And we would have sold our own honor for nothing."

"Not just our own, but the honor of our whole Brotherhood. 'Trust one, trust all.' If we do not hold to our oaths, if we cannot be trusted, we are not Mercenary Brothers, we are just killers."

Parno nodded. A few of the soldiers nearby had stopped in the middle of afternoon tasks and were looking in their direction.

"Calm down," he said. "You're attracting attention."

She stepped in until her nose was almost touching his.

"Am I not acting naturally, given the circumstances which will, as you well know, be all over the camp in twenty more heartbeats?" Though the corner of her mouth twitched, Parno could see the cold light of rage was still in Dhulyn's eye.

He took his Partner by the elbow and started them back toward their tent.

"You have a plan?" He used the nightwatch whisper, hardly louder than breathing.

"You think I'll let him get away with this?"

"And the Tegrian invasion?"

"What invasion?"

Parno found himself standing still as the full meaning of Dhulyn's question struck him.

"Your Vision said the Nisveans would win. Against all odds they would win," he said, his voice still nightwatch quiet.

"Was that the Tegriani force the world has been led to expect? The troops that never tire? Whom weapons do not touch? Against *that* force we should not have won. Regardless of any advice or help *we* gave, against the army of the Blue Mage, the Nisveans should have lost—" Dhulyn broke off her whisper to nod at the cavalry's head stableman as he passed without stopping. Evidently news of the events in the war commander's tent hadn't traveled far enough in the camp to reach the old man's ears. "As Balnia lost last season."

"And Demnion and Monara the season before last," Parno agreed, taking Dhulyn once more by the arm. When they were again on their way, he continued. "The Nisveans are being used. The prince was meant to lose, maybe even to be captured or—"

"Or worse," Dhulyn said. "Remember that Tegrian arrow."

Parno gave a silent whistle. "And the commander either knows or doesn't want to know."

Dhulyn was nodding like a Schooler pleased with her student. "Which tells us what?"

Parno grimaced, tasting acid in the back of his throat. "Nothing is as it appears."

"Except our oaths and our honor."

They reached their tent, a gift from their grateful employer in Berdana, and Dhulyn stepped ahead to lift the flap and duck inside. It was larger than they needed, but they'd put it up nonetheless. As the only Mercenary Brothers with this portion of the Nisvean soldiery, they had reputations to maintain, and that could be done as much with a show of wealth as a show of skills.

Once they were inside, the flap down and tied, Parno acknowledged Dhulyn's signal and sat down cross-legged facing her, close enough for their knees to touch. Dhulyn was frowning, her eyes focused on the heavy silk-lined bag that held Parno's pipes. He laid the tips of his fingers on her knee and waited for her to speak.

"Turned your heart a bit, did it, when Kispeko spoke of saving his homeland?" she said, without turning her head. "Took thought for your own House and Imrion there a moment, didn't you?"

Parno smiled, shaking his head. "It was only the once I wanted to visit my home and family. But if you're truly asking me whether I'd put the safety of Nisvea before our Brotherhood . . ." He shrugged. "I'll be honest and say I'm glad that breaking our Common Rule and letting them keep Prince Edmir would change nothing for the Nisveans. It makes what we have to do easier for me." He caught her chin and turned her head until they were eye to eye. "But I would do it, easy or not. Set your mind at rest."

"I believe you." Dhulyn sighed. "But consider this. Kispeko is no fool, when all is said and done. He knows the truth of things as well or better than we do—he's had the Blue Mage on his doorstep all this time, while you and I have been to the East. So he must know that returning the boy will do nothing. And yet he insists on doing so."

"As you say," Parno said. "There is more here than meets the eye."

"Which changes nothing for us." She pressed her lips tight, fingers tapping on her knee. "This is going to take us even farther out of our way."

Parno studied her face, unable to decide whether she was annoyed or merely stating a fact. They had been on their way to Delmara, where a traveler they'd met in Berdana had told them there was a Seer, perhaps even more than one. Seers were the rarest of the Marked, far rarer than Healers, Menders, or Finders. Everyone thought the Mercenaries were going to Delmara to consult the Seer—and they let everyone think so. What they told no one was that Dhulyn was a Seer herself. Since she had lost her Clan before her Mark had shown, however, she'd had no one to train her, and her Visions were erratic and unreliable. Even with the ancient set of vera tiles she'd acquired in Imrion—Seer's tiles used like a Finder's bowl to focus the Mark—she still needed training. They'd been working their way west to Delmara when they'd run into War Commander Kispeko's recruiters.

Dhulyn had turned her eyes away again, and Parno saw that she hadn't been looking at his pipes after all, but at the olive-wood box lying in the center of her bedding. The box that held the vera tiles. She had a way of blaming him for it whenever he suggested she use them. Still . . .

"This might be a good time to try the tiles."

A warm breeze blows from the east, making the banners and pennants flutter, the stiffened cloth rattling softly with a sound like a flock of birds taking flight. There's a mixed crowd of people before her, some wearing the longer gowns of nobility, many in shorter, more workmanlike dress. Most stand, though there are a scattering on horseback, looking over the heads of the rest. Prince Edmir sits on a thronelike chair on a raised platform, the focus of the crowd's attention. He is wearing robes the brilliant blue of the sky in winter, there is a circle of leaves shining gold against his dark hair, and he holds a long two-handed sword across his lap. A fair-haired woman, expensively dressed in a cloth-of-silver gown with a smaller, jeweled circlet around her head stands to Edmir's left, and an armsman in chain mail to his right. Edmir begins to speak and the crowd hushes. . . .

Hands that are her own push back the lid of a plain wood chest small enough to stand on a tabletop. Inside, resting in a bed of pale silk, is a blue crystal as long as her forearm, and perhaps as thick around. It shines blue like the deep ice that has trapped the glow of the stars. Dhulyn reaches down. . . .

At first Dhulyn cannot see what it is that disturbs the forest. Small animals scatter away. A crashing noise to her left and she turns her head, expecting to see perhaps a deer, perhaps even a small bear. There is too much noise for a forest cat, who even in desperate flight makes no more sound than the wind in the branches. Instead, a young boy—younger than the prince, yet taller, thinner, with long hair the color of old blood escaping from his braids—comes stumbling onto the narrow path, almost falling when his feet find the leveled ground. Dhulyn puts her hand up to her own blood-red hair, and her lips part, but she does not speak. The boy, clearly an Espadryni like herself, would not be able to hear her. He looks up then at a noise that only he can hear, whites clearly showing around the sharp blue of his eyes. There is the mark of an old bruise on the left side of his face. He tries to slow his breathing, taking a deep breath, but his diaphragm spasms, and he cannot manage a second one.

His left hand at his side, the boy sketches a complicated sign in the air with his right hand. There is a tug at Dhulyn's memory and she knows that she is frowning now, knowing that something should follow, but cannot think what it might be. Nothing happens, and the boy turns and runs toward her on the path, chest heaving just as Dhulyn catches the sounds of the men hunting him as they too crash through the forest. . . .

"You sure it was Edmir crowned and on his throne? It wasn't some naming day ceremony?"

Dhulyn stopped rubbing her temples and took the cup of warm water Parno handed her. "He was older than he is now, that I'm sure of. And he'd have had his naming day already, surely?"

Parno nodded, his eyebrows drawn together as he concentrated. "What about the other boy? Do you think he made it? *Some* other of your kindred must have escaped—you can't be the *only* one."

Dhulyn shrugged and drained her water cup. "That event might be years old, there's no way for me to be sure. Fashions don't change much among Horsemen."

Parno studied her face, but she seemed at peace. "And what he was doing—" Parno mimed the movement Dhulyn had described. "You don't know what that was?"

"It seemed familiar," she said. "Something should have happened, but I don't know what." She looked up, her blood-red brows drawn down in a vee. "And I don't know *why*." She raised her hands to her forehead.

"The prince on his throne, though, that seems pretty clear."

Dhulyn stopped rubbing her temples and looked up at him. "That's what you always say. It never seems so clear afterward."

Parno grinned. She'd *already* found a way to blame him. "So the only question is, do we make a great show of leaving and then sneak back into the camp? Or do we decide to leave in the morning and make off in the middle of the night?"

"That is not the only question, my heart, but it will do to begin with."

Parno returned to the tent some hours later carrying a freshly filled wineskin over his shoulder, bought from their friend the old stableman. As he pushed aside the flap, Dhulyn was setting the bright red cavalry cloak down on the battered, leather-covered chest they used as a table, next to his unwrapped pipes, a bright metal flask, and two Tenezian blue-glass cups.

Parno pursed his lips and looked from one side of the tent to the other. Everything his Partner considered essential—except his pipes—had been packed into two sets of saddlebags, and two largish packs that would ride on their horses' cruppers. That still left a considerable pile of bedding, extra clothing and weapons, to say nothing of the tent itself.

"I hadn't realized we'd accumulated so much," he said, frowning.

Dhulyn began rolling up a piece of thick canvas sewn with little pockets that held a set of knives. "Lucky for us, as it turns out; it explains the need for the extra horse." Dhulyn eyed both saddlebags before choosing one and stuffing the roll of canvas down one side of it. She hefted it and nodded, satisfied that the weight was balanced.

"Which I've bought." The twist to her mouth told Parno how unhappy she'd been with the bargain she'd made, but an extra horse they had to have. "And I've moved all four of them over to Randle's tether."

"I've gone around telling people we're off in the morning," he said, putting the wineskin down on one of the two large packs. "Anyone asked, I told them we'd be heading down to the Mercenary House in Lesonika to lodge a complaint."

"And they believed it?"

"Why shouldn't they? It's on our way to Delmara, more or less. Most of them think we're complaining of losing our chance at Prince Edmir's ransom. Even those who know the real reason agree with the Commander. It seems when the subject of the Blue Mage enters the discussion, all minds except ours run along the same paths."

"As Jedrick said, it's not our country. There was a time you would have felt the same about the Mage and ridden against him for your House and for Imrion."

"I admit, even now, I wouldn't like my House to fall, nor Imrion either for that matter. But there's little chance of that."

"I'm sure that's what Balnia thought two years ago. How goes their thinking now?"

Parno moved closer to his Partner and dropped his voice to the nightwatch whisper. "They've got him in a tent close to Kispeko's, small enough that there's only the one guard, walking around it."

"*Blooded* amateurs." Any other time Dhulyn's look of disgust would have made him smile.

Parno shrugged. "They don't expect anyone here to let him out, and they don't expect any of his own people to come and rescue him."

"They are right about the second, that's certain."

"Making it all the easier for us, so we won't complain."

She shot him a glance out of the corner of her eye even as she agreed. "Getting out of camp with the prince was never the hard part. It's keeping out of the Nisveans' hands after that will be the trick."

"Then we'll just have to make sure they've no reason to come after us."

"Moon rises at the end of the second watch, sets at the beginning of the fourth. We'll have to be back in our places by then."

Parno jerked his thumb at pipes and wineskin. "I'm ready when you are."

"Then I shall go and find Cavalry Squad Leader Jedrick." She picked up the red cloak and frowned at her hands, lifting them to her nose. "Do I smell of blood?"

Parno reached out and brought her right hand to his lips. Her skin was roughened and cold. "You washed last night, and you smell wonderful. Are you sure you can manage it with Jedrick . . . ?" The words suddenly dried in his throat and he gestured at the red cloak in Dhulyn's long-fingered hands.

"You think I can't?"

"The man makes no attempt to disguise his dislike of you."

She smiled her wolf's smile and Parno found himself smiling back. "You think that means he actually dislikes me? What he can't disguise is his annoyance that I bested him at the knife throw. There's not many see only the woman and not the Mercenary Brother, but he's one of them. And it's for that reason he'll not forgo what he'll see as a kind of triumph," she said. "His ego will play him right into my hands."

"I still think we should switch places. You do the horse trick, and I go for the prince," he said. "An alibi's all very well, but there's no one more recognizable in the whole blooded camp than you."

And there was no arguing with that, he thought. Even if you set aside her Mercenary's badge, there was still her height, her slimness, to say nothing of her blood-red hair, woven and tied into tiny braids, and her distinctive dress, loose trousers tucked into the knee-high boots of the Western Horsemen, her vest quilted from scraps of leather, bright velvets, silks and ribbons, leaving her arms bare.

"You have it exactly backward," she said to him. "No one will make a wager against me that involves horses—you they're not so sure of. And it's my very distinctiveness will help me vanish in the shadows." She glanced around until her eye fell on the small pile of clothing left unpacked. "Watch." She picked up what he recognized as an old, dull green tunic of his own and slipped it over her vest. She pulled a brown felted hood over her hair and turned back to face him.

"I'll change my trousers, and put on a pair of low half boots instead of these Semlorians everyone has seen me in. It will be dusk by the time I try it," she pointed out. "And no one will know me from any other soldier walking through the camp at dusk."

"By the Caids," Parno whispered. He wanted to tell her she was wrong, but the truth was . . . even without the boots and trousers, the bulky tunic alone, the covering of her hair—"I think I'd walk past you myself, without a second look."

"Then it's in Battle?"

"Or in Death," he agreed.

Two

ONCE PARNO HAD GONE, Dhulyn quickly stripped off her disguise; that was for later. She pulled off her vest, practice allowing her not to snag its laces in the braids and loops of her blood-red hair. She quickly unwrapped and discarded the length of silk scarf she used as a breastband before pulling her vest back on, adjusting the ties to push up her breasts and make them seem more round. Parno knew the plan, but there was no point in rubbing his nose in her part.

The cavalry leaders' tents were in the same southern corner of the camp as their own, but Dhulyn took a roundabout route, stopping once or twice to answer questions and taking care to acknowledge the hails and calls of the soldiers she'd been working beside for most of the past moon. She turned down several chances to join celebratory groups anxious to include a Mercenary Brother. Participation was Parno's role; her part of the plan was to be noticed now, and not later.

Her luck was in. Jedrick, his copper hair shining in the late afternoon sun, was sitting on a camp stool between the two squad leaders with whom he shared his tent.

"We hear you're leaving us, Mercenary," the small dark one seated to Jedrick's right called out as she neared them. The dark one's voice was so carefully neutral that even Dhulyn could not be sure of his opinion on the matter of Prince Edmir's captivity.

"We are," she said, coming to a stop just beyond arm's length of the man she'd come to see. "I thought I'd see if you wanted a chance to win your cloak back, Jedrick." She held up the scarlet wool she had over her left arm.

Jedrick was leaning forward, his elbows on his knees, his hands, scarred and callused by the reins, loosely clasped. He glanced at his tent mates before replying, half a grin on his face. "So you admit you cheated?"

Dhulyn shrugged, rolling her shoulders in a way that made her breasts bounce. "If the wind blew in my favor, I hardly think that is accounted cheating."

Jedrick blinked, cleared his throat, and raised his eyes to her face. "What wager do you have in mind?"

"I had in mind we could discuss it in private." She held his eyes a long moment before giving a pointed look at his two companions, showing them her wolf's smile.

Jedrick rose to his feet, smoothing his mustache with his right thumb and forefinger. "Would Parno Lionsmane not object?"

"Parno? Why would he? He's my Partner." Dhulyn had fielded such questions before, so it was easy to look puzzled. Very few outside of the Mercenary Brotherhood—and some within it for that matter—understood what it meant to be Partnered.

"I'll never understand the Mercenary Brotherhood," Jedrick said, shaking his head with a smile.

"And that's how we like it." Dhulyn reached out and gave him the merest nudge on his shoulder.

Not that Jedrick was truly concerned, she thought, as the man gave his fellow officers a mocking half bow and prepared to follow her. Dhulyn wished Parno were here to see how easy it was to seduce a man who claimed to dislike you.

On the other hand, perhaps it was just as well that he was not.

The route she took back to her tent was more direct than the one she used to reach Jedrick, but even so, a good many people saw them together. All part of the plan.

Once in her tent, Dhulyn tossed the cloak down on the bed, and glanced over her shoulder in time to see Jedrick tying down the tent flap. She bit down on her lip to keep from smiling. There were always men who were too sure of themselves.

"This is an interesting flask," he said, coming to stand next to her. He picked it up and hefted it in his hand as if to weigh the contents.

"I was given it in Berdana," she said, taking it from him and letting the tips of her fingers linger on his skin. "It comes from the Tin Isles, and leaves the brandy's taste unchanged."

"Given it? Then you would not wish to trade it for my cloak?"

"I think you mean *my* cloak."

"I thought that was what we were here to . . . discuss?"

Dhulyn had to stop herself from rolling her eyes. Sun and Moon, this was almost too easy. "I've Imrion brandy here," she said, holding up the flask. "Shall we toast our wager? I warn you, though, it's quite strong." She turned her back to fill the blue-glass cups.

"Is it to be a drinking contest, then?" His breath, smelling not unpleasantly of wine, was warm on her cheek, his voice a soft murmur in her ear. But when she looked at him Dhulyn saw the same hard gleam in Jedrick's eyes that was always there. How was it possible that eyes the same clear amber color as Parno's could be so cold?

She handed Jedrick one of the two cups, picked up the other and tossed its contents down her throat in a single quick swallow. Lowering the cup, she licked her upper lip slowly and smiled. Grinning back at her, Jedrick downed his own brandy just as quickly, smoothing his mustaches as he handed back his cup. Dhulyn raised her brows in a challenge, refilled the cups and, her eyes fixed on his, lifted her own to her lips, taking two long, slow swallows before lowering the cup again. She matched his smile with one of her own, careful to keep the small scar from turning her lip up in a snarl.

Jedrick took three good-sized swallows, and as he lowered his cup from his lips, Dhulyn put her heel behind his, tipped him backward onto the cot, and threw herself down on him slowly enough to let him start twisting out of her way. The trick, she reminded herself, was to dampen her natural reflexes enough that Jedrick actually thought he was besting her. She telegraphed her next move to give him time to grab her wrists—a little too roughly for play, she noted—and flip her over onto her back.

Dhulyn turned her head quickly enough to avoid his chin as he collapsed heavily on her chest.

"Ah, iocain," she whispered as she wriggled out from under the unconscious man. "Works every time."

Dhulyn dug her fingers under Jedrick's jaw and checked his pulse, counting carefully. She'd measured the dose with great accuracy and calculated she had at least two hours before it would begin to wear off. That should give her more than enough time.

She stripped Jedrick and carefully marked his back with several strategically placed scratches. She then sat on her heels and frowned. After a moment's thought, she rolled him over and, using sometimes her closed fist, sometimes the side of her rigid hand and sometimes the tips of her fingers, made what would later be telltale bruises on Jedrick's torso and limbs. She then bit him once on the neck, and once above the right nipple.

If she knew her man—and she was sure she did—when faced with such evidence Jedrick would never admit that he had no memory of what had passed between them.

Dhulyn straightened to her feet and took a slow deliberate breath, listening with all her training to the sound of the camp around her. Did she hear the drone of Parno's pipes in the distance, or was it just wishful thinking? She shoved Jedrick's leg aside and sat down to pull off her boots.

Parno tossed back the slightly sour wine in his cup and concentrated on the story the man in front of him was trying to tell around the bellyful of beer he had in him. This particular campfire was well out of sight of their tent, and even if he wanted to keep an eye out for Dhulyn, Parno couldn't see her from here. He'd chosen this particular gathering around this particular fire for that very reason.

Parno distracted the storyteller with another mugful of beer and picked up his pipes, settling them at his side. As they saw what he was about, several others, having lost confidence in the beer drinker's ability to find the end of his tale, began to call out.

"That's it, Lionsmane."

"Give us the one about the Finder's apprentice!"

Parno moistened his lips and tested the bag for air.

"Oh, I know a better one than that."

There. That sound was Parno's piping, no doubt about it. With tunic, boots, and hood in place, Dhulyn felt for the ioca leaves she'd tucked into a fold of her sash. Satisfied they were secure, she rolled under the rear edge of their tent and stayed crouched, making sure the shadows covered her, before straightening slowly to her feet. Dhulyn tugged at her hood and set off in the direction of the tent that held the prince, hunching her shoulders and dragging her feet a little, in contrast to her usual freely swinging stride.

She angled her progress through the camp so as to draw the least possible notice. Her pace was neither purposeful enough that it drew the questioning eye, nor casual enough to prompt the friendly invitation. And, further, she'd timed her approach to Prince Edmir's tent for the middle of the second watch, when the moon was not yet up. Most of the host had found their beds, and the few souls hardy enough, or drunk enough, to be still awake around their small campfires reliving the unexpected triumph of the day before, paid her no mind.

Sun and Moon grant you do not find cause to regret your victory, she prayed. Considering her present errand was unlikely to bring the Nisveans any good, the least she could do was wish them luck.

As she drew nearer Prince Edmir's tent, Dhulyn left off her slouching walk and began the Stalking Cat *Shora*—the real reason, to her way of thinking, that the rescue of the Prince was *her* part of tonight's work. Like all Mercenaries, Parno had been Schooled in the twenty-seven basic *Shora*, the patterns that made up their intensive training. But Dhulyn was an Outlander, and the Stalking *Shoras* in particular came as naturally to her as sleep. Now, as her mind settled into the Stalking Cat, her breathing slowed, her thoughts focused. The smell of the camp surrounded her. Unwashed bodies, burning wood and oil, cooking smells—mostly onions. Behind this she sensed the warm, clean scent of the horses tethered off to her left, and beyond that, the smell of old blood and death from the river valley.

Between her and her target, she could smell the beer being drunk by two women around a pinewood fire, hear the murmur of their voices, and the gurgle of the liquid as it poured into their cups. In the near distance she thought she could still hear the melodic drone of Parno's pipes. Ahead and to the right, was the stench of the latrine ditch, unmistakable even under layers of shoveled dirt. She turned her feet toward it.

As she went, her eyes adjusted, making full use of the available light, the campfires, the occasional torch smelling strongly of pine resin and oil. Even the starlight helped her as she slid easily into every shadow large enough to hold her—and one or two which she knew would appear too small to do so—moving only when her senses, heightened by the *Shora*, told her no human eye observed her.

A flicker of movement—and she froze just as she was skirting six sleeping figures rolled in rugs and cloaks with their feet toward the embers of a fire. She turned her head slowly. One of the camp's cats eyed her from the shadows, but the animal recognized the scent and stance of a fellow predator, and allowed her to pass with only a slashing tail as comment.

She froze again as, circling around the back of War Commander Kispeko's tent, she heard voices. No. Only one voice, Kispeko's own.

"I will see to it, my lord."

Dhulyn frowned. The man's voice was oddly flat and toneless, and who could he be calling "my lord"? No one outranked Kispeko here in camp.

"He will die as he tries to escape," Kispeko said. "I will see to it, my lord."

Don't put money on it, she thought. No one else had any need of escape. Kispeko must be speaking of Edmir. But to whom?

Dhulyn waited, but Kispeko made no other sound. She concentrated, letting her awareness float. When she was satisfied that, strange as it was, only one person breathed within the commander's tent, she continued on her way.

Think about it later, the voice in the back of her mind instructed.

Dhulyn finally came to a stop in a patch of shadow created by an uneven pile of cooking supplies covered over by a canvas tarp, her toe brushing against what felt and smelled like an empty wineskin. If what Parno had told her was correct, the prince was ahead and just to her left, in a plain, square-sided tent about twice the size of their own. Either the prince had no lamp lit, or the tent's canvas was thick enough to show no shadows.

Her awareness increased another notch as her immediate prey, the human guard, walked around the far corner of the tent and came within reach of the Stalking Cat *Shora*. She let him make three circuits around the tent, timing his pacing, matching her breathing to his, before she fell into step behind him, as close as his own shadow.

The guard did not falter, but kept up his steady pace. Dhulyn moved with exactly the same rhythm, imitating even the slight hitch in the guard's right hip, their breathing matched, their hearts beating in time.

As they entered the shadows at the rear of the tent, Dhulyn glanced down at the rope stretched from one of the tent pegs on the short side. Only if you were looking very carefully could you tell that it had been sliced almost through.

Well done, my heart, floated through her thoughts in time with her moving lungs. On one of his ramblings from fire to fire, or perhaps on a visit to the latrine, Parno had managed to pass unnoticed by this spot.

The guard turned the corner, and as soon as he was out of sight Dhulyn dropped to her belly, snapped the cut rope between her hands, and snaked into the tent.

The prince was sitting at a camp table, a shaded lantern casting a shaft of light on the open book in front of him. He had frozen in the act of dipping a pen into a small pot of ink. So, she thought, not a book to read, but one to write in. Dhulyn rolled to her knees and held a finger to her lips, tensed to spring until she saw the young man relax. The tent they'd given him may not have been much, but the accessories— judging by the quality of the carpet she knelt on—were the best the commander could supply. As were Prince Edmir's clothes. His own boots, brushed and polished, lay neatly to one side of the camp bed, but his borrowed nightshirt was fine linen, and the tunic and leggings folded on a small table were likely from Commander Kispeko's own chests.

The prince shifted, and Dhulyn was beside him, her hand over his mouth, while he was still drawing in breath to speak.

"Stay silent," she breathed in the nightwatch whisper. "Dress as quietly as you can. If you need to speak, mouth the words against my hand, slowly, do you understand?" When the prince nodded, Dhulyn relaxed her hold on his face, leaving her fingers lightly in place over his lips.

"The guard?" he asked. Dhulyn had to ask him to repeat it before she understood.

"Will be distracted. Trust me and dress."

Dhulyn had to give the boy credit; he moved as quietly as she'd ever seen a town man do. They had one bad moment when he couldn't bend his injured leg to pull the leggings on, but he let Dhulyn help him without sign of embarrassment. *Probably has a dresser,* she thought. He hissed when her hand brushed against his wound, but stifled it quickly enough that the sound drew no notice. She touched the wound more carefully with the back of her hand, frowning when she found it markedly hotter than the surrounding skin.

"Did they give you nothing for the wound?" she asked, laying her fingers once more against his lips.

"Fens bark tea," he mouthed.

Dhulyn nodded. They had sense enough for that at any rate. Cleaning the wound, plus an infusion to keep the fever down, was the most anyone could do in the absence of a Healer. And she shouldn't be surprised that Kispeko had used his own Knife to attend the prince, rather than asking either of the Mercenaries for help. She smiled in the darkness as a clever thought occurred to her. She could use that in the morning. But for now, she felt for and removed the ioca leaves from her sash. "Chew this," she said, handing him one. "It will dull the pain."

When Edmir pulled the tunic on directly over the nightshirt, Dhulyn shook her head. It was the long formal tunic a noble might wear to dine, not the short surcoat of a commoner. She waved the prince closer to her and pulled out her knife.

"I'll have to cut that short," she said in his ear. "We need to look like a pair of common drunks."

Again Edmir nodded, this time taking her hand and placing it on his mouth.

"Soon?"

"Listen for it, and be ready."

"My Partner, Dhulyn Wolfshead, has never been unhorsed," Parno said, folding his pipes against the now-emptied air bag. "Not even in practice, though I grant you she's 'fallen off on purpose' when she's had to, just to make a point." He paused, furrowed his brow as if a thought had just occurred to him. " 'Course, she *is* a Red Horseman."

"I'll concede that, horseman to horseman, the Mercenary Brotherhood often matches trained cavalry, and might well be able to unhorse almost anyone. But the question was a man afoot, and such an encounter never ends badly for the one ahorse." Nilo was the closest of the five cavalrymen sitting around the fire. He wiped his mouth on his sleeve and offered the wineskin.

Parno shook his head. "I've heard you say this so often, Nilo, you must believe it's true." Two carefully chosen songs and a little subtle prodding had finally led the discussion where he wanted it to go. Not that it usually took much to get professional soldiers to brag about their own specialties.

Nilo covered a burp with exaggerated care. So exaggerated that Parno began to wonder if he was the only one more sober than he wanted people to think. "Perhaps," the cavalryman said, "I should say no *true* horseman can be unseated from the ground—barring archers, of course."

"True horseman be blooded. *I'll* do it." Parno stood and let himself sway ever so slightly, as if he'd actually drunk all the wine that was in the skin at his feet. "Caids, I'll wager that I not only unhorse you, but I do it unarmed."

Nilo also managed to stand, his hand on the shoulder of one of his fellows. "What's the wager, then, Mercenary?"

There it was, the calls in the distance, the flaring up of fresh torches as the word was passed and men and women rose from their sleep in answer to a summons that had them laughing and calling out odds.

"Here it comes," Dhulyn said, barely breathing the words as she drew Edmir toward the place where she'd rolled into the tent. The shadow that was the prince's guard had stopped his steady pacing and seemed to be listening to the din.

"The Lionsmane's going to unhorse Cadet Nilo," called out a woman's voice.

"I'll take a piece of that wager," the guard answered.

"Which way?"

With the guard distracted, Dhulyn shoved Edmir through the gap in the tent, following closely behind him. Once outside, she lifted him to his feet and swung her left arm over his shoulders. She was slightly taller, and it was easy for her to take a good grip on the youngster while making it look as though *he* was holding *her* up. She headed him toward the horse lines.

Don't worry, she told herself, *Parno's done this before*. The boy winced and Dhulyn loosened her grip. Apparently she was doing a poor job of convincing herself. Apparently it was one thing when Parno was practicing and it was Dhulyn on the horse, and another thing entirely when it was someone else.

Parno stood with one hand held above his head. When he was ready, he would let his arm fall, and Nilo would ride his cavalry horse straight toward him. There was a popular belief among nonsoldiers that horses would not run people down, or even step on them except by accident—but Parno knew that warhorses had been trained to do exactly that, and worse. He had to be careful, the hooves could slash at him from the side, as well as from the front. His arm still raised, he began to slow his breathing in the Python *Shora*, the Wrestler's *Shora*, used for hand-to-hand combat only. *You've done this before*, he told himself. *Do it again now. Just like in practice.*

His awareness narrowed until the tents, the people watching, the flaring torches died away. No sounds, no smells, nothing existed in the world except him and the horse. Time slowed. The horse's breath hung in the air like a cloud.

He let his arm drop.

Through the soles of his feet he could feel the ground shudder as the hooves hit. Watched the spurts of dirt jump backward from the slow, regular strikes of the churning hooves on the earth. He bent his knees, allowing the muscles in his legs to coil, to become springs. Focused, counting the time as each hoof fell, he dodged, feeling the horse's breath on his face as he darted to one side, grasped the mane, bounced off the powerful springs of his legs, swinging his body, knees up, under the blow that Nilo was only now bringing down from above. Long seconds too late.

And just as he had done scores of times in practice, he planted both knees in Nilo's midsection and catapulted the cavalryman neatly from the saddle. Parno let momentum continue his movement until he was sitting sideways on the horse, in the spot Nilo had occupied a moment before. As the animal faltered, Parno twisted to lie stomach-down on the saddle, swinging his legs again until he was sitting astride the horse's back.

Suddenly there was a flash of movement, the yelp of a dog, and the horse twisted violently to one side, almost going down, and only by force of will did Parno manage to stay in his seat.

The cheers and catcalls changed to cries of alarm as the spectators came running up, Nilo first among them, to catch at the bridle of his horse. Parno slid to the ground and joined the man where he was running his hand down the horse's off foreleg. Nilo was frowning, and the horse seemed shy of putting weight down. Parno glanced aside, pressing his eyes shut as the woman crouching over the limp body of the dog shook her head.

Could have been me.

"I don't want to cost you both your money *and* your horse," he said, turning back to Nilo. "Let me take him to my Partner. Dhulyn Wolfshead can tell us what, if anything, is wrong."

As he walked beside the cavalryman, encouraging his horse to walk slowly through the camp, Parno hoped he'd given Dhulyn enough time. He was sorry for the dog, but this couldn't have turned out better if he had planned it. He'd intended to ask Nilo—or whoever made the wager with him—back to the tent for some Imrion brandy. Now it seemed that half the camp would provide Dhulyn with her alibi.

As long as she was back.

The tightness in his chest relaxed as he saw the corner of the tent flap was folded back a scant palm's width. He bent down to toss it back completely, loudly calling out for Dhulyn as he crossed the threshold. Nilo, waiting with his horse, ducked his head to look inside. When he began to laugh, everyone who was close enough crowded forward to get a look. Dhulyn's white southerner's skin glowed in the torchlight as she sat up, yawning and rubbing at her eyes.

"What's all this," she asked in a voice fogged with sleep. "Can't people have a moment's privacy?"

Clear on her skin, and clear on the skin of Squad Leader Jedrick as he, too, sat up, his eyes clouded by what everyone there would take for exhaustion, were telltale bruises and marks of fingernails. As if their nakedness and disheveled hair did not already speak very clearly what they had been doing before they fell asleep.

The cheering and catcalls began again. Clearly the crowd felt this entertainment was just as good as a horse wager.

***

Avylos the Blue Mage let his head fall against the high back of his chair. His eyelids fluttered, and for a moment he struggled against the languor that followed taking power from the Stone. If he slept, he would dream, and it was rarely anything that he wished to see. His lids shut, and the dream began. . . .

"MAMA, MAMA, LOOK! I CAN DO IT, MAMA!" AND HIS MOTHER'S FACE WAS TRANSPORTED BY JOY, HER EYES SHINING, HER MOUTH IN THE WIDEST OF SMILES, AS HE MADE THE PINECONE LEAP INTO HIS HAND. ONCE AGAIN HE SAW THE LOOKS ON THE FACES OF THE BOYS HE THOUGHT OF AS HIS FRIENDS. THEY NUDGED EACH OTHER AND SMILED, NODDING; HIS YOUNGER SELF MISUNDER-STANDING, SAW HAPPINESS NOT MALICE, PLEASURE NOT TWISTED GLEE. HIS MOTHER STROKED HIS HAIR AND KISSED HIM, AND RAN FOR HIS FATHER.

WHEN HIS FATHER CAME, EVERYTHING CHANGED. HIS FATHER PUT A HAND ON AVYLOS' SHOULDER, BUT WHEN AVYLOS OFFERED TO SHOW HIM THE MAGIC HE HAD FINALLY LEARNED TO DO, HIS FATHER HAD LOOKED AROUND HIM, FIXED ON ONE PARTICULAR SMILING FRIEND, AND CLOUTED THE BOY ON THE SIDE OF THE HEAD.

"BEGONE, YOU BRATS! YOUR FATHERS SHALL HEAR OF THIS!"

AND THEY RAN. LOOKING OVER THEIR SHOULDERS, GIGGLING NOW, THOUGH THERE WAS A LITTLE FEAR AS WELL, FEAR OF WHAT HIS FATHER WOULD DO, AND WHAT THEIR OWN FATHERS WOULD SAY.

"BUT, TERAVYL—" HIS MOTHER SAID. "IT WAS A TRICK," HIS FATHER TOLD HER. "THE OTHERS WERE DOING IT, AND LETTING AVI THINK IT WAS HIM. HE IS SRUSHA, MY DEAR."

AND HIS MOTHER, CRYING, TURNED HER FACE AWAY FROM HIM, BUT NOT BE-FORE HE SAW THE FINAL GRIEF IN HER EYES. HIS FATHER STROKED HIS HAIR, BUT HIS FACE TOO WAS FULL OF PITY, AND REGRET. AVYLOS STARED AT THE PINECONE IN HIS HAND, WISHING THAT IT WAS A KNIFE. . . .

Avylos' consciousness fell back into the living world, his breathing coming fast and sharp as rage coursed hotly through his veins. He ran his hands along the cold stone cylinder he still held, as thick as his wrist, as long as his forearm, and his fingers trembled. He still held the Stone; had he continued taking power from it while in his dream?

Quickly, he spoke the words that closed the ritual, grasped the end, and twisted it to the left. He replaced the Stone in its cherrywood cas-ket on his worktable, and shut the lid. He did not believe he could drain the Stone completely, but he *could* drain that portion of the Stone's power available to him. So far as he could tell, the Stone trapped *all* the power fed to it, but he simply did not know the proper chants or settings that would release that reserve to him.

He looked at the books in his room. One day he would know; one day that power would be his.

Not that he had needed any power to crush his tormentors. They had all been dealt with long ago. Before the power had finally shown itself, before the Stone had come to him and he had begun to understand the truth.

He stood and headed for the door before he could be tempted to use the Stone again. He needed no more dreams today.

He shut the door of his workroom behind him and strode into the corridor, stopping just inside the wide, metal-braced door that closed off his wing from the rest of the Royal House. He straightened his robes until he was sure they fell gracefully from his shoulders. His hair, the color of old blood, had been left loose that morning to dry, and he ran his hands through it, pushing it back from his face. When he was sure he looked presentable, he opened the door, startling the young page who stood outside it into giving him a very awkward bow.

"I will go to my garden, Takian," he said. "See that the queen knows."

"Of course, my lord. At once, my lord." Another short bow, this time more gracefully accomplished.

"My lord *Mage*," Avylos corrected.

The boy's face, flushed with embarrassment a moment before, drained of all color.

Avylos smiled. "It's all right, Takian, you cannot remember everything on the first day."

"Thank you, my lord *Mage*," the boy said carefully, his eyes fixed on his shoes.

"There. You'll soon remember." Avylos waited until the boy had gone on his errand before drawing his robes more closely to him and heading toward the open stairwell to the far left of his door. The stairwell was square, taking up the interior of a small tower in the southern curtain wall of Queen Kedneara's palace. The door at the lower end of the stairs opened into an irregularly-shaped courtyard, once the palace laundry's drying place, but now the private garden of the Blue Mage.

Avylos seated himself on the wide stone edge that surrounded the still pool in the center of his garden and breathed deeply, in and out, three times. Though they were not wet, he rubbed the palms of his hands on his robe. He felt strong, his magic was at its peak. He did not, for the moment, require any more power.

But he wanted it.

He put his hands up to his face and pressed his fingers into the bone above his eyes. "I will find the secret," he promised himself, not for the first time. Taking another deep breath, slowly releasing it, he focused on the still water of the pool. He needed distraction, and the pool could give it to him. With the ease of practice he narrowed his awareness until he saw only the pool. Then he focused his mind and his attention further, until he saw through the pool, to what it could show him.

Night. An army's camp. The moon not yet risen, but enough starlight to see by. A tall slim man, drunk from the look of him, with his arm around the shoulders of a younger, shorter man, who helped him stagger along. The younger man raised his head and the starlight fell on his face.
Edmir.

"Sun burn and blast you." Avylos struck the surface of the water with his closed fist, scattering the image of Edmir's escape into the sudden ripples.

"Something wrong, Avylos?"

Only Kera was allowed to use his private stair, come into his private garden. Kera and the Queen her mother, of course. The princess was standing in the open doorway, her hands tucked into her sleeves, sun on her red-gold hair, her dark brows drawn down, her forehead wrinkled in a frown.

"I'm very much afraid that things have not gone well for your brother, Kerusha. The battle has been lost."

The girl stepped forward, her hands falling free. "Lost? Is Edmir . . . ?"

"I can see no more. But, Kera, I fear you must be prepared for the worst." There, the seed was sown. "You counseled against his going— Oh, do not look so surprised, I knew none of this could be of *your* advising. But I could not foresee . . ."

"But your magic, why did it not work?"

Avylos shrugged and slowly shook his head, as if the weight of the world was on his shoulders. "The magic was prepared, Edmir well instructed. For some reason he did not call upon it—or he was prevented. I have not found all there is to know, but I swear to you, I will."

The girl's face was white, and Avylos stood, putting out his hand. But her chin firmed, and her spine straightened.

"I must tell my mother the queen." Her voice was very small.

"Let me accompany you," Avylos said. "The queen will have questions."

The girl nodded without speaking, thrusting her hands back into the sleeves of her gown.

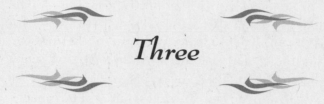

Three

"NO PRACTICE THIS morning, Mercenaries?"

She recognized the voice, so without looking up, Dhulyn continued to draw one end of a long strap around the bundle that was the tent. It had been struck and rolled as compactly as she and Parno could manage between them, but it was still bulky.

"Not this morning, nor any other morning," Parno answered, as Dhulyn had known he would. "You slack-wits will have to find someone else to teach you which end of the sword is sharp."

There were disappointed murmurs mixed in with the laughter. She and Parno had been sharing their morning practice with the interested portion of the Nisvean force for the better part of a moon, and there were more than a few who'd miss the benefit of that workout, now that the Mercenaries were going. Dhulyn tossed the loose end of the strap to Parno, who caught it as he straightened to his feet—grimacing as the muscles of his lower back reminded him of his exertions of the night before.

"I'll go for the horses if you like," Dhulyn said, carefully not smiling as Parno arched his body first one way and then the other, bracing both hands on his lower back.

"Oh, Caids," Parno said. "A day in the saddle. That's exactly what my back needs."

"Teach you to get drunk and do acrobatic tricks." Dhulyn easily dodged the half burned stick he tossed at her from the cold embers of their breakfast fire and picked up her sword, thrusting it into her belt and tugging her vest into place.

"Are you Dhulyn Wolfshead?" The voice broke halfway through her name and Dhulyn wasn't surprised that the boy was blushing when she turned.

"I am, and it's pronounced 'Dillin.' "

"Come with me if you please, Mercenary." Embarrassment momentarily making him lose touch with his common sense, the boy spoke more gruffly than many would have considered polite to a Mercenary Brother.

"And if I don't please?" Smiling her wolf's smile, Dhulyn narrowed her eyes and put her hand on her sword hilt, exactly as she would have done to anyone older, and taller, who had spoken to her in that tone. As she had expected, rather than frightening the lad, it only made him clear his throat, and stand on his dignity.

"The Commander Lord Kispeko has sent for you, Dhulyn Wolfshead." This time the tone—and the pronunciation—was perfect. The lad was clearly the younger son of a Noble House, perhaps even Kispeko's own. Dhulyn looked down at her Partner. Parno, in the midst of wrapping the strap once more around the bundle of tent, shrugged one shoulder and winced.

"I would be pleased to accompany you, Camp Messenger." Dhulyn picked up a pair of gloves and began to draw them over her hands.

Parno pushed the end of the strap through the last loop and tied it off. "Has the prince's wound gone bad?"

The boy licked his lips, clearly of two minds as to what he should say. "What makes you ask?"

"I've been expecting Kispeko—your pardon, I meant Commander Lord Kispeko, to send for one of us since last evening. The prince is injured, you have no Healer, and my Partner and I between us have more experience than any of the Knives that ride with your army."

It would be part of the boy's errand to report what they'd said, and he'd say that it was Parno, whom everyone considered "the talkative one" who had asked.

"The commander will explain, I'm sure," the boy said. "If you please, Dhulyn Wolfshead."

"Be so kind as to lead the way." Dhulyn grimaced when the boy's back was turned. She *was* Senior Brother, so it was natural for Kispeko to send for her alone, and in fact he'd done it many times. But she couldn't shake the feeling that she and Parno were being split up because it would make them easier to take. Not that she could do anything but act in the most natural manner herself, and that meant going along with the boy as if she had nothing on her mind but being on their way while there was still good daylight.

Mindful of the part she played, Dhulyn glanced at the position of the sun, sighed, and addressed the arrow-straight back in front of her.

"Will this take very long, do you think, Camp Messenger?"

The boy shot her a look over his shoulder that told her at once how pleased he was at being addressed by his title, and how nervous he was at not being able to tell her what she wanted to know.

"An improper question, and I withdraw it," she said, acknowledging what was no more or less than the truth. "We awoke so late after the excitement of the night that we're setting out much later than I had planned."

A few people called out to her as they walked through the camp—not so many as would have called out to Parno, perhaps, but enough to allow her to answer back in a manner she hoped was relaxed and confident. Not at all the manner of someone who had robbed the Nisvean army of its greatest treasure.

They arrived finally at Kispeko's tent. A few of the lower-ranked officers hovered outside, their faces for the most part hard and unfriendly. Jedrick, wearing his red cloak once more, frowned and raised his eyebrows at her. The edge of a bruise showed where his shirt was open at his throat. Dhulyn gave her head a tiny shake and followed the young boy into Kispeko's tent.

Parno would have said something to the Commander and the two high officers with him. Asked some question or made some polite noise. He'd been the son of a High Noble House himself, in Imrion, before becoming a Mercenary Brother, and still had court manners. Dhulyn merely rested her crossed wrists on the hilt of her sword and waited for Kispeko to speak. The commander sat behind his campaign table, as he had the day before. But this time only his two subcommanders were with him, two brothers from the Nisvean House of Olesev. As part of the cavalry section, Dhulyn and Parno had reported to the elder, Romenec. He sat relaxed in his seat to Kispeko's right. The younger brother, Renic, stood behind the commander's left shoulder, his brows drawn down in a heavy scowl.

"Would you have any objection to an escort of cavalry along your way, Dhulyn Wolfshead?"

She let her mouth fall open and her eyes go wide. Then she smiled her wolf's smile. "You've lost him, haven't you? *Blooded* fools and amateurs that you are, you've lost him." She relaxed her shoulders, shaking her head with a low whistle. "I should take offense, Kispeko, at what you ask of me. I should, but it would be mean in me. You may give us an escort. Sun! You may search our gear and baggage, if you'd like. Though how you'd think we've hidden the princeling in amongst our spare boots and extra blades . . ." She shook her head again.

"You can account for yourself last night, Wolfshead," Subcommander Renic spoke up. The harshness of his tone showed how little amused he was.

Dhulyn grinned. "I can. From the end of the first watch at least. That is, Cavalry Squad Leader Jedrick can."

Kispeko signaled to the messenger still standing near the tent entrance and the boy disappeared, returning in moments with Jedrick. The squad leader did not acknowledge Dhulyn at all, but saluted his commanders and stood to attention.

"The Mercenary Brother Dhulyn Wolfshead tells us that you can account for her whereabouts last night, after the end of the first watch?"

"I can, Commander." Jedrick spoke without emphasis. "We were in her tent from that time until almost the end of the fifth watch." His mustache trembled and Dhulyn was certain Jedrick had almost smiled. "At which time," he continued, "many others can attest that the Wolfshead and I were both there."

"And half the camp can swear as to where Parno Lionsmane was and what he was doing the whole of the night, Commander," Romenec said from his seat next to Kispeko. From the dry tone of his voice, it was evident he'd heard nothing new to him. "I tell you there is no point in continuing this line of inquiry."

Dhulyn almost bit her lip. Romenec was a good man, he trusted her, and it went against the grain to trick him. But he had supported his commander against her request that their contract be honored, and that placed him out of the reach of her sympathy.

Kispeko was already nodding. "As you have guessed, the prince has escaped. We can find no trail, no sign. Mercenaries are skilled beyond the usual, will you find him for us?"

Dhulyn lifted one blood-red brow and waited. Apparently she was the only one to appreciate irony when she heard it.

"Yesterday I called you Oathbreaker," she said finally. "And told you none of my Brotherhood would take service with you again. That was my final word, Commander Kispeko."

Romenec, the brother she'd worked under, showed no surprise at this; the other, Renic, wrinkled his nose in disapproval.

"There is a Finder in Jarasev, at the Royal House. We will be sending for her."

Dhulyn shrugged. "Then you will have no need of us."

Renic leaned on the table to speak again, but Kispeko raised the fingers of his right hand and he fell silent.

"If that is all, Commander, my Partner and I would like to leave today." Dhulyn carefully ignored both subcommanders.

"Very well. Should I decide to lend you an escort," Kispeko said, "they will find you on the north road?"

Dhulyn inclined her head the exact depth courtesy required. "We go to Broduk, to take ship there," she said and turned to go. Jedrick was holding aside the tent's closure for her.

"I would walk with you to your tent, Wolfshead."

She grinned at him, careful not to let her upper lip pull back. "Sure you don't want to give me that cloak after all," she asked him. "It looks much better on me."

"It gives a nice color to your skin, when you are lying on it, that much is true. But I must keep it to remember you by."

Dhulyn laughed and tapped the man on his shoulder with her closed fist, lowering her eyes as if embarrassed. *He'll think it's because we did,* she thought, *not because we didn't.* Tricking Jedrick was even more fun than she'd expected.

As they neared her camp space, Dhulyn could see Parno sitting on the large bundle that was their packed tent with a smaller figure next to him looking at something in Parno's hands. He'd sent someone for their horses while she was with Kispeko, or had gone himself, since all four beasts were there, waiting for saddles and packs.

"Wolfshead, a moment."

Sun and Moon, what does he want now? But she turned with a friendly look and raised eyebrows. The camp was alive around them, but no one was near enough to hear what they said to each other. Jedrick was frowning again, and looking at his feet. *Blood.*

"We had no time to take a proper leave of one another," Jedrick said. "We were . . . interrupted. I never had opportunity to ask you if—" He straightened his shoulders and looked her in the eye. "If all went well last night?"

Dhulyn hoped he couldn't hear her heart thumping in her chest. Or perhaps it would be better if he could. "I thought I made that abundantly clear last night," she said. "Come now, Jedrick, I didn't think you were the type who needed to be praised and complimented."

Now Jedrick flushed, and Dhulyn, waiting for the next question, the obvious question, wondered what she would answer.

"No, of course not," was what he finally said. "But with you a Mercenary Brother, and an Outlander . . ."

"Of course," she said, tapping him once again with her fist. "I understand. Let me say then, that I won't soon forget you."

"Nor I you, of course," Jedrick said, a little too quickly, his relief clear. "Nor I you."

"Come, say farewell to Parno Lionsmane."

Jedrick fell into step beside her once more, though it seemed to Dhulyn that his shoulders were lower, and his arms swung with more ease. *Nice enough in his way*, she thought. *But he still has too good an opinion of himself.* After a few more paces she came to an abrupt halt. It was Sjan, the young horse girl who looked after Randle's tether, sharing Parno's seat, but that wasn't what caught Dhulyn's eye and made her press her lips together. The larger horse pack was still open, road rations waiting on the ground beside it. The spare bows lay next to their oiled wrappings, and Parno's pipes—stowed into their special bag with one or two other small valuables before she'd been called to the commander's tent—were out again, as Parno was showing Sjan how to fill the bag of air.

"Sun, Moon, and Stars, didn't you finish?"

Parno looked up. "Back already? Sjan here brought us our horses, so I thought, just to thank her . . ."

Dhulyn rolled her eyes, calling on her gods to witness the nonsense she had to put up with, and sighed elaborately. "Can we finish *now*? I'd like to be on our way sometime today."

"Of course, my soul." Parno sprang to his feet. "What did they want, anyway?"

"The prince has escaped."

Parno was halfway to the bag of pipes that Jedrick was helpfully holding open for him when Dhulyn's words stopped him, and turned him around, eyes wide and mouth open.

Don't overdo it, Dhulyn thought.

"The blooded fools," Parno said.

"That's what I told them." Dhulyn pulled the laces of the large bag shut more sharply than necessary and dragged it over to the new pack-horse, clucking at the animal as it rolled its eye at her. "After they'd made sure it wasn't us, Kispeko asked if we'd track the boy."

"*Now* they want our help." Parno stowed his pipes into their bag and nodded his thanks to Jedrick. As Parno dealt with the bag's closures, Jedrick went to help Dhulyn lift the heavy travel pack on to the new horse.

"My thanks, Jedrick," Dhulyn said, tugging the pack forward slightly on the packhorse's back. "Those saddlebags on our mounts, if you would be so kind. Parno will help me with the tent," she added in a voice filled with menace. Jedrick grinned at her, and she winked at him.

The bundle of tent was awkward, but their old packhorse, called Stumpy due to his short legs, had carried much worse and merely snorted at their efforts to balance the bundle on his back. With Sjan's help they had the tent tied securely, and Dhulyn surveyed the rest of the camp. Saddlebags on Bloodbone and Warhammer; tent, extra weapons, clothing and food packs distributed between the two pack animals; finally she nodded and turned to where Jedrick stood in the empty space where their camp had been. "I believe this is farewell, Squad Leader. Again, I thank you for your assistance."

"It has been a pleasure, Dhulyn Wolfshead. I hope we may meet again." Jedrick gave her a short bow and a wide smile.

Dhulyn swung herself on to Bloodbone's back and settled into her saddle, checking that sword and knives were within reach. "Sun and Moon shine on you. Wind at your back." She nodded, and turned Bloodbone's head away, urging the mare forward with her knees.

Almost at the edge of the camp Dhulyn looked back, catching Parno's eye. She could just see Jedrick in his red cloak, still standing where their tent had been.

"Still there," she said.

"Of course." Parno rolled his right shoulder with a grimace. "He had a good look at everything we'd packed—"

"Which you so cleverly left half-packed for him."

"Just so. And once he'd satisfied himself that I didn't have Prince Edmir in my pipe satchel, he'd want to be sure we were really on our way."

"I hope this is all worth it," Dhulyn said.

Parno raised an eyebrow.

"I really liked that cloak."

The north road to Broduk was well conditioned, and they rode through the afternoon, stopping twice to check the packs and retie the tent bundle, but eating their road bread and smoked meat while still in the saddle. The horses were fresh and eager for the exercise, and Dhulyn wanted to put as much distance between them and the Nisvean camp as they could.

When the afternoon turned into evening and the first stars began to appear, Parno called a halt, looking up into the heavens.

"If we turn off here, we can pick up the road to the pass and cut off a great deal of the country."

"As well as getting us off the road they'll expect to find us on."

Parno turned in his saddle. "You think they'll send someone after us?"

Dhulyn had been turning that question over and over in her mind, and had an answer. "No, I don't think they will," she said. "That's what Jedrick was watching us for, to make sure we went where we claimed to go. But in two or three days, when their searching proves fruitless, they'll think of us again. By then, we'll be over the border."

The place Dhulyn finally chose for their campsite—she'd learned early in their Partnership not to leave such choices to Parno—was a small clearing in the center of a thicket of young pine trees, with a larger clearing close by to leave the horses. It wasn't a perfect camp. They were closer to the road than Dhulyn would have liked, and there was no nearby supply of water, though they were still carrying plenty. The sky was darkening swiftly, however, and they could not continue much longer. They threw the reins over their horses' heads, hobbled the new packhorse, and went together to take the heavy bundle of tent from Stumpy's back.

They eased it carefully to the ground, untied the lacing, and pulled it open, exposing what they had hidden with such care within the stiff folds of canvas. Dhulyn dug her fingers under the side of Edmir's chin and held her breath, counting.

"Give him an hour," she said, "he'll come to." She peeled down his leggings, knowing from experience that it would be better to inspect his wound while he was still unconscious.

"How's it look?"

"Not as well as I'd like," she said. "Get my kit and I'll clean and re-dress it now."

                              ~

"Slipped it right out from among the Lionsmane's pipes, I tell you. So there's your great Mercenaries for you." At these words Jedrick paused, fully expecting Nilo to make an appreciative remark. Though perhaps that was expecting too much, considering the amount the younger man had lost wagering against Parno Lionsmane. But when Nilo said nothing at all, Jedrick turned from where he stood in the doorway of his tent, ready to make a sharp remark of his own about sore losers.

The remark died on his lips.

"Nilo?" he said instead, taking a step toward where the younger man lay slumped forward over the square chest that stood between the cots and served them as a table.

Jedrick's immediate fear faded. *Dead men don't snore*, he told himself.

Nilo's cup was still rocking on an uneven spot on the carpet that formed the flooring of the tent, where it had fallen from his hand. The cup of Imrion brandy Jedrick had poured out of the Mercenary woman's flask.

"Nilo," Jedrick said, putting his own untouched cup down carefully to one side. "Nilo?"

An hour later he stood in Commander Lord Kispeko's tent, watching the commander's body servant being carried out, not snoring, but just as unconscious as Nilo had been.

"Call in the search parties," the commander said to Subcommander Renic. Kispeko's voice was harsh, as if his throat was tight. "There must be some way to turn this to our advantage." He turned to Romenec as Renic left the tent.

Jedrick kept silent, fearing to be dismissed, as the cavalry subcommander thought for a moment, his teeth worrying at his mustache. "We could send a messenger to Probic," Romenec finally suggested. "To the Blue Mage—no, to Queen Kedneara, at once."

"And how will that advantage us?" Kispeko sat on the edge of his worktable.

"We tell the Tegriani Queen that the Mercenary Brothers have kidnapped their prince."

"No one would believe such a thing of Mercenary Brothers. They are neutral, always have been." Even in his rage, Jedrick knew this much.

Romenec spread his hands, lifting his eyebrows. "We were as surprised as any. All we know is that they took him, and kept him, contrary to what we all understood of their Common Rule."

"It will be enough." Lord Kispeko was nodding. "People in doubt will choose to take no chances and withhold their aid from them. The Mercenary woman is an Outlander, remember. Perhaps blame can be placed on her." He fixed his eye on Jedrick. "It isn't the Brotherhood itself we have to convince, Squad Leader, nor even popular opinion. Only Queen Kedneara. And if we play our tiles carefully, we can make this almost as great an advantage to us as the Prince himself." He turned to Romenec. "There is something else?"

"Commander, it is imperative that ours is the story the queen hears first. I will pick an escort, and go myself." Romenec turned to Jedrick. "They went north, this is assured?"

Jedrick nodded. "As they would, if they were truly heading for Broduk."

Romenec spread his hands and gripped the edge of Commander Lord Kispeko's worktable, leaning forward to better study the map clamped to the table's surface.

"Then they will be heading for the Eagles Pass and from there to the Queen's Royal House at Beolind." He pointed to their own location in the Limona Valley. "We, however, can use the Limona Pass to reach Probic first, and tell our tale to the City Lord there long before the Mercenaries reach anyone of consequence in Tegrian." He tapped the "X" marked "Probic" with his right forefinger. "In the meantime," he continued, "I would suggest that a small party, a select group, be sent after the Mercenaries. Pick from among those who have not fought and trained with them."

The Commander was nodding, but before he could speak Jedrick was ready. "Permission to go after them myself, Commander," he said.

Kispeko held up his hand. "Romenec, choose your escort and go, lose no time. Jedrick, remain, I wish to speak to you."

Jedrick swallowed. This could not bode well.

Kispeko seated himself once again behind his desk, drumming his fingers on the top.

"She made a fool of you," he said quietly.

Jedrick pressed his lips together. He knew better than to answer.

"You are an ambitious man, Squad Leader. This episode won't do much to further your ambitions, will it?"

"No, Commander."

"No." Kispeko beckoned Jedrick closer. "But there are other ways to gain recognition, Squad Leader. Other ambitions to aspire to. How many men do you think you would need to take these Mercenaries?"

"If I may speak frankly, Commander." Jedrick prudently waited for Kispeko's nod. "I would take archers. It would be easier to kill than to capture them alive."

"And in that case?"

"Five men, counting myself. If they were the right men."

"Choose the right men, then, Squad Leader."

Jedrick drew himself to attention. "Thank you, Commander."

Kispeko did not dismiss him, but leaned on his elbow, tapping his lips with his fingers. "Squad Leader, the prince need not return with you. It will prove to our advantage if the Mercenary Brothers have killed him. Do you, and your ambitions, understand me?"

What he saw in Jedrick's face must have satisfied him.

"You may go, Squad Leader."

$\sim$

"Dhulyn—"

Dhulyn held up her right forefinger, sipped from the shallow metal ladle in her left hand, swallowed, and nodded before speaking.

"Only my Brothers may call me Dhulyn," she said to the prince. "To anyone else I am Wolfshead, or Scholar, and my Partner is Lionsmane, or Chanter. And your question?"

Prince Edmir blinked, as though he was unaccustomed to being given instructions, but he swallowed and dropped his eyes in a way Dhulyn didn't like.

"I don't understand how you managed to trick Jedrick into drinking the iocain without drinking any yourself," he said, as he took the cup of rabbit broth she passed him with a nod of thanks. His injured leg, the wound repacked and bound with fresh-boiled cloths, was stretched out straight in front of him. Dhulyn had made a small fire, using the fireproof cloth she and Parno had purchased in Berdana so as to leave no mark on the ground. Even if, at some future time, someone found their campsite and managed to deduce what it was, there would be no way to tell how many of them there had been.

"I didn't trick him," Dhulyn said, ladling a measure of broth with a few chunks of rabbit into a bowl for Parno before she served herself. "I've done three drug *Shoras*, ioca among them, so I could drink the iocain and feel no effects."

"Neither good effects nor bad," Parno added. "Because of the *Shora*, she can't chew the leaves for pain as you did when she brought you out of your tent, nor can she use the drug to sleep through a surgery or recuperation, as you did today."

"Not ever?"

Dhulyn swallowed the bit of rabbit she was chewing on before answering. "Well, no. That's the drawback to the drug *Shoras*."

"And the reason so few of the Brotherhood learn them." Parno took another mouthful of his own stew.

"You needn't look quite so worried, Lord Prince. There are other pain drugs I can use, if I wish to."

"She never wishes to," Parno said. "Don't listen to her."

The young man looked between them, a smile flitted across his face, and then he lowered his eyes again.

Dhulyn knew that look. *Something he's trying not to think about.*

"But *you* may wish to take iocain again tonight," Dhulyn said, as if it was a thing of no consequence. "After sleeping all day you may have trouble falling asleep naturally. A little iocain will help you drop off, and you will awaken in the morning refreshed."

Before Edmir could answer, Parno held up his finger. "Let's see how much there is left before we start dispensing it. There may be a greater need for it later."

They had unpacked very little, merely relieving the horses of their burdens and taking the bare essentials required to make a quick camp. Among those essentials, Parno's pipes had been set down on the bedroll he and Dhulyn would take turns using. Parno set down his stew bowl and dragged the bag closer to him. He undid the closures, slipping his hand past the bulge of the pipes into the bottom of the bag.

"Dhulyn, my heart," he said after a moment. "Did you take out the brandy flask already?"

"No," she said, a note of warning in her voice.

"Well, it isn't here now."

Dhulyn set down her own bowl and took the bag from her Partner. She took out each piece of his pipes, the air bag, the chanter, the drones, and laid them beside her on the ground. There was one of her books, a travel volume, the paper cut and bound between covers. A roll of thick felt proved to contain only the blue-glass cups she expected to find. There was no sign of the flask of iocain-laced brandy.

She looked up at Parno, as a mental picture of Jedrick handing the bag to him flashed through her mind.

"Jedrick," they both said at once.

"He admired the flask," Dhulyn said. "He asked me for it and I said no." She could feel her ears burning. How had she relaxed her guard so much?

"This is my doing." She began replacing the contents of the bag. "I was so sure I was tricking him, I did not watch for his tricking me."

"That may not have been his purpose—the snail dung may simply have wanted a flask from the Tin Isles."

Dhulyn pulled the bag's ties closed once more. The fact that Jedrick might only be a thief would not save them. "It's only a matter of time until he tries the brandy. He may have done so already."

Parno was shaking his head. "The horses are too tired—look who I'm advising about horses! *I'm* too tired; never mind the horses. We can't go on tonight."

"I'll take the first watch." Dhulyn stood, picked up her sword and crossbow, and stepped into the dark beyond the fire's light.

Four

EDMIR WOKE SUDDENLY, a hand over his mouth. For an instant he thought he was back in Commander Lord Kispeko's tent, but the pale dawn light filtering through the trees, and the feel of cool air on his face soon told him where he was—as did the stiffness in his leg. The Mercenary Brothers had wrapped him well, using all their own bedding as well as their cloaks, but after Dhulyn Wolfshead had put out the small campfire by the simple expedient of kicking it apart and then smothering it in the folds of the fire cloth, the night had grown colder and colder.

When he sat up, the Wolfshead spoke in that eerily quiet way they called the nightwatch voice.

"Five horses come down the road. They must have stopped just long enough to rest during the night, and started after us again long before dawn."

"Five? All they sent was five men? Are they mad?" Lionsmane squatted on Edmir's other side.

"Mad or not, they will reach us before the sun clears the trees."

Edmir froze. *How could she know that?*

Lionsmane whistled softly between his teeth.

"Give me up," Edmir said. "Leave me. Don't come to harm because of me." He clamped his mouth shut, glad it was too dark for them to see his chin tremble. He pushed the images of the battlefield, the dead and the dying back into the darkness in his mind. *No more.* No more dead because of him.

"Speak more softly, Lord Prince. You'd be surprised how far sounds will carry, even here among the trees." The Lionsmane began to unwrap Edmir's bedding, carefully easing the folds of cloth from around his injured leg.

"I say leave me." He took hold of Parno Lionsmane's wrist.

"We will not." The Wolfshead had risen to her feet and her whisper now floated down from above.

"Might they pass us by?" Edmir stifled a gasp as his leg was jarred.

"They might at that," the Lionsmane said. "They might be farmers going to market." He shot a glace at the Wolfshead and flashed her a grin. "Or a flock of sheep and not men on horseback at all, if you really believe my Partner could be mistaken. But do you know what the Mercenary Brotherhood calls those who prepare for what *might* happen, instead of what *can* happen?"

Edmir shook his head.

"We call them the dead. Up you come, Lord Prince."

Edmir looked at Parno Lionsmane's outstretched hand and swallowed. His thoughts seemed to throb in time to the pain in his leg. It shamed him, but he was relieved that the Mercenaries hadn't accepted his offer to leave him. Relieved that his mother wouldn't have to rescue him at the Caids' alone knew what kind of diplomatic price. But he didn't think he'd be walking—let alone fighting—any time soon. Not with his leg.

"I don't think I can," he said, even as he reached up. Parno Lionsmane grasped him by the forearm, and Edmir in turn locked his own hand around the Mercenary's wrist.

"Not to worry," Dhulyn Wolfshead said. "Parno Lionsmane can carry you."

Edmir grimaced. Yes, of course he could. The Wolfshead could probably carry him herself, if she had to. He took firm hold of his lower lip with his teeth as the disappointments of the last three days came crashing down on him. All he'd wanted to do was show his mother that he was as capable as any of her generals. What would she think if she saw him now? Unconsciously, he stood up straighter, choking back a hiss as he put his weight on his injured leg.

But Parno Lionsmane had seen it, and gripped him once more by the arm, placing his callused hand under Edmir's elbow.

Edmir held up his free hand. "Wait," he said. Even in his own ears, his voice sounded tight and breathless with pain. He took a slow deep breath to steady himself.

"Dhulyn Wolfshead," he said. "Are there more of those ioca leaves? I might be of more use to you if the pain was dulled."

The Wolfshead turned back into the clearing, reaching into the small pouch she kept at her waist and withdrawing a fold of oiled silk. She opened the tiny packet with care, frowning as she exposed the ioca leaves.

"These are the last. Let's hope we find no reason to regret using them now."

Edmir took the two almond-shaped leaves from the woman's long fingers and placed them on his tongue. It seemed that as soon as he tasted their sharp bitterness his leg throbbed less.

"Bring him to the horses." Dhulyn Wolfshead took two steps, and vanished.

Edmir looked at the spot where she'd disappeared. It was darker there, beyond the edge of the clearing, but surely not *that* dark. Edmir glanced at Parno Lionsmane, looked back again, and closed his mouth. The Lionsmane twitched the unrolled bedding off the ground one-handed, slinging it over his shoulder.

"Come," he said, handing Edmir the bag that held his pipes. "We'll want you with the horses."

Once in the thicker part of the trees, the light from the rising sun seemed to make the dark places darker, and the shadows more mobile and deceptive. Edmir had to be careful where he placed his feet, as his leg was apt to turn under him—just because he couldn't feel the pain, didn't mean the injury wasn't there. The Lionsmane, on the other hand, walked as though he was on a city pavement in the full light of the sun. Once Edmir stumbled, and the Mercenary turned back to help, but Edmir waved him on. He'd thought that his own training, supplemented by weeks in the field with the army, had toughened him. But a few hours with the Mercenary Brothers were enough to make him feel he was no soldier, but an actor playing a part. And a poor actor at that.

Well, I am *injured*, he said to himself. *That has to count for something*.

They slowed as they neared the other clearing where the horses had been left, the Lionsmane making comforting sounds under his breath both to warn and reassure the animals. This clearing was larger than the one in which they'd camped, the canopy of the trees thinner, and there was enough light for Edmir to see clearly.

Or maybe my eyes have finally adjusted. When they had camped the night before, the Mercenaries had not unpacked more than the night's bare necessities, though they had unburdened the horses for comfort. Only one, the larger packhorse, was hobbled. Of the other three, Edmir recognized the two cavalry horses, the gray and the spotted mare, from his first encounter with the Mercenaries. The fourth was a sturdy bay beast and looked to be what his mother's stableman called "a horse-of-all-trades," useful for both riding and hauling. Each animal stood near a tidy stack of packs, saddles, and saddlebags, though the gray gelding left his position and came to snuffle at the Lionsmane's hands.

"Hah, Warhammer, no fruit for you, greedy beast," Lionsmane said to the horse, rubbing its nose before he pushed the large head out of his way.

Dhulyn Wolfshead was on her knees, unrolling a long bundle that lay among the packs of the hobbled horse. From it, she extracted two unstrung recurve bows, and two shorter thicker bundles that Edmir recognized as quivers. She tossed one bow to Parno Lionsmane. Could they shoot in this light? He shook his head. They were Mercenaries. They could probably shoot blindfolded.

The Wolfshead gestured with the end of the unstrung bow in her hand. "Edmir can set up over there. Leave the horses where they are."

"I'll come with you and help," Edmir corrected her.

"You'll help best by staying here with both crossbows, Lord Prince," Lionsmane said, unhooking the two crossbows that normally hung from their saddles. "If anyone gets around us, it will be for you to stop them and keep them from the horses. So if you hear someone coming, shoot them."

"What if it's you?"

"I said shoot anyone you *hear*," he said, pushing the bundle that was their tent to one side. "Come, sit here." Edmir obeyed, setting one crossbow on his lap and laying the other down on the ground to his left next to the extra bolts. These were light bows, meant to be fired from horseback, and easily armed by a man sitting down.

"Where will you be?"

"Closer to the road."

Dhulyn Wolfshead had finished stringing her recurve bow and set it down against its quiver on the ground. She then went from horse to horse, catching and holding their heads in her hands, while she breathed into their nostrils, and spoke, murmuring words in a language Edmir had never heard before. The two warhorses quieted instantly, as did the other, smaller horse, but the fourth horse, the hobbled one, took a little longer to soothe. "What is she doing?" Edmir said, as the Lionsmane drew near him.

"Asking the horses to stay quiet and still, no matter what they see, or hear, or smell."

"Will it work?"

"It always has before."

"That's good," Edmir said. *That's good*, he thought again as he watched them disappear into the dark. The Lionsmane was right. They made no noise.

When they were nearly at the wide track that served as the road through this section of the Nisvean West Forest, Dhulyn stopped Parno with a click of her tongue, signaling him with a patting motion of her hand to wait as she stepped out into the road. Holding her bow out to her left, she squatted on her heels, resting her right hand on the track. Her eyes were closed, her head tilted as she listened. The colors of her Mercenary badge were bright in the light of the rising sun.

She straightened, made sure he was looking at her and tapped her ear, silently asking, "Do you hear them?"

Parno pressed his lips together and shook his head, then raised his hand to say, "Stop." There. A muted thunking of horses' hooves on the packed dirt of the road, a murmuring of voices in the still air. Dhulyn rejoined him under the trees. He pointed upward and, when she nodded, made a cup of his hands and braced himself as she placed her foot in it. She disappeared into the branches over his head with no more sound than the wind would have made moving the leaves. After several seconds a silk rope as thick as his thumb fell out of the trees over his head. Parno hung his bow across his shoulders, grasped the rope with both hands and pulled himself upward.

Dhulyn had found a place where a thick limb of the oak tree grew almost parallel to the ground. She pointed at it, then at Parno; pointed at herself, then at another fork just above where they were standing. With the habit of caution, Parno glanced around. From here they had good angle and height on the road. And they could reach the ground quickly if they had to. He beckoned Dhulyn closer and put his lips near her ear.

"Permit me to point out—just this once—that I suggested the sea route," he said. "It was you who insisted on going overland through Nisvea. I won't mention it again," he added. As he leaned away from her, Dhulyn grasped his shoulder and pulled him close again.

"You do, and it will be the last thing you ever mention."

"Now, now, be careful. You know they say Partners don't survive each other."

"It would be worth it."

Parno grinned at her disappearing shadow. "In Battle," he whispered.

"Or in Death," she said.

Avylos the Blue Mage ran his index finger along the spines of the seven books he kept on the high shelves behind his worktable. To the untutored eye, they were unremarkable, three herbal lexicons, two works of early philosophy based on the writings of the Caids, and two books of poetry. Avylos took down the larger of the philosophic works and sat down at his table. He centered the volume carefully on the tabletop, opened it to the middle, exposing the blank center pages. Noticeably different from the other pages of the book, these were folded once from a single piece of parchment made from the skin of a pure white kid goat. Matching pages, cut from the other half of the skin, and as identical as two halves of the same thing can be, occupied the central position in another volume of philosophy. One that did not sit on Avylos' table.

He waited until the rays of the setting sun moved to shine directly upon the blank pages. He made a sign in the air above the book.

"At my command," he said. "Speak to me."

"*I am here.*" As he watched, the words appeared on the page as though they were being written by an unseen hand.

"You have failed me," he said. For a moment it seemed the page trembled.

"*Please my lord,*" appeared on the page. "*It was the Mercenaries.*"

"Tell me."

"*Two Mercenaries,*" appeared on the page. "*A man, Parno Li-*

onsmane, and an Outlander woman, Dhulyn Wolfshead. They discovered and claimed the prince. I refused their claim, but they tricked us and took him. I have sent men after them, trusted men who will follow your instructions."

"Do they know the instructions are mine?"

"No my lord."

Avylos straightened, his shoulders pressed against the carved back of his chair. Mercenaries. He had met a Mercenary Brother once, a long time ago. The Brotherhood was ancient, much respected. Followers, some said, of the Sleeping God. He drummed his fingers on the tabletop.

"See that your men are successful," he said. "Make sure of it. In the meantime, send out word that Edmir of Tegrian is dead."

A pause before the words appeared on the page. *"I don't understand, my lord. You mean before we find and deal with them?"*

Avylos cracked the knuckles of his left hand one by one, resisting the desire to look at the casket that held the Stone. "These are Mercenary Brothers," he said dryly. "How would it be if you do not 'find and deal with them'? Let us prepare for the possibility that they might yet escape with their captive. Announce, therefore, that the man the Mercenaries took is not the prince. Prince Edmir died on the battlefield, and these rogue Mercenaries play some trick of their own. Find a suitable corpse, and use the excuse of its return to Tegrian to march on Probic."

"So the original plan holds? And I am still to have Probic?"

"Of course."

Another long pause. Avylos could almost hear the other man thinking. Finally. *"Very good, my lord."*

"At my command," Avylos said, and the page turned blank once more. He shut the book, and sat very still, with his hand on the cover.

Many spans away, Commander Lord Kispeko looked down at the blank pages in front of him and let go the breath he was holding. *So, that's the way it will be.* Not exactly the way Avylos had planned it, but this was better for the Nisveans. Let the Mercenaries be blamed for everything. If anyone could deal with the Mercenary Brotherhood, it was the Blue Mage. Kispeko shut the book and rose to return it to the chest beside his camp bed.

Parno was settling into the spot Dhulyn had found for him—back braced against the trunk, but at an angle to leave his bow arm free— when he heard the slow notes of the owl call that was Dhulyn telling him the troop of Nisveans were in sight. He did not see them himself until a few minutes later. There were five, as Dhulyn had said, and— what she couldn't have known—one of them was Jedrick.

He must have asked for the privilege, Parno thought, baring his teeth. Though it remained to be seen whether the man would still think it *was* a privilege in an hour's time. The trail was wide enough for the Nisveans to ride two abreast, and Jedrick occupied the leader's position in the center of the men. The two in front rode as scouts, three or four horse lengths ahead of their comrades, the two in back the same distance behind. One of those in the rear guard was Nilo, Parno realized, and he recognized the others as well, though he did not know their names. Friends of Jedrick's, without doubt.

The two in front were his. Dhulyn's greater elevation would allow her to reach the two in the rear. As he watched, the forward scouts slowed, finally stopping entirely as they allowed the others to catch up. Parno could almost feel Dhulyn's disapproval at this carelessness wafting down from the branch above him.

"It's along here," the taller of the two forward riders said, pointing into the trees as Jedrick stopped next to him. "If we leave the road here, we'll strike an old hunting trail that will get us to the pass in half the time."

"We'll catch them if we go this way?" Jedrick said.

"We should get ahead of them," the tall man said. "They don't know the country, and they *certainly* won't know the hunting trails. They'll have to stay along this road to the village of Tesnib, where the road to the pass crosses it."

True enough, Parno thought. That was exactly what they would have done, if they hadn't been Mercenary Brothers, for whom the positioning of mountain passes and the maps they appeared on were part of their Schooling.

"Jedrick." That was Nilo. "What made sense last night doesn't make sense this morning. You're right about killing the Mercenaries— we couldn't hope to capture them alive—but the prince is worth any ransom, we could slip him over the border ourselves, none the wiser, and say we got to them too late."

"Do you want to change my orders, Nilo? Is that what you're saying?" The other man stayed silent. "We're to kill them all. Those are our orders. Commander Lord Kispeko has his reasons."

A bit of tree bark struck Parno on the left hand. Without looking, his fingers working automatically, Parno let fly his first arrow, watched it sink into the left eye of the tall man, the one who knew the hunting trails so well. At the same moment, Nilo caught an arrow in *his* left eye. Parno's second arrow caught his other target in the throat as the man spurred his horse into the trees on the far side of the track, the spray of blood showing the man was dying as he went. As fast as he and Dhulyn were, however, Jedrick and the second rear guard managed to turn their horses and take flight down the road, back the way they had come.

Dhulyn's second arrow took the closer man in the small of the back, just where his armor left a gap as he leaned forward, but Jedrick, his red cloak bright in the light of the rising sun, was racing farther away.

Dhulyn beat Parno to the ground by the simple expedient of stepping off her branch and letting herself fall straight down, meeting the ground with bended knees. She ran quickly into the road, dodged the milling horses with a few quick steps, putting arrow to the string as she went. She still had a clear shot, but there was a bend in the road perhaps ten spans away, and the red cloak was quickly approaching it.

Parno opened his mouth, and shut it again as Dhulyn brought up her bow, released her breath, and let fly. Parno held his own breath. He'd seen her hit targets at greater distances—Caids, he'd done it himself—but that was with the longbow, and a still target. If she missed—he turned to grab the bridles of the two nearest horses.

Then he heard the cry, and saw the red cloak that was Jedrick hit the ground.

Dhulyn dropped her bow and swung herself up on the nearest horse, the animal instantly becoming calm and ready when it felt her in the saddle.

"Demons and perverts," Parno called after her as he struggled onto the back of the other horse. He was a good horseman—he *was*, even by Mercenary standards—but not compared to Dhulyn. Precious time was wasted as he persuaded his new mount that he was going to stay on its back, and that they were both going after the other horse. By the time he caught up with Dhulyn, however, she was already off her horse.

Jedrick must have been turning to look over his shoulder, for Dhulyn's final arrow had caught him in the neck with enough force to knock him off his horse, but it had missed any major arteries. Blood streamed from the wound, and he would die from it if he did not meet with a skilled Knife, but that death was still some time away. Jedrick's foot had caught in the stirrup as he came down. As Parno rode up, the man was trying keep the horse between himself and Dhulyn at the same time as he remounted.

Dhulyn grabbed the horse's tail, twisted it, sidestepped the stamping hooves to maneuver herself to Jedrick's side. She caught hold of the arrow shaft that protruded from the side of his neck with her right hand, swept his feet out from under him with her left foot, and pushed the point of the arrow into the ground as he went down. The horse snorted, backed away a few feet and stopped, shaking its head and blowing foam from its mouth.

Dhulyn squatted down on her heels next to the fallen squad leader. Parno swung himself off his own mount, but stayed back.

"Squad Leader," Dhulyn said. "No fear, I will not go without giving you the Final Sword. Though you are no Brother of mine, I won't leave you to die slowly on the road."

"I won't tell you anything." Jedrick's teeth were clenched and there was sweat on his forehead.

"We're to be killed, and the prince with us," Dhulyn said. "You have nothing further to tell us. Kispeko would have told you no more than that."

"I had to follow my orders," Jedrick said then.

Dhulyn nodded, pulling her knife out of its sheath in the small of her back. "You have your orders. We have our Common Rule." She covered Jedrick's eyes with her left hand and cut his throat with her right.

When it was over, Dhulyn wiped the knife off on Jedrick's shirt and straightened to her feet.

"*Blooded* snail dung," she said. "He's gone and bled all over my cloak."

Avylos the Blue Mage sighed at the muted sound of unexpected voices and put down the book he was reading by the light of the candelabra next to his chair. It was late at night, and only something very momentous would bring even Kedneara's royal pages to make such a noise in the Mage's wing.

"My lord, my lord Mage," called out a voice.

He rose and went into the corridor, pulling the door shut behind him to keep in the warmth of the small charcoal brazier under the table. A glance at the door of his workroom showed the magics intact. When he reached the door to his wing, it was to find two white-faced pages waiting for him.

"The Royal Guard Commander Lord Semlian sends for you, my lord Mage. A horse messenger has arrived from Probic for Kedneara the Queen." The taller page, the queen's page, spoke up before Avylos' attendant could. Avylos frowned, he knew this boy, a Balnian recently come to court, and ready to put himself forward.

"From Probic," he said.

"Yes, my lord Mage, changing horses all the way."

"I will come immediately." There were only two or three pieces of news from Probic that would warrant a horse messenger, and Avylos was curious to know which it would be.

This was one occasion, Avylos thought as he followed the new page through the almost deserted corridors to the stairs which would eventually take them to Kedneara's rooms, in which it might have been handier if he slept in the consort's apartments, rather than in his own wing. But he was more than the consort, more than Kedneara's bedwarmer—much more—and it was vital that people keep that always in mind. Long after Kedneara was no longer queen, he would still be the Blue Mage.

It was certainly not as consort that he was being sent for now, and sent for by Lord Semlian, not the queen. Possibly Semlian thought Avylos knew something about the news that had arrived, or possibly the guard commander suspected the news would hit the queen hard. Avylos began to walk a little faster.

One of the first things he had learned about the magic, even before the power finally found him, was that it did not affect women the same way as men. When it affected them at all. He'd asked his father about it, when he was still a small child, before they had all turned their faces away from him, and the old man had laughed, saying, "No power is without limit, Avi, least of all any power over women."

So it was ironic that the one woman it was relatively easy for him to influence and affect with his magics should be Queen Kedneara. Even the armies were almost all male now for that very reason—though he carefully made *that* magic temporary; troops who could never be killed or injured had a way of rebelling against their masters. But the queen's health had begun to fail early, as had her father's before her, and the magics that allowed Avylos to heal her—not *Heal*, as one of the Marked could have done, but better than anything the Royal Knives had ever achieved—also allowed him an access to her mind and spirit he did not have with other women.

Whatever the news was, it had not weakened her. Avylos could hear Kedneara shouting as he turned into the corridor of her rooms. The guards standing at her door looked up in relief when they saw him approaching, and threw open the doors to the anteroom. He nodded them aside and went in, putting his hand to the latch of Kedneara's sitting room door, and hesitated as the thick oak shook under it. Kedneara was throwing things. He must stop her, or she would strain her heart.

"But, my Queen." That was Counselor Csezik's voice. "We can send a complaint to the Mercenary House in Lesonika, and you can confidently expect—"

"What, send a nice well-mannered clerk to ask them to explain themselves?" There was enough sarcasm in Kedneara's tone to sour milk. "*Complain* that they've kidnapped my son? Are you mad? I want them banished. I want every Mercenary Brother out of my realm by midday tomorrow or I will send you all to the Black Dungeons! I want them GONE. Tegrian is closed to the Brotherhood. Do you hear me? CLOSED."

Everyone in the room found something to look at that wasn't the queen. No one wanted to be the one to explain that midday tomorrow would not be enough time to clear the country of Mercenaries.

Kedneara stalked back and forth over the cold stone tiles like a caged cat. She had thrown on a light robe of fine red wool embroidered with golden dragons, but was barefoot, her waist-length hair—still as dark as Edmir's—flying loose. The robe's trailing sleeves swung as Kedneara paced, and she kicked the train out from under her feet as she turned and saw him.

"Avylos!" She seized him by the front of his tunic. "Find him. Find Edmir!"

"Though I am not a Finder, my Queen, I might—"

"Are you not a Mage? Do something! Where have they taken him?"

Her breath was coming in short gasps, and there were two red spots high on her cheeks. If she did not restrain herself, she might easily have an attack. Almost as if she heard his thought, Kedneara took a deep breath, and then another, though she retained her grip on his tunic.

"Perhaps they only bring him to me? That's possible, isn't it? They are Mercenary Brothers, after all, they are to be trusted, aren't they? Of course they are. Perhaps all is well and Tzanek is an old woman who should be relieved of his post."

Here was the opening Avylos was hoping for.

"Let me sit a moment, my Queen, let me see what I can learn. I was about to say that I am not a Finder, but where your children are concerned I have taken certain other steps, and I may be able to tell you—"

"A chair for the Blue Mage, quickly, quickly, and whatever else he needs."

It was almost pathetically easy to convince them that he was performing a great feat of magic, as he took out his silver dagger, called for new, unlit candles and a bowl of the darkest wine. However, he had faked magics before, long ago, before his power found him, and he'd learned then that a good show would convince its audience of anything. It soured his stomach a little to fall back on those tricks now, when he had real power at his fingertips—but he had no intention of using up real power for this.

After a suitable passage of time, and very visible effort, he set his dagger down, blew out the candles, and took the queen by the hands. "Sit down, my Queen. I must insist."

Kedneara was so white her eyebrows stood out like stains on her face.

"I fear to give you this news, my Queen. You must be strong, for all of us, for Tegrian. For your remaining child."

The screams, Avylos thought with carefully concealed satisfaction, must be audible down in the Great Hall.

*　　*　　*

Hours later Avylos shut the door of Kedneara's bedchamber, letting the latch down slowly until it caught without making a sound. The outer room was now blessedly empty, and Avylos leaned against the doorframe, rubbing his face with his hands. He took a deep breath, tugged his robe straight, smoothed back his hair, and strode across the room to the outer door. The two guards stationed in the anteroom leaped to attention as he came out.

"My lord Mage," they said simultaneously as he emerged.

"Guards." A cool nod to them, another to the pages who stood up from their couches as he passed, and he was at the door to the queen's apartments and through it into the wide corridor beyond.

How fast did horse messengers travel, he wondered as he took the shortest route back to his own rooms. And two Mercenary Brothers? How quickly did they travel, considering they had an injured prince with them? The official proclamation of Edmir's death would be made by the queen from her throne tomorrow, but there were one or two people who needed to know now, tonight. Could he afford the power?

It was late, and even taking into account the news which must be even now spreading through the Royal House on the lips of every servant, page, guard, and noble, Avylos passed only three servants who quickly stepped out of his path as he returned to his own wing. His workroom, when he reached it, was deserted, though the wards he had placed on the door showed what he expected. Two people had attempted to open the door in his absence and been thwarted. He made a mental note of their identities, and the people most likely to have sent them. Princess Kera had also attempted to enter, and had been successful.

He smiled, entered the room and swung the door shut behind him. Without conscious decision, his feet took him directly to the casket that held the Stone and he had one hand on the lid and the other hunting in his pocket for the key before he caught himself and stopped. He breathed in slowly, lifting both hands and taking a step back. As an added precaution, he clasped his hands behind his back as he considered.

If he used the Stone again now, who did he have to draw upon to refill it? There was the Champion Archer, his talent and art still hot within a body almost too old to the pull the bow. The second assistant cook who made those marvelous peach pastries—a pity to use her at all, really. Even though the recipe had been passed on, that particular cook would never again create something so good. There was power and talent left yet in both of those. And, finally, this morning, Lord Semlian had come to him about that ambitious new commander in the Royal Guard. The commander who hadn't yet learned that in order to advance in the Tegrian Guard one must be either talented, *or* ambitious. Not both together.

Avylos thought a moment longer. Yes, that should be enough.

The key was in his hand, the casket was open, and the Stone glowing in response to his touch before the thought was even complete. The Stone had seven symbols etched into its otherwise smooth surface. Four were evenly spaced—like compass points—the width of his smallest finger from one end of the cylinder. A circle with a dot in the middle, a simple straight line, a rectangle, and a long triangle like a spearhead. A finger width farther in was a plain circle, all by itself. Around the other end were only two symbols, though these were larger. One he knew, having drawn it in the air many times, the three-line symbol for "light." The other, using only two lines, he did not know; though he'd tried drawing it, nothing had ever happened.

"You have more power than you are giving me," he told the Stone, stroking the warm, smooth crystal. "And when I have found your secret, then I shall need neither queen nor realm."

"*Gehde. Gehde. Monos. Aharneh,*" he said.

The Stone glowed brighter. He took hold of it by either end, and twisted.

The world disappeared in a blaze of blue light.

When the light had faded, and the world returned, the Stone still glowed faintly but perceptibly. Avylos let out a long sigh. He would leave it set, and ready for the morrow, but in the meantime, the Stone would go back into its box, he would shut the lid, turn the key, and put it away once more.

Temptation behind him, Avylos took one of the two books of poetry from the shelf behind his worktable and opened it to its central, blank pages. Like the philosophical work he'd used earlier in the day, these pages had been made from half a sheet of parchment, itself the treated skin of a pure white animal, in this case an albino calf. Avylos threw open the tall window shutters and let in the moonlight. The moon was not quite full, but there was more than enough light at this hour to illuminate the surface of the book.

He sat down at the table, placed his hands palm down to each side of the open volume and spoke.

"At my command," he said, and waited. For a long moment nothing happened, and he frowned until he remembered the hour. "At my command," he repeated. This time the answer came.

"I am here, my lord Mage," appeared in script on the page before him.

"I have grave news to tell you, City Lord Tzanek," Avylos said. "Prince Edmir has fallen."

"But, my lord——" the writing broke off, almost as it would if a pen point had broken, before starting again. *"Surely you are mistaken? How is this possible?"*

Avylos bit back his irritation. How dare the man question him like this?

"Do not concern yourself unduly. Kedneara the Queen's Messengers will be sent out tomorrow to inform the country of this tragedy, but there may yet be a service you can perform in the meantime."

"Name it, my lord."

That was better. "It concerns the two Mercenary Brothers who were said to have taken the prince. If they should appear, you will arrest them in the queen's name."

"I do not understand, Lord Mage. If there are any to be trusted out of hand, surely the Brotherhood——I did not understand the Nisveans' declaration, though I passed it along to the queen, of course——and now you say the prince is dead——"

"Enough. The queen has banished the Brotherhood from Tegrian. See that you make this generally known." The man was a chatterer. Not for the first time Avylos thought how lucky it was that the writing did not remain permanently on the pages.

"Of course, my lord Mage." Now the writing appeared hesitant, as if the man on the other end was not very confident in what he was saying.

"My magics tell me there is some deep deceit afoot," Avylos said. "Some plan of which I see only the edges. If you should see the Mercenary Brothers, they may well have a young man with them, a man they will say is the prince, but you will not be deceived." Avylos waited, but again, the reply was slow in coming. He placed the fingertips of his left hand on the edge of the blank page. "I say that you will not be deceived."

"I will not be deceived."

"The young man they have with them is not Edmir."

"The young man they have with them is not Edmir."

Did the writing seem to be in a different, yet very familiar hand? Avylos smiled.

"You know Edmir well, have known him from a child, and you will not be deceived."

"I will not be deceived."

"Mercenaries who have killed a Prince of Tegrian, even accidentally, would wish to make themselves appear innocent. Clearly the person with them is not Edmir."

"Clearly. The young man they have with them is not Edmir. I will not be deceived."

"Excellent. It is a comfort to be counseled by someone so able as yourself. You will inform me, if you have occasion to arrest these people."

"At once, my lord Mage." The subtle difference in the writing was gone.

"At my command," Avylos said, and closed the book.

———⌇———

"We'll saddle these three," Parno said, turning to Edmir and indicating the gelding, the gray mare, and the sturdy bay. The Mercenary had returned alone, silently, and in answer to Edmir's questioning had told him that they could now move on.

Edmir was just tightening the girth on the smaller horse he took to be his own when Dhulyn Wolfshead suddenly materialized on the animal's far side. The horse merely rolled an eye at her, but Edmir had taken a step back and put his hand to his belt before he registered who it was.

The Wolfshead smiled, the small scar making her lip curl. "At least you were going for your weapon, my princeling," she said. Edmir opened his mouth to reply, but she had already turned to the spotted mare, picking up the saddle pad and slinging it over the mare's back with a practiced flick of the wrist.

"I took the horses into the wood on the far side from the bodies, and told them not to worry. They'll work themselves free when they feel like it." Edmir looked from one to the other. Parno Lionsmane had finished with his gray gelding and had turned to sort through the packs that were still on the ground. Apparently nothing more would be said of the five horsemen on the road. Dhulyn Wolfshead was studying the ground in front of her, frowning, but it was the frown of decision making.

"We were heading for the Eagles Pass," she said, taking up a bit of broken branch lying to one side and beginning to draw on the dirt in front of her. Edmir recognized the curves of the Limona River, and the road they had been following. "The one on the north road from Limona, and the one that would take us most quickly to Beolind, and your mother." She nodded to Edmir. "And that is where they will look for us again. The pass of Limona itself—" she drew in the road that Edmir's army must have followed. "Clearly we cannot retrace our steps and use it. But there is another." She cast a lightning-quick glance around the clearing. "We won't be able to take everything with us, however. The horses must be lightened."

"There's no other pass," Edmir said. "Not in this part of the border." He hadn't spent all that time with his tutors for nothing.

Dhulyn Wolfshead didn't look up from her drawings. "None on any maps, no. But a pass there is, nonetheless."

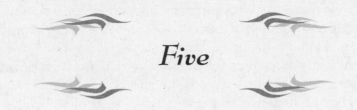

Five

EDMIR WINCED, SUCKING IN his breath. When she heard it, Dhulyn Wolfshead called out to her Partner to stop and, scrambling around her mare on the uneven ground, had the back of her hand against his cheek before Edmir could move out of her way.

"Fever, for certain," she said, shifting to touch his forehead with the backs of her long fingers. "How much pain is there?"

"Not much." The next thing Edmir knew his chin was being held in a grip that felt like iron and the Wolfshead's gray eyes were boring into his soul.

"What a liar you are," she said. "Your breath is short, your skin is white around your mouth, and there are lines on your face where there were none before. You are not yet in so much pain that you cannot move, but it grows." She nodded. "And it brings fever." The two Mercenaries exchanged a long look.

"He should not be afoot." Parno Lionsmane said finally from his position in the lead. "It will slow us, but he should mount. And the sooner we find shelter . . ."

"The better it will be," Dhulyn Wolfshead finished.

Any protest that Edmir thought of making died before he could open his mouth. One moment he was standing, the reins of the small horse, Stumpy, in his left hand, the next Dhulyn Wolfshead had grasped him by knee and elbow and he was in the saddle, Stumpy steady but snorting under him. He still had the reins in his hand.

And the Mercenaries were right. Sore and aching as his leg now was, the pain was nothing compared to how he'd felt walking on it. He realized, now that his weight was off it, that he could not have gone very much farther.

Dhulyn Wolfshead took Stumpy's reins, and let her own horse, the mare Bloodbone, follow of her own accord. Ahead of them, Parno Lionsmane led both his horse Warhammer and the packhorse, burdened now only with their travel food and what extra weapons the Mercenaries could not do without—which seemed, to Edmir, to be all of them. He would have preferred they pack a few more blankets, but everything else, including the much sighed over tent, had been left hidden—hoisted up into the trees—in the clearing in the woods where the horses had been the night before.

"No way to know if we can ever come back for it," Lionsmane had said as he'd hauled on the rope. "But we've at least a chance that anyone looking for Jedrick and his boys won't find this as well."

The sun had now been up for some hours, and they had been leading their horses up increasingly steep hills, jagged and treeless, since they had left the main trail. The trees had changed from the oaks of the forest below to pines and the occasional aspen. They were still climbing, and as far as Edmir could tell, they'd left any real path behind. Between the trees there was nothing but rocks, tufts of dried grass, and hardly a flat spot at all. His head felt heavy. *There's no pass here*, he thought. Stumpy shifted abruptly to the right, and, jolted, Edmir looked up, aware that he had started to doze in the saddle. Parno Lionsmane had stopped, and was looking upward, as if the rocks around them could speak to him.

"Are you sure of the way?" Edmir asked, unable to keep a note of irritation from his voice. The light seemed much too bright.

Dhulyn Wolfshead pointed. "We are now."

Edmir followed her pointing finger to where the silhouette of a bird hung in the sky far above their heads, the shape of its wings marking it for an eagle of some kind. As he watched, the bird stooped, falling so sharply that Edmir exclaimed, certain that it had miscalculated and would dash itself to pieces on the rocks.

Instead, it pulled up in the last possible second and landed, talons outstretched, within easy bowshot of where Parno Lionsmane stood. Warhammer only tossed his head, backing a pace, but the packhorse shied, its hooves sliding on a patch of loose earth, and Dhulyn Wolfshead dodged forward, grabbing its mane and placing her hand over its eyes as she crooned into its ear. *Thank the Caids*, Edmir thought, that Stumpy had only wiggled his ears. If the short-legged beast had so much as tossed its head, Edmir was sure he'd have fallen straight off.

Instead, Edmir reached for the crossbow that hung from his saddle, but found his wrist suddenly engulfed in Parno Lionsmane's rough hand. "Wait," he said. "It's a Racha bird."

Edmir's mouth fell open and Stumpy took a grudging step forward before deciding to ignore the involuntary tightening of his rider's knees. *A Racha*. Edmir had read of them, companion birds to the Cloud People of the Letanian Peninsula. He had even seen a Racha once, as a child in the public square in Beolind, his mother's capital, but he had never seen one so close. If, that is, the Mercenaries were not mistaken. Though large, this bird seemed very much like an ordinary eagle to him.

Scrambling around the horses, Dhulyn Wolfshead reached a rock outcrop about half the distance between them and the waiting bird. She faced the Racha bird, but turned slightly, so that Edmir had her in profile. *And so she can see us in her periphery*, he realized. She was a Mercenary Brother, after all.

"I am Dhulyn Wolfshead," she said, pressing her tongue to her top lip before continuing. "The Seer."

Fingernails bit into his palms as Edmir tightened his fists. *A Seer*. By the Caids, was she *really*? Or was she something else? The Marked were rare in this part of the world, though not unknown. But *Seers* were rarest of all. Edmir couldn't even think of anyone who'd ever met one, though there was supposed to be one in Delmara. He shivered, suddenly feeling cold despite his fever. Why had they not told him before?

The Wolfshead turned her head as the Racha bird shifted and the light caught her hair, the color of old blood.

The color of Avylos' hair. And she was pale like Avylos. And an Outlander, like Avylos. Was Dhulyn Wolfshead also a Red Horseman, or was all this just coincidence?

And was it coincidence, then, that these particular Mercenary Brothers had been among the Nisveans? The only time that Avylos' magic hadn't worked? Coincidence that they were bringing him back to Avylos now? Edmir swallowed past a lump in his throat. He lifted a hand that weighed like lead and rubbed at his damp brow. Why couldn't he *think*?

Surely, he was concerned for nothing? Outlanders were not so very uncommon—nor was red hair. And even if Dhulyn Wolfshead had been a Red Horseman, Mercenary Brothers had no pasts, no lives before the Brotherhood; everyone knew that was their Common Rule. Besides, Edmir rubbed at his face again, he needed them, he could not even get down off this horse without help. He *had* to trust them. He had no choice.

But his brain kept arguing. What other magics were they hiding? He squeezed his eyes shut.

"I was Schooled by Dorian the Black Traveler," Dhulyn said to the waiting bird. "And I have fought with my Brothers at Sadron, at Arcosa, where I found my Partner, Parno Lionsmane, and with the armies of the Great King at Bhexyllia. We have come from the battle of Limona, where the forces of Nisvea have triumphed over the invaders of Tegrian. We have with us a charge of honor, and we seek help, shelter, and passage."

The Racha had watched her while she spoke, turning its head from side to side as it looked first from one bright golden eye and then the other. When she fell silent, the bird waited a moment, as if to be sure she had finished, before bobbing its head, shaking out its wings, and launching itself into the sky. It did not fly immediately away, however, but hovered and beat its wings once, twice, three times, and was gone.

Dhulyn turned, feeling two days without sleep in every tired muscle, and in the grit in her eyes. "Clearly we are to wait."

"Wait for what?" The words were bitten off and spit out of a tight mouth.

Dhulyn glanced at Parno, but her Partner only raised his eyebrows. She turned to the prince, schooling her face to serenity, her lips to a smile.

"The Cloud People, of course."

"Cloud People? There are no Clouds in Tegrian." The prince's voice shook.

"Is your pain worse?" Dhulyn took a step toward him.

He shook his head, leaning away from her. "There are no Clouds here. What really comes?" Dhulyn would not have thought it possible that a person could sound both angry and resigned, but somehow Prince Edmir was managing it. She rubbed at her face, but the gritty feeling never left her eyes. She rubbed at the pain in her lower back and stretched, exaggerating the movement as much as she could, loosening the muscles in her shoulders, before looking around her, and finally sitting down on a nearby outcropping of rock.

Prince Edmir yawned, his body responding to the messages of fatigue and exhaustion hers had sent it.

What was biting the boy? He was looking at her as if she'd threatened to kill his dog. Parno looped the packhorse's lead around his wrist and, as if aping her, rubbed at his own eyes, and in that gesture, she understood. Had it frightened the boy to know she was a Seer? Was that it? True, the Marked were rarer as you went farther west, but their skills were valued the more for it—any Mender, Finder, or Healer could set their own prices, though most followed the rules of their Guild. She had never heard that there was any particular prejudice against the Marked in Tegrian. She glanced at Parno, scratching her nose using the fourth finger of her left hand. Let him be wary.

"There are no Cloud villages here, truly." She answered the prince's declaration as if she had not seen the sullen look that made him seem so much younger than he was. "No settlements as there are in the Antedichas Mountains between Imrion and Navra. But there *is* a small colony of Racha birds here, and where there are Rachas, Clouds will always come for their Life Passage, to attempt to bond with the infant birds."

"And that is all that comes now? No squad of the Tegrian Guard? Not . . . not my stepfather?"

"Your stepfather?" Parno straightened from securing hobbles to the new packhorse against the return of the Racha, and stepped forward so that he stood between her and Prince Edmir. "Are you expecting him?"

The prince wrinkled his nose and looked away. *Sun and Moon.* Dhulyn narrowed her eyes. That had not been the look of a young man, a commander of an army. That had been the look of a frightened child, a child whose world had changed under his feet, and not for the better.

She sighed. "The Racha bond only with Clouds, Lord Prince, as apparently you do not know. I had not heard that the Blue Mage was a Cloud, or had any Clouds among his followers. Am I incorrect?"

The prince now looked at her with narrowed eyes. "No."

"Then I do not know who, or what it is *you* expect," she continued. "But the Lionsmane and I expect Clouds."

"And a good thing that is, yes? Since that's what you're getting."

Dhulyn had not heard the woman approach, but iron discipline kept her from showing any surprise.

"I greet you, Seer." The raven-haired woman stepped lightly from rock to rock as she came down the slope toward them, the seven gold feathers tattooed on the left side of her face clear in the afternoon sunshine. "I am Ayania, once of Pompano, yes? And now of Hrylesh."

"My Partner, Parno Lionsmane the Chanter, and our charge of honor, Edmir of Tegrian."

"*The* Edmir of Tegrian?" Ayania had reached their level finally and, her eyes on Edmir, had tentatively stretched out her hand. Dhulyn touched her own fingers to the Cloudwoman's.

"According to my Partner, and to the prince himself, yes."

"Who was it you *were* expecting then, Lord Prince of Tegrian, if not a Cloud?"

Edmir studied his hands, clasped together on the pommel of his saddle, and did not speak. Dhulyn shrugged and answered the Cloud herself. "He seems to think his stepfather has something to do with us."

"No room for the Blue Mage in our caves, that's certain, yes? Room for the three of you, however, since it's not the season for young birds. So long as you don't mind close quarters, yes? Ho! What's to do with him?"

Parno had moved fast enough to catch Edmir before he'd done more than tilt slightly out of the saddle, helped by Stumpy's shifting over. The beast was well-trained.

"He's had an arrow through the leg, followed by hard usage. You won't have a Healer with you?"

"Too right, we won't," Ayania said. "But we've herbs and medicines. Between us and two Mercenary Brothers, we'll have enough experience to keep him alive and on both feet, yes?" She raised her head and smiled at the bird that hovered high over their heads, almost too far away to see. "We can leave him on the horse if we go 'round the long way. Once we're in the caves, we'll see to his leg, yes? And what else did you need?"

"Sleep." Dhulyn said. Sleep where it was safe, where there was no need for either of them to keep watch. It wasn't every Mercenary Brother who could get those things from Clouds. But as a Seer, she could.

The Cloudwoman smiled. "This way, Seer, if you please."

Dhulyn blinked. By the angle of the moonlight coming through the smoke hole in the roof of the cave, she'd been asleep several hours. She could hear three people breathing, Parno right behind her on the soft mass made of their combined bedrolls, Edmir a few feet away on one of the cots, Ayania nearby on the other. The sleeping chamber was otherwise still and silent, with Ayania's two apprentice Racha Clouds sharing the watch with their birds in the outer cave. Dhulyn shifted, checked that there were several layers of cloth between them before pushing her back firmly against Parno. She shut her eyes again.

By the time they had reached the caves the evening before, the spasms that had started in Dhulyn's lower back had moved to her abdomen, and she was certain the pain from her woman's time would keep her from sleep. But her inability to take the major drugs for pain—and to have them used against her—did not prevent her use of minor drugs and remedies. While Parno and Ayania had tended to Edmir, Ilyan, the older of the Cloud's two young apprentices, with five feathers tattooed on the left side of his face, had heated stones for Dhulyn, while his fellow apprentice warmed water with valerian in it. Both had watched her out of the corners of their eyes, even the Clouds' legendary reserve insufficient to stifle their curiosity.

They would have helped her with the stones, too, anxious to perform a service for a Seer, had not Parno shooed them away. "Best you don't touch her skin to skin," he'd told them. "Her Visions come more often and stronger with her woman's time, and you don't want her to See anything about you, now do you?"

From what Dhulyn had seen in their faces, she rather thought they did. And it seemed that Parno had seen the same expressions.

"Better you shouldn't know, believe me," he'd told them. "If it's good, it makes your delight in it smaller, and if it's bad, you'll only feel your pain and your fear for that much longer."

"We could avoid it, though, couldn't we? The thing that would cause the pain and fear?" The younger apprentice, with two feathers tattooed on her left cheek, showing that she'd had her Racha only two months, had said before Ayania had cuffed her quiet.

"You might, if Dhulyn Wolfshead's Visions were clear, complete, and either you or she could understand them," Parno said. "When I say it's better you shouldn't know, I speak from knowledge."

"Leave the Seer be," Ayania said. "She's not here to help us, yes? We are here to help her." An attitude that Dhulyn had been counting on. She rarely revealed her Sight, but the Cloud People considered themselves the ancient and traditional protectors of the Marked, and she was as safe with them as she would have been with her own Brotherhood.

Dhulyn shifted, trying for a position that would relieve the pain in her back. What Parno had said was true, her Visions *were* often incomplete, and for that reason misleading. All the same, she thought now, as she drifted off to sleep, she should try to See in the morning. Her Visions were stronger, clearer, at her woman's time, as if the blood brought them. And sometimes a partial glimpse of the future was better than none.

When Dhulyn woke again, daylight was coming in through the hole in the cave's roof, and her stomach was rumbling from the smell of cooking meat. She was alone in the bedding—in fact, alone in the sleeping cave but for the prince in his cot.

The stone against her belly had gone cold, but it seemed the worst of her pains had gone with the heat, as was often the way. Dhulyn tossed back the coverings Parno had heaped on her and rolled to her knees, automatically making mental note of the location of her boots, her sword belts, gloves, and weapons. All close at hand. She got to her feet and stretched, holding each position until the stiffness in the muscle slowly loosened. She squatted by the prince.

They had unwrapped and cleaned the wound, packing it with herbs they had brought with them to draw out the poisons. The Clouds had no iocain, but poppy syrup they did have, laced with fens bark tea, and Edmir still slept, his breathing heavy under its influence. His black hair, thick and curly, had fallen back from his face, and only his scanty beard stubble betrayed his age. Otherwise his face in repose was as unlined and innocent as that of a young child.

He had one hand tucked under his chin. Lower lip between her teeth, Dhulyn wrapped her fingers around his exposed wrist.

Edmir's hair is still curly, but the black shows streaks of steel, and his face is more oval, now that he has a grown man's forehead. There's a straight scar on his left cheek. And his hair is shorter now, much shorter, the close-cropped head of a man who regularly wears a helm. He is wearing a heavy wool tunic, finely woven and warm, with a dark red lining thrown over his shoulders. It is night, and Edmir is alone.

This is a tent. There is torchlight shining faintly through the canvas behind him. He is sitting at a camp table, like the one Commander Kispeko had, like many Dhulyn has seen. Edmir is writing; his ink, in a ceramic bowl, is kept warm over a small burner that provides both heat and light. The point of his pen splits. Cursing, his breath making small clouds in the cold air, Edmir searches the tabletop before rising and fetching a knife from the belt pouch that hangs on a tent support.

He lives, Dhulyn thinks. *And he keeps the leg. . . .*

A tall woman with hair the color of old blood hanging in a thick braid down the center of her back strides along a path in a small formal garden. Dhulyn has Seen this woman before, and knows this Vision is of the past, and not the future. But what would bring her mother into a formal garden? When and why? Is it before Dhulyn herself was born? Her mother looks younger than the last time Dhulyn has Seen her, and she wears a pale blue gown, embroidered with vines and leaves in darker blue lines. She turns, and Dhulyn prepares to be greeted. She know this much about the Sight, that if she can See her mother, her mother can also See her. But the expected smile does not come, instead her mother's brow furrows, her smile fades, and she reaches for the weapon that does not hang from her belt. . . .

A hawk-faced woman with hair the color of summer wheat sits at a narrow table polishing something in a dark blue cloth. Dhulyn's heart skips a beat, she has SEEN this coloring before. A lamp like nothing Dhulyn has ever come across is attached by a metal bracket to the side of the narrow table, and light shines straight down on the woman's hands, and reflects upward to harshen the bladelike planes of her face. She peels back the polishing cloth, revealing a blue crystal rod. She smiles, satisfied, and fits a jeweler's lens to her left eye. She picks up a carving tool, so fine Dhulyn can hardly glimpse the tip of the blade, and begins to work close to the edge of the cylinder . . .

The vibration of sword blade striking sword blade shivers through the hilt she holds in her right hand. Another thrust—the man whips his blade around hers, but he's not fast enough to disarm her. She leaps back, dodges forward with her blade, avoids the parry, and draws blood from her opponent's arm. A lunge to the right, followed by two steps back, he jumps on a bench and begins to rain blows on her from above—she *knows* this *Shora*, but if this is practice, why, then, has blood been drawn? The next blow comes from . . . there, and can by countered with—a gasp of indrawn breath as her sword enters her opponent's side. But it is Parno who falls to his knees as she withdraws the blade from between his ribs. She puts out her hand to touch his face.

Wait, this is wrong. This is not how Parno dies—she wills herself to wake, the Vision to clear, before the decks slant, and the wall of water comes to wash Parno overboard into the churning sea . . .

<hr/>

Dhulyn sat back on her heels, lifting her hand from Edmir's wrist. Her heart was racing and there were tears in her eyes.

<hr/>

"Never seen the *Shora* before?" Parno dropped down next to Edmir on the rock shelf that served the Clouds as an outdoor bench. He had a fold of soft leather in his hands, along with a few knives that needed cleaning.

The prince turned toward him, wincing as his body began to follow the turn and his leg moved. Parno knew the arrow wound had much improved in the two days since they'd come into the Clouds' mountain stronghold, but a little more time would be needed to be sure all the heat was gone from the wound. The Racha woman Ayania was very pleased with the healing, and none of them were in any mind to undo her good work. Before going off into the hills in the early morning light with her apprentices and their Racha birds, Ayania had handed Edmir a walking staff, with the warning not to press himself too far.

"Lionsmane." Edmir acknowledged Parno's question with a nod.

"I've seen my mother's Guard practice what they call *Shora*. But though there have been Mercenary Brothers at her court from time to time, I have never seen . . ." At a loss for words, the prince gestured toward Dhulyn. "She doesn't even look down."

"That is the Mountain Goat *Shora*," Parno said, putting down the bundle of knives between them. He turned his own eyes to where Dhulyn Wolfshead moved as surefooted as the *Shora* she was practicing. *About two thirds of the way through*, he noted. "It's specially designed to perfect your technique on rocky terrain. If you'd been up earlier, you'd have had a chance to watch me."

"Can you do that?"

Parno nodded. "The Mountain Goat's one of the twenty-seven basic *Shora* all Mercenary Brothers must learn to be considered Schooled. There's eighty-one all told, some with more moves, some with less. I know a few more than the basics," he shrugged, unrolling the bundle and laying out on the wide strip of soft leather five knives of differing lengths, along with the honing stone. "Not as many as Dhulyn Wolfshead, she must know close to sixty now. But then it is her ambition to be a Schooler herself one day, if she lives. If we both do." Parno fell silent, picking up the honing stone in his left hand and a long straight dagger in his right. *We'll live*, he thought. He caught Edmir's worried look and raised his eyebrows at the boy. But the prince turned away before speaking.

"Will she not use her magic to stay alive?"

Parno fell silent again, automatically finishing the stroke on the blade before he let his hands relax into his lap, and looked at the prince with new eyes. There was a tension to him, a staring to his eyes, that had nothing to do with pain from his wound.

"What has my Partner done to you to deserve that tone, besides rescue you from an embarrassing captivity?"

That drew Edmir's head around. He tried to draw himself upright, difficult to do on the uneven seat of the stone. "I may use what tone I wish," he said. "I am the Lord Prince of Tegrian."

Parno blinked, but even the long-practiced habits of courtesy could only do so much. Dropping the stone, he slapped his knee, and laughed out loud. Dhulyn froze in her *Shora* and looked their way.

Color flooded the prince's face. He began to stand, but Parno took his elbow in an iron grip before he got very far.

"Sit down, you blooded brat." The words were harsh, but Parno was still half laughing. He released Edmir's arm and the boy sank down until he had perched himself on the edge of the bench. Parno picked up the stone, and ran it once more down the long blade.

"You speak to a Mercenary Brother," he said, keeping his eyes on his work. "Not to one of your Tegrian Houses—though the Caids know, if it comes to that, I left behind me a more noble House even than yours when I became a Mercenary Brother.

"But I did leave it behind me, so I'll say no more of it. Courtesy is something you owe all men, Lord Prince, even those you intend to kill—and even those who have rescued you," Parno continued. "And it's for the sake of that courtesy I'll explain to you now."

He glanced up. Edmir was watching him out of the corner of his eye, but his mouth was twisted to one side in what was clearly a sheepish apology.

Parno smiled, put down the cleaned weapon, and picked up the next, a wrist knife. "Dhulyn Wolfshead is no Mage. First and last, she is a Mercenary Brother, and my Partner. Though she is the younger, she is Senior Brother, having been a Mercenary longer than I. She is also Marked—you know the Marked?"

Edmir nodded. "I've seen some, a Mender and two Finders, though no Healer has ever come to be licensed at my mother's court."

"Licensed?"

"They say that in my father's time there was a rash of fakery in the country, a group of people claiming to be Marked, and cozening all who came to them for aid. My father arranged for anyone claiming to be Marked, or claiming any other kind of magic, to be brought to the capital to be examined and licensed. It's gone on ever since, but fewer and fewer come now."

When Parno glanced at him, Edmir was looking to where Dhulyn Wolfshead once more fought her invisible foe. The boy licked his lips. "And there's never been a Seer."

"Not surprising, they're so rare. What have you heard of the Seer at Delmara?"

"Only that there is one again, after so many years that the Seers' Sanctuary stood empty. And that news came fairly recently."

"If there are Marks living in Tegrian, licensed, why do their numbers grow fewer?"

Once more, Edmir nodded, as if it was a question he'd thought of himself. "We have no Guild here, so most of the newly Marked go elsewhere to be trained, to Imrion for the most part, or Berdana. They rarely come back." Edmir shifted in his seat until he was facing Parno more directly. "That's one of the plans we have," he said. "My sister and I. We want to send to the Tarkin of Imrion for help to establish a Guild here in Tegrian, so that Marks can be trained here, and stay to help the people as they do in the lands to the east."

Parno blew out a sigh. "There's fewer Marked even in the east these days, though your plan is a good one, for all that. You're the elder child, correct? And it's your mother who's the queen? Not your father who was the king?"

"That's right. He was the consort, just as Avylos . . . as the Blue Mage is now." The boy looked down and away, but Parno took note of his stumbling over the Mage's name.

"And is the Blue Mage licensed?"

Edmir squirmed on the hard seat. The last thing he wanted to talk about right now was Avylos. But he'd taken heart at what Parno Lionsmane had said about putting his own past behind him. And the man was right, he owed the Mercenary Brothers for saving his life, and rescuing him from the Nisveans. And if information was what they wanted from him . . .

"He's the only Mage, so far as I know. Certainly I don't remember any others. Though he wasn't the Blue Mage when he first came. He called himself that, but he had only small magics." Edmir looked at Lionsmane out of the corner of his eye. "Real, mind you, not the tricks of the stage magicians. He could light candles, cause small objects to come to him. Sometimes he could tell you what people were doing in other rooms. Such things. He was very kind to us when we were children, my sister Kera and I. He and my father were friends, and my father gave him a place among his retinue, and helped him in his studies." Edmir swallowed and fell silent.

"Lord Prince. Clearly there is some heavy matter between you and the Blue Mage. That was not *all* fever talking the other day, nor is it fever that makes you avoid speaking of him now. Consider what I'm telling you." The Lionsmane waited until Edmir raised his head and looked him in the eye. "Either my Partner and I are in league with the Mage, in which case we already know what you are keeping to yourself. Or, we are what we seem to be, your friends and rescuers, and what you know may be vital to keep us all alive."

What Parno Lionsmane said made sense, and Edmir's instinct was to trust the man, not that either his instincts or his judgment had been very good of late. Why hadn't he listened to Kera? She'd warned him nothing good was going to come of this.

"I wanted to show my mother the queen I could be a good commander, as my father was." Edmir licked his lips and swallowed. "I planned a small foray over the border—just a display of tactics and strategy—"

The Lionsmane coughed. "You mean something your mother could explain away as youthful high spirits, something that didn't violate the treaty that exists between Tegrian and Nisvea?"

Edmir felt the heat rise into his face. "Something like that, yes. But somehow the Blue Mage learned of it, and instead of forbidding it, somehow it became, because of his backing, a true test of Nisvea's defenses, not just—as you call it—youthful high spirits, but something that could be useful in the future. Still, we'd keep it secret, so that my mother the queen could deny any knowledge of it diplomatically."

"So the Blue Mage *was* supporting you, and your forces should *not* have lost."

Edmir rubbed at his eyes. "The magic didn't work. There's a . . . a ceremony, a ritual that the Blue Mage gave me and I swear I did it properly, just as I had practiced it."

"But it did not work."

Edmir shook his head.

"So perhaps he isn't as friendly to you now, as he has been in the past." The Lionsmane set down the dagger he was working on and stood, stretched by putting his fists in the small of his back and leaning into them before sitting down again. "And so they've prospered, these studies of his?"

Edmir blinked at the change of subject. "He's had books and scrolls brought from everywhere, and Scholars are always coming with more. He's commissioned copies of many." Edmir frowned as he considered the full depth of the Mercenary's question. He hadn't really thought about it until this moment, but there were so many magics Avylos could do now, that he couldn't do before. "Yes. I'd have to say his studies have prospered."

"Dhulyn Wolfshead is called Scholar, but she's not that kind. And though she's Marked, you understand that the Mark's not magic, it comes down from the Caids."

"A gift from the gods isn't magic?"

Lionsmane picked up another, shorter dagger and examined one edge of the blade with a critical eye. "The Caids weren't gods, however much they might seem that way. Go to any Scholars' Library and they can tell you, show you the old books. They were people just like us, very long ago." He squinted along the other edge and rubbed at an invisible spot. "True, they knew more, could build better, but they were people just the same. There were Marked among them, and so the Mark's passed down to our time."

"Like curly hair or blue eyes?" Edmir smiled, sure the man must be joking.

"Well, yes. Though I think of it more like a good singing voice, or a good eye and hand for knife work." He gestured with the blade in his hand.

"The Scholars who taught me said nothing of all this."

The Lionsmane put down the dagger and picked up the last weapon, another short knife with an almost triangular blade. "Scholars have a way of teaching you what you've asked to be taught. And their knowledge of the Caids is not complete; they don't like to admit such things outside their own Libraries. But if you went to them, and asked, they would tell you."

"How do you know all of this?" The man was not as old as he sounded, Edmir realized, looking at him more closely, only about as old as Edmir's mother the queen pretended still to be. Easy to see that his name "Lionsmane" came from his coloring, skin and hair both a golden brown, the hair showing no gray.

"Dhulyn Wolfshead spent a year in a Scholars' Library before she took her final vows to the Brotherhood, and she's never lost the habit of reading. She can tell you that there's a link between us, that is, the Mercenary Brotherhood, the Scholars, and the Jaldean priests of the Sleeping God. The writings say we were all charged with keeping the knowledge of the Caids. The Brotherhood their physical and fighting skills, the Scholars their acquired knowledge—whatever *that* might mean—and the Jaldeans the secrets of the Sleeping God."

"So there *are* gods? The Sleeping God?"

The Lionsmane was silent for so long, his hands unmoving, that Edmir glanced up. The man was looking at his Partner, who had fallen still as a statue, her blades catching fire from the angle of the sun.

"Yes," the man said, his voice quiet. "The God's real." He blinked, took in a deep breath and turned to Edmir. "But the Wolfshead is no Mage. And as for what lies between you and your stepfather? You should know that the arrow we pulled from your leg was a Tegrian arrow."

The wound in Edmir's thigh throbbed.

They had needed the rest, and the time to let the prince's leg heal, but Dhulyn was glad, three days later, to be back on her horse, with the hills, the Clouds, and the Racha behind them. And the walls of Probic a dark mark on the horizon ahead.

"Once we're in the city," Edmir was saying, "I can give you an official welcome, and I'll be able to repay your hospitality, and your aid, in a proper fashion."

It was obvious that the rest had done the prince good. There was less of the injured boy in the way he sat the saddle, and more of the thoughtful prince. Not that she cared either way, Dhulyn reminded herself. She might well be reluctant to return Edmir to his people, considering what Parno'd had to tell her of the Blue Mage, but it was the boy's decision. However much it went against the grain to rescue him and see him back to health, only to then turn him over to the very people who had let him get that way in the first place, they could hardly force themselves on the boy.

And just to add more water to wine that wasn't very good to start with, so far this engagement was a net loss.

As they neared the gates of Probic, Dhulyn automatically scanned the walls, mentally counting the bastions and calculating the number of guards it would take to man them fully. As the town closest to the Nisvean border, Probic was most at risk from invasion—if any Tegrian town could be considered at risk from invasion since the Blue Mage seemed to know when any sizable band of men, or pack of dogs, crossed the border. Still, for so small a place, Probic's walls were impressive, and Dhulyn would wager that the number of guards would be the same.

Whether it was the time of day, or because this gate was closest to the border, they were the only party approaching. The gate stood open, and as they drew nearer, Dhulyn made out the passage through the walls, a dark and invitingly cool tunnel, at least six horse-lengths deep. Any other town of this size, and Dhulyn would consider the walls to be unusually thick, but again, this was a border city.

There would be archers in the bastions, though she could not see them, and likely holes in the passage itself to allow defenders to either shoot or pour boiling water and oil on any invader who managed to pass through the gate.

Just stepping out from the opening itself were three guards in deep blue tunics, showing them to be part of the Royal Army. Dhulyn frowned.

"Two of the guards have crossbows, cocked and with bolts ready to fly," she said. "Unusual, surely, even for a border town?"

"If any of those who escaped from Limona made it this far," Parno said, "I'm not surprised the guards come armed."

"I should think they would keep the gates shut in that case."

"They can see we're only three—" Whatever else Parno might have said was lost as Edmir spurred his horse forward, heading straight for the waiting guards. Dhulyn hissed, gave Bloodbone her head and dashed after him, calling out to Stumpy and leaning far out from the saddle, reaching out for the smaller horse's bridle.

Stumpy was fighting his reins as Dhulyn came alongside the prince, using Bloodbone's greater height and weight to nudge Stumpy aside just as the crossbow bolt passed harmlessly to their left.

"Are you insane? Did you not hear me say they were armed and waiting to shoot?"

"But I'm the Lord Prince, I . . ." The boy was white with shock.

"And how are they to know that? Where's your escort? Where's your horse of state? Where are your blooded clean clothes for that matter?"

Edmir looked down, but his nostrils were flared, and Dhulyn knew that was the only acknowledgment she'd get that she was right. The boy wasn't stupid, it just hadn't occurred to him that his own people wouldn't know him.

She shook her head in disgust. What were his people thinking to let him grow up this way? Were they *trying* to get him killed?

"Easy, Lord Prince," she said. "I know you are anxious to be finally at home, but we go carefully, even here."

He took a deep breath and nodded. Dhulyn released Stumpy's bridle as Parno joined them.

"They're watching us now," he said, his arm lifted in salute to the waiting guards. "Slow and easy should keep us with whole skins."

Slow and easy was the pace they set, riding in a line, Edmir between her and Parno, the extra packhorse trailing behind them. As they reached the three waiting guards, she let Edmir move slightly into the lead, so that it was he who spoke to them.

"I am Edmir of Tegrian," he said, his clear, educated voice raised enough to be heard by any unseen but listening guards on the walls.

"Prince Edmir's dead, you lying weasel." The young guard on the left took a step forward, and the office in the center jerked him back into his place and cuffed him with his open hand.

Edmir sat openmouthed and frozen. Dhulyn's blood suddenly sang, and she could feel Parno become alert on the prince's other side.

"Four archers watch us," the officer said, ignoring Edmir, his eyes going first to Parno, then to Dhulyn. "I see by your badges that you are Mercenary Brothers. Can I rely on you to act sensibly?"

"So long as we *all* act sensibly," Dhulyn gave a hard look to the young man who had spoken out of turn. "I am Dhulyn Wolfshead, called the Scholar," she said. "I was Schooled by Dorian the Black Traveler, and I fight with my Brother, Parno Lionsmane."

"And I am Parno Lionsmane, the Chanter. Schooled by Nerysa Warhammer."

"I assure you I *am* Edmir," the prince said. Dhulyn smiled. His voice was steady and showed only a very little of the strain he must be feeling. "You and I have not met, Watch Leader, but there are others in the city who know me. City Lord Tzanek for one. Perhaps you would be so good as to send for him."

"We'll take you to him—under escort, with no offense intended," the watch leader added to Dhulyn.

Dhulyn composed her features, eyed the crossbowmen, then shrugged. No one was going to say aloud that the Guard wouldn't send for the City Lord at the request of a boy in torn and dirty clothing who claimed to be a dead prince.

"That seems *sensible*," she said. "I hope it's the custom in the City House to offer ganje to guests," she added. "I could use a cup."

There was ganje in the room they were asked to wait in when they reached City House, hot and strong the way Dhulyn liked it, but she was ready for a second cup long before Lord Tzanek arrived. Everyone they'd met with was being very careful. In case Edmir spoke the truth, the House pages had put them into a small but comfortable waiting room, and seen that ganje was served promptly. In case Edmir was lying, there were two guards on the outside of the unlocked door. Parno appeared to be taking advantage of the delay to take a nap in one of the padded chairs, his hands folded on his chest, but Edmir couldn't sit still. He kept getting to his feet and pacing across the small carpet that covered the polished oak floor, only to sit down again as his leg bothered him.

"You'll see," he told them more than once as they waited. "This is some misunderstanding. Old Tzanek's known me since he was a senior adviser in Beolind—he was a friend of my father's. He'll clear this up."

"And then it's hot baths and soft beds?" Parno said, his eyes still closed.

"Well, yes, among other things."

A bustle of footsteps and voices at the door signaled the arrival of Lord Tzanek. Parno stood and put his hand on the back of the chair he'd been using. Dhulyn stayed leaning against the small table that held their ganje cups; Edmir surged to his feet and strode closer to the door.

The man who came in, short beard well sprinkled with gray, was dressed for the court or the audience chamber. His half boots were low-heeled and sueded, his tunic a fine wool, ankle-length and belted with a wide embroidered sash. There was an ink stain on his left hand. He stopped short just inside the door.

"You did not take their weapons?"

The watch leader's wide eyes showed his surprise. "But, my lord, they're Mercenary Brothers, why would we disarm them?"

"The Mercenary Brotherhood has been banished from Tegrian."

Dhulyn's mouth dropped open in shock. *Banished.* It was like stepping onto a staircase in the dark and finding it gone.

"And as for this boy, I know Edmir well, since he was a child, and I will not be deceived," Tzanek said. "The young man they have with them is not Edmir."

"Tzanek." Edmir's voice was disbelieving. He took two further steps forward, with his hands outstretched. "It's me, it's Edmir."

But the man's face did not change. He turned back to the watch leader.

"I will not be deceived. This is not Edmir. Seize them."

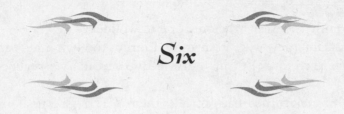

Six

FOR A MOMENT, NO ONE moved. The watch leader cleared his throat.

"My lord," he began.

Dhulyn gave herself a mental shake. Whatever the City Lord meant, banished or not, they were here, and had more pressing problems. She measured the distance between herself and the three guards. Parno had his right hand on the back of his chair, ready to knock down the City Lord with it—the man wasn't armed, so that would take him out. Edmir was on his feet, but he was white with shock, and unlikely to be of any help. Only one of the guards had even put hand to weapon, and she was the farthest away. Once Lord Tzanek was down, Parno would deal with the two closest to him, and Dhulyn would take the third one herself.

"What are you waiting for? He is an imposter, I tell you. Seize them all!"

The watch leader looked from Tzanek to Dhulyn and back again, clearly weighing the possibilities in his mind.

"Come," Parno said, beckoning the guards forward with his empty left hand. "See if *we're* impostors."

Noises at the door spoke of reinforcements, and Dhulyn drew her sword left-handed, but the page that burst in was alone.

"Lord Tzanek," he gasped. "Nisveans . . . already in the gates . . ."

Dhulyn shot a glance at Parno, and found him looking at her, eyebrows raised. How had the Nisveans managed to overpower the gates? How had guards so careful to inspect the three of them before they were even close to the gates overlooked an invading force of the Nisvean army?

"How . . . ?"

Apparently she wasn't the only one to wonder.

"They said they were returning Edmir's body." The page was now in better control of his lungs. "By the time we realized they lied—"

Lord Tzanek turned back to face them. "This is your doing," he said. "While you distracted us, your fellows have invaded."

Dhulyn did not even bother to shake her head; the man was clearly deranged. What he said made no sense whatsoever. Not that any of this was making any sense. *Banished*. She held out her right hand, index finger extended.

Parno threw the chair. Lord Tzanek went down and Parno leaped over him, elbowing the first guard in the face while drawing his sword and giving the second man a sharp rap on the side of the head with the pommel. Dhulyn slid into the gap, knocked the remaining guard's weapon up with a twist of her own blade, and struck the woman between the eyes with the heel of her right hand.

The page, evidently no fool, turned and ran. Parno followed him as far as the doorway where he stopped and looked both ways before beckoning them forward. Dhulyn grabbed Edmir by the upper arm and pulled him away from the prone City Lord.

"He should have known me," Edmir said, twisting his head to look back at Lord Tzanek even as Dhulyn tugged on his arm.

"How long since you were here?"

"You don't understand," Edmir said. "I didn't just meet him a few weeks ago. I've known Tzanek my whole life."

They stepped out into the corridor. Parno had gone right, to retrace their route from the entrance, and was waving them on where this passage met another, clearly impatient at their delay.

"He has no reason to dislike you personally?" Dhulyn said, more to keep Edmir moving than because she thought it important.

"He taught me to throw darts," Edmir said. "One night when I'd been allowed to stay up with my father, after Kera had been sent to bed. Of all my father's friends, he had the best eye, no one could beat him." Edmir looked behind him again, as if part of him still wanted to turn back.

If he had no personal reason, Dhulyn thought, then he must have had a political one. Either way, dangerous.

When they reached Parno he led them around the corner to the left. They'd only gone a few more paces when he signaled and Dhulyn pulled Edmir into a doorway, glancing at him as she did. The whiteness around his mouth had not lessened. She thought she knew exactly how he felt.

There were people ahead in this larger passageway, but the chaos and confusion with which they moved was ample evidence that all was not well in Probic. As Dhulyn waited for Parno's signal to continue, guards in uniform, some only half dressed and scantily armed, ran past them, followed by pages with white faces, most—but not all—heading for the gates of the House.

Parno moved them onward with a jerk of his head, leading them away from the main gates and toward what should be the kitchen wing of the House. Just as Dhulyn thought they would be able to leave unremarked, they were challenged by three guards with weapons at the ready. Dhulyn pushed Edmir behind her and pulled her dagger out of her boot, tossing it up until she held it by the blade.

"I assume you want them left alive?" she asked.

"I . . . yes." Edmir stuttered.

Dhulyn shrugged. "Takes longer," she said as she dove forward on her knees under Parno's left arm and knocked two of the guards sprawling. Once they were down, she used the heavy handle of her dagger to knock them out, while Parno dealt with the remaining guard.

"Here." Parno hustled them around another corner and into an empty room. This had the look of a pantry, with stone floors, and two plain trestle tables for the preparation of plates.

"Let's give everyone some time to return to their posts," Parno said. "When there are fewer people in the halls, we'll only have the regular patrols to deal with, rather than every guard we come across."

Edmir was rubbing at his leg, and Dhulyn made him sit on one of the tables. She wasn't afraid for the wound, but she knew that it was still all too easy for Edmir to overtax the damaged muscles. She needed to distract him.

"How did Tzanek become City Lord here?" she asked.

"When my mother the queen remarried, and the Blue Mage became consort, she rewarded and recognized many of my father's friends. Tzanek was one of the first."

"Getting the old husband's friends out from under the new husband's feet," Parno said. Dhulyn nodded.

"So he might want to get back to the capital," she said. "He might be sick and tired of being City Lord out here in rustic Probic."

"And how could denying the prince get him that?" Parno had the door cracked just slightly open, and he turned his face away from it to speak.

Dhulyn leaned her hips against the other table. "You said the Blue Mage found out about your expedition. Who might have told him?"

"My sister told me not to accept his help, but the others were so enthusiastic . . ." Edmir's voice faded into nothing.

Without turning, Parno made a chopping motion with his hand, but Dhulyn hadn't moved toward the prince. She knew that the least show of sympathy would only make the boy feel worse.

"One or two of the younger Houses were with me—we knew my mother the queen would be turning her eyes to Nisvea soon enough, the treaty is over next year. We thought just a quick strike across the border, something to show her that men were willing to follow me—" He stopped. His voice had quavered on the last few words, and his jaw trembled until he clamped it shut. After a few seconds he continued. "We wanted to know what it was like, to be invulnerable, even if it was only for a few hours."

"Look me in the eye," Dhulyn said, with enough command that even Lord Prince Edmir of Tegrian blinked twice and met her eyes. "What happened was *not* your fault, do you understand?"

Dhulyn expected some reaction from the boy, but the change which came over Edmir's face was all out of proportion to her words.

"What is it?" she asked, beginning to look behind her.

"Wait," Edmir said, grabbing at Dhulyn's arm in his turn. "There's something wrong."

Parno put up his hand like a junior Scholar in a Library. "I know," he said. "We're trapped inside a fortress and the city's under attack."

Dhulyn rolled her eyes, but Edmir ignored them both.

"No. I mean Tzanek. I was looking right at him, straight into his eyes, as I looked into yours just now, and I saw nothing. Do you understand? No hidden message. No recognition. It isn't just that Tzanek *said* he didn't know me. He *didn't* know me."

"Can you be sure?"

Edmir nodded. "My sister and I used to play at disguises, and see who we could fool among the court people and the servers. I know what it looks like when people know me and when they don't." He rubbed at his forehead. "And what it looks like when they know me and are pretending they don't. Tzanek doesn't know me."

"And who do we know that might be able to do that?"

"The Blue Mage," Dhulyn said. She exchanged a glance with Parno behind Edmir's head. She could see that they shared the same thought. Was the Mage working alone, or was the sister in it as well?

"If you will take these to the House Seamstress, that will be all for today."

Princess Kera indicated a bundle of Edmir's cloaks and watched Metrick the page gather them up make his way slowly to the door of Edmir's quarters. She wondered if he would have been so ready to help her if her brother wasn't dead. Metrick was one of the new pages, from a High Noble House in Balnia—not that she could remember which one just at the moment. There the Noble Houses had long had the custom of sending their children for a final polish of manners and service to their Tarkin's House, and since Tegrian had conquered them, and their Tarkins were no more, those sons and daughters came to Queen Kedneara instead.

"Be careful what you say in front of that one, Lady Prince." Sharian Tzeczova, Kera's own senior lady page was taking folded shirts out of Edmir's clothespress. "The other pages are already saying that he's too ready to run with tales to others."

"He's like a badly trained dog," Kera agreed. "He goes begging to everyone in the room, and performs his tricks for everyone."

"Well, to be fair," Sharian said. "He's just a House page at the moment, and doesn't really have a master yet. Though it seems to me, since your brother's death, he's thinking you'll do."

"I'll have to be careful, then."

"Do so. His House is a good one, and he might fancy himself at your side. You're Lady Prince now, remember."

Kera turned her face away so Sharian wouldn't see her grit her teeth. As if she could forget. As if she wasn't here, right now, in Edmir's room, going through his things because Edmir was dead.

"Sharian, would you mind leaving me here a while?"

The lady page couldn't really mind, whatever she might think, and however often she might serve as an informal tutor.

And besides, it would seem natural to anyone that she would like to sit a while in her late brother's room, by herself, where she might think about him, and what his absence now meant to her.

Sharian picked up the shirts she'd been sorting and headed for the door, bestowing an understanding smile that put Kera's teeth on edge. As soon as the door shut behind the older woman, Kera jumped to her feet and went to it, pressing her ear against the opening. Sharian's house shoes made no noise on the smooth wooden floors of the passage outside Edmir's rooms, so Kera counted to twenty before looking to assure herself that the passage was empty. She shut the door, latched it from the inside, and threw the bolts. The outer room secure, Kera went into Edmir's bedroom, directly to the fireplace that took up much of the far side of the room.

The hearth was surrounded by an elaborate mantel built up of several different kinds of dark wood, and large pieces of stone on which the faces of animals had been carved. It took only a few seconds for Kera to find the face of a fox on the left-hand side of the fireplace and press its nose with her thumbs. The stone gave under the pressure and a square of wood lower on the right-hand side popped soundlessly open.

Kera knelt and stuck her hand into the opening, smiling as her fingers brushed against a leather corner. Just as she'd thought, Edmir had *not* found a new hiding place for his journals. She pulled them out one by one. Altogether there were seven books, all showing wear and one a chewed corner where a favored puppy had once got hold of it. The two most recent were made from the newer, lighter-weight paper, cut and bound with the pages sewn together, and stiff covers made from leather. She opened them, and found both were filled from cover to cover with Edmir's neat handwriting.

Of course. She sat back on her heels. The latest one, the one he was writing in now, must have gone with him to Nisvea. Kera tilted her head back, taking a deep breath and blinking to forestall the tears. Where would it be now, her brother's last journal? On the battlefield somewhere, soaked in Edmir's blood? Did the Nisveans have it? Or the Mercenaries who were said to have taken him—might they have kept it?

She hadn't really thought he'd leave it. Edmir was always writing in his journal. But she'd hoped to be wrong. She'd hoped to have this chance to find out why Edmir had ignored her advice. Without his journal, she would never know what possessed him to change his plans, to listen to the Mage.

She gathered together the hem of her gown, making a pouch in which she could stash the journals. There was a satchel in Edmir's clothespress that would hold them all, and she could use that to transport them unseen to her own secret hiding place. As she reached into the hole, making sure that she hadn't left a journal behind, one slipped out of the fold in her skirt and fell open onto the floor. Kera caught sight of her own name in Edmir's handwriting.

Princess Kera and the Seven Suitors, were the words at the top of the page. *There are seven silver fish in the garden pond of the Queen of Tegrian*, the story began. Kera sat heavily on the floor and touched the ink with her fingertip. Edmir had once made up a story that the fish in her mother's pond were really princes who had been turned into fish when they'd come, one by one, to beg for her hand. One had been a pirate prince, she remembered, who'd tried to steal her away. She'd never known that Edmir had written the story down.

This time, she could not stop the tears.

"Troop of six pikemen just ran by," Dhulyn said. They had made it past the kitchens, and were at a scullery door that would take them out into the courtyard and stables. "They're joining others leaving by the gate into the city." She turned back to the door crack in time to see another small group, this time armed with swords and small round shields, heading in the same direction as the first. She needn't have bothered being careful; none of the soldiers were looking her way.

"They'll be coming from the guardhouse, at the other end of the courtyard." Edmir tried to see around her, but Dhulyn kept her elbows out.

"And heading for the walls, though from the sounds of things, those are already breached."

"How is any of this possible? The strength of Probic's walls is legendary . . ." Edmir shook his head.

"All it takes is one man to open a door," Dhulyn said. "And if they tricked their way in, as that page said . . ." She shrugged.

"But who would do such a thing?"

Dhulyn just stopped herself from sighing aloud. The lad would have to get more cynical than this if he expected to be king one day. "The same person who doesn't seem to know you any longer, I would judge. Or someone that he sent."

"But the Blue Mage . . ." Edmir's voice died away, and he drew down his brows as he processed the idea that Dhulyn had lent him.

She knew what he would have said. That fear of the Blue Mage—or respect for his powers, which amounted to much the same thing—had kept Tegrian free of invasion for the last three seasons at least. Why and how had that changed now?

And what other change had resulted in the banishment of Mercenaries from Tegrian?

"Edmir. Can the Blue Mage communicate with others over long distances?" Racha Clouds could with their birds, she knew, but she had never heard such a thing about the Blue Mage.

"Now is not the time for such questions, my heart." Parno gestured Dhulyn forward with a tip of his head. She shrugged and turned back to the door. Her Partner was right. She hovered in the doorway for another few heartbeats, shaking her shoulders loose, moving her head from one side to the other, as she began the Stalking Cat *Shora*. Her breathing slowed, her heartbeat slowed. Her hearing grew more acute. She toned down her awareness of Parno and the prince so that their breathing and their heartbeats would not distract her.

She tilted her head to one side. She held up her left hand, pointed to the open doorway of the stables, and held up one finger. From the corner of her eyes she saw Parno nod. She moved out of the scullery and over to the stable door, noting the shifting of air as Parno and Edmir fell in behind her. The prince was very quiet, but she could hear both his breathing and his footfalls. She pointed downward with the index finger of her left hand and they stayed back, allowing her to approach the stable alone. She paced to the left, staying out of line of sight for the single person she knew to be inside. When she reached a point to the left of the opening, she squatted on her heels and took a quick glance inside the building, her mind and eye automatically registering all within.

She beckoned the others forward, easing back from the edge of the opening. "A table between us and him. Some bowls, tack, and harness on it. Stool on our side," she said, using the nightwatch voice. She looked at Parno. "I went last time."

Parno shrugged. "True." He sheathed his sword, pushed his hands through his hair, and sauntered loose-footed into the open doorway so naturally and so casually that he had the tall, three-legged stool in his hands before the man shutting the stall gate on the opposite side of the table even felt his presence as a threat. The stableman was no amateur, however, and was turned around in one heartbeat, an ax in his hand the next.

The prince pushed against Dhulyn's arm. "He's got an ax."

"And Parno has a stool. Calm down. This will only take a moment."

As if prompted by her words, Parno smashed the stool down on the tabletop, breaking off the seat and leaving himself with two of the stool's stout legs, each as thick as three of Dhulyn's fingers, and as long as Parno's forearm and hand.

She drummed her fingers on the doorframe and blew out a breath.

Parno tossed the hair out of his eyes, and leaped onto the table, kicking horse brushes and pots of liniment at the stableman. The man's eyes widened at the sight of Parno's Mercenary badge, but almost without hesitation he took a step back, lessening the advantage of Parno's elevation, and swung the ax in a controlled sweep at Parno's legs. Without taking his eyes off the man's face, Parno jumped over the moving blade and moved the chair legs once—a blow numbing the stableman's arm with a swing of his left hand—and twice—clubbing him to the ground with a swing of his right.

"They don't pay this man enough," he said, as he jumped back to the ground and held his fingers at the man's throat.

"Will he be able to collect more pay in the future?" Now that she was in the stable, Dhulyn whistled and saw three heads pop out over stall doors along the left-hand side of the stable: Bloodbone, Warhammer, and Stumpy.

"Of course, what do you take me for?"

"I thought you might have been a bit rushed." Dhulyn pushed past him and ran down to Bloodbone. The horses she'd known would be here. What she hadn't expected was to find their own packs and saddlebags sitting in each stall, at the horses' feet.

"Not even opened," she said. Their extra weapons, even the crossbow Parno had hooked on his saddle, were lying untouched on top of the packs.

"Our reputation precedes us," Parno said, as he stepped past her and opened Warhammer's stall. Edmir looked between them frowning, clearly bewildered. Parno indicated the unopened packs. "Not a buckle, not a flap, not even the knots in the laces have been disturbed. Someone's told them we booby trap our packs, that's why they've not been opened."

As they spoke, Dhulyn opened the pack at her feet, slipping the buckles loose and pulling the ties open with one practiced flick of her wrist. If you knew your knots and ties—and there were *Shora* for ropes and bindings—a bundle you had tied shut yourself was as good as open, however confounding it might have been for someone else.

She reached inside, took out the two leather gauntlets she'd packed on top, and pulled them on, settling the knives they held along the inside of her forearms. She bit her lip. Her other throwing knives were in their roll in the saddlebags, no time to fetch them out now. But the small hatchet slipped easily into its place down the back of her vest, and two more daggers went into the tops of her boots, along with a moon razor.

There, now she felt properly dressed.

"We leave the packhorse," Dhulyn said. She picked up Bloodbone's saddle pad and threw it over the mare's back. "Saddlebags, weapons, and camp gear only, and then what food we have room for."

"We don't take everything?"

"We must travel faster now," Parno said. "And the packhorse will slow us down. As for food, unlike an army, we can feed ourselves as we go."

"Hunting won't slow us down?" He might be questioning them, but Edmir was already moving to open Stumpy's stall.

"Not the way we hunt," Dhulyn said.

The prince hesitated, his hand on Stumpy's saddle pad. "Can't I take one of the better horses?"

Dhulyn continued saddling Bloodbone. "Better how, Lord Prince? Stumpy's trained to our ways, and we've no time to train any of these."

"And besides," Parno added, "at the moment we want to get away unseen, and unnoticed. Old Stumpy here draws no one's eye, and you've more chance to be recognized on a good horse."

And judging from the look on Edmir's face, it could go unsaid that recognition, with invaders already inside the gates, was the last thing they wanted right now. The prince was not stupid, Dhulyn thanked Sun and Moon, just inexperienced.

They left City House finally by the simple expedient of joining the tail end of a small contingent of guards and riding out of the gate after them. It appeared that the banishment Tzanek had spoken of was not widely known.

"Don't skulk, Edmir," Parno said in an undertone. "Shoulders back, chin up, ride as though you belong here."

Edmir straightened his shoulders and lifted his chin as he followed Dhulyn through the gate. His grip on Stumpy's reins was too tight, he could feel the tension in his forearms already, but he didn't seem to be able to relax. No one took notice of them, however. Once outside into the city proper there was so much else to notice. More noise, for one thing, the unmistakable sound of steel striking steel in the distance, cries and shouts, and the smell of burning. Edmir gritted his teeth and tried to push the images of the battle of Limona out of his head.

They took the first turning they came to, and found themselves suddenly alone in a small square with a stone pillory in its center, raised above the cobbles of the square itself on three granite steps. The iron arms, with their hooked ends for tying off ropes and prisoners, looked innocent enough, but Edmir licked his suddenly dry lips when he saw the stains on the pillar, on the granite steps, and on the flagstones immediately around them. The pillory's long shadow stretched almost the length of the square. The late afternoon sun cast their own shadows before them.

Dhulyn Wolfshead touched him on the elbow and Edmir jumped.

"This way."

Seven

THEY LEFT THE SQUARE just in time to avoid a small group of four mounted guards wearing Probic's town colors of green and rust, their uniform tunics torn, their weapons bloodied, one being steadied on his horse by a comrade. Even in these smaller streets and alleys Parno could hear the sounds of fighting, the clash of metal, the far-off yells and even the occasional blast of trumpet or horn as signals were given to troops too spread out to hear their orders.

And there was the smell of fire as the poorer, wooden quarters of the town were set ablaze.

Dhulyn stopped, holding up her right hand. Three men in dark blue tunics—wall guards—crossed the alley in front of them without even so much as looking their way.

"It goes against the grain to leave the fight behind us," Parno said, as Edmir caught his eye. "But we have nothing but enemies here."

The prince nodded, his teeth clenched, and at Parno's gesture fell back into position between him and Dhulyn. She set a steady but unremarkable pace, neither chasing nor running from, the best way to avoid unwelcome attention. As they got farther away from the City House, the streets became quieter, deserted, and doors were clearly bolted. Dhulyn stopped once more, tilted her head like a Racha bird catching its partner's thoughts. Then she relaxed, glancing at Parno and indicating upward with her eyes. *Yes*, he thought, following her glance, there *was* someone watching them from behind a third-floor shutter. He touched his fingertips to his forehead in the Mercenary salute to the silent watcher. Banished or not, it seemed not *everyone* here was their enemy, after all.

Two men wearing the long leather aprons of smiths, dragging a corpse in Nisvean colors by the heels, turned into their path and stopped abruptly—looking first at them, down at the corpse, and back at them again. Parno tried hard not to smile as, without speaking, Dhulyn turned her head and tapped the side of her face, indicating her Mercenary badge. The two smiths stood aside then, dragging the corpse out of their path, and watched as they passed by. Once again, Parno touched his forehead to them.

They hadn't gone much farther along, and Dhulyn was signaling a turn to the left as their alley approached the square in front of a Jaldean Shrine, when the unmistakable sound of a woman screaming brought Dhulyn up short.

Out in the late afternoon sunlight that filled the square, a young woman hung between two men, not much bigger than she was herself, who were twisting her arms up behind her back. Her spangled head scarf lay on the ground at her feet, and the taller, wider man in front of her had hold of her white-blonde hair in his right fist, his left cocked back to hit her again. Her face showed signs that she'd been punched at least once already, but she was still screaming, and kicked out—a well-placed blow that had her attacker bent over and bellowing as she caught him squarely in the groin. The man holding her left arm laughed, but the man holding her on the right pulled his knife from his belt and held it to her throat, yelling something in her ear. The girl stopped squirming, her eyes almost crossing in her attempt to look simultaneously at both the man and his knife.

Dhulyn finished her turn into the new alley, but Edmir stopped, hauling back on his reins as Stumpy tried to follow Bloodbone.

"Wait! Aren't we going to stop them?"

The Wolfshead reined in and looked over her shoulder at the prince with a frown. "Why?" she said.

Edmir looked from Dhulyn to Parno and back—his head whipped round again at the sound of tearing cloth.

"I'll go."

Parno grabbed Stumpy's reins just in time. The boy didn't even have a weapon out.

"I've no stomach to leave her, my heart," he said. "It's not an act I'd find easy to live with."

Dhulyn turned Bloodbone back to face the opening to the square.

"*Blooded* nobles. We'll be food for crows ourselves if there are archers in the square. Oh, but we'll be able to live with ourselves—no, wait, we'll be dead." She unhooked the small crossbow from her saddle harness. "Come on, then."

Dhulyn dug her heels into Bloodbone's sides and shot straight into the square, screaming out a challenge as she went. As soon as she cleared the buildings, she ducked, leaning far enough out of the saddle that anyone who didn't know her would think for certain she'd fall off. Parno, riding Warhammer into the square at an angle to Dhulyn's left, did not see her fire, but the man holding the knife to the young woman's throat went down with a crossbow bolt through his eye, just as Parno fired and the man on her left caught a bolt of his own. The girl immediately crouched, holding the front of her dress together with one hand, and retrieving the knife from her dead attacker's grip with the other.

The taller, heavier man still stood, having recovered sufficiently from the kick to the groin to have struck the girl again and torn her gown. He whirled around at the sound of hooves but when he saw Parno bearing down on him from his right, and Dhulyn Wolfshead, standing now in her saddle and howling, waving her long sword in her hand as she flanked him on his left, he turned and ran.

"He's getting away!" Edmir spurred Stumpy forward but the horse pulled up at Dhulyn's whistle, almost dumping the prince out of his saddle.

"So would the others have done if they'd been smart enough to drop the girl and go," Parno said. "As it is, to save one we've killed two."

"But they were going to rape her, perhaps kill her." Edmir urged Stumpy closer to Warhammer. "We did the right thing."

"No argument," Parno said. "I've never cared for rapists. I merely point out the cost of doing the right thing."

Dhulyn had reached the girl and dropped down from Bloodbone's back to land at her side. With the bruising and swelling already distorting her features, it was hard to tell what expression she had on her face, but she was holding the knife up, ready to defend herself.

"There now, little Cat, sheathe your claw. I am Dhulyn Wolfshead, called the Scholar," the Mercenary woman said, crouching on her heels just out of striking distance. "That's my Partner Parno Lions-mane, the Chanter, and our charge of honor. Where are your people?"

The girl lowered the knife, grimacing as her swollen lip interfered with her smile. "I greet you, Dhulyn Wolfshead, and I thank you for your timely rescue. I am Zania Tzadeyeu. My troupe and family has our caravan in the Pine Tree Hostel two streets closer to the gate."

"Dancers?"

"Players, dancers, and musicians, Lady Wolfshead. If you would accompany me, my father will amply repay you for my rescue." The top layer of her voice held the cool graciousness of an imperial princess talking to some member of her court who had done her a favor. But under it was the same shock that whitened her lips and made her hands tremble.

Dhulyn helped the little Cat—Zania—to her feet, blood-red brows drawn down. "We are leaving the town, Zania Tzadeyeu, but I thank you for the offer."

"You are leaving Probic? We could all leave together; there's safety in numbers." With a complicated motion of her shoulders Zania shifted her clothing around until she was decently, if somewhat raggedly, covered. Standing at her full height, Parno noted, the girl was rather shorter than his Partner, and more rounded.

"There's ample space for you to ride on Edmir's horse," Dhulyn was saying, but Zania was already shaking her head.

"Please, Lady Wolfshead, with you." Her voice was steady and clear, but the whites showed around her eyes.

Dhulyn flicked a glance at Parno before she nodded, her mouth twisted to one side. Parno stifled a smile. His Partner always made a large task out of helping someone. She turned and mounted Blood-bone, arranged her weapons behind her, and reached down a hand toward the younger woman.

"Do I look diseased?" Edmir asked Parno out of the corner of his mouth.

"You look like a man, as do I. And you may have noticed that the people who bruised her face and tore her dress—and planned to do considerably more, as we think—were also men. I think you'll find Zania Tzadeyeu will be wary of all such creatures for the next while."

Edmir took his lower lip between his teeth. Evidently, that hadn't occurred to him. He glanced toward the two women, and his lips parted.

Parno rolled his eyes—hadn't there been any women in his mother's court? "What do you think, Edmir?"

Edmir flushed red and turned away from watching Zania's legs as she climbed up onto Dhulyn's saddle.

"Sorry, Lionsmane, I wasn't listening."

"At least you admit it. Are you for traveling with the troupe?"

"There's sense in what she said, about traveling in numbers," Edmir said, his eyes returning to Zania.

"I thought you'd say that. Still, it's for Dhulyn as Senior to decide, so don't hope too much."

Tzanek shut the door of his workroom with more force than he intended, and ran to his worktable, holding his temples as he went. His head was throbbing in a most fearsome headache, and any quick movement seemed likely to make it break completely off. He sat down in the chair next to the table and, reaching into the front of his gown, pulled out a key hanging under his clothes by a small chain. He unlocked the oak box that sat to one side on the table and took out the book of poetry the Blue Mage had given him.

Tzanek took a deep breath, and then another. His head pounded with the beating of his heart. His hands trembled as he fumbled the book open to the blank central pages, careful to touch only the very edges of the parchment. He hoped this would work. The Blue Mage had told him the magic was in the book, not in the user, so it should work even though Tzanek was not a Mage, but he'd never had to do this before. And now his head ached so much.

"Lord Mage." Tzanek cleared his throat and began again. "Lord Mage."

Avylos looked up from the scroll he was reading, certain that someone had called him. He went to the workroom door, but when he looked out, he could see that the metal-bound door closing off this wing of Royal House was shut. No page was there calling him.

There it was again.

Avylos lifted his eyebrows, tapping his upper lip with his tongue. Was it possible?

He went behind his worktable and reached up to the books on the shelf, hesitating only a heartbeat before selecting the book of poetry with the central pages of albino calfskin. He laid the book down on the table, and as soon as he opened it, writing appeared on the right-hand page.

"My lord Mage. Thank the Caids! You must send help, immediately. The Nisveans are here, they are within the walls already, and the city is aflame—"

Avylos smiled. After all, Tzanek couldn't see him. "And the Mercenaries, with the imposter they protect, no word of them?"

"It was they who distracted us while the Nisveans attacked, we were—"

"You have them?"

"No, I'm sorry, my lord Mage, they escaped—at least, they must still be within City House. They cannot have gone far."

"Just a moment, Tzanek. Do not go away, but stay silent until I speak." Avylos' fingernails were biting into his palms, and he forced himself to relax, to breathe deeply, to ride the waves of his rage, rather than to let them overwhelm and drown him. Edmir kept slipping through every trap he set for him—Sun *blast* those Mercenaries. This was intolerable. If only he were there, but Probic was five days' ride . . . he rubbed his fingers across his lips. If he could transport himself there—how could he be sure of having enough power left to do what must be done?

There had to be a way. He drummed his fingers on the tabletop, glanced at the window. He could see Probic through the medium of the pond, but seeing it was not enough. He needed a channel through which power could flow. He looked down at the open book before him, where Tzanek still waited for him. *That* channel already existed.

He could do this. He *knew* it. And it would ultimately serve his purpose very well. Still, it would take much, if not all his present power. He looked quickly around the room. There were magics here he could undo, freeing the power for his own use. The other books he should leave, the pond likewise. They were his lines of communication, using little power to maintain, but a great deal to re-create. The Stone also, ready with a single word to trigger it. But the casket. He pulled it toward him. Locked *and* magicked. He traced a design on the lid and sucked in his breath as the lines of fire lifted and flew into his hand. The lock alone would suffice, so long as he left the door to his workroom magicked. Kera could enter, but then she could not unlock the casket, could she?

But the magic that told him who had come to the door, *that* he could remove and regain. The magic that kept the floor warm, and likewise the one that guarded the door to his sleeping chambers. All these could be renewed when he returned and restored himself. He had used up the talents he still had in Royal House, but there was one he'd been saving for an emergency such as this, a carpenter's apprentice who was far too lucky with dice.

He sat back down at the book. "I will come myself," he said. "Place your left hand on the right-hand leaf of the book."

"But, my lord Mage, your instructions—"

"Are superseded. Do it at once!"

A moment passed, and then the outline of a man's left hand appeared on the page. Avylos placed his own right hand on it.

A pulling at his skin, a twist of the guts, dizziness and nausea. For a moment he was sure his heart had stopped.

He coughed, and lifted his left hand from the page. He looked around at the unfamiliar room. Stone walls and floor. A truly horrible tapestry evidently created by a right-handed person using his or her left hand. Avylos stood and steadied himself on the back of the heavy, leather-covered chair. He'd forgotten how much shorter Tzanek was.

And the man hadn't mentioned the towering headache he had. Avylos hated to use any magic to relieve the pain, but he could not afford the distraction. He went to the door of Tzanek's workroom and looked around. He needed the tallest tower, and it would be . . . he rummaged through the mind he was wearing. This way.

On his way to the tower Avylos met only one guard, whom he dismissed with a short, economic gesture that left the woman unconscious and bleeding from the nose and ears. He had to slow down as he took the stairs to the top of the tower; his breath came short and his heart pounded. Tzanek was heavier and older, and Avylos could not spare any further power to improve the older man's body. *Get me to the top and back down again*, he told it. *That's all I need.*

The air was cool on his face when he pushed open the door at the top of the tower. Here, five days' ride from Beolind, the sun was lower in the sky to the west, but Avylos could clearly make out the edges of the battlements, and the colors of the Nisvean soldiers as they took strategic positions in the streets below. He used his Mage's sight to probe the city, noting where the largest gatherings of soldiers were, where the wooden buildings, where storage houses full of grains, hay, firewood, oil. Of the city's four gates, two were closed and barred, but there were still Nisveans entering by the other two.

Avylos drew a symbol in the air, the same one he would have used over the pond in his garden. Without the medium of the magicked pond, he could see Edmir, but very little of his immediate surroundings. The boy was on horseback, and the angle of his shadows showed in which direction he must be.

And close. Very close. He could feel it.

When he was sure where he wished to strike, Avylos raised his arms and sketched green fire across the sky.

The wind rose, and the lightning began to fall.

"I must get some damp cloths for my face as quickly as possible—do I look very bad?" the girl said over her shoulder as they turned another corner. "We've a performance to give tomorrow in a country holding, and I can't go on with my face all swollen. Paints can only do so much."

Since the little Cat couldn't see her, Dhulyn let her lip curl back over her teeth. Didn't it occur to the child that with the invasion there very likely wouldn't be any performance? Dhulyn was already wishing she'd insisted Zania ride with Edmir. The girl's hostel *was* closer to the gate, but it wasn't just two streets over. Either the little Cat couldn't count, or she simply wasn't an accurate observer. And she wouldn't stop talking.

"Here we are."

Finally. Dhulyn slowed to a stop. The hostel itself was a modest one, as befitted a company of strolling players who had their own caravan. They'd want comfortable beds as a change from traveling, and someone else's cooking, but they wouldn't be inclined to pay much for it. It was not the size of the establishment that made the hairs on Dhulyn's neck rise.

"The gates to the stable yard are open," she said, as Parno came up on her left side.

"Any other day, I'd expect it," Parno said in a voice that indicated he shared her thoughts. "But this would be the only open doorway we've seen since leaving City House."

Dhulyn tilted her head back and widened her nostrils.

"Smells wrong," she said. "Get down, little Cat, and stay back."

For all her chattering, Zania must have been well-trained, probably by her actor parents. She caught Dhulyn's tone and obeyed, swinging her leg nimbly over Bloodbone's head and sliding to the ground without argument or questions.

Dhulyn caught Parno's eye and jerked her head toward the open gateway. He winked his left eye, dismounted, and took up his stance at the left of the gate.

"Edmir," she said, as she pulled her sword from its scabbard across her back. "Stay with the dancer." She turned and rode through the gate.

Edmir dismounted and concentrated on looking as innocent and harmless as he knew how. He needn't have bothered. Zania, lower lip sucked into her mouth, had her eyes fixed on the gateway.

"What are they doing?" She took a determined step forward, and Edmir swung in front of her with his hands raised, palms outwards, resisting the urge to grab her by the arm.

"They said to wait, we'd best wait."

"You're not a Mercenary Brother." She looked at him, meeting his eyes for just a second before glancing away. Her eyes were a startling violet color, all the clearer for the darkening around the left side of her face.

"No, I . . ." For some reason his tongue felt thick. "No, they're my bodyguards. It, uh, it was my idea to stop and help you."

"I thank you, good sir, for your courtesy." But she had turned her eyes back to the gateway, and her words sounded rehearsed. In fact, Edmir thought with a twist to his lips, they probably came from some play she had acted in.

Even Edmir was beginning to wonder whether they should go in when Wolfshead and Lionsmane finally came out of the stable yard on foot. The Lionsmane's face was impassive as he picked up Warhammer's reins, except for a tightening around his mouth. His Partner was smiling her wolf's smile, lip curled back from her teeth. Seeing their faces, Zania cried out—the sound strangely natural and real after her affected tones. Edmir took a step toward her and stopped, not knowing what he meant to say.

Dhulyn Wolfshead caught Zania by the arms as the girl tried to run through the gates. "How many in your troupe? Zania!" She shook her until Zania blinked and focused on her. "How many?"

"Seven—six and me."

"There are eleven dead. One is wearing a Nisvean tunic, and four look like they belong to the hostel. You had better come and look, we have covered the worst of it."

What they'd left uncovered was quite bad enough, Edmir thought as he followed the Mercenaries and the girl into the stable yard and the smell hit him full force. For a moment he was back in the battlefield, he swore he could hear the same flies. His stomach sank under a wave of guilt and fear. Then Parno coughed, and Edmir was back in the yard of the hostel.

The stable yard had not been purpose-built, but was formed by the walls of the surrounding buildings. There was no entrance to the hostel at the ground level, though a set of rough wooden stairs led to an upper balcony. A handful of rough stalls lay along one side, and the stable yard was made tiny by the presence of a gaily painted caravan, built like an elongated coach. The coppery smell of blood was everywhere, and the iron smell of burning was following drifts of smoke from the open windows on the second floor.

The Mercenaries had laid out the bodies roughly where they'd found them. The Nisvean and two others in the back rooms of the hostel they'd left inside; of the rest, three were in the public room and five on the cobblestones of the stable yard. Heads and faces were covered with scraps of blankets and other cloths. Six were dressed in the same bright colors and flowing style that Zania herself wore; except for the Nisvean, the rest were in plain dull homespun.

As soon as they cleared the gate, Zania ran to the body that lay nearest the tall wheel of the caravan, and this time Dhulyn Wolfshead did not stop her. Zania knelt and, picking up the corpse's hand, laid her face against it and began to wail, her voice rising higher and higher. Edmir stepped forward, biting on the inside of his cheek as he fought tears.

Movement caught Dhulyn's eye and she turned toward Parno, who gestured her toward the sobbing girl. She raised her eyebrows at him. He rolled his eyes, pointed at Dhulyn, pointed at the girl, and made shooing motions with both hands. Her stomach sank. The girl would have to be cuddled and quieted, and Parno could not do it. Not now, not with the attack in the square so fresh in the little Cat's mind. *It will have to be me.* Was that a grin her blooded Partner was hiding? She gave him a look that told him it better not be, and went to comfort the weeping girl.

I'm no blooded good at this, she thought, as she wrapped her right arm around Zania's shoulders, drew the girl into the circle of her arms, and covered her mouth with her free hand.

"Stop crying, or I'll have to kill you," she murmured in the girl's ear.

Zania stiffened, flashed Dhulyn a disbelieving look, but fell silent, pushing herself free of the Mercenary's arms, and drying her tears with the trailing end of her sleeve.

"Get your things together," Dhulyn told the girl. "We must be gone."

The little Cat straightened to her feet, smoothing her hair back from her face and automatically adjusting her clothing. She looked around her, eyes blinking and mouth twisting in the effort to keep from crying. She coughed, took in a deep breath, and released it.

"I want the caravan." The girl looked from Dhulyn to Parno and back again, her jaw firm with determination, her voice steadying as she spoke. "*My* caravan, *your* horses. We should manage very well together."

"No offense," Parno spoke up before Dhulyn could. "I see the advantage to you, but what's the advantage to us?"

"Because no one looks at a troupe of traveling players and sees Mercenaries."

"And why should that concern us?"

"*He* says you're his bodyguards." Dhulyn wondered what the Prince of Tegrian thought of being referred to with a hooked thumb. "If that were true," the little Cat continued, "you wouldn't be going so quietly, and watching around every corner. The Nisveans and the Tegriani have been squabbling over the border for generations. Why would you need to hide from either side? Why would they interfere with Brothers going about their legitimate employment? Therefore, either you, or the one you guard, must be kept hidden from the Nisveans, or the Tegriani, or both. I can help you do that."

Dhulyn turned to Parno and punched him lightly in the shoulder. "You see? I told you that reading poetry and plays was not a waste of time." She turned back to the girl. "How?"

Zania gestured at the wagon. "In there I have all the disguises and costumes we could need. By sunrise tomorrow, even your own Brothers wouldn't recognize you. As an acting troupe, we can go anywhere unquestioned." She took a deep breath. "And we already have an engagement."

Warhammer and Bloodbone were not cart horses, but this was not the first time they had been used as such. Though they snorted a bit at first, they gave no real trouble, and with Zania's help Dhulyn had them harnessed in very short order. Parno got Edmir to help him move the bodies farther out of the way, and stow their gear into the caravan itself. Dhulyn's Mercenary badge was covered with one of Zania's colorful head scarves and his own with a peaked hood. He and his Partner had armed themselves only with axes and stout sticks, the weapons generally used by travelers such as Zania and her family. Edmir had wanted a crossbow, but Zania insisted that no player would ever expect to use such a thing, except as a prop on stage.

"We're like Scholars that way," she said. "No one bothers us. Or at least, nothing that sweet words or a little money can't turn away."

"That what happened here?" Edmir said.

Zania pressed her lips together and looked at the Mercenaries.

"Likely they were trying to help their friends and got caught up in the frenzy," Parno said when the silence grew strained. "Once killing begins, it's hard to stop."

"And once the dying begins, that's hard to stop as well," Dhulyn said. "Go," she said to Zania, "say your farewells." She turned back to Parno and Edmir. "Is Stumpy tied on?"

"Why not use the packhorse, rather than one of your own?" Edmir said, as he tied Stumpy's reins to the hook near the caravan's rear door.

"What is it you have against Stumpy?" Parno asked. "That's the second time you've spoken against him. He's too small to be paired with either Warhammer or Bloodbone. Those two are closer in size, and that makes a difference. That's the real reason coach horses are matched as closely as possible, not to make things pretty."

Parno was looking up at an ominously darkening sky when Dhulyn stuck her head around the corner of the caravan.

"We go," she said.

"Have you Seen something?" Parno hoped his tone made it clear what he meant.

"Just a bad feeling," his Partner replied, shaking her head. "I'll get the little Cat."

Zania Tzadeyeu returned from saying farewell to her family with her face as stony as bruising and swelling would allow. She joined Edmir on the driver's seat with Parno. It was a tight fit, but he'd rather they were with him than floating about loose where he couldn't see them.

"I'm sorry we can't give them any better rites than this," Dhulyn called to Zania from her position at the horses' heads. "But they'd want you safe more than anything else."

"They're in the hands of the Caids now," the girl said.

They had no more than cleared the gate of the inn, with Dhulyn jogging ahead with the horses, when a bolt of lightning struck the gatepost. In moments the entire front of the inn—old timbers and plaster—was engulfed by flames.

"Dhulyn!" Parno called, but she was already in motion. Their horses were too well-trained to bolt even at this, but Dhulyn had swung herself onto Bloodbone's back, to help calm them even more. Parno let the reins go slack, she would do the guiding for the present. From the stable yard to the north gate was only a matter of turning the right corner and negotiating a few spans of mostly deserted streets.

The ground rumbled and another bolt of lightning fell. Stumpy squealed, but when Parno looked around, he saw the packhorse running alongside the caravan, eyes wide and neck at its full extent. A building ahead of them was already on fire, with people running into the streets from suddenly unbolted doors.

"Dhulyn!" he called again. This time all she did was point to the left.

"Grab hold of something and get ready to lean all your weight to the left, as soon as we turn the corner," Parno told the two youngsters. He wrapped the reins around the cleat in the center of the footboard in front of him and took hold of it himself, his eyes glued to his Partner.

Dhulyn led the horses around the next corner at a speed even Parno found unbelievable. At the very last instant she pointed again.

"Now!" Parno yelled, leaning all his weight to the left as the caravan careened around the corner. Zania fell against him, gripping Edmir's arm with both her hands.

The caravan righted itself, and Dhulyn was already pointing to the left again.

The entire right side of this narrow street was in flames, but Dhulyn kept the horses galloping, and suddenly they found themselves in the small open space in front of Probic's north gate. The gates were open, the portcullis raised, and bodies of guards in dark blue showed how that had happened. Even here the smoke was thick enough to make them cough, and the ground was trembling once more. A ball of flame leaped from the nearest building to the gate itself, and the ropes that connected parts of the mechanisms began to smolder.

Dhulyn spoke to the horses, patted them both wherever she could reach them. Stumpy would not have her presence to calm him, but he was the most phlegmatic of the three in any case—she would just have to hope for the best. None of them could keep up this pace for long, but they had to get as far away from Probic as quickly as they could. Bracing herself with her hands, Dhulyn kicked up until she was standing crouched on Bloodbone's back. The rhythm of the horse's movement was as natural to her as the beating of her own heart, so she wasted no time in turning to face her Partner.

Parno grinned at her, and touched his forehead with his fingertips. She laughed, and did the same.

"That was not natural," she called out.

"The Mage," Parno answered. She should have known he would be thinking along with her.

"Take up the reins," she said. "I'll slow them very soon."

When she saw him comply, she turned back again to face the road, letting herself down once more to a sitting position astride Bloodbone's back. She began to sing, and the horses pricked their ears, waiting for the chorus, when they knew they should begin to slow.

"Sun blast, Moon drown you!" Avylos put Tzanek's left hand on Tzanek's chest, feeling the heart pound like a fast drum, the breath short. He had missed them. Missed them! His right hand formed a fist and brought it down again and again before he turned and started down the stairs that would take him back to Tzanek's chamber.

This time he leaned heavily against the wall as he went.

⟡

With Parno on the reins, and Dhulyn to encourage the horses, they continued traveling well into the night, having turned off the main road out of Probic on the first track leading toward the Household where Zania's family had their next engagement.

"Even if we don't perform, we'll be welcome for the news we bring and we'll be that much farther along our road," the white-faced girl had pointed out.

"At the moment, any road that takes us from Probic is a good one, but first chance we get, we decide where our final road must be," Dhulyn said. All four of them were on foot to spare the horses as much as possible, with the two youngsters taking it in turns to ride up on the driver's seat. Hardy as both of them might normally be, they were not Mercenaries, and it was all they could do to keep up with the horses for even a short while.

"Somewhere safe, is my suggestion," Parno said. When Dhulyn glanced over to him, he winked at her. It was his job to play the prosy oldster when they had to deal with outsiders. Especially young outsiders.

"Well if that *was* the Mage in Probic, he's stopped now," Dhulyn said. "And we've no way of knowing whether it was us he was after." Once again Dhulyn caught his eye and he knew that her thoughts on that matched his own. Too much coincidence, he thought, that they, and the Nisveans, and a freak storm with fire falling from the sky should all arrive in Probic on the same day.

Parno hated coincidence. It wasn't natural.

He was more than ready to stop by the time Dhulyn called a halt, leading them into a clear spot off the track just large enough to squeeze the caravan through the trees. They could not have gone much farther in any case, the waning moon had set and taken what little light there was with it. Parno let the caravan pass into the trees and looked back in the direction they had come. The moon might have set, but there was a glow to the southeast.

"Probic." Dhulyn's voice at his left elbow.

"Nothing else it could be," he agreed. "Amazing there's still something left to burn."

"Mage fire," Dhulyn said.

"I did not think the Mage had such power."

"I don't think anyone did."

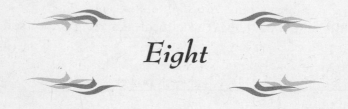

Eight

AVYLOS' FOREHEAD SLAMMED down on the tabletop and
he groaned. Somehow he had managed to bring Tzanek's
headache back with him. He tried to push himself up, but his
head was too heavy; he ended by having to lift it with his hands. Once
upright, he could, with great care, balance his head on the top of his
neck. It felt like trying to balance an apple on the tip of his finger. Fortunately, he had once been very good at that kind of trick.

He did nothing for several minutes but breathe deeply and try to
still the pounding in his head. When he thought he could manage it,
he reached to his left and put his hand on the casket that held the
Stone. Getting the key out of the pocket of his gown almost defeated
him, but after several tries his trembling fingers managed to fit it into
the lock. With the casket open, the Stone in his hands, he already felt
much better, just knowing that restoration was so close.

"*Aharneh.*" His throat was so dry, his voice so weak, that had there
been others in the room with him, they would not have heard the
word. But the Stone heard. His teeth closed on the inside of his lip as
his head fell back. The power washed through him, the headache vanished, and his feeling of fragility lightened but did not disappear entirely. Avylos drew a symbol in the air. It appeared, wavered a moment,
and faded away.

Avylos tasted the blood from his lip. He had used too much power
in Probic, enough that the magics had drawn on the strength of his
own blood and bones. His rage had consumed him in more ways than
one. Instead of filling him once more, restoring his Magehood, the

power he could tap from the Stone had only restored him to normal humanity.

And that was a *lie*. His right hand closed into a fist. He was *not* a normal man, without magic and without power. That was the lie his family, his *Tribe*—his lip curled back and he resisted the urge to spit—had tricked him with for so long. But he had punished them for that, and when he mastered the secrets of the Stone, that lie would be banished forever.

There would be a page standing his post at the entrance to this wing. Avylos stood, dusted down his gown, made sure that the folds of his cloak fell straight, and headed for the door. The page would fetch him Olecz the guard. And the guard would fetch him the dice boy.

"The Wolfshead says we'll stop here," Zania was saying to Edmir, with the unnecessary precision of the exhausted. It was Edmir's turn on the caravan's high seat, and the girl's face, ghostly pale in the darkness under the trees, was peering upward at him from the ground.

"Be careful getting down, Edmir," Parno said as he neared the front of the caravan. "Your leg may have stiffened." He needn't have bothered warning him, the boy lowered himself from the seat with the movements of a man twice Parno's age. And a sick man at that.

"Get inside, you two," Dhulyn said, leaving off stroking and praising the horses to join them. "Find us something to eat and drink—and for the Moon's sake, don't wait for us, eat something yourselves."

She beckoned to him, and Parno joined her at the horses, first rubbing Warhammer's nose and praising him before beginning to undo the harness attaching him to the caravan's central shaft. Dhulyn was doing the same to Bloodbone, crooning to her in the language of the Red Horsemen. Like anyone from a Noble House with country Holdings, Parno had been taught to take care of his animals. Dhulyn's approach made even Parno's training look like neglect, but he had to admit, time-consuming as it was, the results made it worthwhile.

"At least we won't need a fire for warmth, not tonight at any rate," Dhulyn said, as she tugged at a stiff knot on Bloodbone's harness.

Parno nodded. "The bunks are large enough for two to sleep, if they're friendly."

"We'll see how friendly the prince feels."

It wasn't quite a smile Parno could hear in his Partner's voice, but it was close. "What about you?"

"I'm far enough away from my woman's time to share a bed, if that is what you ask." The last bit of harness undone, Bloodbone moved free of her own accord, and Dhulyn coiled up the trailing ends of leather harness and hung them in their places before coming to help Parno.

"Any wagers on which one wants to sleep with you?" he asked, moving aside for her.

"My wager is neither," Dhulyn said. "Since we met with the Clouds, the prince looks at me with eyes that see something uncanny, and the dancer girl is still not comfortable enough in her skin to be close to anyone."

"Don't fret, my heart, that still leaves me."

"We should be so lucky. We'll have to take watch turnabout. Neither of *them* will know what to watch for."

"Do we?" Without meaning to, Parno had glanced back over his shoulder to where the glow from the destruction of Probic could still be seen in the sky. "What did City Lord Tzanek mean when he said that the Brotherhood was banished from Tegrian? The wall guards certainly seemed to know nothing of it."

"Today's trouble today." Dhulyn put her hand on his arm. "We've seen worse than this," she said. "And we are still here to talk about it."

"In Battle," he said.

"Or in Death," she answered.

Free, the horses shook themselves and immediately went to investigate the tufts of grass by the side of the clearing away from the road. Parno unhooked a bucket from the caravan's side and filled it with water from the barrel fastened next to it, as Dhulyn rounded the caravan to untie Stumpy.

"Why do you call her dancer?"

"That's what her name means in the old tongue, the language of the Caids."

"Tzadeyeu?"

Dhulyn slapped Stumpy on the rump and nodded. "The word has changed a bit in the passage of time, as our old friend Gundaron the

Scholar would tell us, but it's the same word." Dhulyn joined him at the water barrel. "Did you see their faces?"

Parno shrugged. "They'll be twitching for hours."

"A long day, and a bad one. For them both." Her fingers felt rough and cold on his wrist. "Play for them. Play them to sleep."

The interior of the caravan was as compact and well-arranged as a ship captain's cabin. Two benches—wide enough, as Parno had said, to hold two people who were friendly—ran lengthwise down each side, and the netting above them held all manner of parcels and packages—and would hold people, too, Dhulyn thought, if the packages were on the floor, and more beds were needed. Cupboard doors under the benches showed where more supplies, and probably the bedding, could be stowed.

Dhulyn left the door of the caravan open behind her as she and Parno climbed in. The two youngsters sat on opposite benches, eyeing each other over the caravan's table, a flap of time-darkened wood that had been let down from where it attached to the wall at the front end. A candle set into a silvered holder reflected light into the space, and illuminated a platter on which rested a partially eaten loaf—yesterday's bread, Dhulyn's thought, eyeing it with sudden interest, half a dozen cold potatoes and a handful of sticks of dried meat.

Parno rubbed his hands together and slid in next to Edmir, leaving Zania's side of the table to Dhulyn.

"And to drink?" Parno said.

Zania lifted a clay jug from the floor at her feet and passed it over the table. Parno pulled the stopper, smelled the jug, and frowned.

"I'll fetch water," he said, and started to rise to his feet.

"There's water here also," Zania said, reaching down for another jug. "I didn't think you'd want it."

"We're Mercenary Brothers," Dhulyn told her. "Not soldiers, not guards. We don't go off duty at the end of the watch."

"And in any case, our watch lasts until Edmir here gets home safely," Parno added, wiping off his mouth with the back of his hand and passing the water jug to Dhulyn. She stifled a smile as she accepted the jug. As Parno had told the prince, he came from a House fully as noble as the prince's own—perhaps more so—and yet here he was pouring water directly into his mouth without touching the jug to his lips as handily as any country man. There was no bumpkin in the man—country or otherwise—and yet Parno liked to play the part. She looked at the faces of the prince and the dancer. Parno's little act did help to set people at ease, she thought. It did that.

"Then the sooner I get home, the better for all of us," Edmir said. "We must get to Beolind as quickly as we can, we must reach my mother."

Parno caught Dhulyn's eye and scratched his nose with his left forefinger. She blinked, and gave herself time to swallow the bread she'd been chewing. "Let us not be hasty, *Edmir*," she said, emphasizing the prince's name ever so slightly. Let him hear her use his name without a title, let him remember, she hoped, that Zania did not know who he was. "It's no return for you if it's not a return to *safety*."

"I know he's Lord Prince Edmir, if that's what you're being so careful about." The girl's tone was at once crisp and smug, like a student who had all the right answers and was ready to show off.

Edmir coughed on the water he was drinking. Dhulyn looked at Parno and saw the twinkle in his eyes. When she smiled back, her Partner broke into laughter. Still smiling, she shook her head at him.

"I didn't tell her." Edmir was indignant.

"No need to tell me." The smugness was now clearly to the fore. "You were declared dead almost four days ago, time enough for likenesses to be made and put up around the town. I saw one in front of the Jaldean Shrine, as well as at the prayer stations for the other gods. They made you look younger and more innocent, of course, but it was you all right."

Parno sat back against the cushions. "Well, this will make things more comfortable."

"For you maybe," Edmir muttered.

"We, at least, can stop watching our tongues when we are in private," Dhulyn said, letting a touch of frost enter her voice. "And you can stop pretending to be an ordinary person."

"And doing a poor job of it." The two women gave each other brisk nods. Parno grinned broadly, took the last piece of bread, broke it, and gave half to her. She took it with a shrug. No point in doing without, it wouldn't last another day.

"Zania's brought up a good point," Parno began.

"What, that he's no actor?"

"Enough, little Cat. I meant that if Edmir's been declared dead, and the country is in mourning, we can't merely turn up at the Queen's Court with him and ask for breakfast."

This time it was the two young people who looked at each other, shared ignorance bringing them together until they noticed what they were doing and looked away.

"Why? If it's not a stupid question?" the girl said.

"There are no stupid questions," Dhulyn said. She sat forward, her elbows on the tabletop. "The prince isn't dead, but someone wants him to be, and going straight to the capital doesn't seem the best method to keep him alive. There are too many questions with no clear answers."

"Who warned the Nisveans you were coming? Because they knew, no doubt there," Parno put in, looking at Edmir.

"Why didn't the Blue Mage's magic work? And why were the Nisveans so adamant about keeping you?" Dhulyn added.

"And why have you been so quickly declared dead, since you obviously aren't?" Zania blinked and lifted her chin to return Edmir's stare.

"And why," Parno said in the tone of someone being careful not to hurt, "did a man who has known and loved you all your life not recognize you, when recognizing you would mean that all the country—including your mother and sister—would rejoice?"

"Meaning that until we find out who wouldn't be rejoicing, it's best we stay hidden." Dhulyn gently tapped the table with her index finger.

"And not just for the prince's sake," Parno said. "If what Lord Tzanek was saying is true, the Mercenary Brotherhood has been asked to leave Tegrian—" He caught Dhulyn's eyes with the look that said, *We'll talk of this later.* "And since we have no intention of leaving Tegrian at the moment, where can we go to both learn things and stay hidden?" Parno asked.

"I still say here's the best place to hide." Zania rapped the table in front of her hard. "The last place anyone will look for you, prince or Mercenary Brother, is performing on a public stage. And we can learn things, too. People are used to passing the news, even letters, along with travelers like us . . ." Her voice faltered. "Like me."

"Agreed," Dhulyn said. "But even players have a destination, a route. And so should we." She bit off the end of a twist of dried meat.

"We can go to Jarlkevo," Edmir said.

Dhulyn, her mouth full, raised her eyebrows at Parno.

"And what's in Jarlkevo?" he asked.

"My aunt Valaika."

"And we can know that she's not part of this—whatever this is?"

Edmir shook his head. His lips were pressed into a thin line. "She's my father's sister. She came with him from Hellik when he married my mother. They had some kind of falling out when I was a child—" Edmir shrugged. No need to say, Dhulyn thought, that he hadn't been interested, or perhaps old enough at the time to remember the details now.

"She wanted to marry someone unsuitable, something like that," he continued. "She left the Royal House, and the Holding at Jarlkevo, part of my father's marriage gift, was elevated to a House and given to her. I don't think she's been back at court since my father's funeral. She didn't come for Kera's naming day, just sent her a nice horse." From the change in his voice, Dhulyn thought Edmir would have liked a nice horse from his aunt as well.

"And will she be disposed to help you now?" Dhulyn asked.

Edmir shrugged, every line in his face turning downward. "I can be sure she had no part in my present circumstances," he said. "That, at least, I can say."

"Jarlkevo it is, then," Dhulyn said.

"Parno," Dhulyn said, once the platters had been cleared away and the tabletop folded to its upright position. "Get your pipes, my soul. Some music will soothe us."

Parno met her glance and made the smallest shrugging motion with his shoulders. Edmir was staring into space again, looking at the Moon and Stars knew what ghastly sight, and Zania's eyes had taken on that hollow look which said "my people are all gone, and I'm still alive." It was a look Dhulyn herself was well familiar with. The girl would be feeling some guilt now, and would feel it again and again, as even planning what she should do next would seem selfish and a betrayal in the light of what had happened to her family. It would be a long process, coming to terms with the events of the past day, but what the girl needed right now was sleep, to give her thoughts at least one night's distance from the events of the day.

And Edmir—how must he feel? *Someone* had betrayed him, the question was, who?

The bag holding Parno's pipes was one of the first things they had brought into the caravan, and it was a matter of moments for him to unfasten the heavy silk cords of the bag's opening. As he set the drones to one side, and took out just the chanter, Dhulyn helped the little Cat bring out the bedding and unfold it along the benches. Edmir lay down without hesitation, his eyes still focused on the middle distance, but Zania shook her head.

"I can't sleep," she said. "There's too much to think about, plans to make." Her chin trembled for a moment, but she soon had it under control again. "There's things that won't wait until tomorrow, now that my uncle is dead—" Abruptly, she stopped and clamped her jaw. Dhulyn guessed that she was seeing once more the blood-drained face, the staring eyes.

Sitting in the open doorway, Parno began to play softly, a simple tune that made Dhulyn smile. It was a variation on a well-known children's song, a game which often involved a blindfold, but played at a tempo that made it a lullaby.

"Tell me your ideas," Dhulyn said, drawing the girl's attention. "What should you be planning? Do you have other family? Another troupe, perhaps, with whom you have ties?"

The little Cat was shaking her head, but her color was better, and her trembling had stopped. "There *is* a meeting place, after the Harvest Fairs have run their course and the Midwinter Festivals have yet to begin, but before that I must finish—If you are going to Beolind, that will suit me perfectly. I can begin there."

"Begin what?" Edmir was not asleep yet, after all. His dark eyes looked even darker in the shadows cast by the oil lamp.

"Your pardon, Lord Prince," Zania said, lowering her eyes. "But my business is my own."

"Fair enough, for now, little Cat," Dhulyn said. "But our road will lie together, and we have pledged to help each other, keep that to mind."

The girl straightened her shoulders. "In part, that's what has been pulling at my thoughts," she said. "Most of our pieces—the ones I know by heart anyway—use my . . . use the whole troupe. But there are others, smaller plays, pieces that would need only two or three players."

"Best think of something for two." Dhulyn patted the bedclothes on the bench and stood up. "Think lying down. Let Parno's music guide your thoughts."

The little Cat drew in her brows and nodded as she obeyed, tucking up her feet and letting Dhulyn cover her.

"I remember we did all manner of things before the troupe split up, when my mother still lived. There are books and scrolls . . ."

"To be looked at in the morning's light," murmured Dhulyn. "Come, just rest your eyes a for a moment. Is it not a beautiful tune my Partner plays?"

Still frowning, Zania closed her eyes. Dhulyn waited, letting the familiar music wash over her as well, loosening the tensions of the day. She glanced at Parno, but his eyes were closed in concentration. Dhulyn let herself out past his sprawling feet and settled on the step outside. She let her head fall back against his thigh and her own eyes closed.

It's summer, late in the day, but the sun still shines, and it is warm enough that the boys all have their blood-red hair braided and one or two are shirtless. They sit on the ground, cross-legged, in a circle, taking turns making gestures in the air, as if they are drawing. One or two are quickly successful, a symbol in light hovering in front of them for a few moments before disappearing. One boy forgets a part of the symbol he is drawing, and it collapses; the other boys laugh. There is one who does not laugh. Only Dhulyn can see him, hiding, watching from behind the hanging awning of a nearby tent. This is not a child, excluded because of age from the business of those who are almost men. He is the same age as the others; his hair is braided, down is forming on his cheeks. Something else keeps him hiding, watching, his hands in fists, with a look of dark hatred on his face . . .

Parno is sitting at a small table, an oil lamp with a curious glass shade illuminating the page on which he is writing. Dhulyn frowns. Usually when there is any writing to be done, she does it. Parno is literate, and in the manner of the sons of Noble Houses in Imrion, well-educated, particularly in history, politics, and economics. But she is the one who has spent a year in a Scholars' Library, while she learned the life was not for her, and it is she who writes a better hand. He frowns, crosses out a short word, and writes something else.

This is an older Parno, Parno-to-come, Dhulyn realizes. The familiar dark red and deep yellow of his Mercenary badge is clear in the lamplight. The lines in his face are more pronounced, his hair is cut much shorter than he wears it now, and there seems to be gray under the gold. Parno lays down his pen and rubs at the wristband on his left wrist. Dhulyn recognizes it. She wears it on her own wrist now. The now of the real world, not the now of the Vision.

Where is she? . . .

Moonlight washes all the color from what must be a beautiful garden surrounded by high walls. A slim man is seated on the edge of a pool of water. He looks down at the surface with great concentration. Perhaps he is a Finder, using the pool as a scrying bowl. Dhulyn can't get close enough to him to see his face, which is turned away and obscured in the faulty light. Nor can she see what it is that so absorbs him in the water. A movement to one side reveals there is a girl sitting on a rough part of the wall, watching the man. He doesn't know she's there. . . .

A redheaded man on horseback, his fur-lined cloak pushed back to free his arms, makes a curiously familiar gesture, drawing in the air in front of him. A blue line of light follows the end of his finger, lingering in the air a moment before it fades. The trail of hoofprints in the snow behind him disappears.

When she woke up, Zania thought for one blessed moment that all the horror—the blood on her aunt's face, her cousin's limp hand—had been a nightmare, and the voices she heard coming from outside were her uncle Jovan and her aunt Ester. But then she remembered. They both were dead, lying in a row, wrapped in blankets in the stable yard of the hostel, and she would never hear their voices again. As the tears began, she turned over to face the caravan's wall, covering her face with her hands to stifle any sound she might make. She couldn't let anyone see her crying. They would lose respect for her, think her no more than an untried child.

When she could finally take a deep breath without sobbing, Zania sat up, throwing off the rugs she didn't remember pulling over her. Everything in the caravan was now hers. Everything. Including the troupe's charter from the old Galan of Cabrea, an age-yellowed bit of parchment that at least in theory gave them free passage wherever they might choose to go. These important documents were here, inside, where her elder relatives normally slept while she, Jovana, and the twins slept under the caravan. But Prince Edmir was asleep in her great-uncle's place, and she couldn't light a lamp now. There were more papers, books and scrolls, performance pieces for the most part, wrapped in oiled cloth and stored in an old chest that was rarely opened, and therefore was kept up top, under the flat pieces of scenery.

But *that* wasn't what she wanted just now. Zania swung her feet off the bench and padded silently to the door, letting herself out before she could change her mind. The cool night air made her shiver, but she didn't expect to be out very long. She heard a horse snort over to her left, but though she waited, holding her breath, she heard nothing else. They were silent sleepers, then, these Mercenaries.

The moon had set, and even the stars had been obscured by clouds. But this caravan had been Zania's home her whole life; she didn't need light to find her away around it. She crept forward along one side, trailing her fingers across the painted surface until she felt the hard edge of the ladder that gave access to the driver's seat. Zania hitched up her skirt, pulled herself up the three short steps and swung into the seat. She ran her fingers over the bits of decorative wooden trim that formed geometric shapes on the front of the caravan. She'd never actually done this herself, but she and her cousin had watched Great-Uncle Therin many times, when they were supposed to be asleep under the wagon.

There. The bottom piece on the left shifted down under her prodding, swung to one side and exposed a flat opening panel about the size of her hand. Zania hesitated, hand lifted, tongue pressing on her upper lip. This was Great-Uncle Therin's secret hiding place, never even to be spoken of. If she had needed any proof that life as she'd known it had ended, and that things would never be the same again, she had it now. She took a deep breath, slipped her hand into the space, and brought out her great-uncle's journal. She lifted it to her face. It smelled like him, of the garlic he loved in all his food, of the herbal rub he used on his lower back and arthritic knees.

She tucked the journal into the front of her gown, returned the piece of wood trim to its original position, feeling the slight "click" through her fingers. She let herself down the short ladder and felt her heart leap as a long-fingered hand closed over her left biceps.

"Stay quiet, there are others who wish to sleep, though you've finished."

The Wolfshead. Though her breath still came short, Zania relaxed. Intellectually she knew—she'd been warned by her aunt—that women could be just as dangerous to a young person as men, but the bare truth was that predatory women were rare, and if she was safe with anyone, it would be Dhulyn Wolfshead.

"There's a chest up top I wanted to check," she said, trying to match the Mercenary woman's whisper-quiet voice.

"In the dark?"

When Zania didn't answer, the Wolfshead gave a short laugh.

"But then, you did not need any light to find what you were looking for in that hiding place, did you? Go back to bed," she said. "I will wake you when there's enough light to see anything."

Zania waited, but it seemed that Dhulyn Wolfshead was not going to ask her anything more about what she'd found.

"I don't know if I can sleep inside," Zania said, closing her mouth abruptly. It was true, she realized, but it hadn't been what she'd meant to say. "That's . . . that *was* the elders' place and I . . ."

"You thought you'd be there one day, but not so soon."

A statement, not a question. A tug on her wrist, and Zania followed the older woman as she led her away from the caravan, under a willow tree whose overhanging branches provided them some cover from the cool breeze. Dhulyn Wolfshead leaned her back against the trunk of the tree. Zania glanced around. *Of course*, she thought. *From here she can see the whole clearing, moonlight or no moonlight.*

"What will be the first thing we need to do, Zania Tzadeyeu, if our disguise is to work? People have only to look at Parno Lionsmane and myself to know that we are Mercenary Brothers."

"I have an idea for that, but we should also see what talents we have among us," Zania said. "The Lionsmane can play, for example. Can he make songs as well? There's money to be made bringing new music to people. Can we all sing, dance? And we must find scenes and plays we can perform with so few players. Not that Great-Uncle Therin takes . . . took so very many parts, I suppose." With the darkness to cover her, Zania tried to imitate the Mercenary woman's stance, chin up, head slightly tilted on an angle like a bird listening, feet shoulder-width apart, knees a little bent, shoulders squared to the torso and arms hanging loosely from the shoulders.

"What did he do, then?"

Zania thought she heard a whisper of amusement in the Wolfshead's voice, as if she'd seen what Zania was doing, and what's more, had understood *why* she'd been doing it. Zania shook herself. "Why ask me all this about the past? We have to plan where we go from here."

"To know where we go, I must know where we have been," Dhulyn Wolfshead said. Her voice was the merest thread of sound in the darkness. "I am the strategist of my Partnership. Let me see how things *were* done, and I can help you to see how things *will* be done."

Zania found herself nodding. That made sense.

"Well, Therin took the parts of the older men, you know, kings, counselors, old Jaldean priests full of advice and the like. My cousin Jovana and I would take all the younger parts between us, pages, young sons or daughters, sometimes the young lovers, if the story called for such."

"Played both parts, did you?" Though the Mercenary woman was close enough to her that Zania could feel the warmth from her body, her voice seemed to come from some distance away.

"Female and male, you mean? Yes, it's easy enough. We were on the lookout for a boy to join us, but all we found were the acrobats. Twins, Nik and Sari. They'd do for spear carriers, but neither of them could act." Zania sat down cross-legged at the Wolfshead's feet. "My aunt Ester played the more important lovers or princesses or pirate queens." Zania was dismayed to hear the note of discontent and envy that had crept into her voice and hurried on. "My uncle Jovan partnered her, taking the man's roles, lords or lovers, the parts Great-Uncle Therin was too old to play."

"And soon you would have taken your aunt's roles?"

"Yes. Well, either Jovana or I would. Depending. It was Great-Uncle Therin decided who played what, and what story it was we acted, for that matter."

"We must all serve an apprenticeship," Dhulyn Wolfshead said. "Mercenaries in our Schools, Scholars in their Libraries, even the Marked in their Guilds. We cannot all begin by playing Nor-iRon Tarkina."

"You know that play?"

"There's a reason I'm called the Scholar," the Mercenary said, "and you have just learned what it is."

"Do you know the play well? We have enough people to do the first act. Parno Lionsmane could play the old Tarkin on his deathbed. You could play the Marked counselor, the Seer Estavia. I'd be Nor-iRon as Heir, and the prince could play . . ." Zania became aware that Dhulyn Wolfshead had stiffened, and fell quiet. The Mercenary was silent for a long time, long enough that Zania's heart began to thump uncomfortably.

"We should leave talk of performances for when the others are with us," she said.

Zania relaxed. "Of course."

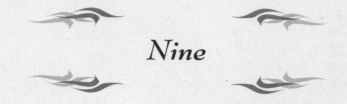

Nine

"I SWEAR TO YOU, LORD Mage, the dice are not weighted, I'm not cheating, I swear it." His hands shaking, Zel-Nobic took the cup of brandy-laced wine the Blue Mage gave him and held it, too frightened to actually lift it to his mouth and take a drink.

"I never thought you were, Zel-Nobic. If I thought you were a mere cheat, I would be very disappointed." The tall Mage's voice was mellow as warm honey, and Zel-Nobic's hands stopped shaking.

"Disappointed, Lord Mage?"

The Blue Mage sat back and rested his elbows on the arms of the chair on the far side of the worktable. "I am not concerned with cheating at dice—that carries punishments, certainly, but not from me. I am looking for something else, something much more important. When I realized that I would not find a teacher, I began looking for an apprentice," he said. "If my own experiences have taught me anything, it is that knowledge is a fragile thing, and we must all do what we can to preserve it."

"Yes, my lord Mage." Zel wasn't sure exactly what the Blue Mage meant, but he nodded, and raised the cup to his lips. The wine was smooth and sweet. The Blue Mage was proving to be very friendly. Really, much friendlier than people here in Beolind had led him to believe.

"Do you think you might be willing to help me in this, my friend? You might become the first pupil in my Academy. Do you think you could try?"

Friend, Zel thought. *The Blue Mage of Tegrian, consort of the queen, has called me friend.* "Yes, my lord Mage."

"Call my Avylos when we are alone together."

"Yes, my . . . yes, Avylos."

"That's better." Avylos smiled, and Zel realized the man was younger than he appeared. "Come, stand by me here."

Zel obeyed Avylos' gesture and came round the end of the work-table to stand at the Mage's side. The top had been cleared of everything except a small wooden chest, plainly carved of a fine-grained wood. Avylos placed a pair of blue-glass dice with white pips on the table in front of him. *Not blue glass.* Zel didn't know how he knew, but he knew he was right. *Not glass at all. Sapphire, maybe?*

"Now, roll these dice for me, Zel-Nobic."

For the next hour Zel did just that, rolling dice over and over. At one point Avylos gave him a different set of dice, green instead of blue, and Zel went on rolling the numbers the Mage asked for. Then Avylos gave him the blue set back again, and Zel rolled all four. Then six, red ones; then eight, another blue pair but these with red pips. When the Mage gave him yet another pair, however, this time smoky topazes, they fell randomly. Zel couldn't even manage to get eight out of ten to fall correctly, getting only three dice to turn up the number Avylos called out.

"No, no, that's fine," Avylos said, patting him on the arm as Zel apologized. "Naturally there's a limit to what the untrained skill can do. We'll take that as our starting point, and work forward from there. How do you feel?"

Zel shrugged. He often played for longer than this. "My wrist aches a little, but otherwise fine."

Zel almost stepped back when Avylos took him by the shoulders, but managed to stay still when the Mage clasped him to his chest, and kissed him on both cheeks.

"Finally." Avylos' voice resounded in his chest. "An apprentice. A brother." The Mage stepped back until Zel could look him once more in the face, his hand still on Zel's shoulders. Avylos smiled, his lips twisted to one side, his eyebrows raised. "That is, if you want it?"

"Oh, yes, my lord—I mean, yes, Avylos." Zel could barely speak around the lump in his throat, the pounding in his ears. He would be a Mage, he would be Avylos' brother. And to think his mother had been worried about him coming to the capital.

"You won't mind, will you, if I ask you to bind yourself formally to the apprenticeship."

Zel almost fell over himself agreeing that no, he wouldn't mind. He'd have to let the man he was working for know, of course, but no one was going to deny the Blue Mage. Already Zel could see himself in a soft linen robe, like the one Avylos was wearing—a different color of course, there couldn't be *two* Blue Mages. And perhaps he could get his sister brought to the Queen's Court. Zelniana couldn't manage the dice as well as he could, but if there was to be training, perhaps she, too, could improve.

Avylos had opened the wooden chest on his worktable, exposing a blue crystal rod, resting in a bed of dark silk.

"What is it?" he asked, regretting his question as soon as it left his lips; in that instant, Avylos' eyes shuttered. But then the Mage smiled and all was well once more.

"It shows well that you are curious," Avylos said. "This is an artifact of the Caids. It will change color if one of us swears falsely, and so it will give us the Caids' blessing on our contract. Lay your hand here, alongside mine, and repeat after me."

Zel put his hand down on the blue crystal, finding it oddly warm and almost soft under his fingertips. *What's it made out of?* he wondered, but stopped himself from asking. Even the most patient teacher, even his *brother* the Blue Mage, wouldn't like to be interrupted too many times. He would have all the time he wanted for questions once his apprenticeship began.

When Zel awoke some hours later, he was behind a table in the taproom of the Archer's Rest Hostel. He licked his lips and blinked. Had he been dreaming? His head felt strangely hollow. Zel cleared his throat, casting his eyes around the room and feeling for his money purse, and his dice bag. All that about the Blue Mage and the apprenticeship, had it been a dream? How long had he been asleep? Had anyone noticed?

To cover and explain the motions of his hands, Zel drew out a pair of dice and idly threw them on the table. Fours. He blinked, and tried again, saying "sixes" to himself as his hand moved. The dice showed a three and a five. "Fours" he said to himself. A two and a three.

No change with a different pair of dice. Nor did tossing with the other hand help. Nor did waiting and trying again. Nor did a cup of ale. Nor two.

Hand shaking, Zel rubbed at his upper lip. *Not a dream*, he thought.

There *was* a hollow inside him, an emptiness that used to be filled. The Caids-cursed Mage had done this to him. Couldn't have another magic man in the place, oh, no, not even a poor boy trying to make his living with dice. No apprenticeship, no brotherhood. Zel had his hands on the table, braced to stand up, before he thought better of it and sat again. What could he do? Who could he go to and say "I used to be able to control the movement of the dice, and the Blue Mage took that power from me?."

Thank the Caids he hadn't mentioned his sister, Zel thought. At least *she* was safe.

"Sun, Moon, and Stars, I tell you. I am not a player, nor do I dance or sing." Dhulyn looked up from where she squatted by the fire, poking the glowing embers back to life. She smiled her wolf's smile, and Parno laughed as the two young people leaned away from her as far as they could without falling off the rocks they were using as seats next to the cook fire.

"That's not strictly true," he said, still grinning as Dhulyn turned her fierce look to where he leaned against the side of the caravan. "You dance very nicely with a sword in your hands, and you have a pleasant singing voice, but nothing, I agree, that people would normally pay to hear."

"All of this is beside the point," Dhulyn said. "Until the little Cat explains how we will not be known for Mercenaries, the singing and dancing are irrelevant."

"Wait." Zania leaped to her feet and dove into the caravan where they could hear her burrowing among the boxes and bags stowed in the overhanging net. Dhulyn shrugged and rolled eyes, letting her hands fall on her knees.

When Zania came back out, she dangled six or seven small linen bags from their drawstrings. She deposited them on the ground, tossed one to Parno and another to Dhulyn before she knelt down and began to work at the strings of a third. It took both fingertips and teeth to loosen the mouth of the bag, but finally she had it open, and took from it a long fall of dark hair. She shook it out, and fitted it over her own short white-blonde hair. Instantly, as the dark hair blended with her sun-darkened skin, she became a Berdanan.

"There are maybe twenty of these wigs," she said, indicating the bags Parno and Dhulyn had in their laps. "All kinds of colors, and lengths. Made over the years from human hair, and sewn onto caps."

Dhulyn had her own bag open and was turning the gray wig it held over in her hands, examining the tiny stitches that attached the hair to the cap. The caps themselves had been made from strips of leather, very supple, and likely able to fit more than one person.

"I thought if you shaved your heads—or at least cut your hair very close like mine," Zania was saying, "you could wear one of these wigs. No one would think it odd if they noticed it. Players must be ready at all times to look like someone else. People would expect us to wear wigs and even costumes to draw attention to ourselves." She indicated her own brightly colored skirts.

Dhulyn sighed noisily, ran her fingers over her hair and tugged on one of her braids. Parno nodded. If she was already thinking about her wires and picklocks, and where she would hide them if her hair was cut, then she was already in agreement. One thing to be said for Mercenary Schooling, he thought. It cured you of useless modesty, and of vanity as well.

"I thought that tonight, at the Vednerysh Holding, Parno Lionsmane could play, and I could dance. And then, you two could give a fighting demonstration—what did I say?"

Dhulyn was shaking her head. "Then we might as well leave our badges showing. Anyone who has ever seen a Mercenary fight, even just a *Shora*, will know us for what we are. The last thing we can do is give such a demonstration."

"But you *can* fake one." Edmir had been silent for so long, Parno had almost forgotten he was there.

Dhulyn froze, her hands in the act of pulling the strings on the wig bag closed again.

"Perhaps you should explain," Parno said.

"You know what I mean," Edmir insisted. "You see performers and stage magicians do things all the time and you know they must be faking it, somehow, even if you can't figure out how. Swallowing swords, making eggs appear out of nowhere. We could do something like that. Make a large show of how difficult it is to do something that is actually very easy for you. Easy for Mercenaries, I mean," he said. Parno looked at Dhulyn, but she seemed just as puzzled as he felt, and Edmir went on. "Do you know the knife-throwing trick? Acrobats and jugglers do it sometimes in the market squares. A person stands against a target and someone else throws knives at them—"

"Sometimes blindfolded," Zania cut in.

"That's right. Or standing with their back to the target. And they make an outline of the person's body with the knives, without ever hitting the person. Or not often anyway."

"But we don't know the trick," Zania pointed out. "We don't know how it's done."

"We don't need to know," Edmir said. "*They* can do it without trickery, can't you?" He looked first at Parno, then at Dhulyn, waiting until they nodded.

"It's not unlike a game we play in the Mercenary Schools called Coward's Knife," Parno said. "Two players throw knives at each other, getting closer and closer. You lost points if you flinched, or if you drew blood."

"As long as no one thinks you're Mercenary Brothers," Edmir said, "everyone will be sure it's a trick. Only we will know it's real."

"I don't know," Zania said. "Oh, I believe you can do it," she added quickly. Dhulyn lifted her hand to rub her mouth, and Parno stifled his own smile. The poor girl actually thought they needed her reassurance. "But this is still Troupe Tzadeyeu, and people will expect plays, not juggling and trickery. I think we must try."

Dhulyn shook her head. "I'm very sorry, but I can't do this. All our Schooling, our *Shora*, teach us to be truer, not to pretend."

Parno frowned and leaned forward, his elbows on his knees. "Dhulyn, my heart. You know how sometimes, when swords are out, it seems that you—" he lifted his shoulders and let them drop. "That you *charm* a man onto your blade?" *Or into your bed*, he didn't say aloud, though he knew from the quirk of her eyebrow and the start of her grin that she'd heard him say it nonetheless.

"The Two Hearts *Shora*?"

Parno nodded. "Try it on Edmir here, but without the sword."

Dhulyn turned to Edmir, looked him up and down. "It would only work standing up."

They all stood, and Dhulyn stepped a few paces away, rubbing her temples and breathing deeply. Parno cut off Edmir's questions.

"Better you don't know what to expect," he said. "Then it will be a true test."

As they watched, Dhulyn lowered her hands from her face and adjusted her feet. Though her hands were at her sides, her feet were placed as though she were holding a sword in her right hand, and was about to use it. Used against a single opponent, the Two Hearts *Shora* had been known to work even on a Mercenary Brother, as it wasn't one of the basic training *Shoras*. Parno knew it, he'd made sure Dhulyn taught it to him, but he wasn't as good at it as she was.

Parno waved Edmir into place in front of his Partner. The prince hesitated, looked once at Parno, once at Zania, before he moved into the opponent's space in front of Dhulyn. The boy was more frightened than he should be, Parno thought.

It was only seconds more until Dhulyn's respiration stilled, coming slower and the breaths themselves deeper. Color rose into her cheeks until she looked flushed. Her lips parted. After a moment, his eyes locked on Dhulyn's, Edmir also stilled. His breathing slowed, until his chest rose and fell in time with hers. Suddenly his color changed, he grew pale, and his breathing quickened, growing loud in the still morning air. He took a step toward Dhulyn, reaching out, and Parno CRACKED his hands together.

Edmir stopped, blinking, and flushed red.

"If you can do that with an audience," Zania said, her voice tight, "we'll be rich."

Kera tugged at the laces on the front of her shirt as she took the chair on her mother the queen's right. She'd come flushed and sweating from her swordplay lesson with Megz Primeau, the current holder of the Queen's White Blade, but from the look on her mother's face, it was lucky she hadn't taken the time to change out of her trousers and boots before answering the summons. Kedneara was seated in the thronelike chair in her anteroom, dressed formally in dark blue robes with white trim, her hair dressed high, with a circle of gold leaves to bind it.

Rage had brought unusual color to her mother's face, but the queen was still a great beauty, Kera thought, taller than both her children, her hair still raven-black. *She's only forty-seven*, Kera reminded herself, though Kedneara had been queen for more than thirty years. *At my age, she was already the ruler of Tegrian*. And at forty-seven, Kedneara's father had been dead already, as Kedneara herself would be, if it were not for Avylos. Kera wasn't sure quite when it was she'd realized that the Blue Mage was keeping the queen alive; it seemed that she'd always known it.

The problem was that Avylos wasn't a Healer, nor had there been one in Tegrian for as long as Kera could remember, and though he didn't like it spoken of, there were limits to Avylos' magic. All Kera knew for certain was that his attempts to magic women were chancy—either the magic didn't take at all, or it didn't last as long as it did on a man.

As if called by her thought, Avylos entered the room, going directly to the queen, bowing low over her extended hand, and kissing it. He took a step back and bowed again—not quite as low—to Kera herself.

"My Queen," he said, in his melodious voice. "Lady Prince."

Kera clenched her teeth. Would she ever get used to being called that?

"Another messenger has come from Probic. The city has been destroyed by fires from the heavens. Is this your doing?" The last words were bitten off. Her mother's breath was short, her hands trembling. Kera almost put out her hand, but stopped—they were not in private, and her mother the queen would not appreciate any signs of concern or even of affection now.

"Please, my Queen, compose yourself. You must be calm, you are putting too much strain on your heart."

At first there was nothing but silence from the queen. Kera risked a glance at her mother out of the corner of her eye.

"Do not take that tone with me, little Mage. I am queen, and you are not Karyli."

Avylos turned so white his eyebrows stood out on his face like slashes of blood. His hands closed into fists. Kera wondered whether she could draw her sword fast enough, or whether it would make any difference if she could.

But Avylos only took a deep breath, and flexed his hands. It seemed the Mage would follow his own advice and remain calm. Kera relaxed back into her seat, though the tension did not completely leave her body.

"It was the Nisveans, my Queen. They were to bring the body of Prince Edmir to Probic, and they . . . they *used* him, Keda." Kera blushed at the Mage's use of her mother's pet name. "*Used* the noble gesture of returning his body to violate the treaty and attack Probic. They spit on his nobility, and on yours. They had to be punished, my love. They had to be destroyed."

"You acted without consulting me." The words were harshly spoken, but Kera could tell the fire was gone from her mother's anger.

"There was no time to call the Houses," Avylos said. "No time to prepare the armies. I needed a faster solution. Quick, deadly, and final.
"I had to punish them."

"And the people of Probic, *my* people?" Kedneara's only movement was the quick rising and falling of her breast as she breathed. Again Kera risked a glance sideways; her mother's face was as cold and hard as the profile on Kedneara's coins.

"I could not pick and choose, my Queen. My magics do not work in that fashion. I had to act quickly. But only think! It will send a message of warning to the Nisveans—to anyone!—showing what will happen if they dare to invade your lands. As for your people, I am certain they would rather die and be held in the hands of the gods than be slaves in Nisvea."

Kera wasn't so sure of that herself, but it seemed that the queen found Avylos' argument persuasive. She was nodding.

"So be it. They are in the hands of the Caids, and let the Caids sort them out."

Avylos looked squarely into the queen's deep blue eyes and bowed. At the very last moment Kera saw a flash of satisfaction pass over the Mage's face.

Kera gripped the arms of her chair, and she was speaking before she was even aware of her intentions.

"How was it your magics prevailed in Probic, when they failed in the Limona Valley?" There. That should upset some of his smugness.

Her mother the queen's face changed, her eyes narrowed in speculation. She reached out for Avylos' forearm, and Kera saw the strong fingers dig in.

"You *knew?* You knew Edmir went to Nisvea and you did not tell me? You failed to either stop or aid him?"

Slowly, reluctantly it seemed, Avylos came to his knees before the queen. "Most assuredly I did not. My magics cannot fail, as you know. But they must be *used*. Edmir was misled somehow, tricked or prevented from calling upon me. The battle was done before I knew of it. Tzanek in Probic was the last to see him, to counsel him. Who knows what may have passed between them?"

"But you did not tell me of his intentions. Who else knew of them? Did *you* counsel Edmir to go to Nisvea? The Houses whose sons went with him—Avros and Redni—they have returned, ransomed. Was this their idea?"

Avylos was still on his knees, his head lowered, but he turned his eyes to Kera and a trickle of cold ran down her spine. Would he speak? Tell her mother the queen that Kera herself had known of Edmir's plan and said nothing? She sat up straight. Well, she'd started this herself by exposing Avylos. She might as well keep control of the tiles in her own hands.

And out of the Mage's.

"Edmir didn't want you to know, Mother." She'd be safe enough, she hoped. Kera was now her mother the queen's only child. Never the favorite, but given the choice, Kedneara would choose her own blood, every time. "This was Edmir's own plan. He shared it with me, and later with the Blue Mage, but I did not counsel him against it. At least, not at first."

"Oh, Edmir." The queen rubbed at her eyes with her fingertips. "He was always so impetuous, so eager. He should have waited for the treaty to be finished."

Kera stifled a sigh. "He wished for your approval," she said. "He wanted to show you he could lead your armies."

Kedneara waved this away. "Of course I approved of him, he was my son. How could he be so foolish?" Kedneara took Kera's hand in both of hers.

From his position still on his knees, Avylos placed his hand atop both of theirs. "Calmness still, my Queen."

"But, Mother, you see, don't you, that Avros and Redni have no blame in this."

Kedneara nodded, and patted Kera's hand.

"Who else knows of the Lady Prince's involvement, my queen?"

Kera was momentarily speechless. She had not thought of what she'd done to help Edmir in quite those terms.

"What do you mean, Avylos?" the queen asked.

"Who knows that the Lady Prince advised her brother in his plans? Wait, hear me out. We had the same motives, Kera and I, to aid our Lord Prince, to enhance his reputation and gain him a greater following among the younger House lords. But—" he turned to Kera. "It could also be said that you deliberately urged him to go, and secretly advised him to reject my aid, knowing that he would very likely meet his death."

There was a sudden buzzing in Kera's ears. "But I would have no motive . . ." Her voice died away. Of course she had a motive. Of course she did.

"Exactly." Avylos was nodding. "You would have your brother's power for yourself. You would have the throne." He turned back to the queen. "And people would believe it, Keda. She is, after all, so much better suited to rule."

Kera thought she couldn't register any more surprises, but she was shocked speechless when her mother merely pursed her lips and nodded at this.

"If it had been Lady Prince Kera at Limona, rather than Edmir," Avylos was still speaking. "She would not have failed. She would have carried the day, magic or no, and we would even now be marching on their capital in her train. Edmir was a fine young man, but Kera will make the better queen, and all know it."

"But people didn't think Edmir was such a fool," Kera said, "or why would anyone have followed him?"

"You are right, Kera. They thought him courageous, and were proud to be among his friends. Still, they will be happier to follow you."

Kera wanted to deny what Avylos was saying. But she knew when she'd been outmaneuvered. Anything she could say now would only sound like false modesty—something her mother the queen would not appreciate.

And besides, her mother was satisfied now, and nothing Kera could say would change that.

"If you have no further need of me." Avylos raised the queen's hand to his lips, lowered it gently, then moved toward the door.

"Avylos."

The Mage stopped with his hand on the door.

"We will not speak of this further, since it could do Kera harm. But you will not act in such a manner again without my orders. *I* am Queen in Tegrian."

Kera made sure to keep her face straight.

Avylos kept his face impassive and his pace steady as far as the door to the consort's apartment. He could not contain himself enough to make it back to his own apartments in the Mage's wing. Rage burned through him like fire through a dry field of grass. He'd come within a breath of reaching out and snapping her neck. The cow. That she would speak to him in such a way—as if his magics were of no account. As if they were not all that kept her alive and on her throne.

She would not speak to him like this if she knew what had really happened to her precious Karyli whom she'd loved so much. She was no different, to dismiss all he had done for her, the conquests he had made possible once Karyli and his foolish scruples were out of the way.

He rubbed his lips with his hand, pushed his fingers through his hair. He could not be seen like this. He must calm himself. He could not afford to treat them as they deserved—both of them!—until he had the full power of the Stone in his hands.

Kedneara he'd expected to have to soothe and explain—she was easy, he understood her. Any explanation that praised her, or her children, would persuade. But Kera! She had been such a pleasant child. She would often come to play in his garden, and he had thought of her—when he thought of her at all—as a sweet child, even his friend. And perhaps she had been, once. Now that she had the throne within her grasp she was just like her mother. They saw him only as a tool, a servant, useful for what they could get from him.

All of them, sneaking, conspiring she-cats. All the women in his life, none of them to be trusted. First his mother—

He rested his forehead against the pane of glass. It was cool, soothing. He needed to calm down, not enrage himself further. And besides, it wasn't true. Not all the women in his life had turned on him, though it had certainly felt that way at the time. . . .

At first he hadn't even been able to identify the feeling, it was so strange to him. He could never remember feeling content, let alone happy. But the troupe had welcomed him, had been impressed by his talents—not only as a magician, but as a mechanic. Inventing the mechanisms to help him in performing his magic tricks had given him several useful ideas that could be used in staging plays as well. When they saw that he was ready to help them and share his expertise, their respect grew.

And there was Marika. No older than himself, but wise beyond his understanding, already a widow with a small child. Matters between them proceeded rapidly, adding to his sense of well-being and contentment.

"For the first time I feel as if I belong," he said to her one night, rolling up on his elbow. He brushed her hair back from her face and kissed her eyes, her cheekbones, her lips. She laughed and rolled up to meet him, pressing her cool forehead against his own, giving him the courage to go on, to say aloud what he'd been thinking of for days.

"Marika, I could not bear to leave you. I would like to stay with you, to become a permanent member of the troupe. Marry me?"

Marika consulted her father, and the others of the troupe, and they had all agreed. He would join them. They would become his family, his Clan, his Tribe. He would not be alone again. Not excluded, not laughed at. Not hunted down.

Three nights later they welcomed him into their ceremony, allowed him, as part of their family, to pray with their household spirits. They showed him the Stone.

And he learned what the Stone could do.

He learned he wasn't *srusha*, wasn't barren, and everything in his world changed, even his history, even his past, now that he understood what had really been happening, and just how badly his own people had betrayed him—before he betrayed them and escaped.

All that he had been, all that he had done, had occurred in order to bring him to the moment when he had first touched the Stone, and had felt the magic within him rise.

He lifted his forehead from the window and sighed. All that was years behind him. He would think of it no more.

When he was calm enough to control his face, and the way he held his body as he walked, Avylos headed back to his own wing. Almost unnoticed around him were the usual activities of the Royal House, the stewards on their rounds, pages, guards, and kitchen servants already beginning the preparations for the evening meal. In a shaft of sunlight from one of the upper windows in the Great Hall, a Knife sat beside her patient as the man—injured by a fall from a ladder while working on the roof tiles of the Westwind Tower—snored under the influence of the poppy she'd given him.

Avylos' steps slowed as he considered taking the Knife, but his pace soon quickened again. She was too useful, even though she could not help the queen. Without the Knife, he might be called upon to waste his magics on just such injuries as she tended now. Instead, he would hold her in reserve; the time might very well come when he would need her. Ordinary skills, talents, and abilities such as the Knife's were useful to him—even if not as useful as the talents of another Mage.

And he might need to feed the Stone even the Knife's meager talents sooner than he'd like.

Kedneara would not be useful to him for very much longer. And Kera . . . Kera would take handling of a different kind. Perhaps everything would need to be handled differently from now on.

Typically, Kedneara had seen the destruction of Probic only as it affected her personally. The woman thought the sun rose and set for her. *Her* message, what happened to people who invaded *her* Tegrian. But Probic's fate carried another message, one Kedneara had not considered. With Probic in ruins, and the army of Nisvea destroyed, Avylos had told the world that the Blue Mage did not need an army.

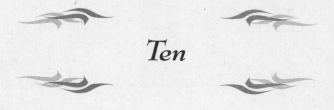

Ten

IN THE END, they did not do a performance at Vednerysh Holding after all. At least, not a proper performance, not to Zania's way of thinking. So much time had been spent earlier in the day making sure the Mercenary Brothers no longer looked like Mercenary Brothers that there had been no time left for learning parts. Neither of them had hesitated for a moment to cut their hair quite short, and the Wolfshead had even insisted on having hers shaved completely.

"It's the color," she explained. "The one thing everyone knows about the Red Horsemen is the color of our hair." She accepted a dark blonde wig which Zania had passed over with reluctance, her fingers suddenly clumsy, and tangling in the long tresses.

"It's my mother's hair, from when she was a young girl," Zania said, when her hesitation became apparent. "It's been worn since of course, many times, but never . . ." She fought to bring her trembling chin under control. "Never by someone outside the family. Please be very careful with it, Wolfshead."

"And speaking of being careful," the Lionsmane interjected. "We must be Dhulyn and Parno to you both from now on, even in your thoughts. Our other names will give us away as quickly as our badges, to those who know the Brotherhood."

Zania considered, her head on one side. That made sense. "If we think of you by your public names, we'll slip up, for certain." She turned to Edmir. "We do the same when we rehearse a new play. We make sure never to think of the other actors by their real names, lest we use them on stage."

Zania had the paste ready, and with a few practiced strokes of the brush applied it to the Wolfshead's—*Dhulyn's*, Zania corrected, *Dhulyn's* head along the front edge of her hairline and over her temples. A very small part of the Mercenary badge still showed, but Zania knew she could cover that with stage paint in an instant. Deftly, she moved the wig into place and pressed firmly along the glued edge.

"You can lift it off from the back it you have to," she told the Mercenary woman. "But the glue should hold for several days unless it becomes wet."

"Keep the beard, do you think?" Parno was saying. "I haven't shaved since Limona."

"Why not? If you're normally clean shaven, the beard will be a decent disguise in itself," Edmir answered. "I wish mine would grow in so well."

"As for you, *Edmir*," Zania said, making sure she emphasized his name. "There's no point in hiding Parno and Dhulyn if *you're* left undisguised. What do you think? I've a powder here that will lighten your hair."

"I could pierce my ears," Edmir said. He took the packet of powder from her, wrinkling his nose as he took a sniff. "I've always refused to do it because everyone at court had it done—Kera thought it would seem ordinary. So if I did it now . . ."

"People would feel sure it wasn't you, though they might not know why. Yes, that's a good idea." Zania's smile felt forced and hollow. She had always thought she'd make a good planner, but to have these people go along with her ideas and suggestions felt . . . She'd often imagined herself in charge of her own troupe, but not at this price. Not at the price of everything—and everyone—else that mattered to her. Belatedly she realized the expression on Edmir's face had changed. She spun around . . . and froze.

Dhulyn, a slight frown on her face, had gone to inspect the clothing Zania had left out for her. After sorting through each piece she had turned her back and pulled her tunic off over her head. Her shirt had come with it, leaving her in just the wrap of silk she used as a breastband.

And a crisscross patterning of scars across her back.

Edmir made a sound in his throat. "The Mercenary Schools are much stricter than I'd thought," he said.

They both stood watching as the scars were covered by a short sleeved blouse with a tight, low-cut bodice, blue as a meadow flower. Dhulyn then stepped into a bright saffron-colored skirt, full and reaching almost to the ankles, covered over with embroidery: black, green, and a blue that matched the blouse. The wig she had caught up carelessly into a knot, letting it frame her face softly.

"Do we have to wear skirts all the time?" she asked, lifting the offending item out from under her feet as she rejoined them.

"It's a wonderful disguise for you," Parno said. "Better even than the wig."

"How beautiful you are." Zania stepped forward, surprise leading her to speak more bluntly than she normally would have.

"Thank the Moon and Stars, my lifelong ambition has been fulfilled." Dhulyn Wolfshead put the back of her hand to her forehead and sighed. Then she dropped the hand and smiled at Zania, letting the small scar curl her lip back. She laughed aloud when Zania took a step back.

"I shall have to be careful, with that, won't I," she said. "It would completely undo the effect of the Two Hearts *Shora.*"

Flustered at having shown her fear so plainly, Zania had stepped in closer than courtesy usually allowed and peered at the scar. "Was it from a knife?" she asked.

"Oh, no," Dhulyn said, laughing. "The tip of a whip flicked 'round and caught me—luckily as it happened. It spoiled my looks for my owner and he sold me. It was while I was in the hands of the slavers that Dorian the Black took their ship and rescued me."

"You don't normally think of it as a 'rescue' when you're taken by pirates," Edmir said.

"You do when the pirates are Mercenary Brothers."

"You'll have to use some of Edmir's powder on your eyebrows." Parno frowned, scrutinizing Dhulyn's face. "Lighten them up a bit."

Slavers? Pirates? Zania looked from one to the other, but there was nothing on their faces to show that they were joking. And Dhulyn *did* have those scars.

It didn't taken long to find clothing distinctive enough to make Parno and Edmir look less like soldiers and more like a couple of traveling players, but the last thing they'd done before repacking and hitching up the horses had been to pierce Edmir's ears. Dhulyn produced two silver-colored wires from the small braids she'd cut off before shaving her head.

"Let me just heat these in the fire and let them cool," she'd said.

"Whatever for?" Edmir said.

"It will help the wounds keep clean and heal faster," Parno said. "All the Knives in the Mercenary Brotherhood do their surgeries with tools heated this way."

"Or soaked in very strong spirits." Dhulyn cut the wires to the length of her forefingers and stood up. "Ready when you are."

The two Mercenaries made Edmir sit down on one of their saddle-bags and Dhulyn brushed the curls—not so black now that Zania's powders had been used—back from his face to expose his ears.

"You'll want to wear your hair brushed back now," she said. "No point in wearing earrings that no one can see."

"I haven't any earrings—ow!" Edmir snatched his hand back from Parno. While Dhulyn had been fussing with Edmir's hair, her Partner had taken the prince's right hand and folded his fingers sharply in toward the palm.

"That hurt," Edmir said, shaking out his hand. "What did you do that for?"

"So that you wouldn't notice your ear being pierced." Dhulyn produced a small pair of metal pincers. "Now hold still while I bend the wire."

"You didn't need to hurt my hand," Edmir grumbled as Parno held the prince's tilted head and Dhulyn worked the wire around into a circle.

"Oh, yes, we did."

"Tell you what," Parno had said, releasing Edmir's head. "I'll let her do the other one without distracting you, and then you can tell us which you prefer."

"That won't be much use—ow!"

"There, all done."

Dhulyn took the first turn at the reins with Zania to tell her the way, while Edmir spent the first hour or so they were on the road whistling a new tune until Parno was satisfied he had it. When they'd stopped to eat, Edmir had taught Zania herself the dance that went with it.

"It's the latest at the Queen's Court," he said. "Usually it would take months for it to filter down to these country Holdings. They'll love it."

And he was right, Zania had to acknowledge. She'd half expected their performance to be canceled, but the Vedneryshi had very quickly overcome the shock of the news from Probic.

"How can they be so calm," Zania had asked Dhulyn Wolfshead, even as she mentally stored the expressions on the faces of the Vednerysho and his spouse.

"So near the border," Dhulyn had replied, speaking in that most quiet of whispers. "They become accustomed to this type of news and alarm. And let's not forget the Blue Mage; since his coming, everyone in Tegrian is less fearful and less cautious than they once were. As for what we've told them of Probic's destruction, I would wager my second-best sword that they think our account greatly exaggerated."

Now as Zania sat down with Edmir after performing the dance, the family seemed completely recovered from the news. The son of the Holding, whose naming day was the reason for the performance, made the Lionsmane—*Parno*, Zania reminded herself—made *Parno* promise to teach him the tune, and Zania could see that the Lady Vednerysh was already imagining herself leading the way in the next Harvest Festival.

Once the young lordling was able to whistle the entire tune himself, Parno had taken the drones off his pipes and accompanied with chanter only the three songs Zania knew best, the ones that really showed off her range and breath control. Dhulyn had joined them for one song by clapping her hands in a complicated rhythm that somehow made the song more exciting, and set toes tapping.

Now Dhulyn herself was rounding up the evening's entertainment by reciting an old poem she said had been written by Tarlyn. She wore her blonde wig loose, and dressed in a simple dark gown that had been Aunt Ester's, with a chain metal belt painted gold. The cut of the gown made her seem much more shapely than her old clothes had. Her voice was good, Zania thought, and her gestures well-timed, if a little wooden. The Vedneryshi would think well enough of the performance, but Dhulyn would have to do better than this if they were to have any real acting in a more discerning House.

The material itself helped, of course. Zania knew Tarlyn as a playwright, but this poem was a wonderful one about a soldier king coming home after long years away at a war, only to find himself declared dead, and his house full of suitors trying to marry his queen and become guardian of his young children.

"You're sure Tarlyn didn't do this as a play?" Edmir whispered to her, as they joined in Dhulyn's applause. His breath made the curls of her chestnut wig tickle her neck.

Zania had been surprised that of the three outsiders, Edmir had turned out to be the most comfortable in front of an audience. *On the other hand, he's probably used to people staring at him*, she thought now, watching him out of the corner of her eye. *He'd have no fear of it, that's for certain.* But how was it he should be so ready to pretend to be someone else? Usually the rich and important were quite happy to be who they were.

"Don't you see Dhulyn as the queen, Parno as the returning soldier king? You and I could, in turn, play the suitors, the children, or the servants, as we were needed."

Zania raised her eyebrows in a conscious effort not to frown where it could be taken as a comment on the performance. But why would he see *Dhulyn* as queen?

"Wouldn't the audience have to know the whole story?" she whispered back. Though Dhulyn was not up to the role, it *was* a good idea—one she should have thought of herself. *She* was the leader of this troupe. Once again her heart caught in her chest. *Not this way*, she pushed the thought away. *I didn't want it this way.* She cleared her throat. "Because for a play," she continued, "we would have to begin as the soldier king arrives home. That's where the action begins."

Edmir waved away this objection. "We could tell them the first part of the story in a prologue." His eyes grew distant. "We'd have to change it a bit, I think. If we made the wife queen, the children could be older and still not inherit. It would give us more opportunities with the characters of the suitors. Some of the suitors would want her only for her position."

"But some would want her for her beauty." Even to her own ears Zania's voice sounded flat.

"Oh, yes, some would."

Zania pressed her lips together and stifled a snort. Fortunately with the applause finishing, she could step forward to join Dhulyn and Parno on the cleared floor space serving as their stage, not caring whether the prince joined them for their bows or not. Edmir's eyes had been fixed on Dhulyn when he spoke, just as if she was the only woman in the world. He'd been mooning at her like that since Dhulyn had mesmerized him that morning. Who would have thought it took so little to impress the Lord Prince of Tegrian? Or perhaps he was the kind who liked women who could kill him?

After all, his mother was queen.

⟡

The Blue Mage's garden was still cool, the sky just beginning to lighten. Dew was forming, settling onto Kera's clothing as she sat on her perch in the hollow made by a forsythia bush and the rough portion of the wall where the repair had been made. This had been a favorite spot of hers when she was a little girl—and still was, though she barely fit into the space any longer. The perch was sheltered, and raised enough above the ground that she could look down on almost the whole garden without being seen.

Even Kera's new awareness of the caution she had to take with Avylos could not change the feelings of peace and calm that the garden still gave her. Strange that she felt closer to Edmir here than she did anywhere else, even his own chambers—or perhaps it wasn't so strange. They'd played here as children, accompanying their father as he helped Avylos plan the garden, turning an old, disused laundry space into the Blue Mage's private retreat.

Kera hadn't thought of those times for a long while, but reading Edmir's journals was bringing so much of her childhood back to her—though, of course, Edmir didn't remember *everything* in precisely the same way Kera did herself. There was that time he'd had three of her gowns shortened, switched them while she slept, and made her think she'd grown a handspan overnight. She didn't remember it as quite so funny.

But what Kera valued most in Edmir's journals was his stories. Many of them were ones she remembered him telling, like the one about the seven enchanted princes. Some she'd forgotten, and only reading them now had brought them back to her. She'd never known that Edmir had been writing his stories down. She wondered now why he'd never told her.

At the noise of the door opening, Kera pressed back against the cold stone and froze to the spot. Footsteps crunched on the gravel of the paths and Avylos brushed past the taller plants, making his way to the edge of the pool. He stopped by the topiary, the one that needed trimming, the mountain cat almost shaggy enough to qualify as a northern lion. It needed seeing to, but Kera knew that Avylos was reluctant to let anyone into the garden to do it. Absently, his eyes still focused on the pond, he moved his hand in the air as he always did when he performed one of his magics, and the ends of the branches shivered, shrinking. He startled, as if just realizing what he'd done, and made a gesture of impatience, but Kera was no longer watching him.

The mountain cat was perfect, its haunches smooth. The branches were not merely trimmed shorter, she realized—he had actually reversed the growth. The plant was now as it had been some weeks before.

"*Blooded* fool," Avylos cursed, as he sat down on the rim of the pool. It took a moment for Kera to realize he wasn't speaking to her, and for her heart to resume beating. Her hands were pressed over her mouth, stifling the cry that had almost escaped when she saw what had happened to the topiary. Could he do that to her? Turn her back into a young child? A baby?

Was that what he was doing to her mother?

Avylos drew another symbol in the air, above the surface of the pool, and it sank into the water, making the smooth surface glow a dull orange. Kera licked her lips. It was more than curiosity that kept her quiet and still as a mouse watching a cat. She *was* allowed here, but she had never come here alone in the night before, and possibly her allowance did not extend to the dark hours. And she should have spoken as soon as Avylos had come into the garden, *before* he'd fixed the topiary, *before* he sat down at the edge of the pool.

If she moved now, he would think himself spied on. She would have to stay quiet, hoping he never became aware of her. Because now Kera *was* curious. What was it Avylos was doing with the pool at daybreak?

At that moment the glow left the surface of the water, and Kera saw a room filled with candles and torches and people dressed for supper. She started to stand up, her mouth open, her brain rejecting what her eyes saw, but she sank down again before she made a sound.

Avylos didn't seem surprised.

At first she didn't recognize the young man she saw wearing the fine brocaded tunic, dancing with a lithe young woman, her chestnut hair an elaborate creation of curls piled high on her head. There were thick silver hoops in his ears, giving him the rakish look of a court dandy, and his hair, an odd shade of light brown, was brushed straight back in the fashion of Imrion. And then he took a turn in the dance, kicked up his foot in a particular way, and she knew.

It was *Edmir*.

She couldn't be mistaken. Kera's hands closed tightly on the folds of her gown. She'd seen him move this way and dance a hundred times. In fact, *she'd* taught him that dance herself. And that little skip he'd added to the turn was a flourish of his own. Edmir, without doubt.

She waited until the pool was dark again, though she would have liked to go on watching her brother dance. She waited until Avylos left the garden. She waited until the sun was up before she finally allowed herself to move, stiff and chilled, from her perch against the garden's inner wall.

Her brother was alive. And Avylos knew it.

⚓

Parno opened the second saddlebag and began lifting its contents onto the blanket he'd spread on the ground. He was positive he'd seen Dhulyn stash her roll of throwing knives in a saddlebag back in the Nisvean camp, and if he didn't find them here, he had nowhere else to look.

"Once more, Dhulyn, please, and look up when you speak."

Parno looked up himself. In the two weeks since they'd left Vednerysh Holding, Edmir had been working on a dramatic version of the poem of the soldier king. He was walking Dhulyn through one of the earlier scenes now.

Their progress toward Jarlkevo not as quick as any of them would have liked, but unlike real players they had to spend time perfecting their disguises—and also unlike real players, they had no store of plays or scenes already learned. Both he and Dhulyn had excellent memories, and had been able to learn the lines of three short plays just from hearing Zania read them, but rehearsing the action meant stopping the caravan, and that slowed them down.

"Blessed Caids, I can't believe it." Zania appeared at his elbow, brows drawn down, mouth pressed to a thin line. "Her voice is so good, and her delivery is so nearly perfect, but she stands like a stick and moves like a broken frog."

Parno mentally sighed. Much could be forgiven in someone who had recently lost their whole family, but Zania's behavior since leaving Vednerysh Holding had become increasing difficult for him to tolerate. The little Cat seemed to alternate between treating Dhulyn Wolfshead as a long lost sister, and treating her like a useless apprentice wished on her by a doting patron.

He eyed Zania now, his hands still inside the saddlebag, and registered the look on the girl's face. *Ah. That's where the problem is.* He pursed his lips in a silent whistle.

"I would have thought your training would make it easier for her to learn new things, but it seems I'm mistaken."

Parno put down the well-wrapped packet of road bread he had fished out of the saddlebag and gave her a hard look. "We're not 'trained,' Zania Tzadeyeu. Soldiers are trained. Acrobats are trained. Dogs are trained. Mercenaries are *Schooled*." He took a deep breath. "And besides, Dhulyn meant what she said before." His hand closed on a bundle with a familiar feel and he pulled out the set of throwing knives with a satisfied grunt. "She has a natural inclination to be truthful, born into her. Slavery did not beat it out of her, and our Schooling simply reinforced it."

"So she *was* a slave? She did not jest?"

"You saw the scarring on her back. Did that look like a jest? Her people were killed and she was taken for a slave when she was a small child. The way her people count their ages, she'd only seen the Hawk Moon eleven times when Dorian the Black Traveler captured the slave ship she was on and offered her a chance to be Schooled as a Mercenary Brother."

He glanced up at his Partner, and his voice softened. "Seeing what she had been, and the use that is made of slave children, it was an offer she accepted gladly."

Zania knelt down next to Parno and began handing him the items that had come out of the saddlebag. "What use is made of slave children, then?"

Parno sighed. He'd no wish to broaden the girl's horizons in this way, but truth was truth, and warnings made good armor. "For the most part," he told her, "children don't make good servants; they're not strong enough for labor, and not yet skilled enough for anything else. People who buy slave children use them as bed partners."

Zania's hand froze with a second packet of road bread halfway to the saddlebag. He'd shocked her, sure enough, if her white face and wide eyes were anything to go by. As good an actress as she was, she couldn't control the movement of the blood under the skin. But she was, as she'd said so many times, a player. She shook herself and rallied, pasting an almost natural smile on her face. After taking a good deep breath she sat back on her heels and pitched her voice in the coy manner of a lady engaged in flirtatious concerns.

"And you, Parno? What is *your* story?" She laid her hand on his arm and stroked his skin ever so lightly with the tips of her fingers.

"Oh, I'm the natural son of the Great King of the West," he said. He looked down at her hand. "And you can stop touching me like that. Even if you actually meant it, you're too young for me."

"You're just teasing about the Great King." She did drop her hand, however. "I could tell you were from a Noble House. *She's* an Outlander. So cold. Can't even express a true feeling. You have more culture and learning than she."

"It's Dhulyn who's the Scholar. And the fact that she expresses her truest feelings with a weapon means I've seen plenty of them." He put the last of the bundles back into the saddlebag and drew the laces shut once more. The girl was still far too close to him. He turned to face her.

"Zania, listen to me. I've not seen so many performances as you, but I know an act when I see one. Do you think no paid companion has ever approached me in a tavern? I'm not sure what your goal is, but it's a mistake to play this game. You can't come between Dhulyn and me. We're Partnered. There is no 'between' where you can fit. You've called her cold. Well, if she's cold, I am her ice."

The girl blushed a deep red, and then paled again just as suddenly. "I don't know what you mean, I wasn't trying to come between you."

"That was clumsily said; no audience would believe it. Zania." Parno sat back on his heels. "Let me tell you what I see. First, you're not truly interested in me as a man—much as it hurts my ego to admit it. Second, you're not as worried by Dhulyn's acting as you claim, or you would be helping her to better it, instead of leaving it up to Edmir. Third, it's Edmir you actually want, and you think my Partner is standing in your way."

Zania stared back at him, her mouth open, but without giving her a chance to answer, Parno called out to the two rehearsing on the far side of the clearing.

"Dhulyn, my soul, I've found the throwing daggers and Zania wants to see a demonstration."

A piece of scenery that was normally stored against the bottom of the caravan was judged suitable for the trial, and Parno stood it upright against the rear steps. Edmir looked ready to offer himself as the test subject, but Parno stepped in before the boy could speak.

"No offense, Edmir, my lad," he said, putting out a hand to hold the boy back. "But the audience will care far more about it if a beautiful young woman is at risk than a young man, however handsome. Go ahead, Zania. Take your place against the board."

With a very firm jaw—no doubt clenched to show she wasn't afraid—Zania pressed her back against the board and held her arms out, away from her body.

"Where do you want my arms—"

THUCK THUCK THUCK THUCK THUCK THUCK-THUCKTHUCKTHUCK *THUNK*

Zania froze, her words still hovering in the air, the blood draining from her face, leaving two red spots isolated on her cheeks. She looked to one side, then the other, saw the handles of the knives protruding scant fingerwidths from her skin. She took a single, measured step away from the board, turned to look at her silhouette outlined in knives. She touched one with the tip of her finger.

"It's like magic," she breathed.

"Don't think that because you've seen her clumsy and inept in one thing, you'll find her clumsy and inept in all things," Parno said. "You players have your skills, and we Mercenaries have ours."

But it was clear Zania was no longer listening to him. Her eyes were opened wide now, and the smile on her lips was pure pleasure as she turned to Dhulyn, her hands outstretched.

"We'll announce you as a royal assassin," she said, taking Dhulyn's hands and tapping out a few dance steps. "Exiled from the Great King's court. You'll wear a black wig and we'll paint your eyes in the western fashion."

Edmir wrinkled his brow. "But they'll know she's not from the Great King's Court, they'll have seen her already, wig or no wig."

"Of course they will, lad," Parno said. "It's because they'll *know* she's not from the Great King's court that they'll *know* it must be a trick. It won't occur to them it's skill and skill alone."

Zania nodded. "They'll be wondering how we're faking it. We can ask for volunteers from the audience, as 'proof' that we're not."

"And that will convince them all the more." Now it was Edmir's turn to nod.

"The cleverer they think us, the less likely they'll think we're actually doing it."

Zania still held Dhulyn's hands. "Do you think you can fumble a bit? Make it look as though it's much harder for you? Squint at the target? We'll need to stretch the action out a bit, at the very least, to increase the drama."

"Certainly, my little Cat. This is the kind of drama I understand."

The smile vanished from Dhulyn's face just as Parno caught the sound himself. They both turned at the same time, Dhulyn dropping Zania's hands and Parno reaching for his sword before he remembered he wasn't wearing one. He slapped the dust off his leggings in an effort to cover the movement and didn't look up until the soldiers who were entering the clearing spoke.

"Don't tell me what you're doing," the woman in the old-fashioned helmet said. "I don't think I want to know."

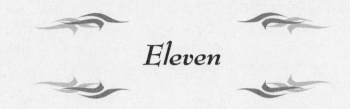

Eleven

"THE BRIGHTEST OF GOOD days to you armsmen, and welcome!" Zania bounced over to the woman who was obviously in charge of the unit of six soldiers and gave her a deep and showy curtsy. Out of the corner of her eye she saw Dhulyn sweep forward, hips swaying in a most obvious manner, to give a curtsy of her own. Parno and Edmir stayed back, though Parno stepped away from the board that held the knives, and both gave good stage bows, sweeping the ground with their hands.

Dhulyn linked her arm through Zania's—and calm swept over her as her hands stopped trembling and her smile became relaxed. *How does she do that?* Zania thought, unaware until that moment that she'd even been frightened.

Dhulyn lifted her free hand to shade her eyes from the sun. "Welcome, indeed. Will you share our camp, Commander? We've no fresh meat, but there's water, dried fruit, and road bread to share."

The woman lifted off her leather helmet and hung it by its strap from the pommel of her saddle, revealing a grinning face and gray-streaked, sweat soaked hair. "I'm no commander, thank the Caids. Just a simple unit leader. Thanks for your offer, but we've no time to stop, worse luck. That was a fine trick you were doing just now, and I wouldn't mind seeing it again." She looked with interest at the knives stuck into the board at the foot of the caravan.

"Don't spoil it for us, Mira!" one of the other soldiers called out, and the unit leader—Mira—laughed.

"Not such a fool. Players, are you? Been camped here long?"

Obeying a slight pressure from Dhulyn's arm, Zania winked at the woman and spoke up. "As you can see, Unit Leader Mira. We're Troupe Tzadeyeu—players, singers, and dancers—at your service. My Uncle Parryn, my Aunt Dilla, my husband Edan, and myself."

As if they had been rehearsing this all morning, Dhulyn chimed in. "Camped here since yesterday evening, practicing away from the prying eyes of our public."

"Heading where?"

"To Jarlkevo, my dear Unit Leader. Sure we can't interest you in a shared meal? We don't have time for a full performance, but we could sing and play. You won't hear finer this side of Beolind." Dhulyn's voice was full of sunshine, and her smile was just as warm. *Why can't she do this on stage?* Zania thought.

One or two of the soldiers had perked up at this renewed offer and even Unit Leader Mira hesitated before slowly shaking her head.

"I believe you, Dilla Tzadeyeu, but we'll have to take our chance that you'll still be in Jarlkevo when our patrol is over. We're due back to our guard tower tonight, like it or not."

"Is the House in residence, then?"

"She is," the unit leader said. "You won't find Valaika Jarlkevoso off in Beolind like many of your fine Houses, with the Steward of Keys left in charge. And good thing for her people, seeing what's happened in Probic—and for you as well, seeing as she's very fond of plays and music."

"What's your errand, if you don't mind my asking?" Parno had come forward and slipped his arm around Dhulyn's waist.

The unit leader's face turned sour for a moment, but her displeasure was not, Zania was sure, aimed at them. When she heard the woman's answer, however, she was glad of Dhulyn's warm arm through hers.

"You'll have heard of the devastation of Probic?"

"It *is* true, then?" Parno said. "We were told, but we found it hard to believe."

"It's true enough, some of us have been there. The very stones are melted in the streets. But some few escaped the Blue Mage's fires, and we're looking for two Mercenary Brothers. Have you seen any such at your performances, or encountered them on the road?"

"Mercenary Brothers?" Dhulyn's voice had just the right hint of confused curiosity. "We understood the Brotherhood was banished—

why, almost a moon ago now. Are these stragglers, then, you look for?"

"I wish that's all it was, Lady." The unit leader shook her head. "A bad business. Word came from Beolind these two in particular are wanted for questioning in the death of Lord Prince Edmir. Them and a young man they might have with them."

Perfectly all right to look shocked and dismayed, Zania thought. *Perfectly normal.* She glanced at Dhulyn and saw her lick her lips.

Parno shifted to his left, until he had his arms around both of them, squeezing their shoulders. "What's unexplained about a death in battle, even at the hands of Mercenaries?"

"Ah, but it's said this wasn't such a death, but rather a case of kidnap and murder by a pair of Mercenaries gone rogue."

"Rogue Mercenaries? Is that even possible? By the Caids, what's becoming of the world?" Parno shook his head, but the hand on Zania's shoulder tightened enough to hurt.

Dhulyn patted Parno's arm. "There, there, my dearest, I'm sure there's some simpler explanation than the end of the world. Should we be worried?" she added, turning to the unit leader. "Is there news of them, hereabouts?"

"No, there isn't, for which we're thanking the Sleeping God, I can tell you." There were shrugs of agreement from among the soldiers at her back. "But formal complaint and a request for outlawry's gone from Kedneara the Queen to the Mercenary House in Lesonika, that's for certain, with banishment for all in the meantime." A grumble came from the soldier who'd spoken up before and there were sidelong looks. Zania had the feeling none of them were looking forward to finding or detaining any Mercenary Brothers.

"Well, best of luck to you, Unit Leader. The Caids bless you, and the Sleeping God keep you in his dreams."

"And the same to you, players."

"Oh, Unit Leader," Dhulyn piped up just as the woman was turning her horse aside to lead the way through the south side of the clearing. "What should we do if we run into these Mercenaries?"

The unit leader frowned, suddenly looking much older. "Do the same you did with us," she said. "Offer to feed them and sing them a song. With luck, you'll get the same answer. In the meantime, if you head southwest from here, you should reach the village of Luk before nightfall, if you'd rather not camp alone." With that, she put her helm back on. The others in the unit nodded as they went past, the second last one giving Zania an appreciative look as he went by.

"Well." When the sounds of movement through the trees had died away, Parno hugged them closer for a moment before stepping back, his hand still on Dhulyn's shoulder. "The banishment's real, then, for all that not everyone we've met has heard of it. But outlawry? *Sons of blooded demons and perverts.* Has there ever been a Mercenary Brother outlawed?"

Dhulyn rubbed her face, let her hands fall back to her sides. "I believe so. Long ago, perhaps even before Pasillon, the scroll I read was unclear on that point. The Common Rule's supposed to prevent it."

"Wonderful. Blooded Common Rule's what's got us into it this time." Parno strode over to the board and pulled a knife free. Edmir looked up as Parno passed him, a furrow between his eyes, his lips pressed tightly together.

Too many hard faces, Zania thought. *Let's have a change of subject.* She turned to Dhulyn and confronted the older woman, hands placed firmly on her hips.

"And how was it you found it so easy to put on an act for those soldiers? You who can barely walk across the stage without tripping over your own feet?"

Dhulyn raised her bleached eyebrows. "But they were soldiers. I understand them and what it takes to . . ." her voice trailed away.

"They were *people*," Zania spread her hands. "And so are the audiences who come to see us every day." Dhulyn gave a slow whistle. "*That's* it, my dear 'Aunt Dilla,' *now* you're beginning to understand. You'll be a fine actress yet, if you stop thinking and just *be*."

Smiling, Dhulyn shook her head at Zania's words, and joined Parno at the knives. "To think it's come to this," she murmured. "My head turned by a few scraps of praise from a half-fledged girl. And this time last year, I was a god."

Parno snorted. "Don't get above yourself. You were only part of a god." He raised his voice so the others could hear. "Zania, what would your people have done, if they'd heard the soldier's news?"

"We'd have gone to the village," Zania answered. "Though to be honest, we probably would have gone anyway, business being business."

"Then let's get packed up. We'll be off to Luk as soon as we've eaten."

Parno waited until Zania had turned away before pulling out another knife. He glanced at his Partner's face as she knelt and unrolled the heavy canvas pouch, ready to slip the knives back into their sleeves. For all of her joking a moment before, now that no one was looking at her, Dhulyn's face was set like stone. She was younger than he, but she'd been longer in the Brotherhood. That made her Senior Brother, and that was all it meant, most of the time. But every now and then, and this seemed to be one of those times, something happened to remind him that for Dhulyn, there had been nothing outside the Brotherhood but loss and slavery.

"I've been Cast Out," he reminded her. "It *is* possible to survive it."

"Your Noble House didn't come looking for you, nor was every hand turned against you," she said, mildly enough.

"We're not outlawed yet, my heart. You won't get careless, will you?"

She fixed him with a sharp look from her steel-gray eyes. "And why should I be careless?"

"My heart, it's one thing to know that the Nisveans are accusing us of murder, it's another thing entirely to know that we've been denounced to our own House, and that we stand in danger of being Outlawed."

"And as you said yourself, we're a long way from that yet." Dhulyn returned the throwing knife he handed her to its pocket in the canvas pouch. "This whole thing started as a way for us to hold by our Common Rule, to keep our honor, and the honor of our Brotherhood. Though it's true we don't look very honorable now."

"There's an easy way for us to clear our names."

"And what is that?"

"Show that Edmir's still alive."

Dhulyn sat back on her heels. "So far, that's got him denied by one who's known him since childhood, and on the run for his life."

"I was afraid you were going to say that."

"Parno, my soul. I'm very much afraid there's no easy way out of this. Any and all might give us the same reaction we had from Tzanek in Probic. They won't know him."

"I don't like what you're saying." Parno pulled out the last knife with more force than necessary.

"It's no longer merely a question of restoring Edmir safely to his home—which the Common Rule still requires of us—now we must clear ourselves as well." She held out her hands for the last of the knives. "There might be only the one way to do both."

"The Blue Mage."

She nodded. "The Blue Mage. My soul—"

He held up his hands. "I'm not arguing, I just don't like what you're saying . . ."

But she'd stopped listening. And she'd stopped putting away knives. Instead, Dhulyn was looking at Edmir and Zania.

"You were very quiet when the soldiers were here."

Edmir shook himself and blinked. "It's one thing to know that you've been declared dead," he said. "You can persuade yourself it's some kind of mistake. But when soldiers come looking for you . . ." His lips were a thin, tight line. "The Mercenaries were right. This *must* be Avylos."

Zania stiffened. "Did you say *Avylos?* Who is Avylos?"

This time Edmir roused himself enough to look at her. "The Blue Mage, of course—ah, I'd forgotten. He doesn't like people to use his name. There's only my sister and I, and my mother the queen, who use it now my father's dead."

"Avylos is the Blue Mage?" Zania swallowed. Her voice sounded far away.

"What of it?"

"Wait." Her heart pounded in her ears so strongly she felt like the skin of a drum. Her hand shook as she thrust it into the pocket of her skirt where she had hidden Great-Uncle Therin's journal. She tore the pocket's edge, getting the journal free. She turned the pages until she found the one she was looking for. "Have you ever seen something like this?"

Edmir's eyes narrowed; he took the book from her and his brows pulled down as he tilted the page until the light fell fully on it. After a moment his brows lifted.

"Where did you get this?" he said. "Avylos has a small casket just like this one on his workroom table." He tapped the drawing of the open casket. "I've never seen inside it, but the clasps, and the handle, are identical. How can you know about this?"

"What is it has you both looking so serious?"

The Mercenaries had approached so quietly that both Zania and Edmir jumped.

"Zania has a drawing of something that belongs to the Blue Mage," Edmir said before Zania could speak up.

"Does she?" Dhulyn Wolfshead looked not at the book Edmir was handing to her, but at Zania. *I must look very odd*, Zania thought. She felt Dhulyn take her firmly by the elbow, and she heard the older woman's voice from far away.

"Parno, my soul, leave the packing. Bring food and strong spirits."

"His name when he was with us was Avylyn," the little Cat said. She held the piece of road bread Parno had given her as if she wasn't aware of it. Parno had found some brandy, and a few swallows had restored most of the color to Zania's face and something of the sparkle to her eye. "If it's the same man," she added.

Dhulyn sipped at her mug of water and swallowed. "Well, we can't know how likely that is until you tell us the full tale. You say the man was part of your troupe?"

Zania nodded. "When the troupe was bigger, the whole family together, and we had other acts—dancers, jugglers, acrobats." She looked around at them. "Shows of magic."

"And this Avylyn was your magician?"

"I don't think I really remember *him*," Zania said. "I was little more than a baby when he left us, walking perhaps, no more. But people spoke of the magic. Small things. He could light a fire even in the rain. He could call a light to sit on the palm of his hand. He could make small objects appear and disappear. I don't know if it was real."

"If it was Avylos, then it *was* real." Edmir sat across from Zania, turning his food over and over in his fingers. His eyes did not sparkle, but burned, cold and dark.

"Or it was the Muse Stone." Zania put her hand on the book in her lap.

Dhulyn put down the strip of dried meat she'd been worrying between her teeth and took another sip of water. Now they were getting to the interesting part.

"This is a drawing of it?" Parno had put out his hand for Zania's book.

"My Great-Uncle Therin said so—but we'd had it, my family I mean, forever, since there was a troupe. It was a relic of the blessed Caids . . ."

Edmir opened his mouth to speak, but Dhulyn silenced him with a negative motion of her head. Time enough later to explain the Caids were no more blessed than anyone else.

"The Ritual of the Stone was what united us as a troupe," Zania said, her voice taking on the singsong cadence of words oft repeated. "What gave us our luck and our prowess, what made us better and more successful than ordinary traveling players. Than what we are now. Until it was stolen from us. We've looked for it since I can remember. All our journeyings have been following news of it." She held out her hand for the book. "There are closer drawings of it on the next pages, and writing, but nothing that I can read."

Dhulyn waited until Zania had found the pages she wanted before reaching out herself. "May I?" she said. "There are only nine written languages," she added, as Zania hesitated. "And three of those are found only in the Scholars' Libraries. I cannot read them all, but even if all I can do is recognize which one this is, it may be a help."

"Come," Parno said. "We know what we are all thinking. This Avylyn of yours and the Blue Mage may be the same person. If so, we are all on the same trail here, and can help one another."

Zania's smile when she finally nodded and handed Dhulyn the book was strained. *And why not?* Dhulyn thought. What a great triumph to find the thing her family had been searching for her whole life—what a tragedy that she would find it alone.

And finding was still not the same thing as having.

Dhulyn took the book and turned it over between her hands, examining it as she'd been taught during her year in the Scholars' Library. There were things to be learned from the whole of the book, not just what was found on the pages themselves. The color and feel of the cow's hide binding told her the book was old, much older than she was herself. The pages were made from very fine paper, such as was found beyond the country of the Great King in the West. It hadn't been so very long—perhaps two generations—that pages were cut and sewn into bindings like this, for easy traveling and storage. This must have been a very early example of such work. The stitches were firm, even, and small, but not in the pattern of any Library she had ever seen. This book had likely been made privately, by some early practitioner of the art.

Finally she opened it. Unlike a copy of a work which already existed, the paper in this book had been bound blank, so it was created to be a journal, or a traveling record book. It was only about two thirds full, the final portion still blank. The same hand appeared throughout, the lettering uniformly even and neat, though larger as it neared the end, as if the sight of the person writing grew longer with age. Still, a practiced hand.

As for the language, Dhulyn smiled. Finally, Sun, Moon, and Stars were smiling on them.

"Were there Scholars in your family? Did anyone, your great-uncle perhaps, ever spend time in a Scholars' Library?"

Zania leaned forward, squinting to see what Dhulyn was looking at.

"Not that I know of," she said, looking at the book as if for the first time. "We can most of us read, but we were taught by the older ones, as we in our turn taught the younger ones."

"This is the common tongue," Dhulyn said, tapping at the words on the page. "Though it will take me some time to read it. It's a Scholar's quick way to take notes, they call it a 'shorthand.' It isn't normally found in any book, just on wax tablets and such that Scholars use to prepare longer pieces and remind themselves of stray thoughts."

"But you can read it, my heart?"

"Not so easily as I once could, it has been a long time, and it will cost me some effort, but yes, I think so." Dhulyn turned to the pages that held the drawings of the Muse Stone. "It may be smart to start here, since the writing will have some reference to the drawing."

At first glance the object Zania had called the Muse Stone appeared to be a fashioned cylinder—most unlikely that it was formed naturally in that shape. Tiny figures gave the dimensions . . . "Is this stone *blue*, by any chance?"

"I believe so, do you read that there?"

Dhulyn kept silent. Clearly this was the same blue crystal cylinder she'd Seen in her Visions, but whether saying so would get them any further just now . . . a detail on the side of the page showed symbols carved near one end.

Four symbols Dhulyn knew very well.

A hawk-faced woman. A blue crystal. A jeweler's lens. A carving tool so fine the point of it seems like a wire.

"Dhulyn?"

"It is nothing, I am well." She swallowed, and touched the drawing again. *This,* this is what that long-ago woman—for though she could not say why, Dhulyn was sure the woman did live long ago—what she had been making.

Parno closed his hand on her wrist. "You see something," he said, the double meaning intended. "Tell us."

"The Stone may or may not be a relic of the Caids, but if your great-uncle has drawn accurately, it *is* a thing of the Marked. You said there were no Scholars in your family or troupe. What of the Marked?"

Zania shook her head while she finished chewing. "How does it concern the Marked?"

"You see these symbols?" Dhulyn tapped the detail with her index finger. "The circle with a dot in the middle stands for a Seer. This straight line for a Finder. This long triangle? Like a spearhead? That's a Mender. And this rectangle is a Healer."

"How do you know this?"

"She's Marked herself," Edmir said. "A Seer."

"But then you can—" Zania fell silent in the face of Dhulyn's raised hand.

"Wait. What I can do may be very little. And the more of the tale I have, the more I can do. Tell me," she said. "What do *you* know of how the stone was used?"

"There was a ritual." Zania looked for someplace to put down the last of the road bread she was holding, and finally Parno took it from her. "I should say, there *is* a ritual. Even though the Stone was gone, we still completed it before every performance, against the day the Stone would be returned. We would take hands and stand in a circle . . ."

Dhulyn caught Parno's eye and twitched her left eyebrow. This was beginning to sound familiar.

". . . and we would recite the words of the ritual, as Great-Uncle Therin had taught us. But, of course, without the Stone, nothing would happen."

"And *with* the Stone?" Dhulyn said.

The girl looked from one face to another, teeth holding her lower lip. Finally, she shrugged. "One night, Great-Uncle got drunk, and he started talking about the 'days before,' the days when we still had the Muse Stone. He said that the ritual filled them with fire, with the spirit of the Muse, the god of players. He talked about how, in those days, you could hear the audience holding their breath during Nor-iRon Tarkina's duel. He said that when he recited the storm clouds speech from *The Mad King*, the heavens answered him with thunder."

The little Cat's mouth had turned down, her eyes had lost their sparkle. "Aunt Ester started to cry, and Uncle Jovan told Great-Uncle to go to bed."

"An enhancer," Parno said. Edmir sat up straighter, his eyebrows raised.

"There are certain drugs that will improve performance . . ." Parno looked at Dhulyn. "Certain *Shora* do the same, though it's thought through focus and concentration, rather than by calling on the gods."

"Finders use their scrying bowls," Dhulyn said. "Seers vera tiles." Her brows knitted in thought. "*Whose* performance was enhanced by this ritual with the Muse Stone?"

"Everyone's. Everyone who participated in the ritual." Zania looked from one face to another. "At least, that's what I always understood. That's why we were so successful. *All* of the acts were improved."

"And it was this Avylyn who took the Muse Stone?"

"My cousin told me that her mother, my aunt Ester, said that when he first came to us, the tricks he did were just that, tricks. He claimed not to believe in any magics, questioned even the actions of the Marked, which no sensible person doubts. He said he would show anyone who cared to see how the tricks were done. Grandfather Devin was troupe master then, and he told him to keep the tricks secret, that it made a better show if the audience thought the tricks were real."

"There's irony for you," Dhulyn said, slapping her hands lightly down on her knees. "Our knife throwing is real, and here *we* are trying to convince our audiences that it is just a trick."

Zania smiled, but her heart wasn't in it. "You know what I mean," she said.

"I do indeed," Dhulyn said. "What's real is a trick, and the tricks are real. That's theater for you."

For a moment Zania looked as though she would argue, but then the light faded out of her face.

"Let me see if I can shorten this tale," Edmir said. "This Avylyn learned of the Muse Stone, learned how to use it, and one day he was gone, and the Stone also."

"And the troupe broke up, first the smaller acts drifting away, the acrobats, jugglers, and jesters. Then the family split up and we have been looking for him and for the Stone ever since." Zania looked around at them, her face set and determined. "I must go to Beolind."

"So must we all. These revelations change nothing for us," Parno said. "If anything, it just makes plainer what our task will be once we are in the Royal House. Confront Avylos, restore Edmir, and regain the Stone."

"Jarlkevo still gives us our best odds of doing that," Edmir said.

Dhulyn shook her head. "I must have time to read the book first," she said. "Who knows what there may be in it that will help us defeat the Mage?"

"But in Jarlkevo—"

"Certainly, if your aunt knows you, and will support you, hide you," Parno said. "But that is a great many 'ifs,' perhaps too many. Dhulyn is right, we need to do this *before* we reach Jarlkevo, in case we do not find an ally there."

"What of this Luk the unit leader spoke of?" Zania said. "It's not uncommon for a troupe of players to stay in one such village several days while they try out a new play. We could be doing both."

Dhulyn looked up from the book. "Did your troupe initiate all its members to the use of the Stone?"

Zania's brows drew down in a sharp vee. "They had to show some talent, I think. Sometimes Great-Uncle would say we were 'ready for the Stone' when we'd done something particularly well." She looked up. "And they could not be people who had joined us for a season. Only firm members of the troupe would be taught the ritual."

"And Avylos did this?" Was it a question, Dhulyn thought, when you knew the answer? "He became a firm member of the troupe?"

"He became my mother's man. He took part in the ritual with the rest."

"And likely found his powers enhanced, and his magics real instead of tricks."

"All this happened when you were still a babe—he's not your father, is he?"

The color drained completely from the little Cat's face. She got to her feet and backed away from them, shaking her head. Before Dhulyn could retract her words, Zania turned and ran, pushing her way through the low bushes into the deeper forest. At a gesture from Parno, Edmir took off after her.

"Ah," Parno said, as Edmir disappeared into the wood. "That went well."

Dhulyn looked sidewise at him and smiled her wolf's smile.

"Zania, Zania stop."

Edmir had caught hold of her sleeve and Zania, out of breath, her heart pounding in her ears, wasn't strong enough to jerk it from his grasp. He took her by her upper arms and shook her until she grabbed the front of his shirt.

"He can't be your father, do you hear me? You don't look like him, nothing like him at all. His coloring's completely different, he's very pale, with dark red hair and very blue eyes. Even if you took after your mother, there'd be *something* in you of him, and I tell you there isn't."

"I just thought . . ." she swallowed and tried to make her fingers loosen their grip on his shirt. "Sometimes it seemed that they treated me with extra care, my family, as if they were watching me. I told myself it was because my mother died when I was still so young. . . ."

"Of course it was that," he said. But Zania shook her head, her eyes squeezed shut.

"Look at me, you half-wit." Shock opened her eyes again.

"Were you a normal girl?"

"What?"

"You're not a blessed Caid, are you? Incapable of doing wrong? Because you could have fooled me. Did you never behave so badly that you made your aunt or uncle—or more likely your cousin, furious with you?"

Heat flushed her face. "Let go of me!"

"They would have said something then, don't you see? If he had been your father, they would have thrown that in your face when you angered them. Any normal person would. People say things they regret when they're angry." As Zania stopped struggling, Edmir lowered his voice.

"They'd have told you if Avylos was your father, to punish you—and to explain to themselves why you were bad. Don't you see, he can't be your father. They would have said."

Her heart resumed beating. "He's not my father. He's not." She rested her head on Edmir's shoulder. He smelled of woodsmoke.

"Zania."

She felt his breath against her ear and lifted her head.

His lips felt very soft and warm on hers.

Twelve

AVYLOS SLID THE THICK glass lens off the map he'd been scrutinizing and let the parchment roll closed. He rubbed at his eyes, and straightened, stretching out his back. He selected the next scroll and unrolled it, using small carved stone weights to hold down the corners. Like the others, this map showed a section of northwest Tegrian, on a scale large enough to display roads and tracks, Houses, Holdings, and even certain Households. The lens revealed tiny drawings, and notations in a neat hand. Avylos moved the lens over to the area he wanted to examine, and blew out his breath in frustration.

When he'd seen Edmir in the pool, he'd seen a clearing in a wood with a fire laid and burning. A sword resting against a rock showed the Mercenaries were still with him, though the magic of the pool did not show any other people. The trouble was that there were so many wooded areas in Tegrian where the particular combination of trees—pine, ash, and birch—could be found. Even supposing that Edmir would choose one of the most direct routes to Beolind from Probic, Avylos had still found four different spots his camp could be in.

And patrols were already in these areas, and none of them had found Edmir, or the two Mercenary Brothers with him. Was it possible that they had left the country after Probic? And gone where?

Avylos tapped his lips with his fingers. Perhaps he should also look at routes to Hellik. It would not be beyond the possible that Edmir would try to reach his relative, the Tarkin.

His eye was caught by his own name magnified by the lens.

"Avylos." The Lady Prince Kera stood in the doorway. "I was told you were here."

And Avylos could guess who had told her. He'd passed that new Balnian page in the corridor. Evidently the blooded boy would babble about anything and everything.

As Kera came no farther into the room, Avylos glanced up again. She must have come from attending her first Royal audience as Lady Prince. She was wearing her brother's coronet, the circlet of twisted gold-and-silver wires almost disappearing in her red-gold hair. Avylos was surprised to note that Kera looked younger than usual, like a child dressed in grownup's clothing. Was she finding it lonely, to be in her brother's place? Could he turn that to his advantage?

"Come," he said, rising and moving one of the other chairs closer to his own seat. "Sit by me. There is something here I would like you to see."

He waited until Kera had sat down next to him before moving the lens once more over the place on the map he'd noted.

"Do you see this writing?"

Kera leaned forward. "It's so tiny."

"It was made using a lens—no, not this one, another, suspended in a stand. This is your father's writing."

Kera leaned still farther forward, this time with interest, not mere politeness, and touched the miniscule letters with her fingertip.

"Your father was my best friend," Avylos said. Kera looked up, blinking, as if seeing him for the first time. Avylos smiled inwardly.

"People forget that, you know." He frowned down at the map in front of them, and then glanced at her from under his brows. "My best friend. I was still a young man when I came here, unsure of my powers and untaught. Pursued by those who would use me for their own ends. Your father's friendship and protection changed all that. He gave me a home, a place to belong, a quiet and safe place to study my art."

Avylos took a deep breath, and tapped the place on the right side of his blue tunic where the consort's coronet was embroidered. "Now everyone sees this and forgets I was your father's friend. No—" Kera had opened her mouth to speak, but Avylos held up his hand. "Even you and your brother forgot. Perhaps especially your brother. It occurs to no one that when your father died, my sanctuary died with my friend."

And so it had, in a way. Karyli had been the brother—the family—he should have had. Avylos had even come to feel that Karyli actually did not care whether he had power or not, whether his magics worked or not. The first person since . . . who had loved him for himself. Who took him seriously, trusted and understood him. Avylos came to feel that he, too, could trust his friend. So much so, that a desire began to form in Avylos' heart, a desire to tell his friend, his brother, what it was he had done. Karyli would understand, Avylos had told himself. Karyli would agree that in the face of the resentment and oppression Avylos had suffered at the hands of his own people, Avylos had done the right thing, the only thing. Karyli would forgive him.

Kera had lowered her eyes, her brow furrowing in thought. Her coloring was so much like her father's. His eyebrow had wrinkled in just that way. Avylos risked a smile. It was working. She was considering what he'd said—what he'd lost, as well as what he'd gained. Kedneara's affections were real, but they were volatile, capricious, especially since Karyli's death—who would know that better than Kera herself? So perhaps Avylos' gain wasn't, after all, as great as it might appear. Kera was considering, perhaps for the first time, that he had pursued her mother the queen not for power, but for the protection of being the consort.

Avylos took another deep breath, letting it out in a shaky sigh. "What I tell you now," he said, "no one else knows. It was not only for myself that I became the consort. After all, I am the Blue Mage, and while my powers were not as great then as they are now . . ." He shrugged. "But your father's last words to me were 'Watch for Kera and Edmir, swear to me you will watch for the children.' "

"I know both you and your brother blamed me for marrying your mother. And Edmir blamed her as well, I know this. But I assure you, Kera my Lady Prince I swear to you, I married your mother in order to fulfill my vow to your father. I could not risk that she would marry someone else, get other children, send me away from you as she sent so many others of your father's circle." He reached out with his left hand, stopping just short of touching her sleeve.

Kera, her eyes still on her father's handwriting, reached out her own hand with the Lady Prince's seal ring on it, and patted Avylos'. There was compassion in her face.

Again, he risked a smile. Kera was a good child, with a kind heart.

She would take her father's place and become his friend. And he would never make the mistake of telling her that his family, his Clan and Tribe, had betrayed him out of jealousy and greed, hiding his magic from him. Never tell her how he'd punished them by betraying them in turn to their enemies. That he'd watched them killed down to the last child, their tents burned, their herds taken or scattered.

He would never have to tell Kera how her father Karyli had reacted not with love and understanding, but with horror and disgust. And had died, moments later, gasping for air.

As he watched Lady Prince Kera leave the map room, Avylos trusted that she would never force him to deal with her as he had dealt with her father.

Kera waited until she was well down the corridor, and even around a turn, before she wiped her hand off on the skirt of her overgown.

❦

"It's not *my* guesthouse, you'll understand." Farmer Bar Wilseyeu, prosperous if her inglera wool tunic was anything to go by, opened the wooden door of the single-story stone structure that made up one of the four sides of the village square. On the other three sides were the farmer's own house—two-storied—the mill, and a Jaldean Shrine featuring the sigils of the Three Planting Gods along with the more customary sign of the Sleeping God.

"I keep it ready in the name of House Jarlkevo, for guests who might need it. Players are always welcome, of course, especially if, well, if there's any chance of a performance." She looked up from under the edge of her leather cap, a tentative smile on her face. Her rough palms rasped as she rubbed them together. "There's time to send word to those who live nearby."

"Send it, my good lady, send it," Parno said, with an actorly flourish of his embroidered gloves. "Give us a chance to wash off the dust of the road, and take a bite of supper, and we'll be at your service."

"Well, as for that, it's late to roast anything, but we've a goodly supply of sausages still, both kinds, and some of the winter hams are just now ready for trial. And there's bacon, which I smoked myself. We'd be happy to have you join us."

"And we'd be happy to come," Parno said. "And perhaps we've news to exchange as well."

"We've heard about Lord Prince Edmir." The farmer's face lost its jovial expression. "All the more need for us to find cheer where we can. The Sleeping God curse those blooded Nisveans—and those Mercenaries, too, if it's true what's being said, and they're involved. Hard to believe it, but there it is. These are hard times." She turned and spit on the ground, saluting the Planting Gods in the farmers' way.

"A true word, my friend, a true word. Has the news of Probic preceded us as well?"

Farmer Wilseyeu turned back, her mouth hanging open a second before she shut it with a snap. "It's not good news, that much I can see from your face. Save it, will you? Tell it but once. Come up to the house when you're ready, and I'll send round to the outliers to come in."

After more than half a moon on the road, even Edmir, not used to fending for himself, was finding the routine of unpacking familiar, and it took them much less time to sort themselves out, choose what they would perform for the local people, and put their hands on scenery and costumes than it had done when they were only a few days out of Probic.

"If it's cheering up they want, I'd say the comic scene from *The Barber's Wife*," Zania said, once they had carried their choices into the guesthouse. Dhulyn thought her voice sounded distant, and the girl was careful to direct her words and attention to Parno—as Edmir was careful to offer his help to Dhulyn.

What has happened between these two? From the stiffness of her smile, and the way she kept her eyes lowered, Zania seemed about ready to cry. And she wasn't the type to cry because Edmir had made advances—more likely, Dhulyn was careful to hide her smile, because he *hadn't*. But now it seemed that something had made these two uncomfortable with each other—unless it was something else entirely. Zania could be excused almost any emotional behavior. Had she not lost all her family and Clan? It had been only, what . . . a moon? A few days more? Dhulyn's own experience told her that these thoughts could never be far from the surface for Zania.

"What about this?" Parno picked up the thick parchment scroll Edmir had just rolled shut, tying it tightly with a loop of leather, and tossed it into the air. He quickly followed it with a painted crown from the open property box in front of him, one of last year's apples plucked from the bowl on the table next to the property box, and the knife he pulled from his own belt. His juggling was clumsy for the first few passes, as each item, different in shape and weight, fell and resisted the push of the air in a different way. In moments he had the feel of it, however, and the items flowed in a smooth stream.

"Here," Dhulyn called and tossed him a thick bracelet to add to the mix.

"I didn't know he could do that," Zania said, her face brightening.

"I'd forgotten myself," Dhulyn said. "I think he once had younger siblings to amuse."

"You *think?*"

Dhulyn turned to her, smiling. "Mercenary Brothers do not have lives before our Schooling began. We leave all that behind us."

For the first time, the little Cat did not flinch from Dhulyn's wolf smile. "And does that work well?"

"Sometimes better than others, but that is the Common Rule."

Parno tossed the bracelet back to Dhulyn, replaced the painted crown, tossed Edwin back his scroll, and with a flourish impaled the apple on his knife, taking a bite out of it before giving them a deep bow. "What do you think," he said to Zania. "Start with a little juggling, *The Barber's Wife*, and music for the rest?"

"Nothing that would weigh too heavy on the heart. A sad song or two, just for flavoring," Zania agreed. "Give them an opening for their grief to leave them. But for the most part, light and happy."

"But not the knife throwing, my little Cat." Dhulyn made it a statement and not a question.

The girl nodded, looking into the middle distance. "Too soon, I think," she said. "We need to work out the patter a bit more."

"Dhulyn, what's Pasillon?"

Thank the Caids, Dhulyn thought. She preferred always to take care of the horses herself, and had sent away the boy the farmer had lent them. Edmir had followed her out and she'd been very much afraid that the prince would use this chance to unburden his soul about whatever had passed between him and the little Cat. Perhaps there had been nothing, after all.

"Where did you hear about it?" She watched him over Warhammer's back. Edmir had gone straight to untie Stumpy, without being asked. For a Lord Prince, Dhulyn thought, he made a decent stable-man, which was more than she could say for many a son of a Noble House.

"This morning, after the soldiers were gone, you said that there might have been Mercenary Brothers outlawed before Pasillon. I meant to ask you then, but," he shrugged, "there were other things to think about."

Dhulyn ran her hand along Warhammer's neck and flanks, taking comfort from the horse's quiet strength. "Long ago," she began, "after the time of the Caids, but long ago for all that, two city-states fought, and Mercenary Brothers carried arms on both sides."

"Fought against each other?" Edmir paused, his fingers on the buckles of the long traces.

Dhulyn looked at him sideways. " 'In Battle or in Death,' it is our greeting and farewell. We are all of us, all living things, walking on a path toward our deaths, and for a Mercenary Brother, to die at the hand of one of our own . . ." She shrugged. "What better way?" She led Warhammer out of the traces and into the first stall. "In any case, one party was victorious," she said. "But at the cost of their prince's life, and so, in their anger, and their grief, they spared no enemy soldier, cutting them down as they fled, killing them they as they lay wounded in the field."

"Like at Limona." Edmir's voice was hollow.

"At Limona they took prisoners for slaves. At Pasillon there was not even that cold hope." Dhulyn turned her attention to Bloodbone, caressing the mare's long nose. "This would have had nothing to do with the Brotherhood, except that in their fury, and the heat of their blood, the victors saw no reason why a Mercenary badge should free anyone of the price they wished to take, and so they began to kill Mercenary Brothers as well."

"Oh, no."

"I see you know enough of our Common Rule to anticipate my story." Dhulyn waited, her fingers working on a knot in Bloodbone's mane. "Those of the Brotherhood who were of the winning faction ran to the aid of their Brothers, but they were outnumbered, and so they died."

"But not all?"

"So the story goes. Against fearful numbers, they held their ground until nightfall, allowing three Brothers to escape. And after that night the victors began to die. Not everyone. Just those who had killed Mercenaries that day. The officers. The lords who gave the orders." She accepted the coil of harness from Edmir and took it into the stable, the boy close on her heels.

"So that's why a request to outlaw a Mercenary Brother has to go through your own House."

"We take care of our own." There was a flaw in the reins, as if the edge of a knife had scored it. She rubbed at it with her thumb. "Defend one another if we are in the right, punish one another if we are in the wrong. We cannot allow others to do it."

"But you *can* be outlawed."

Dhulyn nodded.

"What a play it would make." Whatever Dhulyn expected him to say, it wasn't this. "The leader of the winning side—do you know which it was? His great grief, stained with his arrogance, bringing about his downfall. His growing awareness of the march of his own doom."

Edmir's eyes had taken on that faraway look, the look that meant he was seeing the actors on the stage, hearing the words leaving their mouths. Dhulyn shook her head and left him there, going to join the others.

The evening's performance seemed at least to have restored some of the youngsters' good spirits. Parno's juggling had been warmly appreciated, with contributions from everyone in the audience, especially the children, and the comic scene from *The Barber's Wife*, good physical humor, seemed to have helped release the tension she'd earlier sensed between Edmir and Zania. They came back into the travelers' quarters still buoyant and smiling, even taking hands and dancing a short measure across the guesthouse's dressed stone floor. This had been an audience of farmers and the like, and so the performance had been over earlier than it would have been at a House or even a Holding, where some at least would have stayed up reveling longer into the night. Dhulyn leaned back against the edge of the table and watched, wondering whether the twinges she was feeling in her lower back signaled the approach of her woman's time, or just the unfamiliar exercise of dancing.

"That was well done, very well done, all," Zania said, spinning around to bless them all with her smile. "Only one thing I would say to be careful of and that's for you, Parno." She stepped toward him and put her hand on his arm. "That place where you have delivered your speech to the Barber and you must step to the side, you were supposed to wait, and move at the same time Dhulyn did, so that her movement covered yours. You moved after her, during her speech, and so the audience's eye stayed upon you, and so you drew off some of the effect of her speech. In the future, remember to wait, and move as she does, and you'll be a help instead."

"Like an army in the field," Parno said. "Each doing their part in support of the whole."

"We should have a signal," Dhulyn said, trying to stretch out the muscles of her back, "as we do in the field, to set us right again when we stray. Something the audience will likely not know or recognize."

"Pasillon." They all looked at Edmir. "Something to remind us that we work as a team, and not in conflict with one another."

Parno looked at Dhulyn and raised his right eyebrow. She smiled and shrugged. "Why not? In this endeavor, at least, we are as Brothers."

"Dhulyn, my Dhulyn," Zania sang, dancing up to her and taking her hands. "I have had a great thought, a brilliant thought. I just can't imagine why none of us have thought of this already. You're a Seer, yes? So why don't you See for us? See what we must do next?"

Edmir looked back and forth between the two women. Satisfaction warred with curiosity on his face. Parno caught Dhulyn's eye, his lips pursed in a silent whistle. Dreading the disappointed expectations, her immediate response was to refuse. It was one thing to See for herself and Parno, they both understood the limitations of her Mark. But when she looked at the eager faces of Zania, and Edmir . . .

Had she not just said that they were as Brothers?

"Not a bad idea in itself," Dhulyn said, managing to release her hands from Zania's without hurting the girl. "But let me warn you. Do not expect too much. The Visions are never clear, and even when I think I am directing them, they do not always show me what I ask to See."

Parno ducked into the room he and Dhulyn had chosen for their own and came out carrying the olive-wood box that held her vera tiles.

Edmir cleared the tray holding a jug of cider and clean clay cups from the sturdy square table, as Dhulyn took the box and seated herself on one side. The others took the other seats, watching her as she spilled the tiles out on the table's worn surface.

"But these are vera tiles," Zania said.

"A little more than that." Dhulyn picked up the tiny moleskin bag that held the one unique tile in the set, the Lens tile which was the focus of all Seeing. "You see these tiles here? They're not found in the ordinary sets of vera tiles. You'll recognize these symbols from the drawings of your Muse Stone, the symbols of the Mark. The eye, the line, the rectangle, and the triangle. Seer, Finder, Healer, and Mender, four of each."

Parno sat in the chair next to her and began turning tiles face up, and she slapped his knuckles. "Each of you find a tile to represent yourself. One of the major tiles, Tarkin, Tarkina, Mercenary, Scholar, or Priest, and pay attention also to the suit, Coins, Cups, Swords or Spears. Whichever one feels right to you. Hold it a moment in your hand and give them to me as I ask you for them."

Dhulyn set the Lens tile in the center of the space she had cleared by pushing the tiles to one side. She placed her own tile, the Merce-nary of Swords, just above it, and a Seer's tile above that. Edmir chose the Scholar of Cups, she noted with an inward smile. So the Lord Prince of Tegrian did not see himself as a Tarkin, or even as a Merce-nary. And he did not see himself as Sword or Spear. As she expected, Parno chose the Mercenary of Spears, and Zania the Tarkina of Coins. Trying to make no conscious decision, letting her own internal Sight make the decision for her, Dhulyn placed Parno's tile below the Lens, opposite her own, Zania's to the right, and Edmir's to the left. Next to Parno's she placed a Mender's tile, with its spearhead symbol. Next to Zania's the straight line of the Finder, next to Edmir's the rectangle of the Healer.

She studied the cross formed by the tiles for the space of three heartbeats before nodding, and pushing the remaining tiles back into their box. Keeping her eyes on the tiles in front of her, she reached into the box and pulled out the first tile, setting it on top of her own. Six of Cups. For Edmir, the four of Swords; for Parno, the nine of Swords; for Zania, the three of Coins. For all of them, a Finder, the two of Spears, the seven of Spears, the Priest of Spears. No, the Mage.

The high walls of the garden hold the moonlight like a deep bowl holds water, washing all color from the trees and flowers. The pond is a black diamond held within the setting of its stone rim. For a moment Dhulyn thinks there is someone seated on this stone edge, but it must have been a trick of the light. There is nothing there. She looks up, and there is the girl sitting in a niche created by a rough section of the garden wall and thick piece of hedge almost as tall as the wall itself. Dhulyn waves her arms; sometimes she can be seen by the others who inhabit the Visions, but not this time. The girl watches the pond, as if someone is there, but when Dhulyn looks again, there is no one.

But there *is* an image in the water. Dhulyn moves closer, and the image is clearer, though still without color. It is Edmir, asleep, dreaming. He frowns and rolls over on the bed, his arm sweeping up to cover his eyes. The shadow on his palm created by his curled fingers looks like a curl of hair. . . .

There is Edmir, again on his throne. His robes are the brilliant blue of the sky in winter, there is a circle of leaves shining gold against his dark hair. He puts aside the long two-handed sword he is holding across his lap, handing it to the armsman who stands to his right. Edmir stands and approaches the front of the dais. He raises his hands to speak, and the crowd hushes. . . .

This is her mother, again. Her mother as a young woman, who never had the opportunity to be an old woman. She is in the garden again, dressed in her lady's gown, her hair bound and swinging down her back. She swings a sword . . . a stave. No, it is a sword. And she fights a slim-hipped, dark-haired man who wields a very familiar sword.

It is Parno. When she looks closely at him, the dark wig disappears and she sees his red-and-gold Mercenary badge, with the black line of Partnership threaded through the pattern. In what possible past can this be? In what possible future? Dhulyn looks more closely at the woman she takes for her mother. No, the features are clear. Whoever this person is really, for the purposes of the Vision, she is Dhulyn's mother. Parno is armed with his second-best sword, the one with the nick in the guard, and he is using it to defend himself against the blows of the Espadryni woman. But all he does is defend, and this makes him slow and weak. He will lose if he does not attack. He does not want to kill this woman, but she wants to kill him.

Fight, my soul, she tries to say. *Don't let her kill you. Fight and return to me.*

In Battle, or in Death. . . .

Zania holds a blue crystal cylinder between her hands, thick as a man's wrist, as long as Dhulyn's forearm. Shining blue like the deep ice that traps the glow of the stars. The Muse Stone. A drop of blood falls from Zania's nose to the Stone. There is movement in the room behind her, but Dhulyn cannot make it out in the bright blaze of light that comes from the stone.

Dhulyn pushed back from the table. "Hard to say whether there was anything helpful," she said, her voice coming dry and creaking from her throat. She took the cup of water Parno gave her with a nod of thanks.

"I Saw you on your throne, Edmir, something I've Seen before. And you, Zania, you were holding what appeared to be the Muse Stone in your hands, though I could not see around you."

"But that's good. That means we'll find it." Zania's smile was enough to add light to the room.

"That is one of the possible futures, yes," Dhulyn croaked. "But now you see the limitations of my Sight. *How* will we find it? How can we ensure that is the future we attain? What must we do—and leave undone—for that future to arrive?"

"And are they things we *can* do, or are willing to do?" Parno added.

"But we do know that it's *possible*," Edmir said. "Even if we don't know how *likely* it is."

"True, and so we go ahead." Dhulyn massaged the muscles around her eyes with her fingertips, lowered her hands, and looked around at them. "Perhaps there is something in your book, Zania, that may help make my Visions clearer. It has happened so in the past."

When they were alone in their own room, Dhulyn sat flipping through the pages of Zania's book.

"I Saw you fighting someone," she said, without looking up. "It seemed to be my mother."

"Which is why you didn't mention it to the youngsters."

She nodded. "This is becoming a nightmare," she said, not meaning her Vision.

"Yes, it is," Parno agreed.

"Sleep my soul. I will read."

Several hours later, her eyes gritty with her effort to concentrate on the Scholar's shorthand in Zania's book, Dhulyn got up, stretched the kinks out of her back, and put out the lamp she'd been reading by. In the morning she would have to find paper, something on which to make her own notes. When her eyes adjusted, she made rounds through the other rooms, checking that Zania and Edmir both were asleep and undisturbed. Edmir moved as she started to close the door of his chamber and she froze, but he only rolled over, his arm sweeping up to cover his eyes. He had left the shutter open, and there was enough moonlight to make a shadow on his palm, created by his curled fingers. It looked like a lock of hair. "*Blood,*" Dhulyn said.

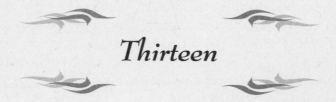

Thirteen

"WHY SHOULD AN IMAGE OF Edmir appear in a pool in a garden?"

Parno rolled over. The open shutter let in enough light to show him Dhulyn standing, fully dressed in her player's clothing, by the window. He propped himself up on his elbow.

"Is that what's kept you restless all night?"

She nodded.

"What else was in the image?"

She turned and moved toward him, silent as a shadow. "At first I thought I saw someone else there, seated by the side of the pool. But I looked again, and nothing. There was, however, a young girl, hiding, watching from some distance away."

Parno scratched at his mustache. "Is someone watching Edmir? I would hate to see the fires that destroyed Probic come to Luk," he said finally.

"By someone, you mean the Mage? All I know for certain is that I saw no one else but the girl. The image was of Edmir asleep in his bed. . . ."

"And possibly his location cannot be discovered from that."

"Possibly."

Parno looked at her. She knew as well as he did how many people could be killed with only a "possibly" to lead the way.

"How long will it take you to read the book?"

"I must have paper."

Parno swung his legs out from under the covers and reached for his leggings. "The Jaldeans will have some."

*   *   *

It was quiet on the steps of the caravan. Zania had been sitting out here long enough to watch the hamlet come to life for the new day. The sun was barely up, but a young girl had come from Farmer Bar's already to bring them breakfast and see to their horses; others had gone out to the fields, and somewhere the milking was being done. This time of year, there would be hay to bring in, if nothing else. But the square itself was quiet.

Zania had woken up sometime before dawn, and finding herself unable to go back to sleep, she'd hoped that coming out to sit somewhere familiar would help to still her racing thoughts. Last night when they'd gone to bed, everything had seemed possible. Dhulyn had Seen the Muse Stone, and even the question of how they were to achieve what the Vision had shown them—well, as Dhulyn had said to her last night, "today's troubles today, tomorrow's for tomorrow."

Somehow, when she woke alone in the dark, the questions had all come flooding back. And now it *was* tomorrow. Zania realized that she hadn't really given much thought to what it meant, getting the Muse Stone back. It had been something Great-Uncle Therin was going to do, with Uncle Jovan. When she'd thought about it at all, she'd imagined a dramatic confrontation, with perhaps herself and her cousin Jovana—Jo in a minor role, of course—a denunciation of the thief, a restoration of their rightful property to enthusiastic applause. To find out now that it was the Blue Mage himself who had the Stone. *The Blue Mage.* Had Great-Uncle Therin suspected anything of the kind? What was she to do now? She was the only one left. . . .

"Where is everyone?" Edmir startled her. He had a meat pastry in his hand, taken from the dish the farmer's girl had brought them. There had been a jug of water as well as the makings for ganje.

"If you mean Dhulyn and Parno, I saw them going across to the Jaldean Shrine a while ago."

"The shrine?" Edmir looked over his shoulder to where the facade of the other building caught the light from the morning sun. "Of course," he added, nodding. "They *are* Mercenaries, they're probably followers of the Sleeping God."

When Edmir turned back, their eyes met, and he blushed.

Zania looked down at her hands, clasped between her knees, hoping she looked relaxed and uncaring. There *had* been one other subject on her mind, other thoughts that had chased themselves around her brain all night. Edmir had said nothing about kissing her. Unless, she eyed him sidewise, unless he'd been waiting for them to be alone.

Though it seemed Edmir wasn't going to say anything after all. He leaned against the corner of the caravan, which put them more or less at the same height, but he was staring off to one side, frowning as if he'd heard Parno play a bad note. Zania cleared her throat.

"Do you think Dhulyn will be able to read my book?"

"Hmm?"

Nervousness changed to irritation. He wasn't even thinking about her.

"You're supposed to lift your left index finger if you're writing in your head," she said in her crispest voice. "If you've lost some precious words of *The Soldier King*, you've only yourself to blame."

Edmir turned to her and smiled. Zania felt her ears grow warm.

"Zania," he said.

Something in his tone made her glance quickly away. *Here it comes*, she thought, her heart speeding up. *Now we'll talk about the kiss.*

"Zania, is the play good?"

"What?" The buzzing in her ears faded, leaving a cold quiet behind it.

"*The Soldier King*, is it a good play?"

Zania was so surprised she forgot her shyness and turned on the step to face Edmir fully and frankly. His eyes were lowered again, and she could see the wrinkle in his forehead, between his bleached brows, the set look to his lips, as he braced himself for her reply. She could make an easy answer—either the quick, cutting slap down or the smooth reassurance—but neither felt right, somehow.

Parno had said that she wanted Edmir. Zania had thought about that, and before their kiss she'd almost persuaded herself that it just wasn't so—that she wasn't interested in Edmir in the way a woman was interested in a man. But if she was going to be honest, there *was* something about him, something she'd never noticed in any other young man. *Of course, he is a Lord Prince; that will set him apart from the others.* But she didn't think it was only that.

Maybe her interest *had* started off that way—many a traveling troupe was sponsored by a House lord or lady who had a lover among the troupe, and what better sponsor than a Lord Prince? If anything, the kisses they had shared yesterday had shown her how easy that could be for them. But they had also shown her something else. Kisses were easy, knowledge was harder. She knew him now, and liked him for himself. Which meant she had to set aside her wounded pride and answer his question truthfully, seriously.

"It is a good play," she said finally. "Among the best I've heard, and I've heard many." She took a deep breath. "But you know this, you've looked through the ones we have in the chest, you've heard enough of the pieces we've been practicing. You know it's good."

"I'm just using Tarlyn's poem."

"No. What you're making is a good deal more than Tarlyn's poem ever was. That's just a story—a good one, maybe, but a story just the same. Your play is different, it's more *real* somehow."

"Thank you. It's not often you say something that doesn't sound as though you were quoting a line."

Zania opened her mouth and shut it again. There was really nothing to say to that. She eyed him more closely. There was a different kind of frown on his face now.

"There's something else worrying you, isn't there?"

"When I think about everything that's waiting for me when we reach Aunt Valaika's House . . ." He shook his head, lips a thin line. He looked at her and tried to smile. "We'll sort it out somehow. My sister says that when she's worried about how something will turn out, she thinks about how things will be afterward, when the worrisome event is long over. What will *you* do when it's all over? Take your Stone and lead your own company?"

"Of course, I—" The words stuck in her throat. The troupe she had wanted to lead was dead in the hostel courtyard in Probic. Weeks dead. And she would never rise to be their leader. They would never vote for her in the fullness of time. That was over. Gone.

Her breath caught in her throat.

"They're all gone," she whispered, sobs rising. "They're all gone, and I don't *know* what to do."

Edmir was appalled, frozen with horror as the girl he'd privately thought so strong and practical, rather hard, really, even if the idea of Avylos as a father had frightened her—the girl he couldn't believe he'd had the nerve to kiss—bent over, face buried in her hands, and broke into wrenching sobs. He reached out a tentative hand to her shaking shoulder, and drew it back. What was the right thing to do? Nothing growing up in the Royal House had prepared him for anything like this. There, the girls took care that he never saw them blotchy-faced and weeping.

He chewed on his lower lip. What would he do if this was his sister Kera? That thought released him. Gently, careful not to startle her, he put his arms around Zania, stroking her on the back and making every soothing and sympathetic noise he could think of.

"We'll think of something, you'll see," he said as the sobs finally began to die down. *She hasn't cried at all*, he realized. *Not at all since it happened*. This reaction was long overdue, and all the stronger for being repressed. "Look at everything we've thought of already. A knife throwing act, a new play. Having the Muse Stone back will change everything. Who knows, maybe the Mercenaries will stay with you."

"You don't really believe that," she said, lifting her head but remaining within the circle of his arms. Her voice was a croaking echo of its normal self. She dabbed at her eyes and nose with the wide sleeve of her blouse. "They're Mercenary Brothers, not players."

"And I'm a prince, not a playwright." Edmir blinked. Those words had come out sounding much more bitter than he'd intended.

Zania moved away enough that Edmir had to lower his arms or look like a fool. "And you'll go back to being a prince," she said, dabbing again at her eyes. Was it his imagination, or did she sound regretful?

For a moment he imagined himself beside her like this for the rest of his life. Writing plays, watching her act in them. Watching their children act. Then he pulled himself together.

"We must deal with Avylos." His voice sounded harsh even in his own ears. How could he tell her that he had to steel himself to push her away?

"Of course," she said. "No use casting the parts before the play is written."

Edmir licked his lips. There was something else he'd like to say. . . .

Dhulyn Wolfshead came around the corner of the caravan, her arms full.

"We've found paper," she said. "The Jaldeans had a supply they were willing to sell us—whatever is the matter? You two look as though someone has killed your pony."

*   *   *

Dhulyn set out her pens, her small bottle of ink, and the paper she'd purchased from the Jaldeans to her right, opened Zania's book, and placed it to her left. The muscles in her lower back spasmed, but the pains had not yet moved around to her belly. They would come soon, she judged, but perhaps they would not be too bad this time.

"Is there anything you need?" Zania was in the doorway. Her voice sounded thick. Obviously the little Cat had been crying, but Dhulyn judged it was not trouble with Edmir. The two had been upset when she'd come upon them at the caravan, but the way they stood with one another showed the problem did not lie between them. The kind of crying that left those signs on a woman's face—Dhulyn recognized those feelings, and knew there was nothing to be done. It was hard to be the only one left, to have no one of your blood, kin or Tribe. Hard not to hate yourself for rejoicing in your own life. Good that the girl had cried, finally.

In the meantime, the little Cat needed something else to occupy her thoughts. And to keep her out of Dhulyn's way.

"I have an idea, little Cat," Dhulyn said. "Do you remember we spoke of *Nor-iRon Tarkina*? While I am reading your book, why should Parno not teach you a *Shora* that you could use in the dueling scene? Slowed well down, it will show very nicely on stage."

Zania gave a dim but genuine echo of her usual smile. "We'll make a player of you yet," she said.

Dhulyn went out with her and caught Parno's eye. They went through possible *Shoras* while Edmir helped Zania pull out the stage swords from their storage spot on top of the caravan.

"Rutting Ram *Shora* it is, then," Parno said. "Two people, one sword each, a series of strong attacks—perfect for the purpose, if I make them clash enough."

"Make up a different name for it," Dhulyn said. "Something grows between these two, and it would embarrass them."

Parno shrugged. "They're of an age. Together all day, every day, with similar tastes and goals—for the moment at least. Of course they're falling in love."

About to head back to the guesthouse, Dhulyn turned to look at her Partner. "This is just a camp romance, then? It will fade away when the campaign is over?"

"Haven't you ever fallen in love?" Parno looked at her sideways.

Dhulyn smiled the smile she gave only him. "No."

"Get to your reading, woman."

"There, that's enough for now. We'll try it again tomorrow, and next day and the next, until I know you won't forget it."

Edmir nodded, breathing deeply, his hands on his knees. Even slowed down, the Mountain Ram *Shora* took strength, concentration, and skill. It had been almost a moon since he'd last held a sword in his hand with any intent, and he was embarrassed to see how out of condition he was. It helped that Zania was also blowing and out of breath, but not much.

"I'm for the bathhouse," Zania said, handing Edmir her sword. "I'll see if Dhulyn is ready for a break from her labors."

Edmir climbed up to the top of the caravan, and Parno passed him up the swords. "Thank you for showing us that."

"It will be useful to Zania to know how this type of thing is done—and good training for you, once you return to your own station in life."

Edmir licked his lips as he slid the swords back into the pack they'd come from and began retying the cords.

"How is it that you came to leave *your* station in life?"

The silence lasted long enough that Edmir became afraid he had somehow stepped over a line. But when he jumped down once more to the ground, he saw that Parno was merely considering his answer.

"You know that the Common Rule holds that we put aside what life we had before the Brotherhood?"

"I know that you've already mentioned your House was nobler than mine," Edmir pointed out a little sourly.

Parno laughed and clapped him on the shoulder. "True, so no reason not to answer your question." Parno continued smiling, but his eyes grew serious. Edmir had a strange feeling that the Mercenary Brother knew exactly what had prompted the question. Which was strange, seeing that Edmir wasn't sure himself.

"I didn't leave my House," Parno said, serious now. "I was Cast Out."

Edmir felt suddenly cold. The man he'd been trusting all this time, admiring, respecting . . . an outlaw?

"Don't look at me like that, lad. Are we not even now, ourselves, being looked for by soldiers and guards?"

Edmir felt his face grow hot. "I beg your pardon," he said. "I didn't think."

"No, well." Parno shrugged. "A kinsman insulted my sister," he said. "The Kir of my House—do you understand? Do you use the term here?"

Edmir nodded. The Kir was the heir of a House.

"Good. I struck the Kir of my House, and . . . disfigured him. He insisted on my being Cast Out. My father had to obey, or he would have lost everything, and my sisters as well. As it was, the eldest of my two sisters inherited."

"And the Kir? Is he now the House?"

"Alas, no."

Edmir answered Parno's grin with one of his own.

But the humor faded from the older man's face, and Parno's eyes narrowed.

"Edmir, listen to me. I thank the gods every day that I am where I am. I *did* choose to become a Mercenary Brother, but my House was already behind me. I would no more have chosen to leave my House than I would choose to leave the Brotherhood now, or break my Partnership—supposing such choice were given me. I cannot break these bonds, these oaths. Nor could I have left my House. My oaths and my bonds to them were just as strong. I would never have *chosen* to break them. Do you understand?"

"Yes, I think so."

"Do you? I would not have left my father, my mother, and sisters in danger if I had not been forced to go."

Edmir's nod was very slow; his head felt so heavy, and his ears were hot with shame. He *did* understand. He knew what Parno Lionsmane the Chanter, Mercenary Brother, was telling him, Lord Prince Edmir of Tegrian. He, too, had oaths and bonds, responsibilities and obligations. He could not choose to break them. Lord Prince Edmir could not leave his sister, nor his mother the queen, in the hands of the Blue Mage.

He would think of such things no more.

*   *   *

Dhulyn studied the page in front of her. The ends of the Stone *twisted*, but according to the notes, they did not stop in any particular place, even though indicator marks suggested they would. She looked more closely. Yes. The indicator symbol on the one end *was* the concentric circles of the Lens, while the symbol on the other end was a crescent moon. Interesting.

She lifted her hands and mimed holding the Muse Stone.

"Gehde. Gehde. Mones. Aharneh."

"No, it's 'aHARneh,' " said Zania's voice from the doorway.

Dhulyn looked up, and slowly straightened her back. She should know better than to sit so long in one position, but it had been years since she'd studied anything with so much concentration. The feeling that she could not let time slip away was nagging at her.

"That's the Chant of Opening," the little Cat said, as she came into the room.

"Then I would take it that 'Ahar Ahar Mones GeDERneh' is the Chant of Closing." Dhulyn frowned down at the book in front of her and made a notation on the paper to her right.

"So we always practiced it." Zania took a seat at the table, pulled a sheet of paper covered with Dhulyn's neat handwriting toward her. "You can read the Scholar's code, then?"

"It's not a code, exactly, just a way to write things quickly. To take notes at lectures, for example."

"And does my great-uncle say where he learned such a thing?"

"Not directly. But he does mention a trip to the Library of Ishkanbar. Apparently when he was himself a young man, his grandfather took the Muse Stone to the Scholars there, to see what they could tell him of it."

"And what did they say?"

"A relic of the Caids," Dhulyn thought, thinking of that fair-haired woman with the long-fingered hands she'd Seen in her Vision. Had she been a Caid, then? For what purpose had she made the Stone?

"According to your great-uncle, at the time it took much persuading to get it back out of the hands of the Scholars." Dhulyn sighed. "If I had time, my little Cat, I would translate the whole of the book for you. There is much here that would be of use and interest, much that has nothing to do with the Stone. It was only when your great-uncle began to feel the first twinges of age—and that was astonishingly

recently—that he thought to write down what he knew of the Stone."
A movement made Dhulyn glance over. "I know. Why use the
Scholar's shorthand if he meant this as a record anyone could use?"

"Do you think Uncle Jovan would have known the shorthand, too?"

Dhulyn nodded. "If, as you say, reading and writing were taught to
you by your elders. Your great-uncle would have taught his son and
heir, never thinking they would both be carried off at once."

Dhulyn grimaced as the light went out of Zania's face. *That* had
been entirely the wrong thing to say. A distraction was needed. She
put out her hand for the page Zania had taken.

"There appear to be at least three other chants," she said. "And
there are symbols on both ends of the Stone."

"So you've told us, the symbols of the Marked."

Dhulyn shook her head. "That is just the one end. On the other are
symbols I do not recognize, though for some reason I feel I should.
See here, I've drawn them larger, do you know them?"

Zania drew down her brows, then her face cleared. "There's a tunic
with these symbols embroidered into it, do you think that's where
you've seen them?"

"I haven't seen a tunic such as you describe," Dhulyn said. Now it
was her turn to frown. "In fact, I know that I haven't seen these particular symbols before, only that they seem familiar."

"What of the other chants? The opening and the closing are the
only ones I've ever heard."

"Your uncle calls the others 'Null Chants.' He says that the Stone
glows when they are spoken, and the ends turn, but nothing happens."

"I wonder if Avylos the Blue Mage has found a way to make something happen?"

"That is a most unpleasant thought." Dhulyn drew her finger down
the list of symbols she had drawn. A crescent moon. Three geometric
patterns—not unlike a Mercenary badge, she thought—a Healer, a
Mender, a Finder, a Seer. And finally a Lens.

<hr>

This is the boy in the woods again, the red-haired Espadryni boy.
Younger, unbruised, unbloodied. But still in the woods. He is drawing
in the air, very slowly at first, and then faster and faster. But nothing
happens. Something should happen, Dhulyn realizes. Colored light

should follow the path of his finger, leaving a symbol drawn upon the air. How does she know this? The boy draws more symbols. Nothing. Nothing. He pounds the ground before him with his fists, grunting in frustration and rage. She takes a step forward and he looks in her direction. But he frowns, chest heaving, tears streaming down his red face, puzzlement coming to replace the rage. . . .

Complete darkness. So dark, so heavy, for a moment Dhulyn imagines she cannot breathe.

Edmir?

⟜

"Dhulyn?" There was worry in Zania's voice.

"I think I've read enough," Dhulyn said. Her own voice sounded hollow in her ears. "Tell the others, we eat, then we ride."

Fourteen

"YOU ARE SOONER THAN I expected you, Squad Leader Olecz." Avylos set aside the ancient scroll he had been studying when the squad leader had been announced.

"We completed our first search very quickly, my lord Mage, and were on our way to the second village when we encountered a patrol sent out from Tsarin with the same errand as ourselves. You did not tell me, my lord Mage, that there would be others."

"No, I did not." Avylos stared until the other man lowered his eyes.

"Of course, my lord Mage." Olecz licked at his lips. Good. Let him remember to whom he was speaking. In the sweat beading on Olecz's forehead was the knowledge of what had been done in Probic.

"Continue," Avylos said.

"Yes, my lord Mage. We found no signs of the persons we were looking for, nor did the other patrol. The only persons of interest encountered were a team of inglera shearers on their way home after their circuit, a troupe of players, five men hiring out for work in the hay fields, and three bandits living in the forest east of Luk."

"Players." A cold grip on his heart. "A large group?"

"No, my lord Mage. One small caravan, with four people. We were told three women and an older man, if memory serves."

"And the bandits?"

"I saw them myself, my lord Mage. A man and two young boys, one of those a runaway servant. Not the people we were sent to find."

Avylos leaned back in his chair, let his hands rest along the arms. "Very well," he said. "Return to your regular duties. Await my future instructions."

The bow Olecz gave him was fully as deep as the one he would have given to Kedneara the Queen. That almost made Avylos feel a little better. Almost. He tapped the arm of his chair with the side of his right fist. He couldn't spare any more magic to keep looking for Edmir in this way. If he kept this up, he would have to recharge the pool in the garden, and he did not have enough power left for something like that. Not unless he could find someone else to tap, someone who had the same level of power as that dice boy.

He would have to follow the trail in a more ordinary way.

He realized that he had placed his left hand on the casket that held the Stone, and pulled the hand back again. No help there, no help until he unlocked the secret of its stored power.

He reached for his maps of Tegrian.

⌁

Valaika Jarlkevo pushed the lists in front of her farther away. She clasped her hands at the back of her neck and pushed her head back against them, trying to loosen the tight muscles of her shoulders.

"That bad, is it?"

Valaika looked up, a smile coming automatically to her lips. Only Sylria would come in without knocking, and only Sylria would ask such a question so bluntly. Valaika released her hands and leaned back in her chair. Any interruption was welcome, but this was better than most.

"Anyone who can read a balance sheet can see we've no more people to spare for Kedneara's armies."

"You mean to say 'Kedneara the Queen.' "

"I mean Kedneara my blooded sister-in-law the Queen, yes." Valaika pulled one of the sheets of paper closer. "As if farming isn't hard enough in these mountain valleys, I sent her every able body *last* season, and we were promised no more would be needed *this* season."

Sylria crossed the room from the door, her house slippers noiseless on the rugs, and seated herself in the wide, padded chair on the other side of the table. Like Valaika, the other woman was dressed entirely in dark blue, the queen's colors, to remind all who saw them that they were directly related to the Royal House, and in mourning. Instead of the usual badge in the Jarlkevo House colors of orange and black, both women followed the custom of Hellik, Valaika's homeland, and wore an embroidered crest, in the shape of a bear's head, on the left side of their tunics.

"I would have thought, after Probic, that Nisvea would have been the last of our worries, but no, Kedneara wants another levy of soldiers."

"What possessed poor Edmir to break the treaty? *That* war should have been at least two years away." Sylria took up the jug of watered wine that sat on the table and poured herself a cup. "And what possessed him to take so few with him. And what, for that matter, possessed the poor child to get himself killed?"

"I should have stayed in Hellik." Valaika addressed her inkpot. "Failing that, I should have stayed in Beolind." She looked up at Sylria. "All right, so I would have killed somebody out of sheer boredom, or been killed myself. How bad could that have been?"

"You've said that many times, and let me remind you of what I've told you, each and every time. If you'd done any of that you wouldn't be House Jarlkevo, important in your own right and not just as the consort's sister. You wouldn't have the land, and the people, and yes, the responsibility. And you wouldn't have Janek to become the House after you, and take the responsibility from you, and, not least I think, you wouldn't have me."

With a grunt, Valaika rubbed her face vigorously in both hands. "You're right, of course."

Sylria leaned forward again and pulled a large sheet of parchment toward her, studying the figures, crossed out and rewritten, and the notation on the bottom of the page. Her brows raised.

"Here I'd been thanking the Caids that spring was early and mild this year, but if your figures are correct, we won't have enough ice in the cellars to keep the stored meat from thawing."

"Of course my figures are correct." Valaika poured a glass of wine for herself. "The question is, should we let it thaw, and salt what we can to send to Kedneara in place of the soldiers we don't have? Or should we cook it all, give the Valley a feast, and tell Kedneara's Steward of War that we have nothing to give?"

Sylria twisted a lock of hair around her finger as she considered. "That would work. So long as the Blue Mage doesn't take occasion to look in this direction. He has uncanny ways of finding things out."

"He's no reason to look this way," Valaika said.

"True." Sylria put the sheet of parchment down. "Don't we have stewards for this work?"

"They're out bringing me more information."

Which Sylria well knew, Valaika thought, eyeing her consort with a frown. Valaika liked to go her own way in more than just the crests they wore on their clothing. Here in Jarlkevo she'd insisted on breaking that ridiculous custom that had spread from the Letanian Peninsula which kept the Steward of Keys confined to the House proper for life, and the Steward of Walls confined within the fortified walls of the town. Hard enough to do in a large House such as was found in the capital. Barbarous to impose here, where winter weather was often bad enough, for long enough, to set the occupants of a House gritting their teeth at each other.

Valaika tapped her lower lip with the feathery end of her pen. "Is everything all right, Syl? I know you didn't come here to go over the accounts with me."

Sylria roused herself from whatever thoughts had put that frown on her face and smiled. "There's a troupe of players come to town," she said. "A small one, but new faces, and maybe new songs, who knows? Janek would love it, and he deserves a treat after the hard work he's put in this winter. Or is a moon not considered mourning enough?" she added, when Val didn't speak.

Valaika leaned back, her elbows on the arms of her chair, and rested her folded hands on her belt buckle. "I hadn't even seen Edmir for six—no, perhaps it's seven years," she finally said. "It would have been at his father's burial ceremonies. Janek was only five, I think, wasn't he? And formal mourning doesn't forbid theater, in any case. Where are these players?"

"Their caravan's in the courtyard of the Hostel Plazan. The players themselves are walking through town singing for business."

"What odds do you give me they won't know any Hellish songs?"

"Is that any reason to go without entertainment?"

Valaika grinned. "Go ahead, invite them up here and send word around the town that as many as can fit into the courtyard will be welcome. Let Janek know he'll be allowed to stay up."

"So this is Jarlkevo?" Zania said the next afternoon, as they stepped out into the street from the courtyard of Hostel Plazan. They'd changed into their brightest clothing, the better to catch the eyes of their potential audience. Parno walked ahead with his pipes, playing familiar country dances, interwoven with the songs children use in their games. Already they were being followed by a few children, escaped from their lessons and chores, and even one or two idling adults.

A familiar series of notes made Dhulyn glance ahead at Parno. Since they had been in Imrion last year he had added that particular children's rhyming song to his store of music, embellishing it as he did everything that touched his ear.

"Technically, House Jarlkevo is the whole of the territory, and we've been in it since the day after we left Luk."

"And 'House' is also the title of the person to whom the land belongs," Edmir added from Zania's other side.

"And who belongs to the land, in the old way of thinking," Dhulyn said. "The House *is* the House. The territory is the person, and the person the territory. Now Jarlkevo House, on the other hand, is the residence of House Jarlkevo. The Jarlkevoso, she'd be called in Imrion, though I don't know whether that's the practice here."

"How do you know all these things," Edmir said.

Dhulyn tapped her temple, where the wig hid her Mercenary badge. "It's our business to know these things." She turned to call out a greeting, blowing a kiss to a smith looking up from his forge, a horseshoe glowing brightly in his tongs. "The town looks prosperous enough, though it's larger than I would have expected in a newly created House."

"It used to be a Holding of the Royal Family," Edmir said. "A performance, good sir," he called out at an elderly man who had paused to watch them and their trail of children. "At dusk in the courtyard of the Hostel Plazan."

"Is there good hunting in the area," Dhulyn asked.

"According to my mother, Jarlkevo was used as a summer Court, and I do vaguely remember coming here as a child—at least I think it was here—before it was made into a High Noble House, and given to my Aunt Valaika."

Dhulyn nodded.

"Yes, madam, yes, good sir, a performance this very night, a small taste only of what we can do, to whet your appetites against the morrow." Zania had stepped ahead of them, holding out her arms and pirouetting down the narrow street.

"Which explains the size of the town," Dhulyn said, as she smiled and blew a kiss at a young man with a wheel of cheese on his shoulder. "Good hunting or not," she continued as Edmir raised his eyebrows at her, "this town is too large for a place visited for just a few weeks out of the year. But as a summer retreat, and now the seat of a Noble House, and at that of the late consort's sister, a woman who is still the niece of the Tarkin of Hellik—or do they call him King there?" Dhulyn shrugged. "In any case. With your Aunt Valaika in permanent residence here as House Jarlkevo, the town had reason to grow."

Just at that moment a young woman in the long vest of a House servant—orange and black with a narrow dark blue band around the bottom edge—stopped Parno where he was playing several spans ahead of them. He listened to what the servant had to say, and turned toward them, a smile on his face.

"We're invited to the House this evening, isn't that lucky?"

"And as much of the town as can make it," the messenger said, loud enough for the townspeople around them to hear.

Dhulyn glanced at Edmir, but other than a slight tightening of his lips, there was no reaction to the invitation at all. *The boy's learning*, she thought. She nodded to Zania.

"Return our most grateful acknowledgment and respectful greetings to House Jarlkevo. We will await her summons after the midday meal."

"We should do *The Soldier King*," Dhulyn said. She turned to Zania. "If you think I'm ready to perform it."

Parno smiled. A capable expert in her own field, Dhulyn had no difficulty bowing to the expertise of another, even if that other was so much younger than herself. They had set up their small table in the hostel's courtyard and were eating a light meal of rabbit stew and dried apples in preparation for the message that would summon them to the House.

"You're ready, though a week ago I wouldn't have believed it possible. That's not what makes me hesitate," Zania said. "It's a long play, and fairly serious . . ."

"The Jarlkevoso would be in mourning, though, wouldn't she?" Dhulyn turned to Edmir. Parno thought the boy looked paler than usual, and he'd been quiet and more thoughtful since the talk they'd had in Luk. Judging by the way he was getting through his bowl of stew, however, his appetite was fine. Edmir nodded in answer to Dhulyn's query, but his eyes remained hooded.

"She'd be expected to mourn six moons at least, though she's not known for her conservative approach to social things," he said. He looked up. "Theater's allowed during mourning, but something serious *would* be more suitable."

Parno smiled at the boy's querying tone. Edmir wanted to see his play performed, but he didn't want to seem to be suggesting it.

"Listen." Dhulyn leaned forward and tapped the tabletop with the end of her spoon. "This may be our only chance to perform it—certainly Edmir's only chance to perform in it himself. After tonight, he will be the prince again, and he will have walked on the stage for the last time."

Edmir's hand stopped halfway to his mouth, the piece of bread he'd been using to sop up the stew's gravy dripping on the table until Zania's nudge brought him back to himself. He smiled guiltily and wiped up the mess with the cloth that had been used as a potholder when the dish was brought out to them. Parno glanced at Dhulyn and saw that she, too, was watching Edmir. So, he wasn't the only one who thought the boy didn't seem as happy as he should be, considering they were taking the first step along the road that would restore him to his birthright.

"There's another consideration," Parno said, and waited until they were all looking at him. "The play's about a king who comes home from the wars after everyone believes him dead, correct? No one recognizes him, and he has to trick his way into his own home before he can reveal himself to his family?" Zania was nodding, and Dhulyn smiling. "Under the circumstances, what better play *could* we put on?"

⬱

Jarlkevo House was an old-fashioned square-towered fortress, standing at the highest point of land within the walled town. What had once been a lonely crag of rock with strategic command of an entire valley was now a steep hillside lined with narrow streets and the openings of houses and buildings that appeared to be hanging from the face of the rock itself. Clearly, space was at a premium.

"I've seen larger courtyards at some country inns," Edmir whispered to Parno, as the Mercenary stopped to try the tautness of the rope securing the screen in front of them.

"You'll not find the rooms within to be very spacious either, I'd wager," Parno agreed as he turned away to check the next rope.

Edmir looked out from behind the screens he, Parno, and Dhulyn had earlier set up across the short end of the courtyard. There were a great many more people out there than the murmuring voices and sounds of movement had led him to expect. A raised platform had been set up perhaps halfway between their stage and the far end of the courtyard. This platform had seats for several people—and children had already taken up places on the front edge, following a bold brown-haired child in deep blue—but there were two padded chairs covered with a canopy which were obviously intended for his aunt and her consort Sylria.

Edmir frowned. He remembered their son, his cousin Janek, as a rather sickly child, coughing and pale, though letters from his aunt had reported the boy much improved in the last few years. Apparently, however, he was not improved enough to attend this evening's performance since there was no chair of state put out for him. Too bad, Edmir thought, remembering the boy's trusting brown eyes as he'd stood next to Edmir at his father Karyli's burial ceremonies. Later, in his mother the queen's private sitting room, they had played a game of tiles while the grown-ups talked. He'd taught Janek and Kera both to play the Sparrow game. He hoped the boy was all right. Janek was his only cousin, and besides Kera, the only living relative of his own generation.

Edmir's stomach clenched suddenly, and he tasted acid in the back of his throat. He was beginning to regret having eaten anything at all; even the half bowl of stew and few mouthfuls of dried apples he'd managed to wash down with watered cider felt like lumps of stone in his belly. Dancing in public was easy, even speaking—he'd done as much before his parents and their Noble Houses since he was a child, to say nothing of functioning as his mother the queen's representative. And he'd thought the half dozen parts he'd done in the last moon or so had accustomed him to acting and the stage. Tonight felt entirely different. This was *his* play, these were *his* lines, *his* words. Even before the battle in the Limona Valley his stomach hadn't felt this queasy. Soon he'd have to step out to give the Prologue—Dhulyn had insisted he should do it—but right now he savored the comfort and safety he felt behind the scenes.

The screens themselves were canvas stretched over light frames of wood, painted on both sides to make the most use of them. Like much of the troupe's properties and costumes, the scenery was normally laid flat on top of the caravan, covered over in heavier canvas against the weather. These particular screens were painted to look like a garden or perhaps a wood on the side currently facing the audience, and like a stone wall on this side. The play opened with the Soldier King coming through the forest where he had hunted as a young man, and the meeting with the old huntsman who would be the only character who recognized him right away. When they were ready, he and Parno would swing the screens around and they would end the play in front of the painted stone walls that represented the castle. Zania, in her costume as the old huntsman, came up on his left side; he grinned at her, glad of the distraction.

"There were more of these when I was a child," she said, running her fingers lightly along the crosspiece of the screen of scenery. "I remember one in particular that was a lady's private bedchamber, with tapestries painted on the walls. I remember my mother standing in front of it. I don't know who has it now." Her voice was wistful.

"This was before the troupe spilt up to look for Avylos?"

She nodded, and then pointed with her chin in the direction of the unseen audience. "Is *she* out there? The House?" On the Mercenary's orders, they'd all been careful to refer to Edmir's aunt by her title only, in case anyone should overhear them, and wonder at their use of her personal name.

"I thought I saw her walking into one of the doorways on the far side of the courtyard, but I'm not sure." He scratched at the pointed chin beard that Zania had carefully glued to his face for his appearance as the Prologue. That, along with the long formal robe he was wearing, was meant to make him unrecognizable to anyone who may have seen him in the Queen's Court. Or on the funeral coins that were already circulating.

So far, at least, it seemed to be working.

Parno rejoined them and put his hand on Edmir's shoulder, giving him a little shake.

"Ready? The House and her consort have just come in and taken their seats."

Edmir, clenching his teeth, shot another quick glance at the audience and nodded. Parno patted him on the shoulder, and Zania squeezed his arm. They each took careful hold of the handles on the screens in front of them and pulled them aside just enough to give Edmir an entrance.

He swallowed again and stepped through. The crowd noticed him and hushed.

"Long ago, and far off," he began. "Among the lands of the Great King . . ."

Valaika leaned forward, chin on hand, elbow on knee, when the Prologue stepped out from behind the screens. He was a tall young man with sun-streaked curly brown hair, wearing a short pointed beard slightly darker in shade. He was richly dressed, like a courtier at a formal audience, and, unexpectedly, his accent was Tegriani. There were not so very many players in Tegrian, and Valaika thought she knew them all. And she was certain that Sylria had said these came from elsewhere.

But the play was beginning now, and she turned her attention to the action.

When she saw the Prologue again, in the second act, it was as one of the suitors of the widowed queen. He wore the same formal tunic, though now he was beardless, and his hair had been brushed straight back from his face, revealing his jeweled earrings. He walked with the kind of swagger that made Valaika hope that, at the very least, this character would not end up winning the queen's hand. He was making the queen—a striking woman indeed with eyes like gray pools in her white face—a very pretty speech, which somehow had an iron threat in the back of it.

"Mother." Janek had come up from where he sat in the front with his friends to whisper in her ear.

"Not just now, my heart, if you please. It's rude to speak during a performance."

"But, Mother, that's Edmir."

"What?" The boy was addled. "Janek, mind your tongue. That can't be. Edmir is—"

"Mother, please. Look at him carefully."

Janek was so insistent, so serious, that Valaika swallowed the reprimand that was rising to her lips and looked back at the stage.

A maidservant—Valaika swore she'd seen her earlier as the aged huntsman—had come on stage to offer the queen and her suitor refreshment in the form of goblets of wine. The queen took her goblet, but the suitor waved his away with a lifted shoulder and a short chopping movement of his hand.

Valaika sat up so abruptly that she banged her elbow on the arm of her chair. She'd seen that movement before. That *exact* movement. The question was, where had this actor seen it?

"See! See!"

"Hush, Janek."

Sylria laid a hand on her knee. "What is it?"

Valaika leaned over so as to whisper in Sylria's ear. "We must invite them to stay after the play. Ask them for music, anything."

Sylria frowned, shrugging her right shoulder in question, but Valaika shook her head and indicated the stage. No point in ruining the show for the rest.

And it was a testament to the play itself, and how well it was acted, that Valaika didn't remember her request until she was standing with the rest of the audience at the end of the play, clapping and shouting.

Fifteen

"WHERE ARE YOUR PIPES?" Dhulyn felt along the edges of her wig. She'd sweated so much under the torches kindled for the final scene—but it seemed the glue still held. She knew she should be pleased at this summons to meet with the Jarl-kevoso and her family. They had been wondering how to get a private audience with the woman since they'd received their invitation to play in the courtyard, but this felt a little too pat, a little too easy. It seemed that since picking Edmir up out of the battlefield, everything that should have gone easily, hadn't. Dhulyn did not think of herself as a superstitious type—like all Red Horsemen, she believed that humans made their own luck, since the gods of Sun, Moon, and Stars had larger things to occupy them—but the fact remained that when it looked as though some god was helping you, that was the time to be most wary.

"Relax," Parno addressed her feelings rather than her question. "What's the worst that can happen?"

She stopped tightening the ribbon laces in her bodice and looked at him. "Oh, very funny."

He put his hand around her wrist, the palm warm and callused against her skin. "Seriously, what is the worst that can happen?"

"We die separately."

His hand tightened. "We are always together," he reminded her. "In Battle."

"Or in Death." And she felt better.

As they followed the two pages who served as their escort through the narrow halls and steep staircases of the House, Dhulyn took automatic note of bottlenecks and potential escape routes. The prince was silent, pale and tense, as she would have expected. For him the next few hours—even the next few minutes, could mean everything. Zania walked beside him whenever she could, at one point reaching over and straightening the cuff of his sleeve. Dhulyn smiled and looked away.

It wasn't long before the pages were ushering them up a short circular stone stair on the western side of the fortress, through a thick wooden door padded with blue leather and into what was clearly the family's private chamber. In addition to the door from the stairway, there were three windows with shutters in the wall opposite, and a smaller, lighter door to the left, in the far wall of the rectangular room. Dhulyn saw no fireplace, though an unlit brazier stood off to one side of the chairs gathered in the center of the room. Obviously the family's summer sitting room, Dhulyn thought, and even now there was a chill in the air that made her glad of the thick rugs still on the floor.

There were three people waiting for them, Dhulyn saw with interest as she made her formal bow from the doorway. Their hostesses were seated with their backs to the windows in large chairs upholstered on arms and seats with brocaded cloth. But beside them, clinging to the arm of Valaika's chair and fidgeting with excitement, stood a slim young boy who had seen his birth moon perhaps ten times. This brown-haired, ruddy youngster would be the son and heir, she thought, Edmir's cousin Janek. There was a smudge of dirt on the boy's cheek, which told Dhulyn much that she liked about his parents. All three were dressed in loose trousers, long-sleeved tunics, and half boots, though there was no mistaking which one was the House, Edmir's Aunt Valaika. She had the same strong features, though her nose was considerably more prominent. Her hair was much fairer than Dhulyn would have expected, with silver threads among the gold, her eyes a piercing blue, and her skin a golden brown not unlike Parno's natural coloring. The consort, Sylria Jarlkevo, was taller, slimmer, with chestnut hair and ruddy skin. Valaika Jarlkevoso had a sword within reach of her hand; both her consort and her son carried only the knives at their belts.

"Here they are, my House," the page said when they were all in the room.

"Thank you, Rudian. Welcome, Troupe Tzadeyeu. Before you sit down," Valaika said, with a smile for her guests, "let me present my consort, Sylria, and our son, Janek Jarlkevo. He's been dying to meet you since he heard there were players in the town." The Jarlkevoso's voice was very rough and low, with a Hellish accent buried deep beneath a few decades of living in Tegrian. So deep, Dhulyn thought, that perhaps she wouldn't have noticed it if she hadn't known the woman was Hellish.

"And threatening to run off with you when you go," the consort said. *There* was the educated Tegrian accent Dhulyn was used to hearing from Edmir.

"We never take people from their homes, young man, until they've reached the age to be apprenticed," Parno said with a smile as they all bowed their heads in acknowledgment of the introduction.

"Please, seat yourselves."

Drawn up to face the two seated women was one backless armed chair with a cushion on the seat, and next to it a small wooden bench with a thin pad made of embroidered cloth. Dhulyn lengthened her stride slightly, to put herself in front, and took the chair for herself, seeing out of the corner of her eye that Parno had claimed the far end of the bench, leaving Edmir and Zania between them. Dhulyn did not have a sword with her—there would have been no manner of way to explain that—but she was more than armed enough, she thought, to deal with either or both of these women, and that included the remaining page, who was no doubt doubling as a guard.

There were no refreshments on the table beyond a jug of water and a single clay cup. None of the cakes or pastries that Dhulyn would have expected, if they had really been invited to sing. She sat forward in her chair, adjusting her center of gravity to make it easier to lunge forward. She'd take the consort, she thought, and leave Valaika Jarlkevoso for Parno.

"We did not know whether you took refreshment after performing," the House said. "May we send to the kitchen?"

"Something light, House Jarlkevo, would suit us perfectly."

Dhulyn suppressed a smile. She'd heard that courtly tone from Parno before. These were manners he'd learned from his own parents, in his own House.

The House glanced up at the page who stood to one side of the door.

"Rudian, fetch ganje for our guests, and jeresh, if you please," she said. "And some of Cook's cheese pastries, and apple tarts." She waited for the door to close behind the page and, turning to Parno, spoke in an entirely different tone. "Would you be kind enough to check that Rudian has actually gone? Occasionally he oversteps."

Parno glanced at Dhulyn, his right eyebrow raised. She gave him the tiniest of nods, and he rose, and went to the door to listen.

"All clear," he said, remaining by the door. "He's gone."

Suddenly the boy Janek shot forward, holding out his hands to Edmir.

"Edmir! It *is* you."

Dhulyn was on her feet, but Sylria had caught hold of the boy's tunic and was hauling him backward. Edmir had also stood, his hands half raised, a look of luminous joy on his face.

That's how afraid he was, Dhulyn thought.

"Just a moment everyone. Janek, stand back, please." Valaika Jarlkevoso narrowed her eyes and leaned forward. "Tell me, young man," she said. "Where did you learn that gesture of shrugging off the servant?" And she made it, the half shrug, half wave that Dhulyn had seen Edmir make a dozen times.

Edmir licked his lips. "Aunt Valaika, I *am* Edmir."

The taller, younger Sylria lifted one hand to her mouth. Valaika Jarlkevoso, sister to the late consort, cousin to the Tarkin of Hellik, moved not one muscle, except to blink, slowly, like an owl. Dhulyn almost smiled. She could like this woman, she could like her very much.

"You see? I told you!" Janek strained against Sylria's hold on his arm.

Finally Valaika unclasped her hands and placed them on the arms of her chair.

"Turn around," she said to Edmir. "Take off your shirt. Show me your back."

Edmir licked his lips again, and turned.

There was no shock, no disbelief, or anger or even hope on the older woman's face. Just a blank and careful mask.

They had all changed out of their stage costumes before answering the summons of the House, and Edmir was dressed simply in woolen trousers, a linen shirt with three-quarter-length sleeves, and a leather vest laced up the front. Standing, he loosened the lacing of the vest and pulled it off over his head. The linen shirt he merely took by the lower edge and lifted as he turned to present his back to his aunt.

"Come a little closer to me, you are out of the light there."

Edmir obliged by taking two short steps back.

As Dhulyn watched, the older woman narrowed her eyes, focusing on the right side of Edmir's back. After a long moment she made a noise in her throat, and, lifting her right hand, traced her finger in a short line just below Edmir's right shoulder blade.

"Embrace your cousin, Janek. Embrace the Lord Prince Edmir of Tegrian."

Now the boy launched himself forward, almost pushing Edmir off his feet with the force of his hug. Edmir laughed, taking his young cousin by the shoulders and holding him a little farther away.

"Let me see you, Janek. However did you know it was me? I wouldn't have known you, you're so much taller." There was great pleasure in Edmir's voice.

"We thought we had disguised him very well," Parno said, still at his post by the door.

"His face is the same," the boy said, as the adults exchanged glances. "His face hasn't changed at all."

"Valaika?" Sylria's voice was a soft croak. The consort was clearly of two minds about what was going on in her sitting room.

"Do you see this scar, my love?" Valaika's voice was tight, and yet there was some triumph in it. She gestured Edmir forward and had him pull up his shirt again. Dhulyn's feet twitched and she had to hold herself back from getting up and looking for herself.

"I know this scar, know it well. And so I should, seeing as I'm the one who put it there. And I'm the one who sewed it up and swore you to secrecy, didn't I?"

"You thought my mother the queen wouldn't approve of your cutting me during fencing practice," Edmir said, smiling.

"And I was right, she didn't approve. How did she find out?" The question was clearly intended as a test, but the tone made it clear that Valaika was already satisfied.

"Kera told her, not knowing it was supposed to be a secret. But it had almost healed by then, you'd taken the stitches out, so we didn't get into too much trouble."

"Speak for yourself, boy, I was almost exiled."

Sylria held up her hands. "Stop. Janek, Valaika, stop a moment. Do you mean to tell me that *this* is *Edmir?* Your nephew Edmir who is de-clared dead?"

"Edmir that we're all in mourning for, yes." Valaika stood. "Edmir." She lifted her arms, hesitantly, as any aunt might do, Dhulyn thought, when confronted with a nephew she had not seen in years. As if the boy might have grown too big for an embrace.

But no. Edmir immediately stepped forward into his aunt's arms. The two clung closely together, and Dhulyn thought she saw Edmir's shoulders shake. Only at that moment did she understand how afraid Edmir must have been, afraid of the possibility that his aunt, too, might no longer know him.

Now Sylria stood also, but only to lower herself to one knee. To her this was no mere nephew, but the Lord Prince of Tegrian.

"You're so much like your father . . ." Valaika's voice faded. "But what did you do to your hair, you miserable brat." Valaika put her fists on her hips. The tension broke. Both aunt and nephew began to laugh, Edmir brushing at his eyes with the back of his hand.

Out of the corner of her eye Dhulyn saw Zania watching everyone closely, as if memorizing what they did, and how they looked when they did it. *Actors*, Dhulyn thought.

"Stand up, Consort Sylria," Parno said from the door. "The ser-vants return. And you do not kneel to players."

"But Val . . ." The woman was already rising to her feet as she spoke.

"In a moment, Syl, they'll have their reasons." The House turned to Dhulyn, "which I'm sure they'll tell us."

As Parno walked back to his seat, filling the air bag of his pipes as he came, Edmir and the Jarlkevo women sat down. Zania hopped to her feet and took up a position to one side of the company, where she would be seen immediately by anyone coming in the door. With a nod to Dhulyn, Zania started singing the "Spring Enchantress," beginning in the middle of a verse, and gesturing to Dhulyn to clap. When the servants entered a few moments later, one carrying a large tray, they were just reaching the rousing finish of the song, and Valaika was clap-ping along in counterpoint to Dhulyn.

"But do you know any Hellish music?" Valaika said, once Zania had taken her bows and sat down again.

"Why do you suppose I've brought my pipes, House Jarlkevo," Parno said. "It's the best accompaniment for Hellish songs."

"I'm not so sure I agree," Valaika said, waving the servants forward. "But take some refreshment first, and then show me."

The second servant fetched another low table from under the middle window and set it between the seats. From the tray they took a jug of ganje, still steaming from the kitchen fire, and a small stone bottle well-corked, two cups made from the rare and expensive Tenezian glass, and four ceramic mugs. When all had been set out on the table, the servants stood back.

"I thank you, and send my compliments to the kitchen. Hellish music is not to everyone's taste, I know," Valaika said. "So you have my leave to be elsewhere." She laughed at the evident disappointment on their faces. "Go on now, I hope to persuade the troupe to favor us with an evening of music, perhaps a dance—" she snapped her fingers. "In fact, prepare chambers for them—you'll stay the night at least—the small suite in the north wing."

"But House Jarlkevo, our caravan—"

Valaika raised her hand. "Can be moved here in the morning. No, I won't hear it. I'll keep you until I've heard every Hellish song you know, and taught you a few of mine."

"Perhaps Janek . . ." began Sylria.

"Sylria, no!" said the boy.

"If you're to stay, young man, it must be quietly," Valaika said. "The first sign of yawns or sleepiness and you're off to bed."

The consort made room for their son on her own chair. It occurred to Dhulyn that she herself must be occupying the boy's usual seat.

The servants grinned and bowed, leaving easily enough now. Valaika was by no means the first Noble House Dhulyn had met, but she was the first to speak to her servants in this free and easy manner. Was it all the Hellish who were like this, or was it just Valaika herself? If the latter, it was easy to see why she had left her sister-in-law's court. Queen Kedneara had the reputation of being a tyrant when it came to protocol. Among other things.

When the door had closed once again behind the servants, Valaika turned back to her nephew.

"Not the best rooms, I'm afraid, Lord Prince, but if you must keep up this masquerade, anything else would give you away. I can't give you better than I would normally give to traveling players."

Parno got back to his feet. "I'll play as softly as I can," he said, as he headed to the door."

"Oh, come now," Valaika said, her brow furrowed. "We have more important things to do than indulge my taste for the music of my homeland."

"Certainly," Parno said. "But don't think for a moment that the servants have gone far, or that others won't be along shortly—curiosity if nothing else will bring them. Best they hear music coming from this room. At least for now."

Valaika pushed her hands through her graying hair and took the glass of steaming ganje her consort was holding out for her. "Forgive me," she said. "I am not thinking clearly." She paused as Parno took up his position at the door and began to play softly, having removed the drones from the pipes.

"It's not every evening the nephew I thought was dead is returned to me alive," Valaika continued under the cover of the music. She turned to Edmir. "But now, how is it we were told you were dead? How did you escape from the Mercenary Brothers?"

Edmir pressed his lips together, wagging his head from side to side. "It isn't just one thing they've lied about, Aunt, it's everything." He looked at Dhulyn. "Shall I . . . ?"

"Allow me," Dhulyn said. For her role as the queen in Edmir's play, Dhulyn had worn the long blonde wig that had been made from Zania's mother's hair. She pushed her fingers under the lower edge, at the back of her neck where the wig had not been glued, and began to loosen and dislodge the glued edges above her ears. In a moment, the wig was free and she pulled it carefully off, revealing her shaven scalp, and, what was more to the moment, the blue-and-green tattoo of her Mercenary badge.

"Caids bless us," Sylria whispered.

"I am Dhulyn Wolfshead, called the Scholar," she said. "Schooled by Dorian the Black. There by the door is my Partner, Parno Lionsmane, called the Chanter, for reasons which are obvious. Schooled by Nerysa Warhammer."

"Was *nothing* we were told the truth, then?" Valaika's words were bitten off, and she looked from Dhulyn to Parno and back again as if she would demand answers.

"My turn," Edmir said. Dhulyn nodded, giving him a stage flourish with her hand that Zania had taught her. This was not a report being made to a Senior Brother, and over the last moon Edmir had shown himself more than skilled at telling a tale. She settled back in her chair, rubbing off the residue of the glue that still clung to her temples and forehead before she replaced the wig.

With the accompaniment of the softly playing music, Edmir began. "We lost the battle at Limona."

Parno had run out of Hellish tunes and was enjoying a cup of jeresh by the time Edmir finished telling the tale of the last moon's adventures. There had been no chance of Janek falling asleep, the boy had been spellbound by his cousin's adventures. Dhulyn had to admit, Edmir had left nothing pertinent out, though he'd glossed over the part involving the Muse Stone, and had made things sound far more interesting than they had seemed at the time.

Valaika had remained quiet throughout the narrative, the narrowing of her eyes and clenching of her jaw her only reactions to what she was hearing. Sylria had exclaimed once or twice, notably at the point where Tzanek, Lord of Probic, had not recognized Edmir.

"I couldn't think of anywhere else to go," Edmir said, as he reached the end of the story. "And so I came to you."

Valaika pounded the arm of her chair with her closed fist. "And you say this is Avylos?" she questioned, through gritted teeth.

"Who else?" Dhulyn said. "A magic that has never been known to fail, fails the only time the Lord Prince calls upon it? Nisveans refuse to release him, when letting us return him would achieve the same results as returning him themselves? An old childhood friend genuinely fails to recognize him? The whole country knows he's dead within days—when does news travel that quickly? If this is not the Blue Mage, what is it?"

"And let's not forget Probic," Parno said.

A short silence fell over the room, even Janek holding perfectly still, though his eyes were alive and round with excitement.

"The queen . . ." Sylria looked around. "I may be prejudiced, but surely she wouldn't countenance this strike against one of her own children."

"If she needed an excuse to invade Nisvea . . ." Edmir fell silent, his eyes bleak.

"Nonsense. Any excuse would do for that. I don't like the woman, never have, but nothing will persuade me that she would put one of her children in harm's way, let alone connive at his murder."

Dhulyn was looking at Edmir and from the expression on his face, his aunt's words did not convince him.

Evidently, Valaika saw it, too. "I know what you are thinking, Nephew. Your mother the queen is a self-absorbed, arrogant woman, the more so since your father is no longer here to laugh her out of her natural tendencies. But you forget that she sees you and your sister as part of herself. Less than herself, without doubt—she would never put your needs before her own—but you would still come before anyone else in the world. Anyone."

"Even if we found an ally in the queen—and there's no way to know that she hasn't been magicked in the same way old Tzanek was in Probic . . ." Parno began.

"She would be a most volatile ally at the best of times—to be handled carefully. She'd find it difficult to believe that Avylos either could or would do anything against her, but once convinced, she would confront him in a rage, without fear or subtlety, and . . ."

"And that might not be the best way to confront the person who destroyed Probic," Dhulyn said.

"Better we should approach him ourselves," Parno said.

"How, precisely, are we to do that?"

Zania leaned forward eagerly, but hesitated as Dhulyn raised her hand, and murmured, "Pasillon."

"We have reason to believe," she said, giving Zania a small smile, "that the Mage's magic is not a natural part of him, like the Mark of a Finder or a Healer. Rather it has an outside source, and we believe we know what that source is. If we can remove it, we remove his power."

Valaika looked at each of their faces in turn. "And you have a plan for this?"

"You can get us into the Royal House, can you not?"

Zania shivered suddenly, and hugged herself, cupping her elbows in her hands.

"I'll light the brazier," Sylria said, getting to her feet.

"Wait." Parno put out his hand. "It's late already, and it's not likely that you'd sit up so long with players you've given houseroom to. Someone will wonder why we've not been dismissed."

"Oh, but surely there's no need to keep up your disguise now?" Sylria said.

"Better cautious than cursing," Dhulyn said. "Can we be certain of everyone in the House? Or the town for that matter? The return of a dead prince is too good a tale for anyone to keep to themselves."

"They're right, Syl. And this is for you, too, Janek. Nothing of what you've heard here tonight can be spoken of—it might very well kill your cousin."

"I was the only one who knew him," the boy replied. "And I told no one but you."

Dhulyn smiled, finding herself well satisfied with the boy's answer. From Valaika's nod, it seemed his mother was as well.

"Come," Valaika got to her feet. "I'll show you to your rooms—I often do so," she said, answering their protests. "No one will think it strange."

"Let's see this famous scar, Edmir."

The rooms they'd been given consisted of two tiny bedchambers which shared a small sitting room, furnished with three short benches, a single armed chair, and a low table on which the servants had placed a stone lamp now almost out of oil, and a triple-branched candelabra with the candles left unlit. Late as it was, they all drifted back into the sitting room after checking their rooms. At Dhulyn's words Zania turned from her inspection of the stars outside the window. Parno had taken the large chair and Dhulyn perched on the arm.

Edmir obeyed her request by stripping off his shirt and presenting his back. Dhulyn took up and lit one of the candles and held it above the prince's shoulder.

"Careful you don't burn him," Parno said.

"Teach your grandmother," Dhulyn answered. She found the scar quite easily. It was, as Valaika had said, a shallow cut made with the edge of an almost dull blade. She could easily imagine the stroke that caused it, an accident pure and simple. She saw another discolored mark lower still, below the kidney, and crouched on her heels to examine it more closely.

"Is that another scar?" Zania peered over Dhulyn's shoulder.

Dhulyn shook her head. The mark was too dark to be a scar, and too well-shaped. "A tattoo perhaps," she said.

"I don't have any tattoos." Edmir tried to twist around to see the thing everyone else was looking at.

"There's a mirror in my side bag," Zania said. "Let me fetch it."

The mirror was brought, and held up at the right angle to permit Edmir to see what everyone else could see, a dull reddish mark like an oval with a smudge in the center of it.

"You're not holding it right," Edmir said. "I still can't see it."

"We are holding it right," Dhulyn said. She caught Parno's eye and summoned him with a jerk of her head.

"Why can't I see it then?"

"It doesn't show in the mirror, lad. It casts no reflection." Parno looked over Dhulyn's head, first at Edmir's back, then at the mirror.

Dhulyn stepped back, her hand rising to her throat, her fingers seeking out a spot on her breastbone, just below the points of her collarbones. "It's not a scar," she said. "It's a . . ." She hesitated, groping for the right word. "It's a ghost eye."

"A type of birthmark?" Zania said.

"I don't have any birthmarks." Edmir jerked down his shirt and turned to face them, his brows drawn down in a sharp vee. "And that wouldn't explain why the thing doesn't show up in a mirror." He reached behind as if to rub the spot and then lowered his hand, thinking better of it. "And how is it you know about them?"

"I had one myself, as a child." Again, Dhulyn touched the spot on her breastbone where the ghost eye had been. "Eventually it wore off."

Zania gasped. "A slaver's mark? But how did Edmir get one? The Nisveans—"

"It was not a slaver's mark, no," Dhulyn said. "I had it before the slavers took me. I had it . . ." she took a deep breath. "Among my people—among the Red Horsemen," Dhulyn corrected. "Children bore these sigils. So we could not be lost." She frowned, concentrating on a wisp of memory that hovered just out of her grasp. Grasp. A memory that involved a rough, callused hand grasping her by the shoulder. "My father used it." She looked up. "It was for my father to find me."

"Your *father?* Was your father a Finder, then?" Parno said.

Dhulyn shook her head, frowning. "You know the Mark doesn't work like this. Finders Find. They don't need to draw signs on things, they just Find. Use a tool, maybe, like a bowl of water, to focus . . . But *this* sigil, the ghost eye, *was* for my father to use. I don't think there were Finders among us, it was . . ."

"We'd better find some way to get this off," Parno said. He looked around at them. "If it's some kind of Outlander magic, and it can be used to find people—if your father used one to find you, than someone can use it to find Edmir."

"I'll wager my second-best sword we know who the someone is," Dhulyn said, the image of Edmir in the pool clear in her mind.

Sixteen

EARLY AS IT WAS WHEN Dhulyn returned from accompanying Valaika's grooms to the Hostel Plazan—knowing that Bloodbone and Warhammer would not allow someone else to harness them—when she returned with the caravan to Jarlkevo House she found the Jarlkevoso already up, dressed for hawking, and with Parno at the breakfast table.

"I've asked that hunting birds be brought out for us," Valaika Jarlkevoso said. "We won't have a quiet moment to talk once the day starts. There's not a room, including my own study, that someone might not walk into. If we're to talk privately without causing remark, we'll have to do it on horseback."

"Nothing would suit me better," Dhulyn said. A morning in the saddle, with well-trained birds, would make a nice change from walking across a stage pretending to be someone else. Parno could do most of the talking—he was good with Noble Houses. "Are the youngsters up and ready?"

Valaika considered this a moment while she chewed. "Leave them here with Sylria," she said after she'd swallowed. "There were Mercenary Brothers at my cousin's court when I was a girl, and I still remember how he relied upon them. Edmir is a grand boy, but I'd rather hear your assessment of events than his."

Back in their rooms, Zania seemed oddly indifferent to their plans, merely shrugging and agreeing with a small smile. Edmir would have liked to go hawking, but saw the sense of his and Zania's staying behind. He closed the journal he'd been writing in and reached for the scrolls of *The Soldier King*. "I can work on that part in act four that feels so flat," he said, eyes already looking into the middle distance.

Dhulyn rolled her eyes to the heavens. His color was better than it had been the day before, and there were fewer lines of worry in his face, but otherwise Edmir was taking his return to his family very quietly. Shaking her head, she changed into her own boots and leggings, topped them with one of Parno's smaller tunics and joined Valaika in the courtyard.

"First, let me tell you now what I did not wish to say in front of Edmir," Valaika said, once they were well out into the fields south of the town. The hawk on her wrist bobbed as she turned in her saddle to speak over her shoulder. "It would take a great deal to make Kedneara turn on Avylos. She will not believe that the man does not love her. And she will not believe that he has killed Edmir, or ordered him killed—else she'd have to admit that she herself made a grave error in judgment. An impossibility in her mind. While she would move the heavens and the earth to keep her children safe, she will do little to revenge them once they are dead, if it means admitting any such unwelcome truths."

"Do you mean she will *not* invade Nisvea?"

Valaika waved that away with her free hand. "She was planning to do that anyway. Though after Probic, does anyone really think an invasion necessary? Say, rather, she would not change a plan she already had in mind. She has no sentiment. Once the child is dead, he's dead. Look at how quickly she married Avylos, and she genuinely loved my brother, insofar as she is able to love anyone. When the children were small, and Karyli still alive, then Kedneara was at her best. Since then . . . she has been queen, with no one to remind her she is also a woman and a mother, for a *very* long time. Any plan we make that includes her must take this into account."

Dhulyn exchanged a glance with her Partner. They had spent two seasons in the Great King's Court, far to the west. Ruthlessness on the part of a country's ruler was something with which they were well familiar.

"This source of Avylos' power, what can you tell me of it?" Valaika said.

They had two beaters with them, but, on foot and positioned well away from the mounted hunters, they were easily out of earshot of those who knew how to speak without letting their voices carry.

The older woman's eyes narrowed, her lips thinning, as Dhulyn told her Zania's history.

"The girl believes the Blue Mage is this same Avylyn that her family has been tracing the last fifteen years," Dhulyn concluded. "And that the secret to his magics is this Stone that belonged to her people."

A rabbit dashed out into the field ahead of them, and Valaika loosed her hawk.

"And this book you speak of, it tells you how to control the Stone?"

"I would not go so far as that," Dhulyn said. "It is rather a description of how Zania's family used it, and some speculations on its origins and true purpose." Dhulyn hesitated. How much did she want to reveal to this woman? "But as for any help in getting it away from Avylos—nothing I have read so far gives me any clues."

"I remember when Avylos first came," Valaika said, her eyes following the progress of her bird as it swung and stooped on the moving air. "He had perhaps twenty summers then, not many more. A dark-haired young man, thin as a reed, but very striking, very handsome. The timing fits with the girl's story."

"And has he grown in his powers, as Edmir believes?"

Valaika tapped her upper lip with her tongue, shaking her head before answering. "That I cannot say. I have not lived in the Royal House for more than fifteen summers. I've only met the Blue Mage twice—no, three times since he first came, and not at all since my brother died." She turned again to look them in the face. "But there is no doubt that until Limona, no Tegriani force has lost a battle, and that is the Mage's doing."

They had reached the place where the hawk still crouched over the body of the rabbit. Valaika called out to the grooms and dismounted, swinging off her horse with the agility of a woman half her age.

"Shhhh, come, Tera, come." She enticed her hawk off the prey, offering her wrist and as a reward, a pellet of specially prepared food. When the hawk was restored to her wrist and hooded, Valaika stepped nimbly back into her saddle.

"Oh, well done," Dhulyn said. "Most people cannot remount without disturbing the bird."

At Valaika's signal, the beaters spread out once more, and they were once again advancing, this time with Parno's bird unhooded.

"What is your plan?" Valaika asked.

Dhulyn was pleased that Parno kept his eyes on the beaters as he answered. A certain amount of clumsiness would be excused, since the servants thought them to be merely players, but it wouldn't do for them to pay no attention whatsoever.

"We saw in Probic," he said, "what could happen if we simply appear, claiming we have Edmir. In coming to you, Edmir thought that with your backing, he could be restored to the Royal House, and we could gain entry ourselves." His eyes narrowed. Dhulyn looked ahead and saw the beaters were moving in on a clump of long grass.

"Once guests in the Royal House," she said, taking up the thread of Parno's explanation, "we would have access to the Mage, and the Stone."

"You say you *wanted* this," Valaika said. "What has changed your minds?"

"Last night we learned something more," Dhulyn said. "Edmir bears a sigil on his lower back, called a 'ghost eye' among the Red Horsemen, used to see or watch the person who bears it."

"Avylos again," Valaika said, in the same bitter tone she'd used the night before. "Can we remove this sigil?"

"The one I bore as a child wore off with time," Dhulyn said. "But perhaps the process can be speeded up. Soap and water, obviously, is not the answer—at least, I would suppose a prince is bathed more often and more thoroughly than a Red Horse child."

A covey of what looked like grouse broke from the long grass between the beaters and Parno loosed his hawk.

"Distilled spirits," Parno said, while his eye followed the flight of the hawk. When it struck, calling out its success, he kneed Warhammer forward, saying over his shoulder as he advanced, "I seem to remember my mother removing a stain from a favorite gown with clear distilled spirits."

"We will try it," Valaika said. "But how will this affect your original plan? Even if you suspect the sigil is Avylos', there has been a general order to be on the lookout for two Mercenary Brothers and a young man, but no one has been sent to any particular place."

"That we know of." Dhulyn shrugged, causing the falcon on her wrist to spread its wings to balance itself. "Your pardon," she said to the bird mechanically. "I do not know for certain what the ghost eye reveals, but my guess is the Mage sees only Edmir and his immediate surroundings. One forest clearing looks much like another, and the same can be said for a village green—or a House's courtyard for that matter. So long as he does not see anyone in House colors, or any recognizable building, there is no way he can tell where Edmir is."

"That's why you agreed to leave him indoors just now."

Dhulyn nodded. "But I tell you, as we approach Beolind there are landmarks, well-known stretches of road; Avylos *will* recognize what he sees, and he will have time to prepare for our arrival. If the Mage has not already bewitched the queen and others to make sure Edmir will not be recognized, he'll have time to do so—and we will lose potential allies."

Valaika nodded. "So Edmir must remain here—or better, our game-keeper's lodge lies vacant just now. It's not far from here, and there is nothing to show the place is Jarlkevo. Like the rooms we gave you last night, it is exactly the type of place we would lend to traveling players who needed privacy and time to rehearse."

Parno returned, the body of a plump grouse hanging from his pommel.

"Then our first task when we return to the House is to see about removing this sigil. All our planning rests upon that."

Distilled spirits did not remove the ghost eye from Edmir's lower back. Nor did animal fat, nor olive oil. Nor hot water and horse brushes.

"I don't suppose you'll consider having it cut out," Parno said as he threw the stiff-bristled horse brush down in disgust.

Edmir spun to face him, hands grabbing protectively at the spot on his back where the sigil was.

"No, I didn't think so." Parno smiled.

"We have no way of knowing whether it *can* be cut off, my soul," Dhulyn pointed out. She eyed Edmir's back from where she leaned against the wall. "There's only one way to find out, and perhaps we should save that as a last resort." She turned to Valaika. "It's as I've said; for now Edmir must remain behind."

"But how is it safer for me to stay here?" Edmir said. "If he *can* see me, Avylos will see me here as well as anywhere else."

"The Blue Mage has never been to Jarlkevo, to my knowledge," Valaika said. "If he has looked this way since your arrival, we must hope he recognized nothing. And to be certain, we are moving you now to another place. As Dhulyn Wolfshead has said, one set of stone walls looks much like any other." Valaika thought, lips pursed. "I can get the two of you into the Royal House," she said to Dhulyn. "After that, it will be up to you."

"How will you explain *your* appearance, Aunt Valaika?" Edmir pulled his shirt on. "It's well known how much you dislike Beolind."

Valaika blew out her breath. "If I come to see my sister-in-law Queen Kedneara, to offer her my support at the death of her son, my brother's child—I could not have come for anything less, but this, this I think they will believe."

Janek was the first stumbling block. It was Edmir who finally convinced him.

"It's like a play—or a battle," he told the boy, when nothing either of his mothers said would change his mind. "Everyone has to do his part. I don't want to go and hide any more than you want to stay here with Sylria, but those are our orders. You wouldn't be allowed to go with us if we were really just players—and you wouldn't go with your mother Valaika to her hunting lodge as she's pretending to do, not if she were really only going for overnight. You'd have to stay here and attend to your studies and other duties. And so you will now."

"It is your carrying on as usual that will provide the rest of us the cover we need," Dhulyn added.

Almost as hard to convince had been Valaika's Steward of Walls.

Sylria had laughed. "Valaika managed to convince him that a caravan load of players was escort enough—he knew better than to argue; old soldier as she is, Valaika avoids an escort whenever she can. It's easier in the last few years, of course. Tegrian has never been so safe for travelers. We have the Blue Mage to thank for that much, at the very least."

There's irony, Parno thought. It was only the work of the Blue Mage that made Tegrian so safe, and here they were on their way to put a stop to him.

"That's the third time you've moved those slippers from one box to the other, and back again." Edmir looked up from the entry he was making in his journal.

"I should be with them," Zania said, not for the first time, as she sat back on her heels and looked from one open chest to the other. "It's *my* Stone."

Edmir understood her frustration—after all, as she'd pointed out, *she* didn't have a ghost eye on *her* back—but he was very glad the Mercenaries had insisted on leaving Zania behind, though he wasn't sure if he should tell her so. The idea that she would be anywhere near Avylos, that Zania might look at Edmir and in that dead voice say that she didn't know him. He shivered and bent back over his journal.

Zania's frustration had taken the form of fussy activity. She'd decided to reorganize her props and costumes, now that there were so few players to use them, and in the absence of any eyes to oversee them here at the gamekeeper's lodge, Edmir had helped her drag the costume trunks into the lodge's large common room from where they normally rode under the caravan. The lodge itself consisted of this large room, with its cooking hearth, oak plank table, carved stools and uneven stone floor, and a single windowless inner room which Edmir had insisted Zania take as her bedchamber. There was nothing in either room to tell the Blue Mage where he was, no clue to give them away.

Edmir glanced up at her again. She certainly seemed to be making very little progress with her organizing.

Could he tell her how happy he had been with the decision to leave them together? He wanted to, that he was sure of, but from the tight look on the girl's face, he knew it would be unwise. It was so much easier to write these things down. On the page in front of him he had sketched in the outline of a short tale, just a few lines detailing a love story. Here, in the pages of his journal, was the one place—the only place—a life with Zania would ever exist.

His talk with Parno Lionsmane had made that very clear.

Best he not say anything to Zania. He sighed and applied himself once more to his story. He had just reached the point where the young prince declares his love to the beautiful lady player when Zania spoke again.

"The Muse Stone *is* mine," she said addressing a pair of boots with turned-down tops. "It belongs to my family." The muscles in her jaw moved as she gritted her teeth. "And Dhulyn took my great-uncle's book as well. They're all I have left."

Edmir swallowed. "Zania, if anything should happen . . . I mean. I want you to know that this past moon has been . . ."

Zania looked up, and her lips twisted to one side in a wry smile. "Better than life at court?"

"That's easily answered. How happy are the nobles in the plays you know?"

"In the comedies, very happy." She tossed the boots back into the chest and stood up, crossing over to lean against the table where he sat. "But your family, you must miss them?"

"I miss Kera, but even with her, lately . . . it's different when you'll be king someday. That sets you apart even from your brothers and sisters." He put the quill he'd been using to one side. "But I have to say, at least *part* of what's made the last few weeks so pleasurable is not being around my mother." He thrust his hands through his hair. "Since my father died— *Caids*, it's like putting down a weight."

Zania moved the inkwell Edmir had been using and perched on the side of the table, doing her best not to look down at what Edmir had been writing. "What weight?" *Part*, her heart said. *Part of what's given him pleasure.*

"The weight of her disapproval, the weight of not meeting her standards. She expects you to be perfect the first time, without giving you a chance to practice. You tell her you've done your best and she tells you to try harder next time, not to be so lazy." He smiled, but to Zania's practiced eye, it looked forced. "She was different when we were younger."

"So *that's* why you're always asking whether the play is good. I was thinking that for a prince, you needed an awful lot of reassurance."

"None of *you* seems to think that there's anything wrong with praise—Dhulyn acts like she thinks praise will make you try harder."

Zania drew up her feet until her heels were on the edge of the table, and she could wrap her arms around her knees. "And so it should, if it's earned. Then you'll do as well or better the next time, in order to be praised again."

"Do you think you should have your feet on the table?"

"What, are you turning into your mother?" She smiled when she said it, but she lowered her eyes. Edmir picked up his pen.

"With the Stone," she said. "I could start a new troupe."

"Well, fresh material—new plays, I mean—that might help you attract some new actors." She looked up then and met his eye.

Only part *of what's made him so happy*, she thought.

I don't want to go back, he thought.

Sylria waited for the moon to rise before leaving her bed. She and Valaika were not in the habit of having pages sleep in the ante-room, something she was very glad of now. No questions to answer as she lit the lamp standing on the table in her chamber, drew on a dressing robe over her nightgown and stepped into the corridor. A right turn and a short flight of stone steps brought her to her own workroom.

Sylria liked having her own room, where she could close the door behind her, and look around with the satisfaction she always felt when she saw the orderly papers, inkpots well-stoppered, pens carefully cleaned and laid out in a neat row.

"You should have been a Scholar," Valaika had always said to tease her. Well, her father had been one, and Sylria had always wanted a home life, not a life spent chasing down a new theory, a just-discovered scrap of the Caids' writings, an untranslated poem in some unpleasant ancient tongue.

She took a book of poetry from her shelf, threw open the shutter of the narrow window and set the book down on the ledge, where the moon would shine directly on it. She turned to blow out the lamp, and when her eyes had adjusted to the darkness, she opened the book to the central, blank, pages. She laid her index fingers on the lower corners of the open pages and spoke.

"My lord Mage," she said. She had time to wish she'd thought to bring a cup of water to the window with her—time enough for second thoughts, time to wonder whether she should just shut the book before any writing appeared. . . .

"Tell me."

And then it was too late.

"I keep our bargain," she said, whispering the words into the cool night air.

"Tell me."

"This will be the last time. With this, I pay my debt in full." She hadn't meant it to sound like a question, but she was fairly sure how it would appear in the book that was a twin to hers.

"Tell me."

"The Lord Prince is here, in Jarlkevo, near at hand." In the game-keeper's lodge, where whatever the Blue Mage visited on him would be far from Janek.

"The Mercenary Brothers?"

Sylria's mouth was too dry to swallow. She'd been right to call him, she thought. He knew so much already, really, it was impossible to hide anything from him.

"They have gone, with my House, to Beolind. Here is only myself, and the prince."

"Kill him."

Sylria fumbled with the book, in her shock she nearly let it fall to the floor from the stone window ledge. "You cannot ask this of me," she said, when she had her voice again. "You wanted only news of him, you never said—"

"Does your son walk? Does he take food? Does he breathe the air? Grow? Laugh? Do you wish this to continue?"

Sylria sank to her knees, her hands still carefully maintaining the position of the book in the moonlight. *Janek, oh, sweet Caids, not Janek.* And yet she saw, with a sickening coldness in her belly, that this was exactly what she should have expected. Valaika was the one who had brought the child to term, for the House could only pass to blood, but Janek was Sylria's—*she* had nursed him, *she* had held him, rocked him, dealt with his fevers, coaxed him to eat, and watched him grow, but thin, hollow-eyed, and weak. Not thriving as other children did. And there would be no other. Valaika had waited too long; she could not have another child.

Sylria had watched as Janek's illness took its price from Valaika as well, making her thin, her hair dull, the bones of her face showing like a skull.

When she could not find a Healer, Sylria had gone to Avylos. And the Blue Mage had helped her. And she had promised him anything, *anything* to save their child.

And now she knew what *anything* was.

"I cannot," she whispered, and then roused herself. What was she saying? "I cannot promise," she said. "What if I am not successful?"

"I will help you. Put the palm of your left hand down on the right-hand page."

When Valaika Jarlkevoso had said that Beolind was a day and a half's ride from the gamekeeper's lodge, if both weather and horse were good, Parno had given Dhulyn the look that meant "we'll laugh about this in private." He remembered that look when, almost exactly a day and half later, they entered the city of Beolind. Valaika was greeted with salutes and attention, and a runner was sent ahead of them to inform the Royal House of their approach.

"Are you all right?"

Dhulyn nodded, but Parno thought she looked pale. "This is the first time I've passed through city gates without declaring myself a Mercenary Brother," she replied, using the nightwatch voice. "Let's hope we never have to do so again."

He and Dhulyn, both in short dark wigs, wore tunics in the same orange and black as the cloak Valaika wore, the better to disguise them as retainers of Jarlkevo. Parno moved his shoulders. The tunic was a good fit, but he was getting awfully tired of wearing borrowed clothes. He looked at Dhulyn as she swung herself onto Bloodbone's back. If *he* was getting tired of it, he could only imagine how Dhulyn felt.

Warm, he thought, as she rolled back her sleeves. After all these years, she still found it too warm here in the north.

"This way," Valaika said once they had passed through the lengthy gate passage that led through the walls of the city. "I have my own suite in the western wing of the Royal House, and we can go straight there."

As they followed Valaika through the city, Parno noticed Dhulyn looking around, frown lines between her brows. He knew that look. She was remembering something she had Seen in a Vision, and comparing it to what she saw now.

A man on horseback came along, calling out to make way for the Royal Guard. Valaika could have stood on rank herself, but instead she moved to one side.

There were only five people in the party, two nobles on horseback, and three in the dark blue tunics of the Royal Guard walking along with them. As the group drew abreast of them, Dhulyn suddenly stiffened and called out in a language Parno had never heard her use.

The taller of the two on horseback turned around at her call, and Parno saw what Dhulyn had seen. The man had the distinctive blood-red hair of the Red Horsemen. Now the two Outlanders were calling to each other, Dhulyn smiling and excited as she pushed through the crowd to the man. As Parno started to follow, Valaika grabbed him by the arm.

"Don't," she said. "Don't move. That's Avylos."

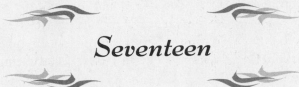

Seventeen

"**C**OUSIN!"

Dhulyn spoke without thinking. When the men rode out of the shadow of a Jaldean Shrine into the sunshine, and Dhulyn saw the taller man's face clearly, and his hair—blowing back from that remembered face and red like old blood—the greeting had burst from her. She had spoken in the old tongue, the language of the Espadryni, that she hadn't used since her Schooler, Dorian the Black, had found her in the slaver's ship.

She was urging Bloodbone forward even as the man stopped and looked at her. It *was* the boy, the one her Vision had shown her being hunted in the woods, much older, but still recognizable as the prey running in the forest of her Vision. So it was the past she'd Seen.

"How can we be kin?" he answered her, also in the old tongue. His deep blue eyes were narrowed, calculating. The foot guards with him exchanged glances, round-eyed, but they stayed silent. He looked over behind her, his eyes narrowed still further, and he inclined his head— not a bow, but as someone who acknowledges an acquaintance. He had seen and recognized Valaika, Dhulyn thought, so this was evidently someone from the Royal House.

"We are the same Tribe, if not the same Clan," she said, willing his attention back to her. Now that she *had* spoken, and drawn his notice, she'd better make the best she could out of this. "What does that make us, in this city of northerners, if not kin?"

He tilted his head. "You speak the old tongue. The Hunter Moon has passed more times than I wish to remember, since I have heard it last. You have the voice, but not the look of an Espadryni."

"It is easy to change the color of one's hair," Dhulyn said. "I will be pleased to prove our kinship, but not here, in the street. I was Dhulyn of the Darklin Plain Clan. My mother Asmodhul and my father Fentlyn."

"You say you *were?*"

"The Darklin Plain is empty. The horses and cattle run wild. You know this as well as I."

"I do. I was Avylyn of Forest Plain Clan. My father Teravyl and my mother Werlyn. Come with me now, and if what you say of yourself is true, you shall be welcomed here as though we were of one blood." He put out his hand, palm down, in the manner of their Tribe.

A cold knot formed in the back of her throat and Dhulyn cursed herself—she was even more a blooded fool than she'd thought. She recognized the name. She knew what his next words would be.

"Here I am known as Avylos, the Blue Mage."

She took his hand, palm to palm, turned their wrists until her hand was uppermost and released him. She let Bloodbone fall into step beside his horse. What else could she do, but find some way to salvage this? As she rode away from her Partner, she stretched up her right arm, as if adjusting the fall of her cloak. First she extended her thumb and index finger only. *Follow and watch.* And then, she closed her fist. *In Battle.*

"And in Death." Parno mouthed the response from where he sat on Warhammer, pushed up against Valaika's horse, automatically giving the open hand signal as he did. Then both his own hands closed into fists, and he forced them to relax.

"I thought you said he had dark hair?"

"He did when I knew him." Valaika said. "What now?"

"Follow and watch," Parno said.

The older woman took a deep breath and let it out slowly. "Then it's a lucky thing we're all going to the Royal House."

Parno hoped the smile he gave her was more confident than the feeling behind it. "We wanted to get into the Mage's quarters. Well, now we're in."

Avylos' hand trembled slightly as he adjusted the magic that locked his workroom door. A woman of his tribe. What if she was? How much did she know, and how many others had survived? He would have to kill her—it was the only way to be sure, to be safe. But she was younger, what if she knew nothing? What if she *was* the last?

And there was more to consider than her parentage. He had never felt such a strong manifestation of power as he had when the woman, Dhulyn, had taken his hand. Espadryni or not, she was Marked. That was beyond doubt. When he was young, he no more thought the women of the Espadryni were Seers than he'd believed the men were Mages. Tricks and illusion—that's what he'd told himself before the Stone had shown him that magic truly existed. But now, with the power of the Stone pulsing through his veins, he could see the Mark for himself, a glow somewhat like the young dice boy's, only . . . thicker. *Could* he feed it to the Stone, even if he wanted to?

An Espadryni. A Seer. The use he could make of her—what if she was of more value to him alive? Would it be a waste to feed her power into the Stone?

"All the rooms in this wing are mine," he told her as he pushed open the door and led the way in. "But this is my workroom, where I conduct my private business."

"Your pardon, Lord Avylos, but you are the consort, are you not? Do you have any private business?"

Avylos pressed his lips together, glad that his back was turned as he opened the shutters to let in the afternoon light. He could not let her see how her casual disrespect had cut through him like a knife.

"As consort, perhaps not, but as the Blue Mage, much of my business is private," he said through gritted teeth. Perhaps he should show her the Stone after all, and sooner rather than later.

He turned back toward her and found her standing, perfectly relaxed, looking around the room with an expression of polite interest. Her face was a long oval, her skin coloring naturally pale, like his own, showing little or no darkening from the sun. Her eyes large, a steel gray in color. Her mouth was full, but there was a small scar on her upper lip. As if she felt his eyes on her, she looked at him and smiled. For a moment the scar caught at her lip and made her seem about to snarl, but then her mouth softened again, and her smile was gentle.

"Of course," she said. "You must excuse my ignorance. I know nothing of Mages and their responsibilities, but surely they must be heavy. In my excitement at finding a kinsman, I may speak too familiarly. Pray believe that I do not wish to offend."

Avylos found himself smiling. He'd forgotten what the Espadryni were like. This Dhulyn was plainspoken, not disrespectful. Open and straightforward, nothing sycophantic in her tone or carriage. But he remembered, and sobered again. How much did she know?

"What do you remember of your time among the tribes?"

She shrugged. "I was so young when the tribes were broken, that I remember very little about the life. I have learned some things since through study—I can read—but I was not sure . . . were there many Mages among the Espadryni?"

"No," he said, and then smiled to soften the bluntness of his answer. She *didn't* know. If she didn't know that, she wouldn't know that he'd been *srusha*. "But I did not start to come into my powers until after the tribes were broken. No doubt, as a child, much was hidden from me."

"No doubt."

"But please, seat yourself, let me offer you some jeresh." When she nodded, he unstoppered the bottle sitting on the table to his right and poured out two portions into the waiting glass cups. He handed her one, and raised his own in salute.

"To proofs," he said.

The woman raised her own cup, took a sip, and lowered it again. She looked at him steadily for a long moment, as if she were considering something of great weight. Finally her lips formed the smallest of smiles.

"I am ready," she said. She set her glass down and lifted her hands to the back of her head. She pushed her fingers into the dark brown curls on her neck and her hair moved. The hairs on Avylos' own neck shivered for an instant until he realized she was wearing a wig, and was lifting it off. She pushed her hands forward until her fingers were scraping at the hairline around her face, and in a few moments more the wig was lying in her lap.

She rubbed her hands quickly over her scalp, brushing off loose bits of the glue that had held on the wig. There was stubble exposed on her shapely skull, perhaps three days' worth, a deep red, a blood color almost identical to his own. But something else was exposed as well. Something that cast all his half-formed plans into the fire.

"You are a Mercenary Brother." He tapped his upper lip with his fingers. Edmir at Jarlkevo, and now this? He was wary of coincidences.

"I am. I am Dhulyn Wolfshead, called the Scholar. I was Schooled by Dorian, the Black Traveler. I have fought with my brothers at Sadron, Arcosa, and Bhexyllia."

He waited, but it seemed Dhulyn Wolfshead had finished. "You had better stay in my rooms until I can find you another wig, Dhulyn Wolfshead—a red one by preference, though I do not know where I will find one so fine as yours. Kedneara the Queen does not feel well-disposed toward Mercenaries, just now."

"The very reason for this." She picked up the dark brown wig and laid it aside on the table. "As you see from my colors, I am employed as a House Guard for Valaika Jarlkevoso, and have been for six or seven moons now. When we heard what was being said about the Lord Prince's death, and the banishment, the Jarlkevoso advised me to cover my Badge and wait."

"Do you believe what is being said?" *Can I believe what's being said?* Had she been all this time with Valaika? Or had she come more recently? And with a princely companion?

"No," she said, looking directly at him with her steel-gray eyes. For a moment he believed she had read his thoughts. "The Brotherhood does not murder—but the Queen of Tegrian will not be the first grief-stricken person who puts blame in the wrong place."

Avylos leaned against the edge of the table, propping his elbow in his free hand. "Do you know why the Jarlkevoso has chosen to come to Beolind just now?"

Dhulyn Wolfshead shrugged, but seemed to give his question some thought. "A group of players came to Jarlkevo. They did a play where a king returns from war to his family. Perhaps the story reminded the Jarlkevoso that her nephew would not be returning from his battle, and that her sister-by-marriage Kedneara the Queen might be bereft." Again, she shrugged. "I was not told anything of the matter."

Avylos nodded. It *could* be. It *was* possible. The players he had already heard about, and if she was merely a guard—however valued, as a Mercenary Brother would be—she might know nothing of the arrival of Edmir. Valaika would bring her to Beolind to keep her from finding out . . . And whatever else she might be, she *was* Espadryni, and Marked. So long as he had her here, in his hands, surely she was more asset than liability. "However did you become a Mercenary Brother?"

"I had seen the Hawk Moon perhaps five or six times when the Espadryni were overrun. My parents were killed, and I was sold to slavers. Sold several times, in fact—I don't believe we make good slaves, we Espadryni. When I had seen the Hawk moon eleven times, the slave ship I was on was taken by Dorian the Black, the Mercenary Schooler. He said he would teach me to kill my enemies, an offer I was happy to take."

Slavers. Avylos hoped she did not see him shiver. "I was luckier than you, I think," he told her. "My Clan was near the forest that is found at the western end of the plains, and I escaped into the wood when we were overrun. I was found and hidden by farmers—folk we'd often traded with. They would have made a home for me, gladly, for their family was not so numerous, but I could not settle to that kind of life. And then my powers began to come, and the news out of Tegrian spoke of the Consort Karyli's gathering of the gifted and Marked to be licensed. So to Tegrian I came, and to Beolind. And I have been here ever since."

"Are you happy here?" There was something different in the tone Dhulyn Wolfshead used to ask this question, and to his surprise, Avylos answered honestly.

"I have been glad of the time to study, to increase my powers. I have done much here in Tegrian, and will have a chance to do more, as Kedneara the Queen extends her rule. But tell me, what brings you to Beolind?"

Not for the first time, Dhulyn wished she had Edmir's gift for telling tales. Already she was losing track of what she *had* told him, and she was keenly aware that she was taking too long to answer now. But she was just as certain that she had to tread carefully. Avylos reminded her of Delmarin Hammerfist who had been Schooled with her, a person quick to feel slighted, and who needed frequent reassurance. Parno was better at handling this kind of person than she was.

"I might easily say that you are yourself my reason to be in Beolind, Lord Avylos. There was talk of you in Monara, and someone who claimed to have seen you, described you in such a way that I thought you might be Espadryni, and so I came to see. I had been, as I said, six moons or more with House Jarlkevo, working my way here, when the news came of the Lord Prince's murder and the banishment of the Brotherhood. House Jarlkevo, knowing of my intention to seek you out, in her generosity chose me to be one of her guard when she came to see the queen." She picked up her glass and took another sip of jeresh. "I did not dream I would be so lucky as to see you on the street. Will you speak for me to the queen? Ask her to exempt me from her order of banishment?"

Avylos leaned back again in his chair and Dhulyn breathed more easily. If he was relaxing, perhaps he believed her.

"I will be happy to speak to her," he said. "But if you take my counsel, we will wait. Give her more time. My assurances will help her to act justly, but you will not gain her favor unless we wait. And I wish you to gain that favor. You may stay here as long as you desire—as you said, we are each of us the closest thing to kin that either of us has left in the world." Avylos hesitated, as if these words had stopped his throat. "I must ask that you remain here in my apartments for now," he continued. "Or, if you will resume your wig, in my garden. Others cannot enter here without my knowing. Give your own hair time to grow out more. If I can claim you as kin, our assurances to the queen will be stronger."

"What of your escort? Will they not speak of me?"

Avylos shook his head. "I will tell everyone that you are ill, and that you must stay in my care until there is no danger."

Suddenly he came around the table and took her hands in his. They were cool, and strangely rough as if his calluses were in the wrong places. There was a softness in his eyes, and for a moment Dhulyn thought he was going to kiss her hands. She widened her eyes and lifted her brows.

He smiled and the moment passed. "I am expected to join my wife the queen for supper, so I must leave you. Let me show you into the garden, you will be safe there. If you can be patient and wait, I will bring you a meal myself later in the evening."

"I am used to going without food," she said. "It is part of our training." She picked up the wig and pulled it on. It fit well enough, even without the glue, to fool anyone who would only see her in a garden.

As soon as she was alone, Dhulyn made her way back to the Blue Mage's workroom. Once there, however, she stood outside the door tapping her upper lip with her tongue. The door was now a plain, smooth expanse of painted wood. There was no door latch, no sign of hinges. It could be a decorative piece of paneling, for any evidence to the contrary. Knowing it to be a waste of time, she nevertheless felt over the smooth surface, paying particular attention to the spot where she had seen the latch when Avylos had used it.

Still nothing. She blew out her breath in a noiseless whistle and turned back to the garden. So much for sneaking into the room, grabbing the Muse Stone, retrieving Bloodbone and the bulk of her weapons from the stables and riding away while the Mage was elsewhere. She would have to think of a new plan.

Dhulyn expected to find the garden familiar, even though this would be the first time she had seen it directly, and in the clear light of day. There was no mistaking the pool, for example, in which she'd seen Edmir's reflection. She sat down on the pool's wide stone edge and trailed her hand in the water. Too bad she couldn't use the Mage's ghost eye to see Edmir for herself. Though if she was wishing things, she'd prefer to see Parno.

Escaped into the woods, she thought. *I wish I could believe him*. But she couldn't, not really. In her Visions Avylos had been terrified, granted, but there had been no sign of what he'd been running from. And while Avylos had been young, he was old enough to hold a sword and die beside his family—or at the very least old enough to lead other, younger children away into the woods, to escape as he had himself. Why hadn't he done so?

Why would he have run without even trying to help? Dhulyn rubbed her hands dry on her leggings. Were her questions reasonable? Or did her thinking reflect that of a Mercenary Brother, and not that of a young Espadryni boy? She'd always assumed that what had made the Mercenary School feel so right for her was that it had provided the same sense of unity she remembered feeling as a child, riding behind her father on his horse. The unity that would keep one Mercenary standing over an injured Brother until the fight—or their lives— ended. In Battle, or in Death.

If Avylos had not felt this, was the fault in him, or in her own memories?

Even if she were willing to believe that part of his story, what of the things he *hadn't* mentioned? There could be no doubting now that he was the same Avylyn who had been a member of Troupe Tzadeyeu. Even if the names had not agreed, there was that plain wooden casket she'd been so careful to ignore, sitting on the end of his worktable, that matched so perfectly the drawing in Zania's book. Dhulyn put her hand where she could feel the edge of the book under her tunic. She stood up once more and followed the path on the far side of the pond. It led to a section of wall that had obviously been rebuilt at one time. In this light, and from this angle, it seemed likely she could climb the wall, when the opportunity presented itself.

"Oh, yes," she muttered, still in her mother's tongue. "I'm *sure* he spent ten summers living on a farm, *that's* likely." But a short time on a farm, and then a second escape to the players troupe? That was far more likely. And if the Stone enhanced what powers he did possess— or somehow triggered powers which had been latent? *That* would explain a great deal. It seemed likelier still that he had taken it and fled for the greater protection of the Royal House of Tegrian.

She stepped back from the wall, propped her left hand on her hip, and tilted her head to one side.

"Aren't you going to miss your supper, loitering about here?" she asked.

After a long moment the girl Dhulyn had sensed sitting behind a flowering bush on a rough protruding stone in the rebuilt section of wall stood up and picked her way down to the ground level.

Dhulyn's face relaxed into a smile. She knew who this girl must be. Her hair was the same red gold as Valaika Jarlkevoso's, though obviously without the gray. And while her face was more oval, she had her brother Edmir's strong nose. Dhulyn raised her hand—

Older. Perhaps ten years older. On horseback, a white horse with deep blue saddlecloth, crested. Her light red hair clubbed back away from her face, smoothed down to take the helm. Her deep blue shirt and cotte covered by a hammered silver cuirass, worked around the edges with lapis lazuli inlay, and crested with the crowned mark of the princes of Tegrian. The soldiers around her, clearly awaiting her orders.

And just that suddenly the Vision was over.

"Avylos can't tell when I'm there," the girl said, half question, half statement.

"I'm not Avylos," Dhulyn said. But the girl's observation was interesting. "Are you often in his garden unknown to him?"

The girl shrugged, and in that movement Dhulyn saw Edmir again. What was the name? Kera, that was it.

"You are wearing Jarlkevo colors," the princess said. "Did you bring the Mage some news?"

"I may have news for you, Princess Kera."

"I'm called Lady Prince now," the girl said, looking away. The corners of her mouth turned down.

"That may be," Dhulyn said. "But you have no right to the title. Your brother is alive, Princess. He misses you, and thinks of you often."

The girl took a step back. Suspicion and anger fought each other on her face. "How do you know?"

To answer, Dhulyn once again pulled off her wig.

~

"Don't point, don't even look," Parno said, walking just behind Valaika's shoulder, where a good personal guard would naturally be. "When we're looking in some other direction, tell me relative to *that* where our objective is."

"The trouble with you Mercenaries is that you think no one but yourselves knows how to do anything." There was amusement in Valaika's voice. "Believe it or not, I was practicing this kind of misdirection before you were born."

Parno grinned. That was exactly the reaction he'd expected. It had been only a few hours since they'd arrived in the rooms permanently set aside for Valaika and her family in the Royal House—rooms within the Royal compound, but actually in a separate building from the queen's own residence. Valaika had sent word to the woman who had been her sister-in-law as soon as they'd arrived, but it seemed the queen was in no hurry to acknowledge Valaika's presence.

"From here you can see the road we used to come into the city," Valaika said, coming to a standstill at the top of a short flight of stairs that raised them to the level of a small square tower which would provide shelter to the night guard in bad weather. "The wing we want is behind us, and slightly to our left. When we turn to go back, look for where a section of wall has been repaired with lighter stone. Behind that section is his garden."

Another thing Parno hadn't needed to tell her was not to say the words "Mage" or "Avylos" aloud, lest they catch the wrong ear.

When they reached the doorway into the square tower, Valaika turned and they began to retrace their steps. As the personal guard he was pretending to be, it was natural for him to scan their perimeter, easy to look in the right direction. The repaired wall stood out, just as Valaika had said it would. Apparently the Mage took as his apartments the very end of a long ell built against the outer wall of the Royal House. It would have windows giving on both the courtyard and the outer world.

The young man with a Balnian accent who had escorted them to Valaika's apartments had already told them of the gossip that was circulating, that a cousin of the Blue Mage had arrived and was recovering in his apartments from the crying fever. A young woman whom he was isolating for fear she would spread the infection. But she was alive, and she was expected to appear in public as soon as her recovery was complete.

Parno concentrated, fixing the image of the Mage's wing in his mind for later consideration, even as every muscle in his body wanted to launch himself across the distance separating him from his Partner. *Now.* He wanted to go *now.* See her with his own eyes, touch her with his own hands. Make sure she was not looking at Avylos with a heart that said, "Cousin."

Just as they were nearing the stone stairway that would return them to the grounds, and the path that would take them back to Valaika's wing, a page with a crown embroidered on the left side of her deep blue tunic came toward them with a determined step.

Valaika stopped and signaled the young girl to approach.

"Good morning, House Jarlkevo. I bring greetings from Kedneara the Queen. She welcomes you to Royal House, and looks forward to seeing you the second morning from now, at her audience."

"I thank you, Page. Tell my sister, Kedneara the Queen, that I anticipate with great satisfaction seeing her, and my niece, the Lady Prince Kera."

"I will tell her so." The page gave an abrupt nod that set her dark curls bouncing and turned on her heel. Parno watched which way she went. Her errand accomplished, she was headed back to the pages' room where she would wait until sent on another.

"Well, only a three-day wait altogether. The Great King's been known to keep even his own mother waiting for longer than that."

Valaika shrugged and turned once more to the entrance of her suite. "It's not as though I'd asked to see her with any urgency. I may be aunt to the next ruler, but since my brother died, there are Noble Houses closer to the throne than I."

"And related to the Tarkin of Hellik?"

They had reached Valaika's door, and she paused, hand on the door's handle.

"That is why I'll be kept waiting only three days."

"All to the good, then," Parno said, following her in. "Any particular reason to invite you only to this audience and not a more private meeting?"

"Oh, yes," she said, her smile twisted to one side. "There's reason."

Eighteen

CROSS THE PASSAGE AND down three paces from the mag-icked door to the Blue Mage's workroom, was another door, this one with a plain wooden latch clearly in view. It opened, Dhulyn found, into what appeared to be a more personal sitting room. Here, in addition to a wide wooden bench covered with bright cushions under the narrow window, there was a small round table with the shelf for a brazier pan between the legs, a short cabinet of the type used to hold plates and cups, several large, well-padded chairs, and niches holding oil lamps decorated with the patterned glass shades for which the city-state of Tenezia was well known. As in the other rooms, winter rugs had been removed, revealing a tiled blue-and-green floor.

It was here, Dhulyn imagined, that Avylos received social guests—if he had any, for she noticed that only one chair showed signs of re-peated use—and took his meals away from his workroom, where all his focus and concentration was needed for his magical pursuits. During the year she had spent in the Scholars' Library before taking her final oaths as a Mercenary Brother, Dhulyn had been taught that, wherever possible, Scholars should keep their workrooms separate from their living quarters. It appeared that the Blue Mage had been given the same advice.

Since there was no magic on the door, Dhulyn did not hesitate to enter the room. She checked the cupboard—plates and eating utensils as she had expected—lit two of the lamps, and, wrinkling her nose at the honeyed smell of the scented oil, pulled one of the unused chairs over to the table. She angled herself so that the light would fall into her lap, and sat down to read, leaving the door to the hall standing open. It was some hours later that she heard footsteps slow as they approached the open doorway. She closed Zania's book, pushed it into her tunic just above her waist and pulled the laces shut, tying them where they would support the book without outlining it. She crossed her ankles, resting her feet on the brazier shelf under the table and folded her hands on her belly, as if she'd been taking a nap.

As Dhulyn expected, it was Avylos himself who appeared in the doorway, the brilliant blue of his overrobe catching the light from the oil lamps. He was carrying a tray on which rested bread, a large piece of game pie, the meat layered with slices of dried fruit, and a pottery flask of what smelled like spiced crab apple wine, sweeter than she would normally drink.

"Here, let me," she said, getting to her feet and taking the tray from him. "You should be better served than this. Or is it that you're hiding me even from your servants and pages?"

He smiled as though something had mightily pleased him. "Indeed, I've let it be known that you have the crying fever."

Dhulyn raised her eyebrows. "That will be sure to keep away all but the desperately curious."

"Even the desperately curious usually know better than to explore my rooms uninvited."

"I will be sure to remember that."

She set the tray on the table and sat down herself. The portions were generous, but even so, there was only enough food for one. As a Mercenary Brother, held captive however comfortably by an enemy, she should not touch it. But that was not the role she was playing here. If Edmir were writing her lines, and Zania directing her movements, what would they be telling her? If she and Avylos were truly what they claimed to be, the last of their tribe, the only Espadryni either of them had ever met since the Tribes were broken—how would Avylos expect her to act? What would be natural under the circumstances? Dhulyn thought of the surge of emotion she had felt on seeing and recognizing Avylos as an Espadryni. *I would want to trust him*, she thought. Though it went against her Schooling, and the Common Rule of the Brotherhood, she would want her kin to be worthy of her trust. And that gave her a way to turn the Common Rule to her advantage.

"Is the food not to your liking?"

"I was just thinking that if I were anywhere else, or if you were anyone else, I would have to find a way to refuse the food, or to trick you somehow into sharing it with me. It is our Common Rule," she added, "to aid us against eating poisoned or drugged food."

He reached for the plate.

Before he touched it, she laid two fingers on the back of his hand. "I said, 'if I were anywhere else.'" She pulled the plate toward her, took her knife from her belt and cut herself off a bite-sized piece of pie. Avylos smiled and poured her out a glass of the wine, pleased, as she'd thought, that she trusted him.

Sun and Stars—if it is *drugged, I hope it's one I've been Schooled against*, she thought.

Avylos got up and went to the cabinet to the right of the door. He selected for his own use a stemmed blue glass and brought it back to the table, filling it with wine before sitting down across from her once again. "Tomorrow I must leave you for the morning," he said. "I will have food left in the corridor where this part of the House joins the main section. I advise you to be sure no one sees you fetch it. Can you do that?"

"It is another of the things I have been Schooled to, yes," she said.

He nodded, and took a careful sip of the wine before setting it down once more on the table. "I know enough about the Mercenary Brotherhood to know that your commitment there is for life. I cannot—I must not—ask you to abandon the Brotherhood, but would you take work here?"

"In Beolind?"

"In the Royal House. We are kin, as you said. Perhaps the only Espadryni left in the whole world. Certainly you are the only one I have ever seen." He lifted his eyes to her face for just a moment before lowering them again to the glass he was turning in his fingers.

Stick to your role, Dhulyn told herself. What would she say if she were just a lone Mercenary Brother, made such an offer? "The Brotherhood *is* a life tie." That, at least, was no more than the truth, the Common Rule. "We have no pasts once we are Schooled."

"Yet you came looking for me here, thinking that I might be one of the Espadryni. When you saw me, you called me cousin."

She had. Dhulyn tore off a piece of bread and put it into her mouth, buying herself time to think. Despite the Common Rule, despite what she may have thought, when she had seen a Tribesman her heart *had* lifted and she *had* called out to him, instinctively, without conscious decision. As though a part of her had, after all, wanted more than the Brotherhood had given her. She'd often been impatient with other Brothers, who found it hard to put aside the years before they came to the Brotherhood. With Parno, especially, she had been short. Now she recognized that it had been very easy for her to follow the Common Rule and put her past behind her. Until she'd met with Avylos the Blue Mage, she'd had no past.

Blooded fool, she said to herself. Whatever he might make her feel, this man was *not* her past, this was the Blue Mage.

"I will be guided by you," she said finally. "But perhaps I should make no plans until you have spoken with the queen."

He leaned back, smiling. Dhulyn wished she was as satisfied with her answer as Avylos appeared to be.

"While we wait for the time to be right, will you do something for me?"

Dhulyn, her mouth once more full, raised her eyebrows as she chewed.

"Will you See for me?"

Dhulyn let herself fall back against her chair, laid her knife down on the table, and allowed herself to blink and appear startled. No matter what he knew, or how he knew it, that would be the safest reaction to Avylos' question. Stay in character. She could almost hear Zania's scolding her. The sharp spike of fear that shot through her she pushed away, and kept well hidden.

She swallowed. "What do you mean?"

He smiled, and in that indulgent smile she saw the smugness, the arrogance which was what *he* tried to keep hidden.

"As you were so young at the breaking of the Tribes, you may not realize that the Sight was a common thing among our women. But even if I had not known this, I *am* a Mage. Your Mark is as clear to me as the color of your eyes."

Dhulyn picked up the cloth napkin that still lay on the tray and began to wipe her trembling hands. She could do nothing that might betray her excitement. She and Parno had been following the rumors that said there was a Seer once more in Delmara, in the hope that Dhulyn could learn from her. But if Avylos knew the women of the Espadryni were Seers . . . He *was* older. He remembered his life among the Tribes. *Here* might be the source of what she needed most to know.

Even so, she was not here to learn from him, but to stop him. Perhaps, if she were very careful, and played her part well, she could do both.

"A Sight of the future would be of great use to me," he said, as the silence grew.

She leaned forward. "I would do everything within my power to help you," she said. "But how much help you'll find me . . ." She lifted her shoulders and let them drop.

"Now it is my turn to ask what you mean."

How much to tell him? If she were to learn anything useful, she must be as truthful as possible. There was no way to know what detail was important.

"I have long hidden my Mark, and not simply because it would complicate the life of a Mercenary Brother," she said. "It did not come to me until after the breaking of the Tribes, when I had seen the Hawk Moon perhaps twelve times. It terrified me, for I had no one to train me or explain. Seers are so rare, that even the Guildhalls of the Marked have little or no information to help me. So my Visions remain erratic, they do not always come when I summon them, nor can I control what I will see. They are strongest during my woman's time, as though the blood calls them, but few other things have any effect. I was hoping to reach the Shrine of Delmara, where they say a Seer sits once more, to ask for training, but I have my living to make, and even for a Mercenary Brother, that's not so easy.

"You are older than I," she added, placing her hands on the edge of the table and leaning forward. "Did you have sisters? Do you remember any ritual they performed? Any tool they used?" If he knew about the vera tiles, that would tell her whether there was anything to learn from him.

He was nodding. "My magic also came late to me, after I'd left the Tribes. Like your Mark, it was limited and erratic at first. I could magic only myself, or my immediate surroundings." Avylos gestured, and suddenly he was a brown-haired man, with Edmir's dark eyes, then his hair returned to its normal blood red, his eyes their vivid blue. He held out a hand and a tiny blue flame appeared on his palm.

"Then, as I practiced and studied, I could send the magic farther from me." He drew a small circle of light in the air with his right index finger and a flame appeared in one of the oil lamps Dhulyn had left dark. The surprise she did not trouble to hide was not a reaction to the lighting of the lamp, however. She had recognized the gesture he'd used painting the streaks of light in the air. She had seen it, or something very like it, before. She had seen Avylos himself gesturing in the air, but without any light following his finger. And she had seen an older Espadryni man do exactly what the Mage was doing now. Avylos painted another symbol and the shutters opened; yet another, and a small scroll flew in the window and came to rest on his open hand.

"But surely you can magic things even farther away?" Dhulyn said. "Unless you travel with the armies . . . ?

"I have ways of sending the magic farther afield, yes, but nothing I can show you now." He laid the scroll to one side. "And you, Cousin, what can you show me?"

Dhulyn nodded smartly, as if she were only making her decision as they spoke. "If you like, I will try, but you may prefer to wait until my woman's time comes again."

"You asked what I remembered of the women of the Tribes," he said. Dhulyn noticed that he did not say whether any of these women were his sisters. "Sometimes they chanted, or hummed the same tune, over and over, until it seemed they fell into a light trance, and it was then the Visions came. The chants I do not remember, but the trance I can give you myself."

It should work, Dhulyn thought, even as she desperately wanted to say no. The Visions often came as she dropped off to sleep, while her mind was loose and drifting. She knew that certain drugs, those which relaxed and freed the mind, could make the Visions clearer—but a trance would mean being unconscious, and vulnerable, in front of him. Still, there was no way she could refuse without making it plain she did not trust him. And always before her hung the possibility that she might learn something.

"I will try," she said.

An Avylos much younger than the man she knows sits back on his heels. He is in a small tent, just large enough to allow two people to stand upright, though at the moment he is alone and kneeling on a cushion. As she has seen him do when a child, he is drawing figures in the air, but this time lines of light trail after his moving finger. His face is split in a wide smile, as he draws faster and faster. *"Ne foromat srusha,"* he is saying over and over again in the tongue of the Espadryni. "I am not barren.". . .

The room has a floor of polished oak, inlaid with a fine banding of a much darker color near the walls, almost like the edging on a carpet. There are shelves and cubbies for books and scrolls. The large work-table is to her left, placed where it will receive the light from one of two tall, narrow windows, under which a bench has been built. There are cushions on the bench, and a three-legged stool lying on its side. She has seen this room before, but this time the door is closed, the tabletop is empty except for the plain casket. No unrolled scrolls, no open books. The room is empty . . . .

It is night. The moon shines through the narrow windows, illumi-nating the worktable, casting shadows from the bars across the wood floor. She walks into the room and approaches the desk. Her field of vision takes in the room's far corner, beyond the windows, to her left as she approaches the worktable. Something is wrong. She has Seen this before, she has Seen herself walk into this room, over to the worktable, her hands outstretched to the casket that sits there. She should be able to See her other self, her *Seeing* self, but the corner of the room is empty, she's not there .. . .

Zania is wearing a winter cloak, the throat well closed with elabo-rate frogging, the hood pulled up close around her face. Her cheeks glow and her eyes dance. She is singing, and looking down at a bar of blue crystal which she holds in her bare hands. As she sings, she turns the bar first one way, then another, first by the middle, then by each end in turn. Finally, she holds the bar between the flat palms of her two hands, and shuts her eyes. . . .

Avylos is made of light. Beams of light pour from his fingers' ends, from his eyes, from his open mouth, from the ends of his hair. He walks toward her, his hands stretched out and she feels herself step-ping forward, even as she wills herself back.

Her eyes snapped open and he was kneeling in front of her, his face white, his eyes focused on her, searching, as if her features would tell him something.

"What did you See?"

"You were full of light, lord Mage. Full of light."

"More jam?"

"Mmm." Dhulyn accepted the small ceramic pot of nellberry jam Princess Kera handed her and spooned some onto her biscuit while she swallowed what she already had in her mouth. She'd never eaten nellberries before, and was beginning to be afraid that she'd never get another chance. She'd gone down to the castle end of the corridor that morning as Avylos had instructed her, and hadn't been altogether surprised to find the princess had brought breakfast herself. Like anyone of her age, the princess was curious, and as Dhulyn expected, she had many questions.

Dhulyn returned the spoon to the tabletop, where it had been representing the Limona River. "Your strategy was a good one," she said, pointing to the battleground she'd created using the saltcellar, spoons, jam pots, and dried fruit that had accompanied the biscuits and bite-sized meat tartlets that made up their breakfast. "You made good use of the terrain, very good use of your cavalry. Your archers, perhaps, could have been in a better position." She tapped a spot that had been left blank before looking up at the princess. "Your brother had no hand in this plan?"

Kera shook her head without lifting her eyes from the tabletop. "Edmir has no head for strategy. The plan was all mine. Why did it fail?"

Dhulyn held up a finger. Frowned. Licked the jam off it and held it up again. "First, you expected to be outnumbered, but not as greatly as you were." She held up another finger. "Second, you did not know that Parno and I had changed the usual strategy and formation of the Nisvean forces." Another finger. "Third, you expected the magic that has protected the Tegrian armies for the last two campaigning seasons to work this time as well."

"So it really wasn't my fault?"

Dhulyn raised her eyebrows. "Come. You knew as soon as you'd seen Edmir's image in the pool what had really happened."

Kera looked up from the representation of the battle of Limona. "I know. It *had* to be Avylos. Yet, somehow, I couldn't feel *sure*."

"And you are sure now?"

The girl nodded. "Avylos tried to kill my brother."

"And he is still trying."

"Why are you helping us?"

Dhulyn shrugged. "It began as a way to follow our Common Rule. We don't hold for ransom, and your brother was ours to decide upon, no one else's. Then, things grew more complicated. With respect to your mother, an ambitious and predatory queen is a worry for her neighbors, if for no one else. Such a queen with a tame Mage can be a larger worry then." She fell silent as images passed through her mind. "If you had seen what he did to Probic, you would not need to ask me why we are here. We have had some experience, my Partner and I, of Mages and the like who become ambitious for themselves. It is not a problem from which you can walk away. It will follow."

"But he is powerful—" Kera stopped and turned abruptly to face Dhulyn. "Can you call upon others of your Brotherhood? Can you oppose him?"

Dhulyn leaned forward, scanning the youthful face in front of her. The princess returned her look steadily, even raising one eyebrow a fraction. Edmir would already have been fidgeting; the girl was much cooler than her brother, more direct and less dreamy. She would make a better ruler than Edmir, Dhulyn thought, and wondered if the girl herself realized it.

"The short answer to your question is 'no,' " she said. "Even setting aside the banishment, the Brotherhood is not a standing army, not a force that can be called upon. Once, long ago, perhaps, close to the time of the Caids, we were more numerous, but in recent years our numbers have dwindled. Many cities, like Beolind, no longer have a Mercenary House. I would not be surprised to learn that Parno and I were the only Mercenary Brothers now in Tegrian. But—" Dhulyn lifted her hand as the princess opened her mouth to speak. "We *are* here, Parno and I, and we will do what we can to stop him.

"We have reason to believe that the source of his power is a blue

Stone, a crystal as long as my forearm, and perhaps as thick around as this." Dhulyn held up her hands to demonstrate the dimensions. "He may have some latent power or abilities of his own, but the crystal fuels them, gives them power and force."

"And if you remove this Stone, you remove his powers?"

"Yes."

"And that's why you are here."

"Yes."

"But he's the consort, he's been helping . . ." Kera's voice died away.

"He's been helping your mother the queen," Dhulyn finished Kera's thought for her. "Do you think your mother wanted Edmir dead?"

Kera shook her head slowly, her eyes unfocused.

"What will he do next that she does not want? Comes a time, when you must ask yourself, do you wield the sword, or does the sword wield you?"

Kera's eyes narrowed. "Is removing the Stone enough? Will Avylos not try to recapture it?"

Dhulyn smiled. The girl was definitely worth two of her brother; this question had not occurred to Edmir. "We may have to destroy it," she said. "But it may be possible to simply neutralize it. His powers may then return to their latent condition."

"How can I help?"

"I need to get into his workroom. When I tried last night, I could not even find the latch; it was as if the door was simply a solid piece of wood."

"He magics it when he leaves the wing," Kera said, nodding. "But unless he has used something new, I should be able to open it."

"How so?"

Kera shrugged. "Edmir and I discovered this when our father was still alive. When Avylos works a magic on a woman, or against a woman, sometimes it does not work at all, and if it does, it will eventually wear off, and must be reworked. On a man, it seems to last for always—that is, if Avylos wants it to. He *can* magic a man temporarily if he chooses to, as he does with the armies, for example. But with a woman, the magic *always* fades by itself. That's why there are so few women in our armies, and why, I suspect, Avylos won't have female pages nor allow my mother to have them," Kera added in a tone that showed this had just occurred to her. "I don't know if any one else has noticed this, but Edmir and I did. Also," she hesitated as if choosing her words carefully. "It seems that there are times when he doesn't . . . when he *conserves* his magic."

"Again, how so?"

"Well, take his workroom as an example. At times we've noticed he uses what Edmir called magics of concealment, where a thing is simply not visible, like the latch on his door. Other times there might be magics of avoidance, where you approach his door, or the shelves behind his worktable say, and then find yourself in another part of the corridor entirely, or on the other side of the room, looking out the window." Kera straightened the spoon next to her plate. "Sometimes all these magics are in effect. But there are times when there is no magic of concealment, if an avoidance magic would serve the purpose just as well, or where there's no avoidance magics if a lock would do."

Dhulyn whistled silently. "So there are times when the door is magicked, but the things inside the room are not?"

Kera nodded.

Dhulyn would wager her second-best sword that it was Kera herself who noticed this and told Edmir. "And if the magic on the door is an old one, one which has been there a while, you should be able to see the latch, and open the door?"

"I've done it before." Kera studied the jam pot with great concentration.

"Will he know you've helped me?"

Kera spoke without raising her eyes from the empty jam pot. "From what Avylos has said before, he can tell *that* I've been somewhere, like his workroom or the garden. But he can't tell *when* it was, or for how long."

"Nor, from what you said in the garden yesterday, can he always tell when you are actually present, but hiding." Dhulyn drew away from the table. It seemed, then, that she was not the only one whose control over their gift was less than perfect. Perhaps Avylos depended too much on his magics, and that might provide them with an opening. "So his magics can tell him certain things, but not *all* things."

"He learns new magics all the time, though," Kera said. "When we were small, he couldn't tell that we'd been in his room. Then he could tell that someone had been, but not who. Now he call tell who." The girl frowned. "Dhulyn Wolfshead, if Avylos gets his power from this Stone, where does the Stone get its power?"

As her hand strayed to brush against the book under her tunic, Dhulyn scanned the table once more for any food she'd missed before answering. "The Stone is like a well," she said. "You draw power from it, as you would water from the well, and then it must be replenished, as the well is replenished by an underground stream or lake."

"But how is the Stone replenished?"

Dhulyn knew from Zania's book how the players had refilled the Stone. After every performance, they had returned to it the power they took. Old Therin had believed that their own skill, and the heightened energies created by the performance itself, had enabled them always to return at least as much as they had used, if not a little more.

"Avylos is the one who checks new Mages and the Marked, isn't he? For licensing?"

Kera pushed her empty plate away. "Yes."

"And has he issued any new licenses?"

"I wouldn't necessarily know," Kera said. "There have been a few of the Marked, a Finder, I think, and a Mender. Edmir was trying to work out a scheme to get them to return here after they'd been sent to the Guilds in Imrion for training. But if the ones here are already licensed . . ."

"You say the Marked, but what about Mages? How many of them have been found and licensed?"

"Mages?" Kera looked puzzled, her brow furrowed and her lips parted. "None," she said finally. "None that I've heard of, anyway."

"I'd wager that's how he is powering the Stone, then." Dhulyn rubbed at her forehead with her fingertips. "Anyone who has magic within them comes to be examined and licensed. And then he takes their power, and feeds it to the Stone."

"Maybe not just Mages." Kera had turned very white, and her eyes stared into the distance. "There was a harper used to live here at Royal House. She would make new songs for my mother's birthday, and other songs, all kinds, great stirring ballads and light funny tunes. She fell ill, and Avylos tended to her—we have no Healer here, not since before my grandfather's time. When her illness was gone, she couldn't make new songs anymore. She could still sing the old ones, but there were no more new songs."

Dhulyn shivered. No more new songs. That would also fit what Therin had described. The Stone could take in talent of every kind.

"Even if I get you into the workroom," Kera said finally. "What if there are other avoidance magics in the room itself?

"What are the areas he makes you avoid?" Dhulyn said.

"The shelves behind his worktable. There's mostly books, a couple of other things. And the small casket on the table itself. To the left if you're sitting in his chair, on the right if you're facing the table."

Dhulyn nodded, she'd seen the casket, and the bookshelf for that matter. "The casket holds the Stone," she said. "We'll just have to try and see." Another thought occurred to her. "Are Avylos' enchantments just against people? Could I reach the Stone with a weapon? A fire arrow, for example?"

Kera leaned forward, her brows drawn down in a vee. "I've never tried throwing anything into the magicked area." Her brows lifted. "A fire arrow might be very interesting indeed."

"How soon can you get me into the room?"

Kera thought, turning her spoon over and over on the tablecloth. "Tonight," she said. "There's to be a banquet. Avylos will attend with my mother the queen, and won't come back to his rooms until late. If at all."

Edmir sank to his knees, let his face fall forward into Zania's hands, and crushed his lips against her palm.

The audience—four herd children, a dog, and nine of their flock— was silent for two heartbeats before breaking into thunderous whistling, clapping, and stamping of bare feet. The dog barked, and the sheep shied away a few paces before settling once more to their cropping of the clumps of grass.

"I thought there might be too much kissing," the tallest boy said, his fair hair tied back in a tail. "But there wasn't. It was just right."

"High praise, indeed," Edmir said, and swept the boy another bow. When the children had gone their way up the hillside with promises of more dramatics the next day, Edmir turned to Zania. She had taken off the cloak she'd been wearing to rehearse the part of the queen and spread it on the ground before sitting down.

Edmir sat down next to her, feeling light as a feather. He turned his face up to the warmth of the sun. He couldn't stop smiling, and his lips could still feel Zania's skin.

"You don't think you could write me a half dozen more of these before you go back to your real life, do you? This one pleases all who've seen it, but I can't make a living with just *The Soldier King*." Zania ran her hands through her short hair and leaned back on her elbows.

Edmir came down to earth with a thump that almost stopped his heart.

"That's all you have to say," he said finally when he could trust his voice—and his breathing—to sound normal. "You didn't feel anything just now?"

Zania sat up, her eyes turned away. "Of course I did, I was supposed to." She glanced at him, her green eyes dark. "It's the play, Edmir."

He spread his hands, shaking his head. "I must be a great writer then."

Zania took hold of his sleeve between her thumb and forefinger and gave it a little tug. "You are. And I understand how you feel. It's one of the reasons that actors so frequently marry other actors. Let's see how you feel when you're Prince Edmir once again."

"You could come with me," he said. The words were out before he knew it, but once out, he was certain he wouldn't take them back.

"You don't mean it."

"I do."

Zania took in a deep breath through her nose. "Your mother the queen would let us marry?"

Edmir didn't speak, he knew the answer was on his face.

"That's what I thought. You'll be Lord Prince, and then King. What will I be?" Zania stood up and tugged on the edge of the cloak. Edmir waited long enough to be sure she wasn't running away before he stood up also, holding the edge closest to him in his hands. Zania dropped the edge she was holding and started to walk down the hill toward the track that led to the gamekeeper's lodge.

But she *was* walking, not running.

"You could have a theater in Beolind," he said, trying to keep his voice neutral as he hurried to catch up with her.

"Or in Gotterang, or Lesonika or Tenezia. Any city large enough to have the business. Why should I stay in Beolind?"

Because I would be there. But he couldn't say it aloud, couldn't bare his need so plainly. "Because I would ask you to," he said instead. That was as close as he could come.

She looked back at him then and stopped, her feet carefully braced on the uneven dirt of the track. She smiled, but it was a stage smile; her eyes were still hooded and dark. "Yes," she said. "And you could write me plays in your copious free time, between ruling the country, going to war, and making a good political marriage. As for me, I would never know whether my audiences loved my work, or whether they applauded because I was the king's woman."

It was true, what she was saying, they both knew it.

And that's *why she pushes me away*, he thought. Because he would be going back to his own life, and because, when he became Lord Prince Edmir once again, he would have to put his feelings for her aside.

But not because she doesn't feel the same way. She'd been speaking plainly, out here with only the rocks and grass to hear them, and if she didn't care for him, she would have said so. If she did not ask him to stay with her, it was only because she knew what his answer must be.

There was a strange horse tied up outside the lodge, which drove all other thoughts away.

"We're just players," Zania reminded him under her breath. "Nothing to worry about."

"Where are the others?" he murmured.

"Fishing."

But acting turned out not to be necessary, as it was the Consort Sylria who greeted them when they reached the door.

"There you are, I was just coming out to see to the horse. You had me worried a moment, though I could see all was well." She gestured at the orderly room around her. "I have news, we leave for Beolind tomorrow, can you be ready?"

"Tomorrow?"

The older woman nodded. "A messenger came from Valaika. We're to leave for Beolind tomorrow."

"Have they spoken to my mother?" Edmir was afraid to look at Zania.

Sylria came closer to them and lowered her voice. "I would think she had to be careful how much to entrust to a messenger. All I know is we're to go to Beolind." She smiled and patted them both on the shoulder. "Tomorrow."

"Shouldn't we be leaving right away?" Did Zania have to sound so eager?

"It's already late to begin the journey today," Sylria said. "Though I came as quickly as I could." She went to the doorway and clucked at her horse. "My instructions were quite clear. We're to leave for Beolind tomorrow." Sylria smiled again, and disappeared through the doorway.

Edmir shared a look with Zania, their earlier awkwardness forgotten.

"That still doesn't leave us much time," Zania said. "Lucky thing I've repacked almost everything already."

Edmir looked back at the doorway. "Something's wrong," he said, when he judged Sylria was far enough away. "Something in the tone of her voice . . ."

"You think you know her tones so well?" Zania sat down on the bench along one side of the table.

Edmir sat down next to her, taking care to leave space between them. " 'We're to leave for Beolind tomorrow,' " he said. "I know *that* tone—Caids know you've made us all so sensitive to intonation and syllable stress and what all in the last moon. I know I've heard that tone before." He reached for the knife at his belt, suddenly wishing for his sword instead, as the hairs on the back of his neck rose. "And I know where."

He turned to face Zania. "In Probic, that's how Tzanek sounded when he said, 'The young man they have with them is not Edmir, I will not be deceived.' I'll never forget it, never."

"You sounded just like her."

"So you see?"

Zania looked at the doorway, gnawing on her lower lip. "It's like sleep suggestion," she said finally.

"What?"

"It's a stage show trick—or not a trick exactly, but it doesn't need real magic. At least—well, I think Avylos used to do it, but I've seen it done by others I know are not Mages."

Edmir wanted to take her by the shoulders and shake it out of her. "Explain," he said through clenched teeth.

"You focus someone's attention in such a way that they appear to fall asleep, but they can still hear you. Then you tell them to do something, dance, or sing, or beg some stranger to marry them, something to make the audience laugh."

"And they do it?" Edmir had a cold feeling in his stomach.

"Usually, yes, but it's meant to be funny. Or sometimes you give them a command to follow after they've woken up and when the cue comes, they'll do it, even though they're awake. Oh—"

His face must have shown what he was thinking because Zania broke off, shaking her head and hunching up her shoulders.

"I don't know *how* it works, exactly, but it *does* work. And that's what Sylria makes me think of."

"And Avylos can do this." Edmir looked down at his hands. "I don't think we should go anywhere with Sylria. Dhulyn and Parno haven't sent for us, I'm sure of it."

"But we *want* to go to Beolind. If we can't trust Sylria any longer . . ." Zania shrugged. "The only people we *can* trust are there."

"So we go along with her, and look for our best chance to escape?"

"Now you're thinking."

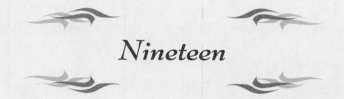

Nineteen

DHULYN WOLFSHEAD FINGERED the edge of the short, blood-red wig Avylos had found for her. He'd been right; it wasn't as good a quality as the one she'd been wearing, the one she'd had from Zania's stock. Nor was the fit as secure without the paste from Zania's well-sealed jars. And, if anything, it had been *more* disconcerting to catch sight of herself in the small mirror that hung in her chamber with hair the right color, but no Mercenary badge. She lowered her hand and brought her attention back to what she was supposed to be doing, waiting for Princess Kera.

Dhulyn had earlier made note of the spot where the corridor of dressed stone widened as it approached the doorway of Avylos' workroom, and made a small corner. It wouldn't appear possible, but at night, with only the light from the sconces in the main hallway, that small corner created just enough shadow for a slim person to stand unseen. Provided that person was using one of the Stalking *Shoras*. Dhulyn pressed her shoulder blades against the cold stone and breathed shallowly. She'd arrived early, but just as she'd expected, she hadn't been able to open the door to the Blue Mage's workroom. Once again, there was neither latch nor lock, just the plain, unbroken expanse of wood.

She had only been waiting for a few minutes when the rustle of stiff silks warned her that Kera was coming. *Loud enough for three people*, she thought. *Good thing I'm the only one here*. And a good thing that she wasn't wearing formal court clothes herself—even her breathing would have been too loud for caution.

"Kera," she whispered as the girl passed her.

The princess squeaked and brought her hands up in self-defense, almost taking off the end of her sleeve with the sword held in her right hand. Squeak or no, Dhulyn noted, the girl held her sword steady, and she'd turned in the right direction, *toward* what had frightened her. Kera lowered her left hand slowly, and peered into the shadow.

"Dhulyn Wolfshead?"

Dhulyn stepped out of the narrow shadow and carefully took the blade out of Kera's hand.

"How much time have you?"

"Not long. I said I was going to the water closet, and then I had to stop in my room for the sword." She looked at it, lower lip between her teeth. "It was my father's," she said.

Dhulyn had already noticed it was a soldier's blade, plain with only a single rough stone in the pommel.

"Best that you don't come in with me, then." *Not that I would have let you, but there's no need for you to know that.* "The door will not open for me," she added.

"Unless he's renewed it . . ." Kera stood in front of the door and slowed her breathing. She lifted her hand to a spot rather higher than Dhulyn would have expected a door latch to be, and an elaborately wrought metal handle appeared just as Kera's fingers closed on it. The door swung open the width of a hand.

"Either he has no secrets from you," Dhulyn said. "Or he thinks there's nothing in there you can discover by yourself."

"I used to think it was the first one." Kera shrugged. "But what need to spell the door against me if I can't open anything once I'm inside?"

"I'll see what *I* can do," Dhulyn said. "Best you be off before you're missed."

Kera looked once more into the room, indecision plain on her face. Finally she took a step back. "Caids smile on you," she said, and ran back down the hallway toward the main part of the Royal House.

Dhulyn waited until the sound of rustling silk died away, and she could both hear herself think, and hear anyone else who might be coming. Standing to one side, she pushed the door farther open with the tip of the sword blade, and listened.

She took four measured strides into the room and stopped, looked about, and took one more step. What she now saw matched what she had Seen in her Vision. There was the angle of dim light from a moon only half full slanting in the narrow window, casting the shadows of the bars across the polished oak floor, with its band of dark inlay around the edges. There were the softer shadows cast by the chairs, the piece of rug that seemed, in this light, to have no pattern and no color. The worktable and the plain casket that stood upon it. And the darkness in the far corner. Where, in her Vision, she was standing with a full view of the room.

But sometimes, in her Visions, the room had been empty. She hadn't always Seen herself.

Out of habit and training Dhulyn moved slowly, her feet making no sound. As she advanced toward the worktable, she felt along the left seam of the shirt she was wearing and finally pulled out a steel wire as long as her hand. She'd bought it off a jeweler in Cabrea, a long time ago, and it was still her best lockpick, though usually she wore it woven into the braids of her hair. She put the lockpick between her teeth, and pulled a soft silk scarf out of the front of her shirt. Among its many qualities, silk was thought to insulate and cleanse. Finders, she knew, often used silk to wrap and store their scrying bowls, and the ancient box that held her vera tiles was lined with it. She wrapped the scarf carefully around the hilt of the sword and, taking it in her left hand, approached the worktable with its small casket.

She was alert for the phenomenon Kera had described, of heading toward the casket and finding herself suddenly on the far side of the room. Dhulyn slowed her breathing, let herself fall into a Hunter's *Shora*, senses alert, focused on her prey, the plain wooden box. The box filled her mind, her vision narrowed. Almost, she could taste it.

Turning her body sideways to present the smallest target, Dhulyn struck with the blade in her left hand, making flashing touches on the casket's lid, then on the right, left and front sides.

Nothing. No resistance, no flash of light, no shimmer such as Finders or Menders had described to her sometimes happened when they used their Mark.

Dhulyn took two steps closer, still focusing her senses on the casket. She laid the sword on the tabletop and wrapped the silk around her left hand, lowering it slowly, alert for any change in either the box or herself. But she felt no reluctance—nor did she suddenly find herself at the other end of the desk, unaware of her intention of moving. Even through the silk, the wood was cool and smooth under her fingers. She could clearly see the faceplate of the locking mechanism, a fine Balnian lock after the old pattern—just as Therin had described it in the journal still tucked into her shirt. It seemed there was no avoidance magic on the box itself, that Avylos was relying solely on the magicked door. It struck Dhulyn as a strange economy of magic, to use both spells and physical deterrents. Was there some strategy she did not see, or was Avylos only conserving power?

Still, the box would not open.

Dhulyn rolled her eyes as she pulled the lockpick from between her teeth. Balnian locks, though good, could be mastered with sufficient practice. The pick went in easily, and after a few tense moments of careful prodding, Dhulyn felt through her fingers the 'click' that signified the lock was open.

She licked suddenly dry lips, picked up the sword once more and backed away from the table. Using the tip of the blade, she flicked the lid open with a twist of her wrist.

Inside the box, nestled in what looked to be layers of dark red velvet cloth, was the Muse Stone. Even if she had not already Seen it in her Visions, she would have recognized it from the meticulous drawings in Therin's journal. A cylinder as long as her forearm, the dark blue of a Berdanan ice sapphire, though the moonlight was not bright enough to make it sparkle. There were lamplighters in a bowl, and Dhulyn used one to light the squat oil lamp on a nearby shelf. The crystal remained dark, as the journal had led her to expect. She frowned, peering more closely. She could not quite make out the markings that should be around the end of the Stone.

Dhulyn took a deep breath and let it out slowly. Both the journal and Zania herself had said that the older members of the troupe had handled the Stone many times and had taken no harm from it. Still, it was as well to be careful. Dhulyn shifted the sword to her right hand, reached out with her left and picked up the Stone.

It was warm. There was no vibration, no noise, but it was warm, like a grindstone recently in use, or a stone crock kept close to the kitchen fires. And now she could see the symbols the journal had described. The *Marks*, circle around a dot, rectangle—though here it was closer to a square—long triangle, and straight line. Each Mark clear, the carving deep, and set at the four compass points within a bowstring's width of the end of the Muse Stone. A finger width farther in, Dhulyn found the fifth Mark, the Lens, three concentric circles. As Therin's journal had indicated, the Lens was placed exactly between two of the Marks, at present, between the triangle of the Mender and the dotted circle of the Seer.

And there were the symbols on the other end. Dhulyn's eyebrows arched as high as they would go. She knew these symbols now, though she hadn't when she'd first seen them in the book. They were like the signs that Avylos had drawn in the air. Like the signs she'd Seen him, and one other, draw in her Visions.

So one end for the Marked, and one for Mages?

She tried to turn the bottom, twisting it as the journal described, but it stood fast, as if in one solid piece. There was no feeling of either resistance or give. In fact, Dhulyn had no sense of a mechanism at all, as she'd had with the lock.

She checked the tightness of her belt preparatory to slipping the Muse Stone into the front of her shirt. With her shirt collar in one hand, she paused, thinking.

A few moments ago she'd questioned Avylos' strategy. A magical lock on the door that at least one person could get through, at least some of the time. No other magics, nothing but mundane locks and bars. She held the Stone out in the light again. Was it all too easy?

A false Stone, set to trap the ignorant? If *she* could think of this idea, *he* could think of it. But unlike any other who might come into the room, she was not entirely ignorant. She tapped the book hidden in her shirt with her fingertips. She could test the Stone. She wanted neither to receive power nor to bestow it, but surely what Therin had called the Null Chant, the empty words which drew no response from the Stone other than to turn the cylinder, *they* would be safe.

Elis elis tanton neel;
Dor la sinquin so la dele.
Kos noforlin sik ek aye,
Kik shon te ounte gesserae.

The Stone grew marginally warmer, as if the stone crock had been moved closer to the flames. Careful not to put her fingers on any of the symbols, Dhulyn tried again to turn the end of the Stone, and this

time it moved. Repeating the lines, she kept turning until the Mark of
the Seer lined up with the Mark of the Lens.

The room disappeared. A great light filled her eyes. A bell began to
ring.

A snowstorm, a voice calls from somewhere to her left . . .

A man with hair the color of wheat sits behind a desk reading a
massive book in an unknown tongue. A large round mirror stands to
his right . . .

A stocky, fair-haired boy looks down into a bowl . . .

The deck slants almost vertical and water pours off in sheets; a
man with a red-and-gold Mercenary badge goes over the side into the
churning waves . . .

The body of a Cloud falls from a great height, his Racha bird keeping pace with him, keening . . .

An older Kera walks toward a throne. A circle of women across a
room . . .

A one-eyed man peers into her face, asking a question . . .

A smiling man with hair the color of old blood matching his huge
mustache offers her a ball of light in the palm of his hand . . .

A horde of cavalry rides over the ridge and darkens the valley
below . . .

A red-haired woman pushes a sword through Parno's heart . . .

Water seeps up through pale gray sand, forming a pool as wide as
her spread hands . . .

*   *   *

She stands in the dark corner of Avylos' workroom and takes a step toward herself . . .

Avylos runs through the woods, falls, gets up and runs again, looking back over his shoulder. Far down the trail, two men with hair the color of old blood give chase . . .

Three sisters hold hands, beckoning toward her, and holding out their free hands for her to join their circle. Each has the Mark of the Seer tattooed on her forehead.

A strange sensation. Her cheek on something cool. Tiles? Floor tiles? She set the palm of her hand down flat. Oak. Hard wood. She thought about pushing herself upright. But her head was so heavy.

A sharp crackling sound, and there was light on the other side of her eyelids.

Footsteps. Feet. Black house shoes with a dark blue trim. Satin? Velvet? Hands on her arms, in her armpits, dragging her upright. How could her head possibly be so heavy? Had she been ill? What was she doing on the floor? Where was she?

Who was she?

Strong fingers on her chin, holding her head steady and upright. She blinked. A long face, pale. Blue eyes. Hair a very dark red. Blue eyes narrowed, dark red brows drawn down in a vee over a long, thin nose. Lips pressed tight together.

She tried to speak, but her throat was thick. She licked her lips, cleared her throat, and tried again.

"Where am I?" she said, finding she could not bring herself to ask the more important question, "who?" "Who are you?"

The man's face relaxed, though his eyes were still narrowed. The hand on her chin became a caress, and the muscles in her neck and shoulders which had been very tight a moment before loosened. Her head still throbbed.

"Don't you know me, my dearest? Has your fever become worse?"

She took his hand and struggled to sit up. Something hard poked painfully into her ribs and she winced, her hand going automatically to the spot. There seemed to be something . . .

"Here, let me help you." The man helped loosen the ties of her shirt and drew a slim book out from under her clothing. He raised his eyebrows, but did not seem in any way surprised or upset. He reached up and put the book on the tabletop above her head.

A sound made them both look to the door.

Kera went directly to Dhulyn Wolfshead's room when she was finally excused from the banquet. She'd never realized, when Edmir was alive—when Edmir was at court, she corrected, Edmir was *still* alive. She hadn't realized, in any case, just how much of his time was taken up with being the Lord Prince, meeting the right people at the right times, attending functions that until now she'd mostly been excused from. Which probably explained why he'd been so much more tense and abrupt in the last few years, without time to play with her. Even his journal entries, she now knew, had been shorter, with fewer of the stories he used to make up for her.

Now that she was Lady Prince, and the heir to the throne, it seemed there were not enough hours in the day. Her feet slowed. If she was being honest, she would have to admit that *she* didn't feel at all tense or abrupt. Even her mother the queen was easier to handle, now that all their contact was strictly formal. And the servants were definitely easier to deal with. Now, when she told them to leave her, they stopped cooing over her and patting her on the head. They actually went. Well, most of them.

Kera turned from the main hallway just before she reached the passage which held Avylos' study, into a much shorter passage which had only one door at the end of it. Kera lifted the latch and stepped inside. The Wolfshead's room was very simply furnished, like that of an upper servant. A bed, a table with a single chair. A brazier under the table, empty, and unlit now in the warm weather of summer. Three wooden pegs attached to the dressed stone wall to hold clothing, also empty. There was enough clothing tossed over the furniture, however, to make it difficult to be sure what Dhulyn Wolfshead was wearing. The bed was rumpled, the pillow showed the indentation of a head.

Had the Mercenary woman returned to this room, then? Or was all this a stage setting, so that if the Wolfshead was found up and wandering around she could claim to have just left her bed?

Kera took her lower lip between her teeth. The room was telling her nothing. The Wolfshead was not here; could she be still in the workroom?

She retraced her steps back along the passage to the main corridor, turned left, carefully eyed the patch of shadow where it widened to assure herself that the Mercenary was not in it, and stopped at the door to Avylos' workroom. The thinnest line of light showed in the opening. She waited, straining forward. Was that voices? She tilted her head closer to the door, and held her breath. Voices, for certain, though she couldn't hear any words. She touched the door with her fingertips, meaning just to open it slightly, but misjudged the pressure, and, dry mouthed, watched it swing fully open.

Kera stood dead still, her fingertips still on the door. Dhulyn Wolfshead was on the floor, propped against the table leg. Avylos had his hand on her face, holding her by the chin, the way a Knife might when he wanted you to stay still for an examination. His head was tilted forward at such an angle that Kera was certain he had been about to kiss her.

Avylos dropped his hand when he saw her, but he did not move away from Dhulyn Wolfshead. Kera saw she had hold of Avylos' sleeve.

Kera stepped forward, speaking before anyone could ask her questions.

"I saw the light," she said, "I thought you were still with my mother the queen."

"Avylos, who is this child?" A thread of accent heavier than Kera had heard from Dhulyn Wolfshead before.

Kera stepped forward with more confidence. Dhulyn Wolfshead would not be speaking in that tone, and asking that question, if there was any trouble. She was letting Kera know that their acquaintance was still a secret from Avylos. But as she got nearer to the two at the table, Kera's step faltered. She expected Dhulyn Wolfshead to pretend not to know her, but that wide-eyed stare, that hint of tension—even fear—that was no pretense. When they were younger, she and Edmir used to disguise themselves and wander through the public portions of the Royal House, and even into the nearby streets when they could manage to get out the gates. They learned very early to tell the difference between people who genuinely didn't recognize them and people who were just playing along with the Royal children's game.

And Dhulyn Wolfshead was not faking. She no longer knew her.

Kera's heart pounded in her ears. Think, *think*. What would be the natural thing for her to say?

"Is this your kinswoman, Avylos?" Kera hoped her smile didn't look as fake as it felt.

"It is, Lady Prince, my cousin. Dhulyn, my dear, this is the Lady Prince Kera, the heir to the throne of Tegrian."

Avylos helped her to her feet, and the woman looked down at Kera with a grave face and nodded her head once.

"I thank you, Lady Prince, and your mother the queen, for your hospitality. I am Dhulyn of . . ." She looked at Avylos, lips beginning to tremble before she clamped her mouth shut firmly enough that a muscle twitched at the hinge of her jaw.

"Of the Forest Plain Clan," the Mage finished for her, and Dhulyn Wolfshead nodded.

Had she been about to say something else, Kera wondered. Was there anything of Dhulyn Wolfshead left? How had Avylos done this?

The evening meal, a simple one of rewarmed rabbit pie, fresh water from the lodge's well, and a few dried apples found in a stone crock near the door, went smoothly enough, with Sylria telling stories of how she and Valaika had met, and Zania telling of how her uncle had once performed *The Galan of Illrya* without the false nose the part required, and how he had done it.

It had been a long, tiring day, so Zania's suggestion of an early night was welcomed. Sylria was surprised when Edmir insisted she use the bedchamber, and tried to defer to his rank.

"I've been sleeping rough the last moon," he'd told her. "Plenty of time for beds when we're back in Beolind."

When the large shutter that was the bedchamber's door was closed, Edmir left the soft pile of sheep and inglera skins that made up his bed and crept across the floor to Zania.

"Shall we keep watch?" he said in as close an approximation of the Mercenary nightwatch voice as he could manage.

"Dhulyn and Parno—" Edmir put his finger on Zania's lips. Trained to project her voice over an area the size of a market square, even her whispers were too loud. Too bad he couldn't read her lips against the palm of his hand, as Dhulyn had done in Nisvea.

"They would say we should keep watch," Zania said.

Edmir nodded. "Sylria sounded her normal self at supper, but I thought she was looking at us . . ." He shrugged. Had he actually seen anything? Or were all his fears the result of too easy an imagination?

But Zania was nodding again, and patting his arm. *Take the precautions anyway*, he thought. What was it Dhulyn was always saying? Prepare for what *can* happen, not for what *might* happen.

"I'll take the first watch."

Edmir crept back to his own bed and watched the shadowy form of Zania lie down again and pull a blanket over her head to block what little light from the half full moon came in with the breeze through the open windows. He left the bulk of his bedding where it was, taking only an inglera hide thick with wool. He shifted over against the wall, made a pad for his back, and sat braced against the stone.

Caids grant I don't fall asleep.

Whether it was the spirits of the Caids or not, Edmir was wide awake when the shutter of Sylria's bedchamber swung noiselessly open, and the older woman, her pale sleeping shift making her stand out in the gloom, padded out into the main room on bare feet. The figure hesitated, looking between the two piles of bedding. Edmir held his breath and shifted his weight forward, prepared to spring to his feet.

Sylria turned to Edmir's bedroll and squatted down on her heels—an unattractive position, Edmir felt sure, that no woman of her age and rank would take voluntarily. She raised one hand above her head, and Edmir was already rolling forward onto his feet when he saw the blade flash in moonlight as it plunged down into the blankets of his bed.

Edmir continued the roll that brought him to his feet, turning it into a dive that took him across the short stretch of floor and into Sylria's left side. He landed on top of her, trapping her blade hand, and, half winded himself, hoping even after what he'd seen that he hadn't injured the woman under him.

"Zania. Some light."

But she was already throwing off blankets and running to the table. When she turned with the oil lamp in her hand, her eyes went first to him, her eyebrows crawling almost to her hairline when she saw where he was, and who he had under him. A sound, quickly stifled, escaped her lips when she saw the weapon.

"Get the knife, quickly."

Zania darted forward, her eyes huge and dark, took the knife from Sylria's slack hand and jumped back. Edmir scuttled backward, heels and hands, until he was brought up short by the wall. His mouth was dry, and his heart thundered in his ears.

"Something to tie her with," he managed to say. As Zania disappeared into the bedchamber, returning with Sylria's sashes and scarves, Edmir crept forward and held his fingers under Sylria's jaw. His hands were shaking so badly he had to take a deep breath and try again. Sylria's heart beat steadily, but her eyes were shut.

"She must have hit her head against the edge of the bench," Zania said, kneeling down next to them. It made Edmir feel less of a coward to see her hands were shaking as well. "Let's get her bound before she wakes up."

Edmir sat quiet, holding a long orange sash between his hands. "*If* she wakes up." He licked his lips.

"Edmir, she tried to kill you."

He looked up, blinking. "Maybe she didn't. Sylria wouldn't want to kill me." He sat back on his heels. "What if it was sleep suggestion? What if it was Avylos?" Not that that changed anything. It didn't make him feel any better about leaving Sylria unconscious. She was still his aunt's consort. Oh, Caids, his aunt. What was he going to tell Valaika?

"Edmir." Zania's voice a mere thread of sound.

Sylria's eyelids were fluttering.

"Move the light away," he said. The sound of his voice brought Sylria's eyes wide open.

"Are they dead?"

The hairs rose on the back of Edmir's neck and cold sweat trickled down his back. He realized that with the dim lamp behind him, Sylria saw only his silhouette.

"Yes," he said.

A look of pain crossed Sylria's face. "I had to kill them," she said. "He would have magicked our Janek, made him waste away. Kill them," she repeated. "Or Janek will waste away. Kill them. Or Janek will waste away."

Edmir caught Zania's eye. She had her bottom lip between her teeth and her eyes were huge in the lamplight.

"They're dead, so you can rest now," he said to Sylria. "Come." He helped her to her feet and guided her back to her bed. She crept in like a small child, and Edmir was reminded of putting his sister to bed when they had both been much younger, and Kera wouldn't sleep unless he tucked her in. He pulled up Sylria's covers and smoothed them over her with the same gentle gestures he'd used then.

"Close your eyes and sleep now," he said. "We're going to —" he cleared his throat. "We're going to take the bodies away with us, so no one will know. Janek will be safe."

"I must go to him."

"No." Edmir glanced at Zania, at a loss what to do or say next. She moved closer and put her hand on Sylria's shoulder.

"You must wait here," she said, her tone calm and authoritative. "Wait until your servants come."

"I must wait until my servants come."

"If they ask, tell them the players have gone to Beolind."

"The players have gone to Beolind."

"Tell the Blue Mage the one he wanted killed is dead."

"The one he wanted killed is dead."

"That's right. Sleep now." Zania backed away, and Edmir swung the shutter closed again. He listened for the sound of the latch on the inside, but when he did not hear it, he wedged it shut with the blade of Sylria's dagger.

"She'll be all right," he whispered, more to convince himself than Zania. "Someone will come within a day or so."

"He threatened their child," Zania said. "The sleep suggestion alone was not enough to persuade her to kill you, the Mage had to threaten their child as well."

"Zania, we should go now. We can't risk being here when she wakes up."

"Of course." She got to her feet with a shadow of her usual briskness. "I'll harness the horses, I'll be faster."

"Zania, we can't take the caravan."

She stiffened, and turned to look at him.

"Zania, even with both Stumpy *and* Sylria's horse, the caravan would slow us down too much. We'd be easy targets. As it is . . . If all goes well, we can retrieve it—look, I know how much it means to you, what it holds of all your family and your life, but it isn't worth *risking* your life for! Everything you are, your family, it's in here." He touched her on the forehead. "And in here." A light touch just above the collar of her gown. "The rest . . . it's just things."

She bristled, and for a long moment he braced to continue the argument, wondering how far he would take it before he gave in. Finally her eyes dropped, and her shoulders lowered as she nodded her agreement.

Twenty

"THIS THING IS VERY HOT." Dhulyn's fingers strayed to the edge of the new wig Avylos had found for her. Somehow, she looked more natural with longer hair, though why he should think so Avylos didn't know; he'd never seen her with long hair.

"Nevertheless you must leave it on, my dear," Avylos said as he sat down in the chair next to where Dhulyn had been served her breakfast in the garden. "The scarring from your head injury will cause too much remark. Town people are suspicious and untrustworthy enough, as I've told you already, without giving them something to worry them."

Dhulyn nodded. "And it is that injury which has affected my memory?"

"Not precisely." Avylos wondered how much it would be useful to tell her at this point. His excitement at finding what was clearly a manual for the Stone kept him fidgeting with his cup of ganje, and pushing his breakfast away. He had spent most of the night in study of the book she'd had hidden in her tunic, but the language in it was like nothing he had ever seen. If Dhulyn Wolfshead was able to read it—and she *must* have been, she had changed the setting of the Stone—she was more valuable to him than ever. And it was safe to keep her now. *Safe.* She remembered nothing of her former life. He could tell her whatever he chose, and with the sleep suggestion, he could control what she remembered. It would be worth it. He took hold of her hand, and held it, rubbing the back of it with his thumb. "I am doing everything I can to restore you completely, but I am a Mage, not a Healer."

"And *are* you my cousin?"

He hesitated. What to say? What might prove most useful in the long run? If she believed they were blood, well, no tie was greater to an Espadryni—but he should not make it too close a tie, he thought, looking at her hand in his, there were other considerations after all.

"A distant cousin, yes," he said finally. "However, there may be no others of our Tribe, and that makes us closer." He squeezed her hand and replaced it on her lap, sitting back in his own chair. A bird landed on the back of a nearby branch, looking with a hopeful eye at the re-mains of Dhulyn's breakfast on the low table beside her. Dhulyn's hand flashed out, and the bird was caught.

"I'm not finished yet, little cousin," she said, holding the bird close to her face. She blew into its beak and tossed it into the air, where it flew off, clearly more annoyed than frightened.

Avylos smiled. As events were unfolding, how right he'd been to put off killing her. It had *not* been sentimental weakness in him, not at all, but strength, and shrewdness. Events were unfolding better than if he had planned them. Not that he'd ever before felt any lack of family. His own siblings, his two brothers, and their sisters, had never looked at him the way Dhulyn did now. On him, she smiled, her gray eyes warm, showing stony only to the pages who had brought their food.

She did not treat him with exaggerated patience, she did not dismiss him as of no value. She did not look on him with pity, when she thought he did not see. He could keep her. He *must* keep her.

And, he thought, looking around for the bird she had released, Dhulyn clearly still retained the physical skills she'd spent a lifetime developing. His hand strayed back to the book that now rested in the pocket of his robe. Had someone sent her after the Stone, or had she come on her own, having learned of its existence from Edmir? Where had the book come from, and *could* she read it? Surely she would not have had the book with her if she had merely been sent by another?

"Tell me, Dhulyn, do you recall what you were doing with the Blue Stone in my workroom?" It had been on the floor when he'd entered and found her there.

"That cylinder of crystal?" She frowned, her eyebrows, growing blood red once more with the removal of the dye, drawn into a vee above her gray eyes. "I'm not sure. Judging from where it was lying, I would say that I had it in my hand when I fell. But I don't remember." She looked up at him. "Is it important? Did I damage it?"

"No, no. It's come to no harm. But it is a very powerful magical artifact, and touching it may have contributed to your memory loss. I must ask you not to touch it again."

The Blue Stone had come to no harm, that was true, but something *had* happened to it—though what he didn't know. The setting was definitely changed, and it seemed active, alive in a way he had not seen before. But its power level appeared the same, neither higher nor lower. Perhaps the Stone worked differently on the Marked? Perhaps the talent was stored in a different way?

Or perhaps it had not drained Dhulyn Wolfshead of her Mark, just her knowledge of who she was. What irony, if it had also drained the knowledge that would help him finally achieve his goal. Now, with the book and this woman of his own blood who could read it, now, he was the closest he had ever been to having total control over the power of the Stone.

Dhulyn cleared her throat and he looked over at her once more. Her brow was furrowed, her breath came short, and she clutched at the edge of the table with both hands.

<hr />

A golden-haired man with tattoos on his temples laughs and holds out a peach . . .

A woman with hair the color of wheat and a jeweler's lens in her eye carves on a length of blue crystal . . .

An older, red-haired man draws pictures of light in the air while she laughs and claps her hands . . .

She stands in the dark corner of Avylos' workroom and takes a step toward herself . . .

She lunges with her sword at the tattooed man . . .

Water crashes across the deck of a ship . . .

*   *   *

She has the blue crystal in her own hands, she is speaking, and turning the ends . . .

Avylos holds the blue crystal in his hands, light streams from it . . .

<hr>

"Dhulyn? My dear?"

She blinked and looked into Avylos' face. What had just happened to her? What did it mean? She swallowed and licked her lips. Better she should say nothing just now. Her cousin thought she was getting better, and she wanted to do nothing that would upset him.

"A momentary dizziness," she said, smiling as naturally as she could.

He got to his feet and held out his hand. "Come, then. Kedneara the Queen has graciously invited you to this morning's audience."

<hr>

In this informal audience chamber, the dais was only two steps up from the floor, but from her seat next to the queen, Kera could clearly see everyone as they entered the room. This was not a public audience where anyone could come to petition the Royal House for judgment or favor, but rather a private gathering of people invited expressly by Queen Kedneara. Petitions would be made here, yes, favors granted and accepted, but there was a pretense of informality and intimacy to the gathering. Servants circulated with cups of ganje, jeresh, and wine, and others with small bite-sized nibbles from the kitchen.

"Be careful not to fall for any of these boys, my lamb," her mother said, just loudly enough to be overheard by the people standing nearest the throne. "Trifle with them if you like—experience is always a good thing, but go no further than trifling."

There *were* High Noble Houses present, and some *had* brought younger kin with them—for the most part unmarried kin, and male. Kera nodded at her mother the queen, and put on her most careful smile. Now that she was Lady Prince, and not to be sent away to seal some foreign alliance, every High Noble House saw profit in dangling their sons before her.

"I'll be careful, Mother." And she would be, too, if not for the reason her mother expected. The throne was not to be hers, no matter what all these people might think. *And no matter what I might think,* said a traitorous inner voice. Edmir would be back. She would not wish her brother dead, not for all the thrones in the world.

As if in response to the sound of her voice—*blessed Caids, let it not be my thoughts he heard*—Avylos turned to smile at her from his position to the left of the dais. He also had his seat, on the other side of the queen's throne, but at these affairs he liked to stay on his feet, and watch those who approached his queen from their own level.

And today, of course, he had Dhulyn Wolfshead with him. Though she still seemed not to know who she really was.

"There is your Aunt Valaika, Kera my sweet, do you see her? The golden-haired woman coming in the door."

As if Kera wouldn't remember her aunt perfectly well from her father's burial ceremonies. Valaika had taken her out hawking, a pastime she still loved, and had sent her a horse for her naming day only last year.

"Though she's getting gray I see, and a little stouter than when I saw her last. Her consort's a woman, you know. Ran off and married her when I married your father, her brother, so you know what *that* means."

Kera managed to refrain from shutting her eyes and sighing. She'd heard the story a thousand times. How Aunt Valaika had fallen in love with her mother, and, of course, how her mother had wanted her father and how Aunt Valaika had been persuaded to go away, and "stop mooning around me" as Kera's mother had always put it, by the granting of Jarlkevo House.

Her aunt had eventually married, Kera knew, and had produced an heir—though no one knew who the father had been. It was not her consort with her today, Kera saw, as she watched her aunt stroll through the room, heading steadily, if not particularly directly, to the throne. Valaika was a High Noble House, and as such had taken her privilege to bring her own retainer with her.

The man who kept correctly just behind Aunt Valaika's left shoulder would make a fine father of anyone's children, Kera thought. On the tall side of average, muscular but lean, the sun had toasted him a golden brown, his skin just a shade lighter than his hair, and two shades lighter than his short beard. As his eyes scanned the room, he seemed to be on the verge of smiling, and he padded along at Valaika's heels with the smooth movement of one of her mother's hunting cats.

Kera had expected to recognize her aunt, but there was something familiar about her aunt's servant as well, something she couldn't quite—

The man suddenly became alert, eyes brighter, focused. Kera shifted her own eyes to see what the man looked at—of course. Dhulyn Wolfshead had appeared almost four days ago, the day after the message had come announcing the imminent arrival of Aunt Valaika. They had arrived in the city at the same time, the man with Valaika walked with the same catlike smoothness as Dhulyn Wolfshead, and he was looking at the Mercenary woman with an expression that made Kera's breath grow short.

And then his eyes met hers, and his expression cleared, becoming again the correct, bland politeness of a personal guard.

I must speak privately with Aunt Valaika.

The princess was not quite so much the stiffly dressed girl child that she looked, Parno Lionsmane thought. Conscious that what *her* eyes could see, others could see also, he dragged his own gaze away from where Dhulyn stood next to Avylos the Blue Mage. He had seen her for the last moon with her Mercenary badge covered, but not with hair her natural color. This is what she might have looked like if she'd grown up in her own Tribe, if she'd never become a Mercenary Brother. What her mother must have looked like, according to Dhulyn's descriptions of the Visions in which her mother had appeared.

She didn't look all that much like the Blue Mage, beyond the superficial similarity of their coloring. But Parno didn't like how closely together they were standing.

He was certain she'd looked at him, but there had been no change of expression on her face. Of course there wouldn't be, he thought, with a mental sigh. His Partner schooled her features better than anyone he'd ever met—even if she *was* an Outlander. She looked calm but watchful, like a person somewhere for the first time. Or like a personal guard.

But she should have acknowledged his signal.

He followed Valaika up to the throne, and when Avylos, too, stepped up onto the dais to greet the woman who was still, to a degree, part of the Royal House, Parno took advantage of everyone's attention being elsewhere to shift over next to Dhulyn. He pretended to stumble and took hold of her arm.

His own arm was instantly in a grip like a Racha bird's talons and he was roughly pushed away.

"Take your hands from me, town man."

In an instant Avylos was beside them, taking Dhulyn's elbow and turning her away.

"Your pardon, Lord Mage, Lady." Parno spoke in the exaggerated Imrion accent he'd practiced for the stage. "New boots have made me clumsy." He peered at Dhulyn as if seeing her for the first time. "Do I not know you? Have we not met?"

"No." Her voice was very cold, very final. "I do not know you." She turned away from him to the Blue Mage

Valaika appeared as Avylos was murmuring to Dhulyn. "Any trouble?"

"Not at all, House Jarlkevo." Avylos turned to face them, keeping Dhulyn behind him. "My ward was startled, that's all. She has only recently recovered enough from her illness to rise from her bed."

"I'll see it doesn't happen again. You." She turned to Parno. "Back to our rooms, now."

It was the only thing Valaika could have done, the only order that would make sense to the audience watching them out of the corners of their eyes. Parno didn't like it, but he had to leave the audience chamber.

He blew out each breath slowly and completely as he went, consciously forcing the muscles in his shoulders, arms, and hands to relax. He would kill that Mage with his own hands. He didn't know when, or even how, but if it took him the rest of his life, he would kill that Mage. Now he knew how Edmir had felt, back in Probic, when that City Lord hadn't known him.

Dhulyn's reaction had been no act. She hadn't known him. His Brother, his Partner, hadn't known him.

Sylria woke with a dry mouth and a head that felt strangely light and empty, as if she'd had a fever and had taken too much fens bark tea. At first the door to the tiny bedchamber seemed to be stuck, but with repeated jiggling and shoving she eventually had it open. Her foot kicked something almost as soon as she entered the main room, and sent it skittering a short way across the cold stone floor.

A dagger.

And then the whole of the previous night came sweeping over her, and Sylria had to sit down, and hold her now too full head in her hands.

"I did it," she said aloud. "I killed him." And not just Edmir, Sylria realized, as she looked around her. She'd killed them both, the young girl as well.

She barely made it as far as the door before she threw up.

When she was finally able to turn back into the room, she was struck by how clean and tidy it was. She must have cleaned up, removed the bodies. Of course. She must have. She fetched herself a cup of water from the bucket that sat next to the fireplace, rinsed out her mouth, spat, and sat down again.

She knew absolutely that she had killed Edmir. But now that she thought about it, she could not remember the actual act. She knew the bodies had been removed, and the players' caravan hidden. She could not remember doing it.

It *had* been done. All of it, of that she was certain. What did it matter that she could not remember the details?

"This comes of Avylos' 'help,' " she said aloud. Even her voice sounded sour. Her stomach threatened to rebel again and she sipped at the cup of water. She simply could not bear to recall what she had done, and so her mind rejected it. There had been a guardsman once, who had lost his wife, but he simply could not retain the fact of her death, and so he had eventually gone mad. Would that happen to her now? Would she lose her sanity? She took in a deep breath, released it slowly. Better that, better anything, than losing Janek.

One thing did remain to be done. Carefully, feeling unsteady on her feet, Sylria went into the bedchamber and came out with her saddlebags. From an inner pocket she took out the book of poetry she'd brought with her from Jarlkevo House. She set it down on the table, in the full light of the sun, and opened it to the middle pages.

Avylos snapped the book shut with a snort of pleasure. It was done. Finally, Edmir was really dead. Finally, everything was falling into place.

The grounds of the Royal House of Tegrian resembled a small park, with sections for fruit and shade trees, and stretches of formal garden with white-pebbled paths. Like all such places, and at this time of the morning, it was busy, with messengers and guards in livery walking to and from the gates, servants on errands to the stables at the southern end, or to the kitchen gardens. No one took special note of Parno Lionsmane as he strolled through, his chanter to his lips, warming up by playing parts and snippets of tunes and runs of notes. In no time, as he'd fully expected and counted on, a group of children were following him, begging for tunes and songs. Anyone who was within the grounds had been passed through the gate, and was safe to play with.

By allowing the children to think they were chasing him, Parno led them close to the repaired wall that marked the Blue Mage's wing. He noticed that the children were not afraid to approach it—and that there seemed to be no special guards or watchfulness on the wing itself. He went so far as to lean his shoulders against the repaired part of the wall, hiking up one knee and making himself comfortable. He began to play a an old tune, a familiar tune, one that he'd both heard and played many times himself, and the children clapped their hands and whistled, beginning to bounce up and down in time with the music. In a moment they had chosen one of the smaller boys to be the Blind Man, and an older girl pulled off her neck scarf and bound his eyes as the rest organized themselves in a circle around him, joining hands.

One eye on the children—it wouldn't do to outstay their pleasure—Parno settled in to accompany them for as long as he could. He was playing not for them, but for his Partner, and the longer he played, the greater the chance that Dhulyn would come into the garden on the other side of the wall and hear him. Would she recognize the tune? He hoped so; she'd been studying this child's game, and the tune that came with it, when they'd been in Imrion the year before, and she had special reason to remember it. Of all the tunes that he could play, he wagered this would be the one to catch at her mind and memory.

Whether the magic of the music would be enough to undo what the Mage had done to her—that was what he couldn't know.

He wasn't sure exactly how long he'd been playing, long enough for the shadows to move a finger's breadth perhaps, but not long enough to dry his mouth unduly, when he saw a page whose colors marked him as one on loan to Valaika, coming toward them down one of the nearby paths. Parno waited until the page was almost standing next to him before lowering the chanter from his mouth. Immediately the children who were waiting their turns to play surrounded him, calling out for him to continue.

"Off with you, fiends and torments! I'm summoned and that's the end of it. Off now, enjoy your freedom while you can." He turned to the page even as he began the walk back across the grounds to Valaika's suite. "I *am* summoned, I take it? Not that I could have played much longer, mind."

"If you please, sir. The Lady Prince Kera has announced her intention to visit her aunt, and our House wishes you to be present."

"Lead on, youngster." Parno was happy to get another look at Edmir's sister. And he was interested in what made Valaika think she needed a Mercenary Brother with her when her niece visited.

⌁

Dhulyn was humming along with the tune she heard rising and falling on the other side of the garden wall, and soon found herself on her feet, stepping two paces to the left, to the right, forward and back, turning and offering her hand to someone who wasn't there. She faltered.

Surely there was a song as well. The words were on the tip of her tongue. She could almost see them—

"What are you doing?"

She turned, smiling, and ran to Avylyn—no, she corrected herself, he was called Avylos here. The Blue Mage. He was smiling, as if he'd had some very good news.

"Did you hear that music? Come, I remember the steps to the dance. Come dance with me."

"Men do not dance." Avylos actually put his hands behind his back, as if he feared she would catch them and pull him forward. "Not our men, anyway, not Espadryni."

She stood still, something throbbed behind her left eye. Was that right? "Do they not? I remember . . . no, I suppose I don't. For a moment there I thought—but perhaps you're right, perhaps it is only women who dance." She shrugged and stepped away from him again. "Then I shall dance by myself." Three steps to the right, two steps to the left. A spin with the arms wide open.

A circle of women, their hair the red of old blood, holding hands, eyes closed, feet moving in rhythmic pacing . . .

An old crone, a young woman with dark hair and a heart-shaped face, a stocky blond man in a Scholar's tunic, and a young boy, thin and round-eyed, holding hands, singing, feet moving in rhythmic pacing . . .

The golden-haired, tattooed man, with pipes in his hands . . .

Water crashes over the deck of a ship . . .

A golden-haired man with tattoos . . .

Avylos with the Blue Stone in his hands, light burning through him . . .

She was standing still.

"Could you dance later, my dear one? Would you come with me, now? I would like you to try something."

"Something to eat, I hope?"

He smiled, but stiffly now, his good humor already faded. *Sun and Moon*, what was wrong with the man? No humor, no fun, stiff as a bow that was never bent. She stopped spinning. That was an odd simile to think of. Perhaps she'd been a hunter?

"Very well, then, Avylos my brother—" The words stuck in her throat, and she had to cough. Odd. "I'll be as serious as a Scholar, nay, as serious as a Mage." She dusted off the skirts of her gown and joined him, linking her arm through his.

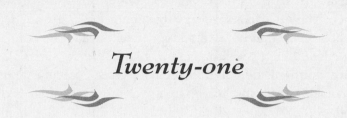

Twenty-one

KERA'S MOUTH WAS AS DRY as winter sand. She held herself
stiffly as she walked, her hands folded at her waist since her
awareness of the need for caution was giving them a ten-
dency to tremble. She had dressed carefully, had a lady page at her
elbow, and she'd rehearsed her speeches to Aunt Valaika until she felt
she could recite them without hesitation or sign of how nervous she
really felt. She put on the face that she'd been taught to use in public. Formality, Edmir had always told her, was a tool to fall back on
when fear or uncertainty nipped at your composure. Informally, she
would have walked directly across the grounds to the section of
rooms set aside for the use of House Jarlkevo. As it was, she and her
escort were walking sedately around the long way, through the
buildings, Kera pausing where appropriate to let her lady page open
and close doors for her.

As she walked along, she used the time to consider—yet again—
what she was doing. Logic said that Aunt Valaika, by virtue of her long
estrangement from the Royal House, and her subsequent isolation in
her mountain fortress, had few ties, if any, that would make her an ally
of the Blue Mage.

But logic made for poor signposts on the road of human nature. Just
because Valaika had no particular friends at court didn't mean she
wanted to make an enemy.

After what seemed like hours, Kera's lady page opened the door to
her aunt's suite and announced her. Kera signaled that the woman
should remain outside, and walked in. Her first thought on entering
her aunt's receiving room was relief that the tall, golden-haired per-

sonal guard was already there. Now she wouldn't have to make up some excuse to ask for him.

Very correctly, Valaika stood as Kera entered, and waited for the door to be shut behind her. Kera stopped just inside the door and let her aunt come to her. Now that she was Lady Prince, she took precedence over even an older blood relative. Over everyone except the queen, herself. As a close blood relative, however, Valaika did not kneel, but took Kera's hand and bowed over it. When she straightened, and would have stepped away, Kera found herself clinging to the hand, warm and rough, in hers. She looked into her aunt's face, and Valaika met her eyes steadily. Her aunt's eyes were the same dark blue as her father's, full of warmth. The same warmth, the same welcome, as the day they had buried her father.

Kera's lower lip trembled, her determination to remain formal crumbled, and she took another step forward into her aunt's arms.

"There, my little one. I'm here. Whatever it is, I'll help you." Even the voice, with its Hellish accent, reminded Kera of her father.

Strong arms around her, hands patting her back. Valaika *would* help her, Kera was certain, though she didn't know how she knew it. These weren't just words. But much as she would have liked to go on clinging to this woman who reminded her so much of her father, there was someone else in the room, and pride made Kera straighten her shoulders and take a step back, clearing her throat and adjusting her brocaded sleeves, trying to regain the composure she'd had when she'd come in the door.

"I thank you," she said in as steady a voice as she could manage. Pride told her to say no more, but curiosity was stronger. "What makes you think I need help?"

"No one stands near the throne and doesn't," Valaika said, smiling to take the sting of cynicism from the words. "I knew that when I was younger than you are now, and farther from a throne."

Kera swallowed. "You're right, of course," she said. "I have come looking for an ally, though to be honest, I'm not sure what any of us can do."

"Start at the beginning."

The deep, unexpected voice made Kera jump just a little, and she brushed a bit of fluff from her skirt to cover the movement. If he were just a personal guard, he wouldn't have spoken, and that meant her thinking was correct. Time to set formalities aside.

"Do you know a Mercenary Brother called Dhulyn Wolfshead?" she said. Her breath caught. "I see from your face that you do."

The man stepped forward until he was almost too close for protocol, and Kera found herself leaning very slightly away from him.

"My name is Parno Lionsmane, called the Chanter. I was schooled by Nerysa of Tourin, the Warhammer. I fight with my Brother, Dhulyn Wolfshead, she is my Partner. Do you know what has happened to her?"

Valaika drew Kera to a seat at the small table, waving to Parno Lionsmane to bring up another chair. There was a plate of small poppy seed cakes and ganje in a glazed jug being kept warm on a metal stand over a small oil lamp.

Kera lowered herself into the seat and rested her hands along the arms of the chair; nodded her thanks as Valaika poured her a cup of ganje. "Five or six days ago the Blue Mage returned from one of his tours with a woman who claimed to be of his Tribe, the Red Horsemen. Avylos let it be known that she was ill—the crying fever was mentioned—or perhaps injured, and that he was tending her in his wing. But she wasn't sick at all, and she caught me spying on her in the garden." Kera paused, checking their faces. The Lionsmane looked solemn, except for his shining eyes, and Valaika seemed about to smile. Kera took a deep breath.

"She told me that Edmir was still alive." A lifted eyebrow was the only reaction to her statement. "It's true, then?" She hadn't really doubted it—it was impossible to look Dhulyn Wolfshead in the face and doubt her—but Kera's heart gave a little skip when both Valaika and the Lionsmane nodded.

"She told me about the Blue Stone," Kera continued, "and together we formed the plan of stealing it." As quickly as she could, she outlined what had happened three nights before—and how Dhulyn Wolfshead had been behaving ever since.

"Did Avylos do this?" The Lionsmane's voice was a low growl.

Kera shook her head. "He seemed just as surprised as I was. The look on his face was almost frightened before he regained command of himself. I wondered—I have heard that if a person takes a blow to the head . . ."

The Lionsmane was nodding. "Certainly. That is possible, though I've only seen memory loss on this scale once, and I've seen many thousands of blows to the head."

"What was done in that case?" Valaika asked.

"A Finder and a Healer combined their talents to restore the lost memory. But that is not an option we have here."

"Could it be the Stone?" Valaika drummed on the polished wood with her fingers.

Parno shrugged, blowing out a lungful of air. "If we had the journal, and we could read it, perhaps there would be something there that would tell us. Zania certainly never mentioned such a possibility. As it is . . . Can you get me into the Mage's wing?"

Kera blew out a long breath, shaking her head. "Something prevents it. My mother or I can enter whenever we wish. But no one else, not even Edmir. We've tried disguising him," she added, as the Lionsmane opened his mouth to speak. "It doesn't work. Besides, what can you do? Dhulyn Wolfshead doesn't remember you."

He fell quiet, his eyes narrow, his lips pressed tight. "We're Partnered," he said finally. "She will remember." He looked up again. "Did you ever try getting someone over the wall?"

"It's impossible to climb over . . ." Kera leaned forward, the heels of her hands on the table's edge. If Avylos was conserving magic, as it seemed he was, would he have bothered to magic a wall everyone considered impossible to climb? She looked Parno Lionsmane over, taking in the hardness of the muscle under the golden hair on his arms. If he could move the way Dhulyn Wolfshead could . . . Mercenary Brothers were *supposed* to be able to do impossible things.

"If you can get over the wall," she said. "I will bring Dhulyn Wolfshead to the garden."

⌐⌐⌐

Parno had looked the wall over fairly thoroughly when he'd been leaning against it, playing for the children as they skipped and danced through their game of Blind Man. Old as it was, the stones of the original wall were still smooth and beautifully fitted. He suspected the lower courses had been laid without mortar, probably by some long-dead craftsman who had studied the technique of the Caids. It was hard to tell from below, but Parno was sure the individual stones had been placed in such a way that the wall actually leaned out slightly from the bottom. At one time, this must have been part of the outer wall of the Royal House. Climbing it might well be as impossible as Kera thought.

The repaired portion, now that was a different tale. Clearly the repair had been made after the courtyard had been created, and this had become an interior wall, no longer exposed to the possibility of an enemy attack. It was not merely the newer, unaged stone that made the repair stand out. It was good, sturdy work, and the unpracticed eye would see no difference other than color from the original wall. But Parno could tell that the newer portion had been created by a much less skilled craftsman than the old. There was more mortar, for one thing, which meant greater possibilities for finger- and toeholds. And he was virtually certain that the wall did not lean outward, toward the climber. If he was right, then all he had to deal with here was an ordinary wall. A little taller than the ones he'd climbed before, perhaps, but still, only an ordinary wall.

Parno and Valaika arrived at the spot Parno picked out as the most climbable while there was still light in the sky. It had to be late enough in the day that the grounds were as good as deserted, but early enough that Parno could take advantage of the minute shadows created by the slanting rays of the sun to find purchase as he climbed. A torch would flicker too much to help him, and would undoubtedly draw far too much attention. As it was, even the torches that burned nightly in the entrances to the main section of the citadel had not yet been lit.

Valaika eyed the wall as Parno shifted his sword around to hang down his back.

"You sure about this?" she said. "It looks too high."

"They all do, from the bottom," he said. "But I was Schooled in the mountains, I won't even need a Climbing *Shora* for this," he added. Climbing was, in fact, one of the few things he did better than Dhulyn, though it was she who had taught him the Sable Monkey *Shora*. However, Parno suspected he knew what Valaika was really asking. If Dhulyn had not known him in the audience hall, why would she know him now?

Because she had to. That was why. Because they were Partnered, and apart they were incomplete. That was why.

He bent down to pull off his boots and folded the tops into his belt. He had taken off the wig covering his Mercenary badge, and replaced it with a knitted hood that fit closely around his face. If Dhulyn was in the garden, he could push the hood off. In the meantime, he still looked like an ordinary retainer of House Jarlkevo.

"I'll hold those for you," Valaika said, pointing to his boots.

"If my Partner is not in the garden," he said, "I may want to look around a little. If I'm fully dressed, I can claim to be lost, but if I'm missing my boots, that might be a little harder to explain."

Parno turned once more to the wall, took several deep breaths, put his hands on the cool stones and looked up. The top seemed much farther away than it had a few moments before.

"Is it too difficult?" Valaika asked. "Perhaps I can get you in, if I asked to visit Avylos . . . ?"

"A moment, if you will," he said.

He rubbed his palms together, dried them on the front of his tunic. He looked up and saw his path, laid out as if drawn on a sheet of paper. There were his first fingerholds, and there the first spots where he could brace his toes. From there he would veer slightly to the left and then . . . He launched himself upward, sliding his fingertips into two uneven spots in the mortar around a stone and pulled himself up.

The last of the sunlight still glowed in the windows of the upper stories, but here in the garden torches had been lit. Dhulyn shifted in her seat, wincing and rubbing her lower back. She set down the tile she had just removed from the board.

"When is this drug supposed to start working?" she asked.

"My mother says in a short span of minutes." The Lady Prince Kera concentrated on the board. "I don't get the birthing pains when my woman's time comes, so I've never needed it."

"Pray Sun and Moon you never do." Dhulyn twisted from side to side. Was the pain subsiding, or was it wishful thinking?

"My old nurse used to say that bad pains every moon meant that real births would come easier."

"It's hard to be glad of that just at the moment."

Dhulyn tried to refocus her attention on the game in front of her. Strange that she could remember perfectly well how to play Two-handed Tailor with the vera tiles, and yet nothing much else from the time before her memory loss wanted to come to the surface. Her hand went once more to her head, as if this time she would feel something different. There was still some pain, and when she moved her head quickly lines of light and color seemed to trail after things, but she could find no sore or tender spots anywhere. She had not, apparently, struck her head. Was it indeed this Stone that Avylos made so much fuss about which had robbed her of her past?

If she touched the Stone again, could she get her past back? And what of those odd visions with their confusing cascade of images? Should she tell Avylos that they were still troubling her?

Princess Kera finally made her move and Dhulyn kept her face carefully still. The princess had discarded the precise tile Dhulyn needed to complete her hand. As she reached for it, she heard the unmistakable sound of feet hitting the ground behind her.

In the time it took for the intruder to circle the pond and close on them, Dhulyn snatched up the only weapons to hand, the jug of iced lemon laced with pain drugs that Kera had brought with her from the Royal kitchens, and the silver tray on which it sat. She whirled, threw the contents of the jug first, followed immediately by the jug itself. But the man, moving in a golden-brown blur, dodged both drink and jug.

"Kera, run for Avylos—now!"

But the man didn't follow Kera, not even with his eyes. Not an assassin after the Lady Prince, then. She must herself be the target. But why would anyone want to kill *her*? To strike at Avylos? Or was this still another thing from her past she couldn't remember?

The man stepped forward again, and Dhulyn hurled the tray like a disk, aiming for the side of his head. Cursing—that wiped off his smile!—he barely got his forearm up in time to keep the tray from striking him.

Without waiting, Dhulyn ran to a row of climbing flowers and wrenched up a wooden stake from out of the garden fencing. It was as thick, though not as long, as a quarterstaff. It felt awkward in her hand, no proper hilt, badly balanced, but as long as she avoided meeting the edge of his sword directly, she could use it. She took up a defensive position, and began circling to the man's right. Perhaps she could angle him so as to get the light of the torch in his eyes.

Dhulyn blinked, even as she kept her own eyes on the intruder. *What is this?* How did she know these things? Why should this knowledge just come to her? What *was* she?

The man drew the sword that hung down his back, and stood ready for her, sword up, knees bent. Dhulyn felt her body automatically imitating his stance and she faltered.

"Dhulyn Wolfshead," the man said. "You don't want to hurt me."

"Will you cut me with words, or do you plan to use that blade?" She leaped forward, feinted a blow to his head, dropped the point of her stake, intending to jab him in the groin—only to be met by the flat side of the man's blade, deflecting her blow and almost knocking the unwieldy thing out of her hand. She brought up her left hand to steady it, and dodged to her right, making the man take two steps to her one in order to keep his sword between them.

But he didn't cross his feet when he moved, didn't drop his guard; and the torchlight wasn't enough to dazzle him.

"Dhulyn Wolfshead," he said. "You were Schooled by Dorian the Black Traveler. You fought at Sadron, Arcosa, and Bhexyllia, where you slapped the Great King's face. You must remember?"

"Blooded nonsense," she said. She leaped up on the white boulder that marked the corner of the rock garden. He was not that much taller, but this would remove even that advantage from him. She struck again, bearing down on the stave, but he blocked her, once more with the flat of his sword so that her wooden stake remained intact.

"I'm your Partner," he said stepping back to avoid a rapid series of blows she aimed at his sword arm, his ribs, and his groin. "Parno Lionsmane, called the Chanter. We met at Arcosa, fighting for the old Tarkin of Imrion, remember? I saved your life."

As he said this he swung at her legs, and Dhulyn was forced to leap up and to the left to avoid his blade. Landing once more on the pebbles of the garden path, she had lost the advantage of height the boulder gave her, but his back was now to the door. When Avylos came, the man would be finished.

"If you aren't who I say you are," he said, warding off her next strike, "how is it you can fight me? How is it you can hold me off?"

The truth was, her body seemed to move by itself, as if it remembered things she did not.

"I'm a Red Horseman," she said aloud, grasping at the only idea she could think of. "We are formidable warriors."

In answer the man reached up and pushed back the hood he was wearing. His close-cropped hair was the same amber gold as his eyes, but had been removed above the ears and along the temples. In its place was a dark red-and-gold tattoo with a black line tracing through it.

"Formidable enough to hold your own against a Mercenary Brother?"

Sun, Moon, and *Stars*, she cursed under her breath. A Mercenary Brother. She felt she should know something about them, but what? A town man, though. He was a town man just the same, Mercenary or not. Town men were liars and brigands, and Avylos had told her it was town men who had injured her and brought on the fever. Without the hood it was easier to see his face . . .

"Sun burn you! You're the blooded spawn of a snail who bumped into me in the audience room. You're nothing to me, or my kinsman would know you."

"He's no kinsman of yours! Listen to me, you have a tattoo just like mine under that wig of yours. How else could you know what you know?"

She feinted again with the stake, but this time let it drop from her right hand to her left, and lunged at his heart.

Or where his heart should have been. He knocked the stake flying out of her hand, but did not attack again. Rather, he dropped back two steps, his point up, his eyes fixed on hers.

"How is it you knew how to do that? And how is it I knew what you were going to do? That was the Mirror *Shora* for two-handed sword-play. Where did you learn it if you are not a Mercenary?"

Could he be telling her the truth? She glanced toward her weapon.

"Dhulyn, my soul, *think*. If you don't remember me . . . where is your horse? Where is Bloodbone? What has happened to her?"

Dhulyn stayed crouched, knees slightly bent. Her horse? She was Espadryni, what the world called the Red Horsemen. So where, indeed, was her horse?

The man smiled. No! He was trying to trick her, take her from her kin. Not again. She could not lose her Tribe again. She threw back her head and as she gave the snow heron's cry . . .

Sword in hand, she fights a one-eyed man in a room with a round mirror . . .

Sword in hand, she fights the golden-haired tattooed man, but she is laughing, pleased . . .

*   *   *

Her own hands lay out vera tiles in a pattern she does not recognize from any game. The floor under her is moving like the deck of a ship . . .

A young woman with almost white hair holds the Blue Stone in her hands . . .

Avylos as a young man, running through a forest; the hunters behind him are Espadryni . . .

With the weird howling still echoing in his ears Parno landed heavily on the courtyard side of the wall. Valaika was there in an instant, pulling up his hood and drawing her own sword. Calls, running footsteps, and torches were heading in their direction.

"Guards, quickly, this way," Valaika called out. "What happened?" she said in a quiet aside.

"Dhulyn almost killed me." His hands were still trembling, muscles twitching. He could not tell her what the worst cut had been. That Dhulyn should cry out for Avylos the second she laid eyes on him—he pushed the thought away. That wasn't the real Dhulyn. It *wasn't*. "If she'd had a sword instead of a garden stake—" he shook his head as two guards in the queen's colors ran up to them, swords out, torches to the fore.

"It came from the other side of this wall," Valaika said, pointing upward with a gesture that both took her sword point away from them, and showed her own Royal colors to good advantage. "The weirdest howling noise."

Both guards grinned and lowered their own weapons, the shorter one going so far as to sheathe his sword as he stepped forward.

"You're the Jarlkevoso, aren't you, Lady? What brings you out this way?"

"Trying to settle my supper with a bit of a walk. Not used to the rich fare at my sister the queen's table. For the Caids sake, what was that noise?"

"Don't you worry, Jarlkevoso, this is the Blue Mage's wing. Whatever it was, it's no concern of ours, nor yours either, with respect. The Blue Mage will manage it, whatever it was."

"Of course." Valaika backed a few paces from the wall, looking upward, and letting Parno trail a little behind her. "I'd forgotten Avylos had this end of the old keep for his use. I'm sorry to have disturbed you."

The guards walked them back to the entrance of the building that housed Valaika's suite of rooms, and bade them good night. By this time the trembling had stopped, and the sweat on his face had dried. But Parno's mind was no further settled.

"She was thinking too much," he said, as they walked into Valaika's private sitting room and shut the door. "That's the only thing that kept her from killing me—and I made sure she thought too much, asked her questions, kept her consciously aware of what she was doing—I'm blooded lucky she didn't break something."

"Are you all right?"

He looked up, blinking. "I'll be all right when I get my Partner back."

"You say he came over the wall?" Avylos sat behind his worktable and pulled at his lower lip.

"He did."

"And what did young Kera do then?"

"I sent her to fetch you."

"Which she manifestly did not do, as this is the first I'm hearing of it."

Red spots appeared in the sudden pallor of his cheeks, and Dhulyn found her muscles readying themselves for action in response to Avylos' anger. Then his gaze shifted from the book he had open in front of him to the small casket to his left, and she relaxed. It looked out of place here—old, plain, and unadorned where everything else was of the first quality. Inside it, Dhulyn knew, was the Blue Stone. Dhulyn waited until he was looking at her once more.

"Perhaps she could not find you," she said.

Avylos' expression told her how much he believed that. She shrugged, for some reason finding herself reluctant to think ill of the

Lady Prince. But Avylos knew these town people so much better than she did herself. She must trust in his knowledge of them.

"Is it possible what he said was true? Could I have been a Mercenary Brother?"

"He is a town man, you say?"

"From his accent and speech, I would say so, yes." Dhulyn frowned, rubbing her forehead. "Though how it is I know this, *that* I cannot tell you." She looked up again. "But you know him, you have seen him yourself. It was that man who jostled me in the queen's audience. The retainer of House Jarlkevo." Avylos' eyes narrowed and the corners of his mouth turned down. Dhulyn felt a trickle of fear run up her spine. Her muscles tensed as she prepared to either flee or defend herself.

"Are you certain?" Whatever it was that had disturbed him, his anger was not aimed at her. Dhulyn allowed herself to relax.

"Of course. *That* I remember perfectly."

Avylos came out from behind his table and took her hands in his, squatting so that she looked directly into his eyes. They were a brilliant blue, and kind in a way that made her draw in a deep breath.

"Are there any other signs of your memory returning?" When she shook her head, he continued. "Can you guess why this man should be so interested in you? No? Nothing comes to mind?" Rising, Avylos released her left hand, and stroked her cheek with the back of his fingers. "Rest easy, my dearest cousin. I will help you, I promise."

"Have there been others like me? Others who have lost their memories to the Stone?"

Avylos hesitated, his fingers still caressing her face, and then seemed to come to a decision. "I will not lie to you," he said. "There have been others. But they regained their memories within hours of touching the Stone. But again, I promise you—" here his hand tightened on hers. "I swear that I will not abandon you, I *will* help you."

Without meaning to, Dhulyn squirmed, lowering her eyes.

"What is it? I cannot help you, if you do not tell me everything."

"I have told you—" She began again. "Once or twice I have spoken of feeling dizzy . . ."

"But there was more?"

There was a hardness under his words that made Dhulyn hesitate. But once begun . . . "I see images, rapidly, one after another. Sometimes things I recognize—you, the Blue Stone, myself fighting the

Mercenary—but often people I don't know, place I have never, to my knowledge, seen. I thought at first it would pass, and so I did not mention it." She let her hand fall into her lap and raised her eyes to his. "But it is not passing. Is this the Stone? Can you help me?"

Avylos did not answer her immediately, and Dhulyn felt a tremor of worry pass through her. Still holding her hand, he straightened. He was thinking, and from his face it seemed as though he debated what to tell her. Finally, he spoke.

"Very likely. These may be some form of waking dreams. It may be that proximity to the Stone has brought out some latent power in you, as it did once with me. You must tell me if it happens again, and what you see. I have promised to help you, and I will help you in this as well."

He kissed her hand. "And to start that help, let me assure you, I have known you your whole life and you were never a Mercenary Brother. It's as you said to him, the Espadryni are formidably skilled, that is all. You were injured, suffered a fever, and have lost your memory, but you are my cousin. You were never a Mercenary Brother."

He paused, and obediently Dhulyn repeated the phrase.

"I was never a Mercenary Brother. I have been injured and lost my memory, but I am your cousin."

"There you are."

Dhulyn waited until Avylos had left her before throwing herself backward into her chair, with a huff of breath. "I was never a Mercenary Brother," she said in the tones of gravest solemnity that Avylos seemed to require. "I have been injured and lost my memory." She leaned back in the chair and rolled her eyes to the heavens. Sun, Moon, and Stars, but grown-ups thought the silliest things were important.

Twenty-two

LATE AS IT WAS, AVYLOS found the Lady Prince Kera coming up the Great West Stair, as if she was heading to his apartments, rather than toward her own. He gestured her into a nearby alcove, empty since the removal of a bust of Kedneara's grandfather.

"But I met a messenger from my mother the queen—I *had* to go to her. I came back to find you as soon as I could," Kera said in answer to his query.

It was a good lie. One that on any other day he might have believed. Had he not been returning from the queen himself, he might very well have believed it. As it was, he fought to keep his face serene against the rage that swept through him, hot as fired metal. Fought to keep his hand at his side when it itched to lift up, draw a symbol in the air and watch her try to breathe through a closed throat.

How dare she. How *dare* she lie to him. Just like her mother, using him, treating him with smiles and now lying to him, turning her back. After all he had done, and was doing, to ensure that the throne would come to her. Well, that was at an end. He saw clearly now. Very clearly. Edmir was already gone, he had accomplished that through Sylria. He had Dhulyn, and she had Seen him full of light. Full of power. What did this mean but that together they would unlock the Stone and he would have all the power he wanted. He no longer needed to bring Kera to the throne. With Dhulyn, and the book, he could bring himself there. He could be Mage King, not over the Espadryni, not over a mere ragtag band of nomads as his father had been, but over the whole of Tegrian and its territories. Over the whole world.

A shifted foot, a cleared throat, returned Avylos' attention to the girl in front of him. However compelling, he must set his vision of the future aside for now. There were still items in the present which required his attention.

"Did you not tell them you were looking for me?" His voice was mild. "That it was urgent?"

"I did." Kera's cheeks flushed. "But it was Lady Mora who came for me, and she refused to listen." Again, on any other day Avylos might have taken her flushed cheeks and trembling lips for embarrassment and frustration at having been thwarted by her old nurse. But today he knew it for a liar's agitation.

"If there is nothing else, Avylos, and your cousin is safe, then I must return to my mother the queen."

"Of course, my Lady Prince."

As he watched her go, walking as fast as dignity and formal gown would allow her, he lifted his hand again, index finger extended, thumb out in the proper position . . .

Avylos let his hand fall. Not yet. Soon, but now was not the time. He should have realized that the other Mercenary would come looking for his Brother. He and Valaika were as yet unaware that Edmir was dead, and their involvement in these events was now at an end. But if Avylos wanted to keep Dhulyn Wolfshead, and he did, he would have to find a way to deal with the other Mercenary—and perhaps Valaika as well. But it was already late, and there was little he could accomplish now that could not wait until morning.

Wait. He had already taken a few paces down the corridor toward his wing when a thought occurred to him. There *was* something he could do, and now was the best time. He descended the West Stair into the Great Hall, but instead of heading toward the East Stair that would bring him eventually to the queen's rooms, he set out across the hall toward the outer doors. The evening meal was long over, and the extra wall sconces were starting to be doused for the night.

Avylos was aware that his anger still burned, a small flame like those in the sconces, deep inside him. Not yet, but very soon he would deal with Princess Kera, and the queen, as he had dealt with Edmir. Soon he would have no further use for the Royal House of Tegrian. He had thought—even hoped—that Kera was malleable, but he now knew she also would lie to him, hide things from him, treat him as though he was a person of no consequence. Avylos took a deep breath, and unclenched his fists. Only Dhulyn repaid his attentions with trust, only she came to him for help, came to him as one does to family.

And her trust of him did not come about through magic. *He* had not removed her memory, nor tampered with her feelings in any way. What he was experiencing—what *she* was experiencing, must be Dhulyn's own natural reaction to him.

Avylos had never thought to see another of his Tribe, of his race. He'd long ago convinced himself he never *wished* to see one, not after all the tricks and lies they had shown him, making him believe he was *srusha*. Once he had encountered the Stone, and it had unlocked the powers those jealous of him had blocked—yes, even his own father, making him believe he was barren and empty of magic—he no longer feared the appearance of an Espadryni. But Dhulyn was different. She was too young to remember what he had done to revenge himself. If he could see to it that she now regained only *parts* of her memory . . . surely it could not be dangerous to keep her, once he'd dealt with the people who had come to take her away.

And her Mark? If it was truly returning, he had only to tell her what she'd told him herself. That it was erratic, and not to be trusted. He could still use it.

The guards at the entrance to the Great Hall saluted him, and sprang to swing open the heavy doors.

The main entrance of the citadel of Royal House was raised above the level of the grounds by five stone steps, each wide enough to be almost a platform in itself. Avylos paused on the top step, letting his eyes adjust until they could see into the darkness beyond the torches that bracketed the doors. A breeze had sprung up with the sun's setting and pulled at his hair and the edges of his cloak, bringing the scent of flowers and greenery with it.

And if her Mark made Dhulyn herself unreliable—Avylos pushed that thought away. He would not think it. He *would not*. She was his kin, something he never thought to want again. But now that he had her, she was his. He would not lose her. He started down the steps.

Avylos did not need light to find the portion of the wall he was looking for. He laid his hands on the stones. The avoidance magic he'd laid on it two moons ago was gone, he could feel no trace of it. The stones were rough here where the repair had been made, and he had noticed before that the better a thing was made, the longer it would hold a magic. Magic or no, however, he hadn't been overly concerned with anyone obtaining entrance from this quarter. The wall was rougher here, but not so rough that it was easily scaled. It would take an accomplished climber to do so. Apparently the Mercenaries Schooled their Brotherhood in more than force of arms. He hadn't been concerned when Dhulyn had managed to get into his workroom. As his father had told him so long ago, women were difficult to magic, and Espadryni women even more so. But if the Mercenary Brother could climb this wall . . .

With his right hand he drew a pattern on the stones. It glowed blue, and held. With his left hand he drew another, a different pattern over the first. It glowed gold, and where the line of one pattern touched another, the colors began to run, twisting and twining.

"You cannot be climbed," he told the wall in the language of the Espadryni. "You have no handholds, no toeholds. You are as smooth as blown glass."

There, let the Mercenary try to climb that.

Sword in hand, she duels with the golden-haired, tattooed man, the mercenary brother . . .

Two men trot down a narrow path in heavy woods. It is early morning, and the sun is just penetrating the canopy of trees. The pines are ancient, so thick that there is little underbrush, and the snow that shows on upper branches has managed to fall to the ground only on the path. This is a wild place. One man has a cloth tied over the right side of his face, and from the blood on it, Dhulyn would guess that he has lost the eye. The other man has his left arm tied closely to his body. His right arm is out for balance as he runs, the hilt of his sword shows over his right shoulder, where it is slung down his back. Both men have hair the color of old blood; both men show other wounds sketchily cared for; both men have the flushed cheeks and bright eyes of fever. The one-eyed man grunts out something Dhulyn cannot catch, pointing ahead. The other man draws his sword, and they break into a run . . .

*   *   *

She fights a one-eyed man . . . the mercenary brother . . . a tall black man stripped to the waist . . . a thickset woman with green eyes . . .

Avylos is on his knees, laughing. He spreads his arms wide, and beams of light pour from his fingers' ends, from his eyes, from his open mouth, from the ends of his hair. And he laughs . . .

A storm rages, pushing walls of water over the rails of the ship washing over the decks. There is so much water it is almost impossible to breathe, one could drown standing upright, clinging to the sheets. She looks down to the deck in time to see a man, his golden hair darkened by the wet, swept off the pitching side of the deck by a wave taller than two men. She wails, her heart breaking, and lets go of the rope she clings to . . .

⌒

Dhulyn woke up tasting tears, her chest heaving. What strange nightmares. She sat up, swung her legs over the side of the bed, taking deep breaths to slow down the thumping of her heart. That golden-haired man, that was the Mercenary Brother. Why should his loss, even in a dream, affect her so? She went to push her hands through her hair and felt the wig. In a daze, almost as though she were still dreaming, she threw off her coverings and went to the round mirror that hung on one wall. The moon was down and it was too dark to see any reflection. She used the sparker laying to one side on the table and lit the oil lamp, carrying it over to the mirror.

With her free hand she pulled off the wig.

Scars covered the sides of her head above her ears. There was no tattoo. The man *had* been lying then.

⌒

The morning's rain made it seem much later, but the sun was only just up when the Lady Prince Kera joined Dhulyn for breakfast in Avylos' sitting room. Dhulyn put her hand out for the crockery pot of nellberry jam the princess was passing her and froze, blinking, her hand suspended in the air. She had the strangest feeling that she had lived through these actions before. What was it that was familiar?

Breakfast? Nellberry jam? She groped after the memory, but nothing came.

Twice she had opened her mouth, about to ask Kera why she had not gone to fetch Avylos to the garden. Both times she'd filled her mouth with jam-covered biscuit instead. Her instincts were telling her to trust the girl—but she didn't know whether she could trust her instincts. For now, she would have to rely on Avylos' judgment.

"I woke up wondering about what that man told me, night thoughts, I suppose," she said instead. "I wondered whether I might have been a Mercenary Brother. So I looked."

"You looked?"

Dhulyn nodded, waving her free hand at her wig. "But it was as Avylos had told me, only scars."

"Do you think the scars might have been caused by removing a Mercenary's badge?" Kera waited, a cup of ganje halfway to her mouth. "Perhaps I should take a look."

Dhulyn held up a finger, turned her head, and a moment later Avylos entered the room. Dhulyn smiled. Now that the Mage was here, Kera did not repeat her offer to examine Dhulyn's scars. The girl *did* have secrets, that was clear. But were they dangerous ones?

"I had a most curious dream last night," she said, reaching toward Avylos. "I dreamed I saw you full of light."

<hr />

The sun was just up, but the rain was making everyone at Beolind's west gate grumpy and querulous. Not that there were many people here, Edmir noticed, just those few like themselves, travelers already out when the rain began. Anyone else with business in the city was doubtless taking shelter, waiting for the rain to stop.

"Members of House Jarlkevo with a report for our House."

Caids, Edmir thought, Zania even *sounded* more like a soldier than he did. He kept his focus on the gate guard's chin strap in an effort to pretend that he was looking the man boldly in the face. Though he doubted that many among the guard at the west gate had any clear idea of what their late Lord Prince looked like, Edmir still felt as though anyone and everyone in Beolind would recognize him.

Or maybe I'm hoping *they recognize me.* Surely Avylos couldn't have magicked the whole city?

Zania flirted a bit more with the guard before they were passed through. Once they had emerged on the far side of the long tunnel that led under the city walls, Zania cuffed him on the shoulder and pointed up the street. Edmir looked, but could see nothing of consequence.

"Try to put an awed look on your face," she hissed through a strained smile. "We're plain country soldiers on our first trip to the capital. Try to look as though everything's new to you. Gawk, you idiot. Gawk."

Edmir did the best he could to follow Zania's direction, smiling and nodding like a fool as she pointed and gasped. She was right, he knew she was. They'd talked about it on the way here, and had decided on this as the safest way for them to behave, as if they were merely plain country folk who had never seen a city the size of Beolind before. Trouble was, Zania was a much better actor than he would ever be. In fact, it was some help to Edmir that he'd rarely, if ever, come into the city through this particular gate, though that hadn't been the reason they'd picked it. His mother the queen always used the north gate, as it would accommodate both carriages and people on horseback, which she felt made a much better entrance. It was far more likely he'd be recognized by the guards there.

The rain did help them by emptying the streets and making their passage much faster than it would have been on a bright day. Still, last night's hasty biscuits and cheese felt a long time ago, and his stomach was growling by the time they led their horses up the final slope toward the sheer stone walls of his home.

Zania touched his elbow and they stopped in an alley just before reaching the immediate precincts of Royal House. He pushed back his hood while Zania reached into her waist pouch for the makeup she had there, leaning forward to touch his face with a few streaks of shading, making his cheekbones seem flatter, and giving his jaw a contour it did not naturally have. This gate would be the real test. The Royal House Guard had seen Edmir every day, though perhaps not from very close up. This was where his lightened hair, brushed back so uncharacteristically from his face, his earrings, and the fact that both he and Zania were dressed in Jarlkevo colors, would be put to the test. He scratched his chin. Along with everything else, he was letting his beard grow in, though it was much sparser than Parno's.

"Perhaps I should cough when we get to the gate," he suggested. "That way I can cover my face."

"Haven't you learned anything? Coughing will only make everyone look at you. I'm telling you, *soldier*—" Zania was careful not to say his name, "Just act as naturally as you can. Look around you, be respectful, let me do the talking."

Just like rehearsal, he thought.

The walls of the Royal House were not as thick as those of the city itself, but thick enough to provide for two offset pairs of gates. Even this early in the morning, even in the rain, these *were* public gates, and he and Zania found them standing wide open. But there were armed guards on watch, and everyone passing through here, even those wearing the Royal dark blue, would have to stop and account for themselves.

Ahead of them were a farmer and his son with a donkey cart, obviously delivering their load of lettuces to the kitchens. Sitting quietly on his horse as they waited their turn was the hardest thing Edmir had ever done. The last time he'd passed through was only two moons ago, he realized with a sense of shock. He'd been on his way to Probic, riding at the head of his escort of twenty handpicked soldiers, most from High Noble Houses with only a handful of the lesser nobility, followed by wagons carrying provisions for the journey, changes of clothing, tents, even musical instruments. His friends, Jenshan of Toron House and SuRohl of Kinton House, had been riding beside him that day. Had either of them made it back to Beolind?

And would they know me, if they had?

He and Zania dismounted, and Edmir saw that both the guards there were strangers to him. He began to relax.

"Members of House Jarlkevo with a report for our House," Zania said again as they drew level with the guards.

"How go things in your mountains, then, Jarlkevos?" the guard asked, as he took in their colors, the Jarlkevo brands on at least one of their horses, and the Jarlkevo bear heads stamped into the leather of their saddles.

"Well enough," Zania was answering with a grin. "More to see here, though, that's for certain, even in this rain."

Just as Edmir was sure the man was going to pass them through without further hindrance, a guard officer stepped into the gate area and approached them. Though wearing the same uniform as the two guards already at the gate, the officer's shirtsleeves showed the shine of silk, and there was gold braiding edging her tunic, not just turned cloth.

"Did I hear you say Jarlkevo?" she said as she came nearer.

Edmir knew her, and he tightened his grip on his reins, to keep from lifting his hand to cover his face. Section Leader Megz Primeau, champion swordplayer, and the current holder of the Queen's White Blade. She had once shown Edmir how to parry her secret thrust, and he had promised never to show it to anyone else.

"Yes, my lady," Zania said, ducking her head.

"I'm section leader, not 'my lady,' " Megz said, her eyes taking in every detail of their clothing and crests. She looked at their faces, and Edmir hastily lowered his eyes. That would be what a young guard would do when faced with authority, he thought. It was what young guards had usually done when he looked at them.

"Well, it seems your House was telling the truth when she said she'd sent all her best people to the queen's armies already. You two look as though you've hardly spent three weeks between you holding a sword." The first guard laughed, but not unkindly.

Edmir judged it was safe to lower his head entirely.

"Do you know your way?"

"Yes, we do, my—I mean, yes, Section Leader."

"Pass them in," Megz said. "Give my regards to your House," she added as she stepped out of their way.

"We will, and thank you," Zania said. She led her horse forward and Edmir was quick to follow her. As they remounted and walked their horses into the clear area of courtyard beyond the gate, heading to the right toward House Jarlkevo's rooms, he risked a look back over his shoulder. Section Leader Megz was still standing under the arch watching them, her fists on her hips.

Valaika Jarlkevo was gray-faced. Her hand kept rising to her trembling lips and sinking again into her lap, as if she didn't have the strength to hold it up. She had aged twenty years, Parno thought, in less than twenty minutes.

"My Lord Prince." She kept repeating it, over and over, her voice drained of all life and substance. Finally she struggled to her feet. Edmir moved forward, but Parno gave the older woman his arm, indicating to Edmir with a twist of his head that the boy should step back. Shaking, Valaika went to her knees before her nephew, and, taking his hand, pressed her forehead to it in submission.

"My Lord Prince," she began again. "I beg you, hold your hand back from my consort. Do not tell your mother the queen. Let me—give me a chance to—"

"But, Valaika." Edmir was white under the tan that a moon of traveling had given him. "Jarlkevoso," he corrected when Parno coughed. His aunt *had* addressed the boy with his formal title. "It wasn't Sylria—that is, she was tricked. But no harm was done, at least not to us. This may even work in our favor. She believes we're dead, and she'll report that to Avylos."

These words didn't seem to help. Valaika shook her head from side to side as if she would never be able to stop.

"She'll report it to Avylos. *My* consort. *My* love. And she'll report to Avylos."

"He threatened her, Valaika." Now it was Zania's turn to speak up. "Threatened your child."

Parno had taken a step back, and leaned against the wall with his arms crossed, the only way he could keep still. This was getting them nowhere.

"Listen to me, all of you." The ring of command in his voice made everyone, even Valaika, even Edmir, turn to him. "Of course it was not Sylria. Avylos magicked her somehow, as we know he's magicked others. She'll be as horrified when she learns of it as you are now, Valaika. *But*—" And here he waited, making sure he had their absolute attention. He must give no one the chance to raise the question of whether the Consort Jarlkevo would put the life of her prince before the life of her son. Let them not think of that. "Sylria won't have a chance to *be* horrified if we don't deal with Avylos. This time, Edmir and Zania were able to turn his trickery to our advantage. As Edmir said, Avylos won't bother watching a dead man, so we now have reinforcements we didn't have yesterday. Get up, Valaika. I grieve for you, but we cannot allow your private grief to slow us, or change our course. We cannot let him win."

This time it was Edmir who offered his arm, and Parno did not interfere. When Valaika had regained her feet, Edmir embraced her. Zania stood watching, tapping her lips with the fingers of her clasped hands.

Parno turned toward the door. "Stand away, Edmir," he said. "Someone comes and we could not explain what a common guard is doing embracing his House."

Edmir did step back, but it was not until Zania took hold of his sleeve and pulled him away that he really took note of what he was doing and where he was standing. They had taken up reasonable positions to the right and left of the doorway, and Parno had seated Valaika once more in her chair when the expected knock came at the door.

"Come." Valaika almost managed to sound like her old self.

The door opened inward, hiding Edmir behind it. A voice announced, "The Lady Prince Kera," and she walked into the room.

Parno kept his hand pressed down on Valaika's shoulder, holding her in her seat. The last thing they needed was for the older woman to rise up and fall flat on her face. Her color was only now returning, and she still looked very pinched about the mouth.

Kera came all the way into the room and waited until the door had been pulled shut behind her. As soon as she heard the click of the latch she ran forward, her hands held out to her aunt.

"What is it?" she said. "What's happened. Is it Edmir?"

"It *is* Edmir," the boy said, striding forward from his place by the door.

At the sound of her brother's voice Kera spun around so quickly the skirt of her stiffened gown swung like a bell.

Well, Parno thought. *He hasn't spent the better part of a moon pretending to be an actor without learning a thing or two about theatrics.*

For a moment Kera did not move, and Parno thought with a sudden sickening drop to his stomach that she, too, had been magicked in the way of the City Lord in Probic, in the way Sylria Consort Jarlkevo had been magicked. And from the look in Edmir's eyes, he, too, feared that his sister would not know him. But then the girl made a noise in her throat that turned Parno's heart over and ran forward.

"Quietly, children. Quietly," he said. "We don't know who is on the other side of the door."

His words checked the brother and sister just as they reached each other. They gripped arms for a moment before embracing fully, Kera with her face buried in her brother's shoulder.

Let this be an omen, Parno pleaded. *So may I be reunited with* my *Brother*.

Kera stepped back, wiping at her eyes. She reached out and ran her hands over his dyed hair, her fingers resting for a moment on the rings in his ears. "How are you here? When did you come? How . . . ? Oh, Ed, I thought you were dead, I read your journals, I'm so sorry."

That brought a smile to Edmir's lips. "It's all right, Kera. Everything's all right."

That was an overstatement, if anything was, but Parno held his tongue.

A small cough reminded him that Edmir had not arrived alone. Zania, her cheeks flushed and the corners of her mouth turned slightly down stepped forward.

"Your pardon, Princess, Jarlkevoso," she said. "But we've had no food today. Before we do anything else—"

"Of course." Valaika looked up at Parno.

"Princess," he said, as he held out a chair for Kera. He jerked his head at Edmir and the prince returned to his position to one side of the door.

Motioning Zania to stay still, Parno opened the door just enough to let the lady page who was waiting there see Kera seated behind him.

"The Lady Prince begs you will see that refreshments are brought," he murmured. The young woman's eyes brightened and her smile spread. Evidently the idea of a trip down to the busy kitchens pleased her more than standing in silent attendance in a doorway. She bobbed her head and went off practically dancing.

Parno turned back into the room to find Edmir setting chairs around the table and Zania at the window shutters.

"Leave them" he told her. "The rain falls in the other direction, and as warm as it is, someone will notice if they are closed."

There was not really enough room around the small table for all five of them to sit comfortably, but the very closeness meant they could speak softly and lessen their chance of being overheard. Parno was about to take what would have been Dhulyn's favorite spot—against the wall between the two windows—when Kera settled the problem by sitting on the arm of Edmir's chair.

"Princess Kera, please." Zania, still on her feet, indicated one of the chairs. "I can stand."

"And eat standing up? I don't think so, you've had hardships enough from the look of my brother." Kera patted Edmir on the head as if he had been a huge dog. She was smiling as she spoke, but the sparkle had gone from her eyes. Parno could see that somehow, there was a shadow on the young girl's happiness. Well, and why not? She might have her brother back, alive and well, but they still had to deal with the Blue Mage.

"Princess," Parno said. "What occurred after my entry into the garden?"

Kera's narrative was interrupted only by the arrival of servants carrying trays of tarts, some berry, some cheese, and others of spiced meat, and a jug each of water and cider. Edmir and Zania listened to the rest of Kera's story with mouths full.

"I don't know that we accomplished anything, except perhaps to make Avylos suspicious of me," Kera concluded.

"We must kill Avylos, or else destroy the Stone." Edmir was quiet, but forceful.

"Both, if we can manage it." Kera seemed as determined as her brother.

Lips parted, Zania looked from one face to another. "I think you forget," she said. "The Muse Stone is my property, mine and my family's. You can't just destroy it, I need it."

"I may need it myself, for that matter," Parno said, before anyone else could answer her. "If it is the Stone that has taken Dhulyn Wolfshead's memories, then it may be needed to restore her."

"You would risk everything on that chance?" Kera asked not as though she would disagree, but as if she actually wanted to know. Dhulyn must somehow have made an impression on the girl, either before, or after her memory loss.

"She's my Partner. In Battle or in Death." *She is my world*, he refused to say aloud. *If I have lost her . . .*

"Does she still have my great-uncle's book?" Zania asked. "Surely, with both the Stone *and* the book, we can find another Scholar, we can learn how the Stone works, and . . ." Her voice trailed away at the look on Parno's face.

"Does Dhulyn remember the book? Or how to read it?" he asked.

Zania subsided, pushing her cup away from her. From the look on her face, Parno thought, she would not agree to a plan that meant destroying the Stone. Any more than he would agree to a plan that meant leaving Dhulyn.

Kera's brow was furrowed. She looked down into the cup of cider she held in her free hand. "It would be best if we could simply put an end to Avylos. But how likely is that, here in his stronghold, with his source of power at hand? And if we fail? We must secure the Stone, not only for your sake, Zania Tzadeyeu, nor for Dhulyn Wolfshead's, but because it is the source of Avylos' power. One of two things will happen if we have the Stone. Either Avylos' powers will eventually wane to the point where we *can* deal with him, or, we can learn how to use the Stone to neutralize him. So, first the Stone, then Avylos."

Parno smiled. He would wager his pipes that Kera was the thinker in the family. Edmir had better not marry her off too far away, she might very well be his best counselor. It took the others a few minutes longer, but soon enough they were all nodding in agreement. Zania, in particular, was all smiles.

"We can get in over the wall," Parno said. "Zania, Edmir, and I."

Kera made a sharp movement that had them all looking at her again. She flushed, almost as though she were guilty of something. "Not Edmir. The one thing we can be sure of is that Avylos wants him dead. He can't walk into danger like that. From here, he could still manage to escape."

"Escape to what?" Edmir said.

Zania put her hand on his arm. "Better a live playwright than a dead prince."

From his angle to one side of them, Parno was the only one who could see the look Edmir gave Zania. It was the look of a man tempted almost beyond his ability to withstand. But perhaps he wasn't the only one who saw something pass between them, Parno thought. Kera was looking at her brother as if seeing him for the first time.

"There would be no point in my escaping without you," he said to Zania. "What use is a playwright without a troupe?"

"Then I will go," Kera put in. "Edmir, we can't risk everyone. One of us must remain alive to keep fighting if we're not successful—"

"Or to tell our tale, if that's what's left to us," Zania added.

"Stop." When he was sure he had their full attention, he continued.

"The one who has the best chance of getting out alive will go in. That would be me. The only other one who can contribute something to the fight will go in. That would be Zania with her knowledge of the Stone."

Kera was nodding her agreement. "I will get Avylos away by telling him that my mother wants to see him. There are often delays in getting to the queen, even for Avylos, and I can make sure there are more than usual. By the time he gets to her presence, you'll have ample time to get to the Stone, and get out again. And then we all escape."

"I will not leave without my Partner." Let them make of that what they'd like.

"But, Parno . . ."

He raised his hand, palm out. "I cannot. It is our Common Rule. Even if Dhulyn Wolfshead was not my Partner, I could not leave a Mercenary Brother behind me in such a condition. I must either persuade her, or bring her with us by force." *Or kill her.*

Parno stopped Kera as she reached the door.

"Did she say anything of me?" No need to say who "she" was.

"She's troubled, that's clear. At times she looks at me almost like her old self, or she seems about to speak and then it fades again, and she falls silent." Kera shot a glance back at the others around the table and then faced him again. "She said she looked for the Mercenary badge and all she saw was scarring."

A cold hand clutched at his heart and stopped his breath. "And is it gone?"

"I don't know, I asked to see for myself, but we were interrupted by Avylos. Could it be a magic? Are they easy to remove?"

"I would not have thought so."

Twenty-three

THIS WAS AN EXCEPTIONALLY good idea. Dhulyn stretched out in the hot water until her toes touched the far end of the bath. The water was scented somehow with pine, and she took a deep restful breath, letting it out slowly. She'd turned the servants out, not because she preferred to bathe herself, but because of their obvious discomfort at the scarring on her back. Or perhaps it was her own inability to explain where the scars had come from that made the bath attendants uncomfortable. Since Avylos had judged her well enough to take part in one of the queen's audiences, Dhulyn had asked to be given more freedom around the Royal House. Her kinsman had not agreed entirely, but he could hardly deny her a trip to the bathhouse.

According to what Lady Prince Kera had told her while bringing her here after breakfast, the Royal Baths had been built years before over a hot spring. Though from the smooth perfection of the stone floors Dhulyn suspected that this was the site of an ancient Caid building, and that certainly the Royal House, and perhaps the city of Beolind itself rested on an old Caid settlement—

She opened her eyes. That seemed like a Scholar's thought. But surely, if she were a Scholar, Avylos would have told her so. And her clothing, she eyed the carefully folded gown and overtunic on the bench against the warm inner wall. That was not the blue tunic and brown leggings of a Scholar. She sighed, closed her eyes, purposefully letting her muscles relax again.

The scent of pine was very soothing. And were the candles not beeswax? The heat was so pleasant.

There is smoke and screaming, the wild flickering of fires, and running shadows. A woman bends over her, though her arms are bare, her face is wrapped in scarves as though against the winter's cold; only her gray eyes show above the folds of material. She is tying similar scarves around Dhulyn's face, and as if that realization frees something in her mind, Dhulyn knows this is her mother, and the scarves are to keep her from choking on the smoke. Her mother speaks, and Dhulyn strains to hear her, trying to force the dream to give up her mother's voice. She fears that, as often happens in dreams (and how does she know this?) she will hear the voice clearly within the dream itself, but will have lost the precise sound of it when she awakens. . . .

A circle of women, their hair the color of old blood . . . Her own hands lay out vera tiles in a pattern she does not recognize from any game. . . . The Mercenary Brother with pipes in his hands. . . .

She is in the garden again, dressed in her lady's gown, her hair bound and swinging down her back. She swings a sword . . . a stave. No, it is a sword. She is in Avylos' workroom, and she fights a slim-hipped, dark-haired man. When she looks closely at him the dark wig disappears and she sees his Mercenary badge, with a black line threaded through the red-and-gold pattern. The steel rings, and rings again, the vibration of sword blade striking sword blade shivering in the hilt she grips in her left hand. There is blood dripping from her right hand, which she holds high to give her balance. Another thrust—she whips her blade around the other, keeping the point away from her skin, though she doesn't manage to disarm her opponent. Another thrust, this time at her belly, another parry, a thrust of her own that draws blood from her opponent's forearm; her satisfaction is short-lived as he changes hands and begins to fight left-handed as well. A lunge to the right, followed by two steps back—this is the Knife-Maker's *Shora*, but why then has blood been drawn? The next blow comes from . . . there, and can be countered with—a gasp of indrawn breath as her sword enters her opponent's side. He falls to his knees as she withdraws the blade from between his ribs. She puts out her hand to touch his face. . . .

*   *   *

A circle of women, their hair the color of old blood . . . Her own hands lay out vera tiles in a pattern she does not recognize from any game . . . The Mercenary Brother with pipes in his hands. . . .

Again the smell of burning. Blood. Now she stands to one side and watches herself watching her mother. She has never Seen herself with her mother before, never from this perspective (what does that mean? *Before what?*) Her mother turns toward her and *sees* her, within the dream itself, as if they were both really there. Even though she can't see her mother's face, Dhulyn knows that she is smiling. She turns the head of the child so that she is looking at herself. She blinks, seeing a tall, slim woman with short red hair and tattoos above her ears. She blinks and sees her mother and the small child who is herself. She puts out a hand, but there is nothing to steady herself against.

"Go," her mother tells her. "Oh, my soul, do not watch. Find your own soul and save yourself. Go now, go."

But she does not go. She sees her mother tell her to hide in a nearby tree. "You'll be found in the morning," she hears her mother tell her. "When they have tired of killing us."

Why did I not remember this? she thinks, as the Vision fades. *Why have I never Seen this before?"*

And what do I mean by before?

She tried to follow that thought, but as she does. . . .

A circle of women, their hair the color of old blood . . . Her own hands lay out vera tiles in a pattern she does not recognize from any game . . . The Mercenary Brother with pipes in his hands. . . .

Dhulyn jolted awake just as her nose was about to slide under the surface of the water.

"My lord Mage."

Avylos kept his eyes focused on the book in front of him, as if by concentrating on the symbols he would be able to force his brain to understand them. When Dhulyn returned from her bath, he resolved, he would show her the book and see if she remembered how to read it. There was a chance, of course, that in doing so the rest of her memory might be triggered, but Avylos thought he had found a solution to that in one of his old texts. A light sleeping trance should do the trick. . . .

The page was still standing in the doorway and Avylos finally raised his head. Though he could not recall the name, he recognized the young man. This was that son of one of the Balnian Houses, recently come to Beolind to give his service to Kedneara. The talebearer and gossip. Though from the shrewd hardness of the eyes above the pleasant smile, there was more to him than a flapping tongue. Perhaps he was more astute than he seemed, astute enough to know that the way to advancement lay through Avylos.

For a moment Avylos considered simply sending him away. Whatever it was he had come to report, it could not be more important than the study of the book. But the young man *was* astute, and only a very good reason would have brought him into the Mage's wing at this hour, when breakfast was over, and no other service would be required for some time.

"Yes?"

"My lord Mage," the young Balnian began again. "The Lady Prince Kera has gone to visit Jarlkevo House."

Avylos closed the book with a snap and leaned forward. Emboldened, the young Balnian came two steps into the room. Avylos had fully expected Kera to remain in the bathhouse with Dhulyn, in a futile attempt to interrogate her.

"The Lady Prince may certainly visit her aunt Jarlkevo if she chooses."

"Of course, Lord Mage. But two newcomers arrived this morning, and must have ridden through the rain to arrive so early. Young guards from Jarlkevo, it is said, with a report for their House."

Yes, the boy *was* astute. The guards must be bringing the news that Edmir was dead. And Kera, no doubt hurrying for a counsel with her aunt and the Mercenary Brother following the unsuccessful attempt of the night before, would learn that her brother was definitely dead.

And Edmir's body? Where would it be now? Sylria, showing good sense, had buried it without mention to anyone. Better he should know where it was, however, in case Valaika was thinking of doing anything with it. He could send Olecz and a few carefully chosen others.

"Come with me."

The Balnian page stood to one side and followed Avylos out of his sitting room, along the corridor and down the steps to the garden doorway. Here Avylos hesitated. It was unlikely that the boy could see anything in the pool, but it was best to be cautious.

"Wait here," he said. The boy took up his post next to the open door and Avylos strode down the path, white pebbles crunching under his house shoes, until he reached the pool. He sat on the wide stone ledge, leaned forward and with his left hand drew a symbol, about a handbreadth above the surface of the still water, as though he were writing on an invisible tablet. When he withdrew his hand, the symbol remained, drawn in light, and the water began to darken.

As the water cleared, Avylos sat up straight, drawing in a sharp breath. He had expected to see first the darkness of earth, and then some hidden forest clearing where the angle of light would tell him in which direction from Jarlkevo lay this gamekeeper's lodge. This was no grave site, however, but the shadowy darkness of a shuttered room, the flickering light of candles. A sitting room. A fireplace freshly cleaned and laid with kindling. The bear's head emblem of Jarlkevo House carved into the thick oak beam of the mantel.

Avylos clenched his teeth. It had not been guards bringing news of Edmir's death who had arrived this morning, but Edmir himself. How was this possible? How had Sylria managed to lie to him?

Rising to his feet, he headed for the door, calling out to the still waiting Balnian page. "Fetch Royal Guard Commander Lord Semlian to the queen's apartments. Run."

Avylos waited until the boy was out of sight before returning inside. He checked his workroom door before following, keeping his pace brisk but controlled. Even now, he could not afford to look as though he were in any way perturbed. Meeting him, no one would be able to guess how loudly the blood pounded in his ears.

Edmir, the Mercenaries who had rescued him, Valaika. All here. Now. His plans unraveling. His pace slowed as his thoughts moved furiously fast. There *was* a way he could turn this to his advantage. A very clever way. A way that might very well solve more than one problem, and speed his plans.

He walked faster.

When he arrived at the double doors leading to the queen's private rooms Royal Guard Commander Semlian was already waiting for him. The Balnian page was nowhere in sight, but the guard commander was accompanied by Megz Primeau, one of the section leaders. All the better. Nodding to them, Avylos threw open the doors, waved aside the startled pages who sat ready for orders in Kedneara's anteroom. He had never done this, never just charged his way into the queen's presence. Until now he had always observed protocols scrupulously in approaching the queen, and it was obvious that none of her pages knew quite what to do. The old consort, Karyli, yes, *he'd* been allowed to flaunt protocol, but never Avylos. It was with unexpected relish that, Lord Semlian at his heels, Avylos pulled open the inner doors and found Kedneara on her feet, her shocked face turned toward the sounds of intrusion.

He went directly to her, taking her right hand in his and going to his knees. "Forgive me, my love, my Queen. I bring news of traitors to your rule."

"Traitors?"

Avylos rose to his feet and slipped his free arm around Kedneara's waist. "Sit, please, my Queen. You must be strong." The lady page who had been pinning the sleeves of her new gown pushed her abandoned chair closer and Avylos lowered the queen into it.

"Tell me." Her face was flushed with anger.

Smiling on the inside, Avylos knelt again and pressed her hand to his forehead. "I grieve to be the one who brings—"

"Tell me."

"It is House Jarlkevo, my Queen."

"Valaika?"

He raised his eyes to her face. "Yes, my Queen. My magic tells me that in her apartments she has an impostor, a young man she plans to claim is Edmir." Out of the corner of his eye, Avylos saw Section Leader Megz put her hand on her sword hilt.

"This is how she repays me." Kedneara's whisper was harsh. "This is what comes of spurning her love, all those years ago."

Avylos blinked, but kept his face steady. Was it possible that all Kedneara saw here was the revenge of unrequited love? Could even Kedneara be this self-absorbed? She gripped the arms of her chair.

"How can she do this?"

"There is a resemblance. I can only guess that he must be a child of the Jarlkevoso's own, a puppet she has been hiding, holding in reserve against a bid on your throne."

"And are you sure . . . ?"

"There speaks a mother's heart." Avylos kissed the back of the hand he still held. "But you know it cannot be. You know he is dead. This is not and cannot be Edmir."

"This cannot be Edmir."

He felt her pulse slow under his fingers. Much as he would have preferred it, it would be dangerous to have Kedneara repeat his words in front of these people.

"Is it Valaika then who is behind all this? Nisvea's invasion? Edmir's death?"

Good. She clearly believed in Edmir's death. "That I cannot know, my Queen. But it seems likely."

Kedneara's face hardened, and Avylos felt her pulse increase. She turned her stony face to the guard leader. "Bring them here."

"My Queen, you distress yourself too much. Let me spare you. Would it not be better—let me go with Guard Leader Semlian. Think of the scandal. Let *me* deal with the traitors. If necessary, it can be made to look like an accident."

"I thank you for your advice," Kedneara said in a voice that meant the opposite. "But I would speak with this woman and with those she uses against me. Bring them here. *Now.*"

As Avylos led Lord Semlian and Section Leader Megz Primeau toward the Great West Stairs, his face was hidden from them and he was able to smile. Kedneara was so easily manipulated, he thought. All he had to do was suggest that he wished to spare her, that something might be too much for her, and Kedneara would insist on seeing the traitors for herself. And if her health was completely undermined by the depth and deviousness of the treachery—one which might even involve the Princess Kera, if she were still in Valaika's rooms—well, who would be surprised?

Parno came out of the room Valaika had given him tugging on the sleeves of his shirt. It was now of fine silk, with wide sleeves and buttons rather than simple lacing, and over it he wore a long formal velvet overgown, open in the front and edged with marten fur. If his trousers were cut more loosely than was the strict court fashion of the moment, he trusted that no one would be looking at him closely enough to notice. He would have preferred to keep his own boots, with their hidden knives and his lockpicks sewn into the trim, but in order to pass as a minor House member, he had to settle for leather half boots.

With her lifetime of practice, Zania had taken less time than he had to change her costume, and was already dressed in a heavily brocaded gown, tightly laced, which left her neck and the upper part of her shoulders exposed, but whose long sleeves reached almost to her feet.

"The laces can be cut," Zania said, "and then the whole gown just falls to the ground."

"Undoubtedly exactly what the designer had in mind," Parno said. "Though I would imagine for a different purpose than the one we have." Zania curtsied, fluttering her eyes before she started to laugh.

"Guess where she has the rope," Edmir said from his perch on the edge of the table. Valaika was still sitting in her chair on the other side, frowning at her own thoughts.

Parno looked Zania up and down, taking two paces around her to be sure. "Around her hips. Oh, don't worry," he smiled, seeing the look of annoyance on Zania's face. "I'd give odds that no one else will notice it, and if they do, no one will remark on it. They'll just think you feel yourself too thin." He was pleased that Zania had come up with this solution. His sword he'd be able to carry openly, but the climbing rope they needed to get Zania up the wall wasn't something they could simply carry through the grounds.

Parno cocked his head, turning toward the door. He automatically moved to place himself between it and the others in the room.

"Someone's coming," he said. "Valaika, any legitimate reasons for guards to be coming to your door?"

The Jarlkevo roused herself. "None," she said, crisply enough.

"Well judging by the sound of their footsteps, guards are coming now." Parno crossed quickly to the door and made sure the latch and locking mechanisms were secure. Not that that gave them much security. The lock was impressive in looks only, meant to give a feeling of security to what should, after all, be a perfectly secure place already. One well-placed kick and the door would open.

As if in answer to his thoughts, the door shivered under a pounding fist. "Open in the name of Kedneara the Queen."

"Quick, the window." At this time of the morning, it was unlikely that anyone would notice their descent. They were only one story up, and the window opened directly onto the wide cobblestone path that skirted the inner wall of the grounds. A short hedge of flowering bushes edged the pathway at this point, enclosing a small orchard of carefully pruned apple and pear trees. The trees wouldn't provide much in the way of cover, but they would at least slow down pursuit.

And if they were very lucky, the guards were all at the door, and none had been left to watch the windows.

"Edmir." Parno caught the prince's eye and jerked his head toward the open casement.

"No," Valaika strode forward, taking hold of Edmir's sleeve and addressing herself to Parno. "You and Zania go first. Edmir and I are the least at risk if it transpires that we cannot follow. Whatever else may happen, you must get to the Stone, that is the most important thing."

Parno hesitated, surely Edmir was the most at risk, but there was no longer any time to argue. "Zania, follow me. Edmir, you're next lightest, and lastly Valaika." He caught the older woman's eye. "I expect you to follow, Jarlkevoso," he told her, with as much meaning as he could force into his tone. He thought he recognized the look on Valaika's face. Defeat, and despair. Now that the planning was over, and she'd been given time to brood, her shock over what Sylria had done had once more taken possession of her mind.

The pounding on the door renewed. With a nod at Valaika, Parno crossed back to the window, drew his sword to keep it from getting in his way should he fall, sat down on the windowsill and swung his legs over. He let himself drop straight down, knees slightly bent, ankles flexed, mindful that he might have to correct for the roughness of the cobbles below. He landed cleanly, and a quick look to the right and left assured him that he'd landed unobserved as well. He sheathed his sword and looked up in time to see Zania's face in the window. He beckoned with his hands, and held up his arms to catch her.

She must have learned something from the tumblers who had been with her troupe, for she twisted quickly in the air and landed in his arms as if she were throwing herself backward into a feather bed. He tipped her to her feet and looked up again. Edmir had one leg over the windowsill, but he was looking back into the room, not down at Parno and Zania.

"Come on, boy, come on," Parno muttered under his breath. As if he'd heard him, Edmir looked down and his lips moved silently, but almost immediately he looked away again. He dropped the hand that was hidden by his body from those within below the level of his waist, and waved them away, already withdrawing his leg.

"What's he doing?" Zania said. "What did he say?"

"Guards must be in the room," Parno said. "He's waving us off before anyone can look out the window. Come on." He took Zania by the elbow and pushed through the hedge beside them. If it had been more than waist high it might have been of some use as cover, but as it was, Parno needed to get them past at least two rows of fruit trees before the foliage, thick as it was at this time of the season, could adequately cover them from anyone looking out the window.

"But what did he say?"

"He said, 'the Mage,'" Parno said. "Avylos must be with them. No, don't look." Parno took her by the elbow and urged her forward.

The orchard turned out to be only three rows deep, but the hedge on the far side was as tall as Parno's shoulder. They burst out onto yet another white pebbled path and just to their left was a stone bench, shaded at this hour of the day. Parno hooked Zania's hand through his bent elbow and led her to the bench.

"Sit." He suited action to word.

"But—"

"We're on a stage," he told her, and felt her immediately relax at this bit of direction. "We're noble lovers in a garden. And that is what anyone who may be looking out a window just now will see."

"Parno, what's happening to them?"

"Nothing we can do anything about. And Valaika was quite right, nothing very serious *can* happen to them, not being who they are—or, at least, who Valaika is. It's not so easy to dispose of a High Noble House, let alone the cousin of the Tarkin of Hellik. It will take time, and in this, time is on our side."

"Surely Edmir will tell them who he is."

"The moment he thinks it will do any good."

"And for us? What now?" She looked up at him and smiled, just as if they were merely a courting couple taking advantage of a shady nook.

He smiled down at her and patted her hand. "We take advantage of the absence of the Mage to get to the Stone."

"How will we get into Avylos' workroom without Kera?"

"We'll worry about that when we get there. Today's problems today. In a few minutes we'll get up, and we'll start off in that direction." Parno nodded to the right. "We'll be strolling, just a couple taking advantage of the rain having stopped, and the sun coming out to dry the paths.

"And if we turn away from others, seeking out the darker and more secluded parts of the queen's gardens and grounds, well, no one seeing a courting couple sauntering about is going to find that unusual."

Avylos leaned against the doorframe, arms crossed, fingers tapping. Lord Semlian had managed to get himself slashed across the arm. Whatever could be said of Valaika, Avylos eyed her, she could still fight. Edmir—*no*, Avylos corrected himself, *I must not even* think *of him as Edmir*. Not that he was very likely to slip up. The young man had fought defensively, clearly reluctant to hurt anyone, let alone kill them. Not an unexpected attitude given who he was—*but don't say it, don't even think it*—typical really, avoid the unpleasant, even when it was necessary. Kera would have done what she needed to do, however much it might have pained her. In that, as in so many things, she was stronger than her brother. All this young man had achieved with his sensibilities was a bloody nose and a relatively quick disarming. Section Leader Megz had him bent over a chair as she bound his wrists behind him. He was smart enough to stay quiet at least.

The two extra guards with them returned from their search of the inner rooms, shaking their heads.

"This is everyone, my lord Mage, Guard Commander," the shorter one said with a nod to each captive.

"There should be at least one other," Avylos told them. He crossed to the window and looked out. What he could see of the grounds looked normal for this time of the morning. The watch was changing, and guards walking in pairs were coming and going from stations around the perimeter wall of Royal House. On a short stretch of lawn toward the western part of the grounds a huntswoman was training a dog. Avylos lifted his head and narrowed his eyes. Near the barracks, someone was setting up butts for archery practice. There were scattered people strolling through the grounds, fewer than normal given that the rain had stopped recently, though there were even a few couples sitting on benches.

No sign of anyone running. Nothing out of place.

Avylos turned back into the room. "Where have you sent him this time?" Valaika did not even raise her head. Avylos wrinkled his nose. "You have seen him," he said to the waiting guards. "The bodyguard who follows Valaika Jarlkevo. As tall as I am but thicker about the body. His dark hair is a wig, remove it and you will see a Mercenary badge." The guards in the room exchanged glances. "If you fear to engage with him, shoot him from a distance," Avylos told them, careful to keep the sneer from his voice. "An arrow will kill a man no matter where he has been Schooled.

"Guard Commander, you will see to your wound and the search. Assign Section Leader Olecz. You others will bring these traitors to Kedneara the Queen."

Kera turned out of the corridor which led to Avylos' wing and started back toward the Great Hall. She ducked into the alcove just before the Great West Stairs that until this winter had held the bust of her grandfather. Her lower lip was caught tight between her teeth, and in her hands was a broken strand of Tenezian glass beads, ready to spill on the floor if she had a sudden need to explain what she was doing standing in such an out of the way place.

Though it was cool here in the alcove, Kera felt a drop of sweat trickle its way down her back. Avylos had not been in his rooms for her to lure away with a false summons to her mother the queen. What should she do now? Find him and make sure—somehow—that he stayed away? Or trust that whatever occupied him at the moment would hold his attention long enough for Parno and Zania to steal the Stone? They could not possibly have reached Avylos' garden yet; she still had some time to decide what to do.

She heard the sound of footsteps coming up the staircase to her left. Kera knelt, tossed the beads on the floor, and bent down to pick them up. It did not sound like Avylos, but . . .

"Allow me, Lady Prince."

Kera looked up. Metrick. Metrick the Balnian. Metrick the gossip.

"I would not keep you from your errand, Metrick."

"I have no errand, Lady Prince, but to find you."

Kera's hands froze for one second before she forced her fingers to continue picking up beads. "Who sent you?"

"No one, my Prince, only, I have noticed that you are frequently in this part of the House, and when I wished to find you . . ."

"*You* wished to find me?" Kera sat back on her heels, not knowing whether to feel flattered or skeptical. She *was* Lady Prince. Metrick of Balnia might very well feel his path to advancement lay through her. Or indeed, more than advancement. How important *was* his family in Balnia? Was he one of the people her mother the queen had warned her against? She realized that he had gone on speaking, and that she'd missed the first part of what he'd said.

"I'm sorry, could you repeat that?"

"You may well be shocked, Lady Prince. I'm sorry to be the one to bring you this news."

But he wasn't sorry, Kera could tell. He was pleased, not at the news, but at the importance it gave him in bringing it.

"Valaika Jarlkevoso has been arrested, along with an impostor she had in her rooms and planned to pass off as Prince Edmir, your brother."

"Where are they now?"

"The Blue Mage has taken them to Kedneara the Queen."

Kera thought quickly. Valaika and Edmir. That meant Parno and Zania were still free. Could they have been already on their way to the Mage's wing when the guards had come? What had brought the guards to Valaika? Not that there was time to think about that now.

And what should she do? If Parno and Zania *were* free, then they would be coming to the Mage's garden. And that's where she should be. She would simply have to trust that her mother would not act so quickly that Valaika and Edmir would be in danger. And surely, surely, her mother would recognize her own son?

"Metrick, go now and fetch—no," she interrupted herself as if she was having a change of thought. "Please take these beads to my apartments and give them to Sharian, my lady page. Explain to her what has occurred." He'd like that, he evidently liked being the bearer of news. "I will go myself to tell the Blue Mage's cousin what delays him, as she may not trust another. Tell Sharian to go to my mother the queen's apartments and await me there."

"At once, Lady Prince."

Kera waited until Metrick was part of the way down the Great West Stairs before turning and running back into Avylos' wing.

⌒

As they walked Parno steered them farther away from Valaika's rooms, seemingly taking paths at random, so anyone watching them would not even believe they had a destination, let alone guess what it might be.

"I think this is the first thing I've ever done where my goal was *not* to attract attention." Zania's voice was calm and measured, but Parno could feel her arm trembling ever so slightly in his.

"Not true," he said. "Remember how and why we started using the code word 'Pasillon'? To remind us that we are not the only people on stage, and that sometimes we must efface ourselves to let others shine, or to let the story unfold of itself? What is that if not a need to deflect the audience's eyes?"

The farther they got from the gardens closest to Valaika's rooms the greater the urge to walk faster. It seemed that every corner they turned led to yet another piece of statuary, yet another formally laid out bed of flowers or ornamental trees. Finally the paths began to widen, and Parno knew that they approached the edge of the garden plantings closest to the section of repaired wall.

Parno slowed down even more; the only person within eyeshot was a kitchen boy passing with a basket of eggs hanging from one arm, and the instant the turnings of the path faced him away from them Parno pulled Zania into the nearest shrubbery. In a moment, Parno had discarded his formal overgown, and had cut Zania's laces, allowing her to drop her own gown and step out of it. She pulled up the shoulders of the simple vest she had been wearing under the gown. At a distance, with her tousled hair and leggings, she could pass for any lower servant. Only the rope wound around her hips was out of place. A wriggle, and that too was on the ground. Parno picked up the coil of rope and slung it over his shoulder.

A trumpet call from toward the front gate—and the guard barracks—made Zania look around and grab Parno's arm.

"Ignore it," he told her. "They call the guard to assemble a search party. By the time they reach us down here, we'll be in the Mage's garden." As he spoke, he took sights from the top of two battlements, and the flagstaff on a tower he knew lay to the north. The repaired part of the wall was to their left.

"Just ahead there," he said. "Follow me." The distance they had to cross was short, and in a moment Parno had his hand on the surface of the wall. He frowned. The wall was smoother than he remembered, much smoother.

"What is it?"

"I may have cut the angle a little short after all, coming through the garden. Wait here." He took three paces to the right, but the wall was equally smooth there. He returned to where Zania marked the spot he'd started from, took three paces to the left . . . and found nothing but smooth wall.

"Zania, you did not move?" He hardly needed her indignant response to tell him that she hadn't. He checked his position again against the closest guard tower, the edges of the garden, and the distant murmur of noise that would be the guard barracks. He had not made a mistake. They were in the right place.

Parno's skin crawled with a sudden chill.

"The wall's been magicked," he said. "He must have been told. Avylos must have been told that I came over the wall."

Zania's face fell. "We'll get our court clothes back on," she said. "We'll have to try bluffing our way in the front doors."

"With everyone now looking for us? No disrespect intended to your ability to bluff anyone into anything, we would still have to find our way through the entire House, to say nothing of the magic that would keep me at least out of the Mage's wing once we got there."

Parno eyed the wall again. Demons and perverts, he needed to *think*. Kera had said that Avylos used as little magic as he could in any given situation—he would not use both an avoidance *and* a locking magic, where he could simply use a lock. That had made sense, given that Avylos' power source constantly had to be renewed. Would it follow that he would be equally parsimonious when it came to placing a magic on the wall? Parno put his hand on the stone and rubbed it back and forth. Smooth, but smooth like a polished stone floor, not like glass or the glazing on a pot. So Avylos had not changed the nature of the wall itself. He tapped his fingertips on the stone as though on the airholes of his pipes. That wasn't exactly the right sound.

"A surface as smooth as this one appears to be should make a cleaner sound," he said aloud.

"It doesn't seem so very smooth to me," Zania said, looking up and squinting.

"Doesn't it? Touch it, would you, and tell me what you feel."

Zania lifted her hand slowly, glancing at him sideways to see if she was doing what he wanted. She laid her palm flat on the wall.

"Move it back and forth a little."

"What am I trying to find?" she asked.

"Can you feel the individual stones, the mortar?"

"Y–yes."

That hesitation told Parno everything he wanted to know. Avylos would not waste his power. He would magic the wall against those, such as Parno, who intended to climb it. Zania, in truth, would be doing no climbing, it was Parno who would bring her up once he had reached the top himself. Evidently that slight difference between them was enough to make them experience the wall differently.

So the magic didn't make the wall impossible to climb, it just made the wall *seem* impossible to climb.

"Parno?" Zania was still standing with her hand on the wall.

"Give me a moment," he said. "I need to try something." He shook out his hands. The Sable Monkey *Shora*. That's what was needed here. Used for climbing trees, rock faces and yes, stone walls, the *Shora* trained the eye to see and recognize holds that would support weight. Dhulyn had taught him the principles, not that there had been many opportunities for him to practice.

Climb, he told himself. *You're a Sable Monkey and you're going to climb this wall.* Nothing. He waited a handful of heartbeats longer and touched the wall again. Still nothing. Was it that he didn't know the *Shora* well enough? Or was it that it would not work.

Sun and Moon. He heard Dhulyn's voice in his head as he'd heard it so many times during practice. *The Shora* always *work. Pattern is always pattern.* Tradition said the *Shoras* came from the Caids. Was that enough for them to counteract the Mage's magics?

Parno settled the coil of rope over his shoulder and took a deep breath, releasing it slowly. This time he concentrated on relaxing his muscles, regularizing his breathing. He repeated seven times the three words that were his own personal *Shora* triggers allowing him to concentrate his focus and draw upon the *Shoras* that he knew. And he *did* know the Sable Monkey *Shora*, Dhulyn had taught it to him only last year, and he'd practiced it since. And he *did* know this wall. It was climbable. He'd already climbed it. His hands and feet knew the pattern. *And pattern is always pattern.* He flexed his fingers in the pattern prescribed by the Sable Monkey *Shora*. *I am climbing, I will reach the top. I cannot fall.*

Parno put up his hands, found the first fingerholds, and pulled himself up. There were the toeholds he had used before. He did not rest or pause, but put out his hands for the next holds, and then the next. He was more than halfway to the top when his hands felt only smooth stone. For a heartbeat his belly turned to ice, and the muscles in his calves began to tremble. How long until his toes felt nothing but smooth stone? How long before he fell?

Parno laid his cheek flat against the stone, eyes squeezed shut, and whispered his triggers, whispered them seven times seven times.

"I am the Sable Monkey," he said aloud. "I will not fall." He opened his eyes, and continued climbing.

Twenty-four

IT WAS HARD TO GAUGE the passage of time, since the water in these baths grew no colder, and Dhulyn had sent the attendants away. She found, however, that she could not recapture the languor she'd felt before falling asleep; just as she felt herself relaxing once more, she was disturbed by the nagging feeling that she had forgotten something. Her laugh echoed sharply in the tiled room. She hadn't just forgotten *something*, she'd forgotten *everything*.

Except she hadn't, not really. Life with Avylos would be considerably easier if she really had forgotten everything. If she didn't have these constant reminders, these surfacing thoughts, these *dreams*. The dreams felt real to her, solid, full of color, sound, and feeling. Her life with Avylos, on the other hand, felt empty and flat, as if it had left no footprints in the pathways of her brain.

There. That kind of thinking. What kind of person had thoughts like those? Footprints. Paths. Arrows. Swords. Surely not someone who had spent her whole life in the Tegrian Queen's Royal House.

Dhulyn rolled her shoulders and flexed her feet. She should try to relax, take advantage of this wonderful bath. It was seldom she ever got the chance for a long soak in a place like this one. In fact, she couldn't remember when—

"*Blooded* Stars," she said aloud, her voice echoing once more off the walls. She sat up and looked around for the towels the attendants had left. There was certainly no point in remaining here any longer, chasing the same thoughts around and around. Surely there must be something Avylos could do. Find a Healer, use a magic on her. *Something*.

And what was she doing wearing this ridiculous wig in the baths? It itched, and there were no servants here to whisper behind their hands at the scarring on her head. Besides, they'd seen enough of the scars on her back to give them plenty to whisper about. She gathered her feet under her and stood, wiping the water off her body with the edges of her hands before reaching for a towel. After wrapping a large sheet of toweling around herself, she sat down on the bench next to the bath and inserted her fingers around the edges of the wig. She would have it off, if only for a few minutes.

She peeled the wig off gently and spread it out along the bench. It would have to be brushed out, in any case, she thought. Dhulyn knelt by the side of the bath and stuck her head under the warm water to loosen and remove the last of the sticky paste that had held on the wig. Her head felt so much lighter now, and so much cooler. She eyed the wig, twisting her mouth to one side. If only she could go without it. What about when her own hair grew out, could it be combed in such a way that it would cover the scarring on her head?

Dhulyn put her hands to her temples . . . and froze. She felt the skin more carefully with the sensitive tips of her fingers. Nothing. No roughness. She trailed her fingertips over her cheeks and forehead, and back to her temples.

It all felt the same. No scarring.

Dhulyn lowered her hands, and pursed her lips in a silent whistle. She tucked the towel around her more tightly and proceeded to the outer room, where clean clothes had been left out for her away from the moist air of the bathing chamber. As she had requested, she'd been left trousers, a shirt, and a short-waisted tunic to replace the gown she'd been wearing. She frowned. The shirt was long sleeved, and the shoes house slippers instead of boots. Why *that* should trouble her was just another thing she didn't know.

She had buckled the sword belt around her hips and was attaching the sword to it before she was aware what she was doing. She lifted her hands away and took a few steps. It felt right. Natural. As if she had often had a sword there. She found herself nodding. *This* was why she'd fought so well against the Mercenary. She *was* skilled as a war-rior. It must be common among the women of the Tribes.

She drew the blade and weighed it in her hand, admiring its balance.

"Is this your doing, Avylos? Did you hope to trigger my memory?"

Dhulyn resheathed the sword. She needed a mirror. She needed answers. And she would find neither of those things here.

Strange how different even your own home can look, when your hands
are bound behind your back and you're being marched along as a prisoner by the very guards who are supposed to be protecting you. On
the other hand, Edmir thought, perhaps it was lucky he *was* bound.
This way no one could see how badly he was shaking. His mother the
queen was never an easy person to contend with, and they had not
planned on having to deal with her until after Avylos had been neu-
tralized. His stomach clenched and he licked a drop of sweat from his
upper lip.

Do I want her to know me, he thought, *or not know me*?

And that thought made him pause. Staying alive was his worry at
the moment, and he needed to focus his attention on that. What
would happen with the rest of his life was only important if he lived.

"Lord Mage," came the voice of Section Leader Megz Primeau
from behind him as they neared the doorway which would let them
out into the grounds. She tightened her grip on his right arm and gave
him a shake. "This one does look most remarkably like Prince Edmir."
Her hand clamped down painfully when she said his name, and Edmir
winced. "May I," another painful *squeeze*. "Suggest that we cover their
heads, lest the whole House know," *squeeze*, "of this imposture? I do
not offend you," *squeeze*, "I trust." *Squeeze*.

Edmir heard enough of Avylos' answer to know that it was in the
negative, but his attention was focused elsewhere. Whether it was his
recent training at catching cues on the stage, or that his present
predicament sharpened his wits, Edmir couldn't know, but he thought
he understood Megz Primeau's message. His arm would be badly
bruised, the section leader had fingers like metal pincers, but her
squeezing had not been random.

Edmir. I. Know. You. . . . Trust.

In that moment, Edmir's perception shifted. With Megz's words,
what happened in the audience with his mother the queen—what she
believed, and what she would say to him—became less important.
Getting through the interview—*that* was now the goal. Section Leader
Megz was the senior guard present, and would undoubtedly be put in

charge of them when they were dismissed from his mother the queen's presence. All he and Valaika had to do was hold out until then.

That, and do everything they could to buy time for Parno and Zania.

Now Edmir lifted his head and looked around him. They were almost across the corner of the grounds between Valaika's rooms and the main citadel of Royal House. From what he could see, they were heading for the entrance known as the consort's door, not the main entrance and the more direct route that would take them through the Great Hall. So Avylos was taking no chances. The fewer people who saw them, the fewer there would be to ask questions and delay them. But just the same, Royal House was full of people, personal servants, cleaners, kitchen staff, pages, and guards on normal patrols. It was impossible for them to march through even the lesser-used corridors without being seen and remarked on.

Avylos said nothing, his set stare was enough to clear their way of anyone they encountered. The other guards were not so quiet, however, and Avylos did nothing to stop their murmurs of "traitors to the queen" and "an impostor."

What Edmir saw when they finally entered his mother the queen's private sitting room made his heart sink. She wasn't stalking back and forth, her long strides making the skirt and sleeves of her gown flutter. That would have meant she was angry. She wasn't standing by her window, leaning on the ledge and looking out into her private garden. That would have meant she was seriously annoyed. No. Kedneara the Queen was sitting in her large chair, the one that most resembled her throne, gripping its arms so tightly that her knuckles were white.

She was in a flying fury. They would be very lucky if blood was not shed.

Edmir lowered his eyes and tried to make his breathing as shallow as possible. It was cowardly of him, he knew, but he did not want to do anything that would bring the full force of that fury down on him.

"Get out," the queen said. Her voice was still musical, but it was as if someone plucked the strings of a harp with a dagger. The three pages who had been waiting with her looked at each other out of the corners of their eyes, but they did so as they were moving to the door. Even the guards holding Valaika shuffled their feet, falling still only when Avylos raised his hand to them. Edmir risked a glance upward, but his mother was looking at Valaika.

"Valaika, you Hellish cow," she spat, as the door was closing behind the last page. "Have you always hated me this much?"

Edmir knew a sudden, though not unfamiliar, pang. Once his mother would have looked at him first, asked about him, even if she thought he was only an impostor. Those days were long gone.

"I never hated you, Kedneara," Valaika was saying. The guards had forced her to her knees. "You loved my brother, you chose him. You were happy, Kedneara, and Karyli was happy with you. That was enough for me."

"You don't hate me?" Kedneara, hands still gripping the arms of her chair, leaned forward as though she would spit in Valaika's face. "You say you don't hate me? Why else would you do this? Join with my enemies to conspire against me, kill my child, come here with an imp—"

Edmir pulled against Megz's grip as his mother's face darkened, suffused with blood. Her mouth was open, but it seemed she could neither speak nor breathe. Her grip on the arms of her chair became, if possible, even tighter, but her body began to heave and jerk. Megz let go of his arm and moved forward, but Avylos reached the queen's side before anyone, holding the others back with a short chop of his hand.

"Kedneara, my Queen, look at me."

It seemed that his mother couldn't raise her head, but she managed to twist it enough that she could look sideways at Avylos through slitted eyes. Froth tinged with blood formed on her lips. Holding her gaze with his own, Avylos took hold of the queen's wrist in his right hand. With his left, he began to sketch in the air. Edmir was not surprised when lines of light flowed from the end of Avylos' finger, and a symbol formed in the air, but the guards, who perhaps had never seen the Blue Mage actually perform from this close a distance, drew their breaths in sharply and took a pace back, leaving Valaika alone on her knees. She watched, tight-lipped, as the symbol glowed first blue, then gold.

"Inhale, my Queen. Inhale." As if Avylos' words were themselves a magic, Edmir's mother suddenly inhaled. The gold symbol flew in between her parted lips and almost immediately the dark color faded from her face, leaving her pale except for a slight blush on her cheeks. Her breathing regularized, she blinked, and sat back in her chair, holding both hands against her heart.

Edmir's own heart felt cold in his chest. This was what they had not known, he and Kera. They had not known how sick their mother was, and how dependent on Avylos' magic. Of course, Kedneara was a woman, the Mage's magic would not cure her once and for all. He would need to renew the magic regularly, perhaps even find new magics when the old ones failed to serve. If he and his friends succeeded in what they were trying to do, if they succeeded in taking and destroying the Stone and Avylos' magic faded away, so would his mother the queen. She would die, if they stopped Avylos.

Finally she looked up, right into Edmir's eyes.

"Edmir," she said, but her voice was so flat, it was impossible to know what she meant, impossible to be sure that she knew him.

"That is not Edmir, my dear one, my Queen, do not let your illness trick you." Avylos was already drawing in the air again, this time in the open space before the queen, short, chopping lines, a symbol harsh with corners. "This is an impostor, my Queen, Edmir is dead. This is not Edmir."

Edmir watched as his mother dragged her eyes from his to focus on the Mage and his symbol. She began slowly to nod.

"Mother," he cried, pushing forward. If only he could get her to look at him again.

But Section Leader Megz Primeau's steely hand on his arm pulled him back. "Edmir is dead," Megz said. "This is not Edmir."

"Valaika, close your eyes," he cried out. "Valaika!" Megz raised her fist to strike at him, but when he lowered his head and turned away, she let her hand fall open again.

"Edmir is dead. This is not Edmir."

His mother the queen, Megz, and the two other guards had spoken in unison. Without looking up, Edmir couldn't be certain whether Valaika had also spoken, or whether she remained unaffected by Avylos' magic.

Two at least of the people affected were women, which meant that eventually both his mother and Megz Primeau would recognize him again—but that eventuality was very small comfort to him now.

"My Queen, do not hesitate, do not let your kind heart lead you astray." Avylos was still standing next to the queen's chair. "You see how insidious they are, what havoc they could cause, do not hesitate I beg you, send them to the Black Dungeons now."

"But the other Houses—"

"Do you believe that any of them will speak for Jarlkevo? Outsider as she is? If you feel the need to tell them, do it after the fact, when the imposter is dead and the danger is past."

At these words Edmir looked up, unable to believe that Avylos gave this advice seriously. Jarlkevo *was* a new House, as these things were counted, but a High Noble House it was, and the idea that the other Houses—so jealous of their rights and privileges as they had always been—would stand meekly and nod agreement when one of their own, even a relative newcomer and outsider, was put to death without trial or hearing . . . No. What was done to Valaika Jarlkevo could be done to any of them, and they would know it, and their reaction would be swift and dangerous.

Regardless of the consequences to himself, Edmir had opened his mouth to say so, but Avylos pointed at him, a flicker like the flame of a candle appearing on his fingertip. The flame flew to Edmir's mouth, and he found he could not speak.

"I will see to it that the other Houses are informed," he told the queen. "Trust me, this you must do, for your own protection."

Edmir looked on, astonished, as his mother the queen nodded, and waved her hand. "Take them away," she said. She had not looked at him again.

"To the Black Dungeons?" It seemed even the other guards could not believe what they'd been told.

"Yes," said the queen. "Take them, now."

It was not until he felt the pain in his throat that Edmir realized he was trying to scream.

<hr />

Parno sat astride the top of the garden wall, his hands shaking, and the sweat drying on his face. He could taste blood; he must have bitten the inside of his lip on his way up. The Sable Monkey *Shora* controlled his breathing and heart rate while he was using it, but now he felt the exertions in the burning of his muscles, and the pounding of his heart.

He spat to one side as he uncoiled the rope and tied one end around his waist before tossing the loose end down to where Zania stood waiting, her arms already raised to catch it. As soon as it reached her, Zania created a loop in the rope, using the knots he'd shown her, and pushed her head and arms through it. When she was ready, she tugged on the rope. Parno swung both legs over to the garden side of the wall, and began to walk down, taking it nice and slow. With his weight to counterbalance hers, Zania would be lifted up the outer side of the wall at a pace which would let her use her hands and feet to prevent scraping or bumping against the wall. This was a trick taught in the Mercenary Schools, and Parno had practiced it many times before, both as anchor and counterweight.

Just as his feet touched the ground on the garden side of the wall, Zania's head popped up over the top. She swung her legs to the garden side of the wall, and, in answer to Parno's waving hands, maneuvered herself over a half a span to her right, where she could use the limbs of a tree to help lower herself to the ground.

"What now?" Zania said as he freed her from the rope and began coiling it again. "Kera is not expecting us until nightfall."

"Can't be any harm in looking around a bit. Who knows, maybe Avylos has left his workroom open."

When he straightened from hiding the rope under the nearest flowering bush, Zania was looking at him with her brows drawn down. "Are you sure it won't be safer to hide somewhere in here? Those hedges against the wall over there would give us plenty of cover."

Parno found his hands had clenched into fists and forced them open, spreading his fingers as far as they would go. It went against the grain to tell his true feelings—his true *worries* was more the point, to anyone except his own Partner. Even to Zania, even after spending all this time on the road with her. But his own Partner had not known him the last time they spoke, she had fought with him, tried to kill him. In fact, the last time the real Dhulyn had said anything to him had been her signaled "In Battle" as she rode away. She had not even seen his response "In Death." He filled his lungs with air, and let it out slowly. They were not dead yet, and if this wasn't a battle, he'd like to know what it was.

"Dhulyn may be inside," he said finally. "I cannot wait here, hiding, knowing that. I must at least try to find her."

Zania was silent for so long Parno turned to look at her. Except for the tiny wrinkle between her brows, her face was expressionless. She glanced up at him, just a flash of her green eyes before she looked away again. "I understand," she said. "Lead the way."

Parno patted her shoulder. He should have known Zania would

understand. He imagined that she would like to know where Edmir was just now. "The door's this way," he said.

The Mage's garden was like a miniature of the grounds outside, but the pathways and plantings were not so numerous that Parno could not remember the layout. He followed one narrow path and came, as he expected, to the small pool. Just beyond it, near the rock garden, was the table and two sturdy wooden chairs where Dhulyn and Kera had been sitting. He stopped and picked up the garden stake Dhulyn had used against him. He put it back down and looked around, mentally counting the paths leading from this spot. When Dhulyn had sent her for Avylos, Kera had run in that direction, he decided, choosing the central pathway. That way lay the door. He gestured to Zania to follow him.

"Will the door be magicked?" she asked, as they drew closer to it.

"Unlikely. But then again, I didn't expect the wall to be magicked." Standing as far back as he could and still retain leverage, Parno reached out with his sword, positioned the point under the metal latch, and lifted. The door swung open outward. Neither locked nor magicked by the look of it.

"Avylos must have thought putting a magic on the wall was enough to keep people out."

"It's as Kera told us," Parno agreed, "he does not waste his power."

The door opened on a small stone landing. Three steps led upward to another, smaller landing where an arched doorway opened onto a corridor. Parno signaled Zania to stand back, went down on one knee, and shot a quick look down each arm of the corridor from a spot just below the height of his own waist. Empty and, except for three closed doors, featureless.

"Which way?" Zania breathed.

Parno held up his hand, listening. He would swear he could hear a distant but rhythmic tapping. He nodded. Running footsteps. For a moment his heart leaped, only to subside again. It was not Dhulyn, he knew every sound she could make, and this was not her.

"This way," he said, turning toward the sound.

Zania took a pinch of his sleeve between her thumb and forefinger. "How do you know?"

"Someone is running toward us, it's only courteous that we go to meet them."

"Shouldn't we avoid whoever it is?" Zania's tone was sour, but she followed.

"From the lightness of the sound, and swiftness of the footsteps, this is a young, slim person wearing lady's house shoes. The only person I can think of who would match that description, and who would be running in this direction, is Princess Kera. But just in case I'm wrong—" he grinned at her to show how unlikely *that* was. "Take this." He pulled his spare dagger from his sleeve and handed it to her. Better careful than cursing, was what Dhulyn would have said.

Parno set a cautious pace, and they had advanced only a few spans down the hall when Zania stopped him with a whisper.

"Parno, this must be the door."

Still with his eyes on the end of the corridor he backed up two steps to come even with her.

"The other two have latches," Zania said. "But look, this one's just plain, no latch, no hinges showing, nothing."

"That's it, then," Parno agreed. "But finding it doesn't get us much further. What is it?" Zania had gone close enough to almost press her nose against the polished wood. She squinted, wrinkling up her nose.

"There's a shadow here," she said, "like a bunch of cobwebs, but if I move, the shadow doesn't change." She waved her hand up and down.

"I see no shadow at all, except your own."

"If only I see it . . . do you think it might be the latch?"

"It's placed higher on the door than these others," Parno said, pointing at the closest door with the point of his sword. "But who knows, that might help the magic." He turned to look down the corridor. The footsteps were getting closer. "Behind me," he whispered, gesturing with his head.

But it was indeed Princess Kera who turned into the far end of the corridor and slid to a halt at the sight of them, her hand pressed tightly to her waist, and her breath coming short and fast.

"Parno Lionsmane," she said, as soon as she had caught her breath and drawn closer to them. "Do you know? Avylos has arrested Valaika and Edmir."

Parno looked past her, but no one was following Kera from the main part of the citadel. "We know," he said. "If Avylos is occupied with them, we must use this time to get the Stone. Do you know where Dhulyn Wolfshead is?""

Kera gave a short nod. "Still in the baths, I should think."

Parno grinned despite himself. "She's always loved baths, that's for certain. We should have time enough, then, so long as we can get to the Stone."

"Have you tried the door?" she asked, stepping around him.

Zania tapped the spot where she'd seen the shadow. "Is this the latch?"

Kera nodded and put out her hand. As her fingers closed on the spot Zania had indicated, an intricate iron latch took form under her hand. She lifted it and the door swung silently open.

Avylos' working chamber was a large rectangular room with two windows equipped with both shutters and bars. The shutters were open, and Parno could see dust motes floating in the sunlight that shone across the Mage's worktable and the dark oak floor. There were shelves and cabinets against the walls of the room, including some behind the table itself, but Parno's eyes went almost immediately to the wooden casket that sat to the right on the table.

"Zania?" he said.

"I think so," she said. "It looks like the drawing, don't you think?"

"You never saw it, not even as a small child?"

"I don't remember." Zania walked over to the casket and put her hand on it. It was locked.

"Well, your touching it doesn't prove there's no magic on it, just that whatever there is doesn't affect women. Let's see what happens . . ." He stood at Zania's side and put his own hand where hers had been on the casket's lid. The wood felt warm. Warmer than it should have felt, even with the sun upon it. Parno frowned.

"What is it?" Kera had crept up beside them.

"It's a Balnian lock," he said. "I *have* opened Balnian locks, but not many, and not recently."

"Dhulyn Wolfshead must have opened it," Kera said. "I saw the Stone that night."

"My Partner has a better hand with locks than I do," Parno said. But all the while he was speaking his hands were busy feeling along the inner seam of his sword sheath, where his lockpick was hidden. The fold of leather was stiff, but he pried it open with his thumbnail and the thin, flat, metal rod popped out into his hand. Dhulyn had found this for him, and had an old smith in Cabrea fashion it to her specifications. Half of Parno's trouble with locks had disappeared once he had a proper tool.

Half his trouble. Not all.

He took a deep breath and looked around. He found himself reluctant to sit in the Mage's chair. "Zania, pull that chair closer, would you?" He indicated where he wanted it to be placed, but the moment he sat down, he wondered if he had made a mistake. The muscles in his legs burned now that he was no longer standing, and he felt a tiny tremor in his hands that did not bode well for the picking of the lock. Since early morning he'd jumped out a window, run across half the grounds of the Royal House, used the *Shoras* to help him climb a magicked wall, and pulled Zania up behind him. He risked a glance at her. Her lips had no color, and there were dark smudges under her eyes.

We're a fine pair, he thought. He had reserves of strength the girl did not have, and she was neither complaining nor trembling. He smiled at her, and was comforted to see her smile back.

No point in putting this off any longer, he was not going to get less tired. There was no *Shora* for picking locks, more was the pity. If they lived through this, he would help Dhulyn make one. He put the lockpick between his teeth, flexed his fingers and rubbed his hands together, before taking hold of the pick once more and lowering his eyes to the level of the lock. One end of the lockpick was formed like a squared-off hook, the metal bent at right angles. That end he inserted into the lock and moved it to feel gingerly to the right and left. Nothing. Up. Nothing. Down. Ah, there was the first catch of the locking mechanism.

He had reached the fifth catch when he slipped, and lost his place. He sat back and took two deep breaths, rolling his shoulders. He would have to release the first four catches again, but having done it once, it would be much easier the second time. So he told himself, and so it proved, as he was soon unlocking the fifth catch and moving along to what he hoped was the sixth, and final catch. There were more complicated Balnian locks, he knew, but he had to hope this was not one of them. Any more catches and he would need a second lockpick, and that he did not have.

The final catch moved with a click he felt more in his fingers than heard with his ears and he was just leaning back to share his satisfied smile with Zania and Kera when a sound made them all turn to look at the door.

It had swung open and standing in the doorway was his Partner, Dhulyn Wolfshead.

Twenty-five

THE WAY TO THE BLACK DUNGEONS was not entirely dark, contrary to what Edmir had always been told. He'd known that the stories told around the fire in the Royal Guardroom couldn't all be true, seeing as how so many contradicted each other. But as children, he and Kera had loved to be frightened by rumors and gossip, and with wondering which tales *were* true. According to one source, the Black Guards never came up out of the dungeons, once their time of service there began. Another said the Guard was a secret duty, and that its members walked about mixing with the House Guard unknown to anyone but themselves. You might sit down next to one at the meal table, and never know.

Some stories maintained the Black Guards were blind from birth, carefully selected and trained, and that the hoods and masks tradition said they wore were used only at the delivery of prisoners, to preserve anonymity. Other stories said they were sighted people, but bred—or helped by magic—to see in the dark. Most stories claimed that once Black Guards accepted their positions, the hoods and masks never came off, and hid their identities not just from guards delivering prisoners, but even from each other.

The only thing all the stories agreed on was that the work of the Black Guards was done in the dark, "neither in sunlight, nor moonlight, nor light of flame." That's how Edmir had heard it. Wisdom that came down from the Caids warned against the witnessing of torture and executions. While such actions might be deemed necessary, those who watched them were in danger of developing a taste for such things. Hence the stories that even the Black Guards themselves were blind, not just dark-adapted.

Edmir did not find it reassuring that the reality was more prosaic than the rumors. He'd been familiar with the entrance to the Black Dungeons his whole life; the circular stone stairwell was in his mother the queen's apartments, and as Lord Prince he'd known that one day he would make the journey down into the foundations of the Royal House to visit the Black Dungeons, as his mother had done before him. No one could rule in Tegrian without knowing what sending someone to the dungeons meant.

Truth to tell, a part of Edmir, *the playwright part*, he was now aware, had been looking forward to that visit, to finally learning for himself which of the stories were true, and which false. *I just never thought I'd find out* this *way*, he thought. *Not as a prisoner.*

When his mother the queen had passed her sentence on them, Edmir expected other guards to be sent for, but it seemed that Avylos had thought of that as well, and Megz Primeau and her companions were senior enough for this duty. At the top of the circular staircase Edmir tried to make them stop, but he still couldn't speak, and when he dug in his heels and pulled away, one of the two guards with Megz Primeau simply tripped him, and toppled him down the stone steps.

"We can roll you all the way down, if you'd like." Megz's voice actually showed some pity. "You could break your neck, but you might prefer that to what you'll find at the bottom."

Edmir shook his head and staggered to his feet, pressing his right shoulder against the stone wall of the stairwell. Whatever it was he needed to face, he'd do it better unbruised, and unbattered. He stood still, therefore, and allowed Megz to take hold of him once more by the upper arm. The larger of the two guards had four short torches in his belt. At Megz's nod, he lit one and began the descent. He was soon lost to sight as the turnings of the stairs carried him away, but the light continued; he used the torch to ignite the evenly spaced wall sconces as he passed them by.

Four torches, Edmir thought. *Two to get us there, and two to lead them back again?*

By the time they stepped off the final stair Edmir's legs were trembling with the strain of keeping his balance with his hands tied behind his back. Megz did not pause, however, but set off along the wide passage. After so many turns on the staircase, Edmir found he could not even guess in what direction they were now heading. The row of wall sconces continued, and in their flickering light Valaika looked gray and stunned, her lower lip trembling as she shuffled in the grip of her guard. She was in no danger of falling, or stumbling, however, as the floors and walls of the passage were clean, neither dusty nor damp, and even the stones underfoot were beautifully fitted and smooth.

Work of the Caids, Edmir thought, remembering what the Mercenaries had told them, him and Zania. The Royal House must have been built on ruins dating from the time of the Caids themselves. These stones were older than his family, older than Tegrian, older, perhaps, than the gods. For a moment, his awe at that immeasurable, unthinkable expanse of time was enough to distract him from his own present. But only for a moment.

The temperature increased, and Edmir realized that, dry as this passage was, they were passing close by the hot springs that surfaced in the Royal Baths. Before he could think about what that meant, the corridor ended abruptly in what was obviously a much more recent addition, a heavy oak door with metal banding, and a thickly barred grate at the height of an average man's head. Above the door, a shaded lantern with a fat candle inside replaced the wall sconces that had lined the passage. The larger guard was there, the candle was lit, and the stubs of the first two torches lay extinguished on the floor. A rope bell pull, stout and tarred such as might be found outside the night door of any respectable inn, hung to one side.

At a nod from Megz, the large guard put his hand on the rope.

"It's not like they couldn't hear us coming," he said.

"Just ring the bell, Tzen."

The sound the bell made was very pure, very sweet, like the bells that hung on the trees in the queen's private garden. Edmir swallowed and blinked away sudden tears.

Tzen must have been right, the Black Guards *had* heard them coming, because the gate was swinging silently inward even as the last notes of the bell faded away.

The man who stepped forward into the opening, and the two others who kept their places behind him, *were* masked, *and* hooded, as tradition had it, but there were eyeholes in the masks, something that would not have been necessary if they were blind. But their eyes *were* huge and dark, with no color showing around the pupils. They were squinting, as if even the shaded light from the lantern was more than they could tolerate comfortably. The Black Guard in the doorway looked at Megz, and said nothing.

The section leader cleared her throat. "Two for the dungeons," she said.

"Are there questions?"

Edmir expected the voice to be rusty from disuse, but on the contrary, it was smooth and warm, even pleasant.

"No," Megz said. "Death only."

Edmir shivered. He had not considered the possibility that there might be torture waiting for them, but his sense of relief was so great that it restored his courage. Everything, even death, took time. He did not wait for the House Guards to push him, but stepped forward, turning to face Megz and the other guards. When he was sure that she was looking at him, he took two quick, short steps to his right, and one back, almost dancing steps, and then twisted, dropping his left shoulder. If only his hands were not bound, but maybe this would be enough to remind Megz, to make her think about the block to her secret thrust—and who she'd shown it to. Who knew? At this point, anything was worth trying.

His heart sank as Megz only looked at him with impatience before spinning him around again to face the Black Guards.

Edmir cleared his throat and opened his mouth, the words that would give him a good exit already on his tongue.

But a soft moan was all the sound he made.

"A mute?" the Black Guard in the doorway said.

"The Blue Mage took his voice," Megz said.

The Black Guard shook his head. "A shame. Often there is much they wish to say before they die." He gestured, and Edmir stepped past him into the dark hallway beyond.

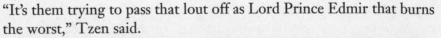

"It's them trying to pass that lout off as Lord Prince Edmir that burns the worst," Tzen said.

Megz Primeau let them talk. All they'd done in leaving the traitors in the hands of the masked and hooded guards of the Black Dungeon was their plain duty. But they were forbidden to talk to anyone else about it outside of this underground passage. Let them have their say here and now, get things off their chests where no one else could hear them.

"There wasn't a member of the family better liked," Granz the other guard said. "Best noble in the Royal House, he was. Even the chamber servants had good words for Prince Edmir." Unspoken was the knowledge that the same most emphatically could not be said for Kedneara the Queen.

"Best noble in Beolind, comes to that," Tzen agreed. "Too good to be king, that's certain."

"And that's why the Caids took him," Granz said. "To save him from that path, poor lad." Again, the three guards shared the unspoken awareness of what every soldier in the Royal House knew: well-liked as Edmir had been, even loved, the Princess Kera would make the better ruler.

"Black Dungeons' too good for those two," Megz said, making her own contribution to the purging of fury and sadness that threatened to rise in her own throat as she thought about Edmir's loss. Why it had been only this morning she'd seen him riding in the west gate . . . She stopped dead in the center of the dark hallway. The other two guards, wrapped in their own grieving, continued several paces before noticing that they were alone. They stopped, turning back toward her. She waved at them to continue.

"I've dropped a buckle," she said, holding her hand over the left side of her harness. "You two go on, I'll check down here first while the light lasts."

Megz waited until the other two had reached the far end of the corridor. She needed to think, and their chattering wasn't helping her. On the one hand, the prince was dead, had been for more than a moon, though no one had seen his corpse thanks to those Caids-cursed Nisveans. But on the other hand—

Two steps to the right, a step back, drop the left shoulder to twist the torso to . . . allow for the block to her secret thrust—*EDMIR*. Megz *had* seen Edmir this morning. She knew she had. She'd recognized the one thing it was impossible to copy or disguise—the way he sat his horse. Maybe she hadn't put her finger on it right at that moment, but when she'd seen him in the Jarlkevoso's rooms, she'd known. She didn't know how or why, but that young man, the young man she'd just left with the Black Guards, *was* Edmir.

"Oh, Caids. What have I done?"

And what could she do about it now?

She looked back in the direction from which they'd come. What could *she* do to get the Black Guard to release the prince and the Jarl-kevoso? Had she ever heard of anyone being released from the Black Dungeons? She tapped her sword hilt with her fingers. Surely there must be a way. She started running back, back toward the heavy oak door, back to the candle lantern. There in the darkness were three masked and hooded people who could answer her question.

Parno's heart leaped in his chest. For a fleeting instant he thought the woman in the doorway was *his* Dhulyn, the Wolfshead, his Partner. Her lip was even curled back in that familiar wolf's smile, though it had been years since she had shown that smile to him. Her hair was uncovered, growing in blood red, and her Mercenary badge was perfect and unscarred. Parno had sheathed his sword and taken three steps toward her before he registered what that wolf's smile meant. He halted and put his hand back on the hilt of his sword.

"Dhulyn."

"Thief."

Parno stood still and spread his hands wide. "Now I'm no thief, and you know it."

"I do beg your pardon. You are not a thief until you leave here with something that does not belong to you. So, you are a would-be thief, since you will not be leaving here." She took a pace forward and the door swung shut behind her.

"I disagree. I *will* be leaving, but only with something that *does* belong to me. You."

"You were looking for me in that box?"

Parno drew his sword, turned back to the casket, and flipped open the lid to expose the Stone. "This is the source of the Mage's power," he told her. "But it belongs to this young lady, making Avylos the thief, and his powers stolen. We came here," he pointed first to Dhulyn and then back to himself, "to restore the Stone to its proper place and function. So again, we'll be taking it with us when we go."

Dhulyn's eyes narrowed, and her brow wrinkled in a frown. For a moment Parno thought she might be remembering. But then she turned sideways, kicked at the door where the metal tongue of the latch protruded. Her heel hit the latch just right, bending the tongue, and effectively locking the door. Parno had to shake his head in admiration. Dhulyn could now ignore the girls entirely, seeing that they could not get out of the room without his help. Habit made him glance at the open windows, even though he remembered the bars. What Dhulyn couldn't know is that none of them actually wanted to leave the room—at least not yet.

Parno moved to his left, keeping his feet shoulder width apart and his weight evenly distributed. Dhulyn would shift to follow him—she would correctly assess that he was the danger, not the two young women—and that would give Zania a chance to reach the Stone. What the girl would do with it once she had the chance, he couldn't be sure, but he had to give her that chance. As he moved, he whistled through his teeth, the same tune he'd played for the children under the wall, the same tune Dhulyn, his Dhulyn, knew so well. She frowned, but continued her own even pacing, as she waited for the inevitable moment when they would be close enough to engage.

"I am Parno Lionsmane," he said, keeping his eyes on hers and his voice even and smooth. "Called the Chanter. I was schooled by Nerysa the Warhammer. I came late to the Mercenary Brotherhood and my first battle was in the vale of Arcosa. That is where you and I first met, fighting for old Nyl-aLyn, the Tarkin of Imrion. We became Partners then. Last year we were in Imrion again, and you sang to this tune, do you remember?"

He began whistling again, and again, her wolf's smile faltered. But she pressed her lips together and shook her head, moving it just once to the left, and back again. Her cold gray eyes never moved from his face. All the while he was speaking, he kept circling to the left, and he and Dhulyn drew slowly closer to one another.

"You have told me this tale before," she said. "Why should I believe you?"

"What do I gain by such a lie? Look in a glass, your own Mercenary badge supports my tale."

Her left hand floated to her temple, her fingers stroked her badge. She was frowning again. "Tell me what you see."

"A Mercenary badge, like this one," he gestured to his own temples. "Yours is blue and green, the colors of Dorian the Black Traveler, who

Schooled you. But the Partner's Line is identical to mine." He traced the black line going through his badge with the tip of his index finger. "You are Dhulyn Wolfshead, called the Scholar. Dorian Schooled you on his ship, called, like him, the *Black Traveler*. He took you from the hold of a slaver's ship when you had seen the Hawk Moon eleven times."

"You tell a fine story, Mercenary, but I think I know a better one."

She moved so fast that only Parno's own finely Schooled reflexes saved him. He arched his body away while at the same moment sweeping her sword down with his own, knocking her point aside when it was only a fingerwidth from his guts. She had moved on the word "think," he realized, and he could not keep the smile from his face.

It was as he suspected. He parried a blow to his head, flicking her blade up and to one side. Dhulyn might not remember herself, but her body remembered her Schooling, whether she was aware of it or not. He feinted to his right and she followed, but not enough to put her off-balance. "To think is to move, to move is to think" was a saying in the Common Rule of Mercenary training. After being Schooled a Mercenary no longer needed to plan out the steps and moves of a fight, for them there was no longer any difference between thinking and moving.

Dhulyn's blade sliced through his left sleeve and he jumped back.

When Dhulyn had attacked on the saying the word "think," it was in unconscious reflection of the Common Rule. He had noticed this in her strategy before, though he could not recall whether he had ever mentioned it.

"You're always doing that," he told her. He swept aside her blade with his left hand, followed through with the thrust he would normally execute into that opening, but slowly enough that she could easily parry him in return. So easily in fact that she wrapped her blade around his and came within a hairsbreadth of snaking it out of his hand.

"You mean I'm always almost killing you?"

He grinned. He could give her no quarter, he realized, or she *would* kill him. Without her memories, she had no reason not to. "Always moving in one of the *Shora*." To illustrate his point he executed an attack in three moves to her throat, which she parried brilliantly. "That was part of the Desert Snake *Shora*," he said. "Your body remembers who you are, even if you do not." *But I'll* make *you remember,* he thought. *I'll keep you thinking, keep you aware.*

Parno saw movement out of the corner of his eye as Zania took advantage of their position to slip behind the Mage's worktable. When Dhulyn's eye flickered in that direction he lunged in, striking like the desert snake. She blocked his sword with the palm of her hand against the flat of the blade, pushing it out to her left and simultaneously stepping in to thrust at his neck. Parno twisted out of the way and took another step to gain himself some breathing room.

He blinked as sweat dripped into his eye. The long muscles of his thighs burned, and he could feel the corded tendons in his wrists and elbows. What else could he do to bring her back to herself?

It was hard to think and plan while keeping her blade from his guts and blood. Switching to the left hand would not help him in this fight, as Dhulyn would simply do the same. He was in the same predicament as he'd been when he fought her in the garden—he couldn't keep up a defense only. Tired as he was, she would kill him. Even in top condition, Parno needed all his speed and all his wits to stay even with her, they were so perfectly matched. As for now, he could feel exhaustion not so very far away, in the burning of his muscles.

As if to illustrate his thought, Parno felt the cold edge of her blade slide through the skin on the upper part of his left arm, as his block was seconds too slow. He had no reserves left after climbing the wall, after fighting his way through Avylos' magic—

The *Shora* had led him through the magic. Without the Sable Monkey *Shora* showing him the path, he and Zania would still be standing at the bottom of the wall, or, more likely, in the hands of the Royal House's Guard. Was he going about this the wrong way? Interrupting Dhulyn, breaking into her unconscious movements, *did* slow her down a bit, but it didn't seem to be bringing her any recognition, it did not seem to be triggering any memories for her.

Should he let the *Shora* have her? If a *Shora* could show him a pathway through Avylos' magic, could one also show Dhulyn the path back to herself?

He blocked a thrust to his groin, and another to his throat, stepping back each time.

What did he have to lose?

Rapidly, he ran through the basic *Shora* for right-handed swordplay, instinctively discarding each one as too simple or too short to engage the level of concentration he thought would be required.

Another thrust, again he stepped back, only to feel against his calves the edge of the bench that ran along the wall. Dhulyn's smile widened, her lip curling back. Parno could not back away any farther, and she would not let him move to the side.

But now he had an idea. He swept his blade at her face, and leaped backward onto the bench as she flinched away. Then, bringing his sword straight down toward Dhulyn's head, Parno began the first movements of what she had once called the Older Brother *Shora*. Parno did not know what its real name was—or even if it had one. Older Brother was not one of the Mercenary Brotherhood's basic twenty-seven *Shora*, though it had been the first Dorian the Black had taught to Dhulyn as a child. A specialty of Dorian the Black's, Older Brother was designed for use against an opponent much taller than oneself, and as such, an ideal *Shora* for children.

It meant a great deal to Dhulyn, and she had once taught it to Parno on a whim. Though taller than Dhulyn, he was not really tall enough for her to use the Older Brother *Shora* against him. So long as he stayed on the bench, it would work, he could keep it up, but if she managed to force him down, he knew he would not have the strength to keep his arms lifted, trying his best to mimic the angles of a taller person.

This would have to work. He had no more ideas, and no more strength. *She will remember herself, or she will kill me.*

"In Battle," he told her. "Or in Death."

Dhulyn and Parno moved so fast that Zania couldn't even distinguish the individual movements of their blades. This was nothing like what she had seen done, and done herself for that matter, on stage.

"Come on, Dhulyn," she muttered under her breath as if they *were* on stage and she was giving the Mercenary woman a cue. "Come back to us, come back." She shivered as the tiny hairs on the back of her neck stood straight. It was one thing to be told that Dhulyn had lost her memories, it was another thing entirely to see her look at Parno with that snarling smile.

Zania sucked in her breath. Blood darkened Parno's sleeve, though she hadn't seen the touch that caused it.

A movement at the periphery of her vision. Princess Kera was waving her hand down almost behind the skirt of her gown, and angling her head toward the worktable, and the open casket. Parno and Dhulyn were along the side wall now, Dhulyn forcing Parno back against the bench. The path to the worktable was clear. Her eyes on the two combatants, Zania began sliding her feet sideways toward the Stone. She had her hand out when she saw another flower of blood blossom, this time on Parno's right sleeve.

Section Leader Megz Primeau was panting by the time she reached the top of the circular staircase. She had run the last few spans in the dark, as the sconces they had lit on their way down to the Black Dungeon had burned out. The Black Guards had been very helpful. It had rarely happened, but as Megz had suspected, there *was* a way to bring prisoners out again. She had to reach Kedneara the Queen, and persuade her to come. Only the physical presence of the queen herself would stop the Black Guards.

The Black Guards were firm but not cruel. They placed Edmir and Valaika into a cell almost as gently as Edmir's own nurse had moved him when, as a child, he resisted going to bed. As the cell door closed with an ominously quiet thud, Valaika seemed to awaken from the stupor that had held her since they left the queen. She turned toward the faint glow of the tiny candle that burned in the corridor, and seized the bars of the grating in the door.

"Wait," she called. "You don't understand. I would *never* do this. I would never bring an impostor to Kedneara . . . this doesn't make sense." The last few words were almost too faint to hear, but a soft musical voice answered from beyond the door.

"We will give you some time to compose yourselves. There is water to the right of the door. You need fear no pain, or horrors. Since there are no questions for you, your deaths will be quick and painless."

"Why? Why are there no questions? Why aren't you going to ask us to betray the rest of this conspiracy?" Valaika seemed to become aware that there was no longer anyone at the door. "Why," Valaika said, as if to herself. "Unless it is because there is no conspiracy."

Blinking, Edmir could make out his aunt as a darker shape among the shadows around the door.

"I don't know who you are, young man; I don't understand what's going on, what's happening. I—you're an impostor, you're not Edmir—"

At this Edmir tried again to speak, but all he could manage was a coughing croak that hurt his throat, making him swallow. He could not bear for Valaika to die like this, not knowing him, thinking him an impostor, not understanding why she should have to die. He knew the magic would wear off, as it wore off all women, but would it be soon enough?

"I brought you to Beolind. *I* brought *you* to Kedneara. But I would not bring an impostor to the queen, try to take her from her place on the throne. What do I care about her throne? She was my brother's wife, he loved her, and I was content. I would not bring her an impostor."

Edmir wished there was light enough for him to show her the scar on his back. It had been the proof that convinced her, back in Jarlkevo, it might have been enough to jog her real memory of him loose. But in this darkness, he might just as well wish to be out and free, sitting next to Zania on the driver's seat of the caravan, arguing about stagecraft.

Still, he had to try something. Reaching out with his hands, he edged closer to where he could just make out her shape. When he touched her, she flinched away, and Edmir braced himself, expecting a blow. But Valaika relaxed, and let him take her hand. Holding her hand in his, he turned his back on her, and pulled her hand toward his back.

Her arm and hand were tense, but Valaika did not pull away. Edmir thought her resistance stemmed from caution, not knowing what he wanted her to touch, rather than fear.

"What is it? What—oh, that's right, you can't speak. Show me, then." Her arm relaxed more. "Your back?" She snatched her hand away. "What could there possibly be about . . . the scar," she said, her voice hollow and cold in the darkness. "You had the scar, I remember. And if you had the scar, then you *are* Edmir. But how? Why did I stop thinking so? Why do I not believe it now, even when logic tells me it must be so? You are not Edmir," she repeated in that dead voice Edmir knew so well. "You are an impostor." But now her voice was rising high and tight. He had to do something more, not leave her in this state of confusion.

After all that she had done for him, risked for him, this is not how his aunt Valaika should spend her final moments.

If only this was Dhulyn Wolfshead, he could speak against the palm of her hand, as he had done back in the tent of the Nisveans. Edmir clapped his hands. If Valaika could not read lips with her hands, perhaps there was something she *could* read.

He felt more than saw Valaika turn toward him, and took her hand once more in his, opening it to expose her palm. Using the tip of his finger, he wrote, "A." She did not react and he tried it again.

"What are you doing, boy, what is it? I don't understand." She pulled her hand away and Edmir let it go. No use upsetting her further if she didn't understand. He rubbed at his face in frustration. If only there was more light. He could do it if he were on stage. Zania had showed him all the tricks for making light appear. Or if he could make a flame appear in the palm of his hand, like Avylos used to do . . .

He grabbed Valaika by the shoulder and turned her toward the door edging her backward until she was the right distance from the opening in the door. Between his teeth he whistled a tune he was sure she would recognize, the traditional bit of music that would accompany the appearance of a Mage or Mark in a play. The sound he could make was faint, his mouth was so dry, but he thought that Valaika heard and understood.

Still whistling he held up his left hand, palm upward. He snapped the fingers of his right hand, and pointed to his left.

"What? I don't see . . ."

Edmir snapped his fingers again and again pointed to his left hand. If he had positioned it correctly, and if Valaika was standing the right distance away, it would seem as though the glow of the candle in the corridor rested on his open palm.

"Oh, Caids. Avylos. The Blue Mage. This is Avylos' work. Avylos and his blooded magic." The change in Valaika's voice told him that the magic was broken. "Then you *are* Edmir, after all."

Edmir stepped into her open arms.

"Oh, my Prince," Valaika whispered. "How I have failed you, and failed myself. Over and over again. My own consort, my Sylria, keeping her debt to Avylos from me all these years, and paying it back in this way. How can I face your father, if he waits for me at the side of the Sleeping God, knowing what I have done. I would rather I had died beforehand, than to bring you to this."

But I wouldn't, Edmir thought. He shook his head, and to be sure she understood him, he took her right hand, brought it to his face, and shook his head again. Holding her right hand still to his face, he took her left hand, tapped himself on the chest, then tapped Valaika, and moved her hand to touch her lower abdomen.

"You would give your life for me?" she said. "Edmir, no."

He shook his head again, touched her belly again.

"For Janek? For my son?" Valaika's breath hitched, as if she were trying to stop crying. "Not my life," she said. "Not Sylria's. It is Janek's life that is purchased with yours."

This time he nodded. In his mind's eye he could see the smiling face of the boy who had been the only one to recognize him. And this time, Valaika stayed quiet. Edmir understood. When it came to herself, or to Sylria, Valaika was his aunt, his father's sister, one of the High Noble Houses of Tegrian and the cousin of the Tarkin of Hellik. She knew where her duty lay, and she would die to save him, Edmir had no doubt. But when it came to Janek, she was a mother first, and she could not bring herself to say that she would trade her son's life for his. Not even here, where a gesture was all it would be.

He patted her cheek, and kissed her. For a long moment, they clung to each other in the dark.

"We are ready now."

Both Edmir and his aunt jerked and jumped away from the door. How long had the Black Guard been standing there?

"One of you will come with us," the Black Guard said. "Do you prefer to choose, or shall we?"

Edmir tried to put himself forward, but Valaika was closer to the door, and she could speak.

"Take me," she said. "No," she added to Edmir as he clutched her arm. "However long it takes for me to die, I would buy you that time."

"Your death *can* be slower," came the voice of the Black Guard. "But there is more pain."

"Make it as slow as you can," she said. "Good-bye, my Prince, my nephew. May the Sleeping God keep us both, and may I meet you at his side."

Good-bye, he said, kissing her again on the cheek. This silent good-bye was the only one he would make, he realized, as he strained to watch them disappear into the shadows. He would never take his leave of Dhulyn and Parno, never thank them for all they had done, and tried to do. They might yet succeed, even now, and he would never know.

And then Kera will be king. His sister would make a better king than he would have, he told himself, wishing that he had the chance to tell her as well. *My best kings would have been on the stage.*

And he would never be able to tell Zania that he was a fool ever to have put his throne before her. Never be able to tell her that he loved her. He would ask for the slow death, he thought. He would find a way to make them understand. He would like to think of Zania as long as he could, and the plays he would have written for her.

Twenty-six

DHULYN SAW THE SECOND WOUND begin to bleed and laughed aloud. Her body moved like oiled silk sliding across skin, as if she knew where the Mercenary's sword would be before he did himself. As if she was Marked, and had the Sight. She felt her smile falter, but her body still moved automatically, parrying each blow as it fell on her from above. He should have picked a different *Shora*, she thought with a frown, he wasn't really tall enough for this one, though the bench did help him there. Still, he was tiring, and she knew this *Shora* so much better than he did, it was almost the first one she'd been taught . . .

She hesitated, blade hovering in the air. Where had those thoughts come from? Just in time, she saw his sword coming down upon her, stepped half a pace closer and blocked it, blade against blade. He bore down on her, taking advantage of his height and weight, and she pushed back—give her an inch or two, and she could twist away. He grunted, and Dhulyn looked up into his amber eyes, so close she could see the individual lashes. As their gazes locked over the crossed swords, he whistled four notes, and something within her loosened, and gave way.

Her own hands lay out the vera tiles, but not for any Solitary game that she recognizes. She chooses one tile, the Mercenary of Swords, covers it with another tile, a circle. Lays out the rectangle, the triangle, the straight line, the circle with a dot in the center. She draws out more tiles and begins to lay them down . . .

*   *   *

The smell of burning, and blood. she stands to one side, watching herself and her mother. Her mother turns toward her and *sees* her. Her mother is smiling as she turns the head of the child. Dhulyn blinks, and with her child's eyes sees herself, a tall, slim woman with short red hair and tattoos above her ears. She blinks and sees her mother and the small child who is herself. She puts out a hand, but there is nothing to steady herself against.

"Go," her mother tells her. "Oh, my soul, do not watch. Find your own soul and save yourself. Go now, go. . . ."

The redheaded boy she has Seen before is squatting next to a map drawn on the ground. The map shows passes, game trails, a wide expanse of plain, the juncture of two rivers. Where the herds will be, and how many will be guarding them . . .

And then the boy is running through the woods, running from the sound of screaming and the smell of smoke. His eyes are wide and frightened, but his lips are pulled back from his teeth in a grimace. Or a smile . . .

A tall black man, the tallest she has ever seen, a triangular scar along the orbit of his left eye. A dead man with a sword in his gut lies between them. The black man pulls the sword free, wipes the blade clean on the corpse's clothing and holds it out to her, hilt first. "Come with me," he says, "and I will teach you to kill your enemies." . . .

She runs along a ship's rail as the motion of the sea causes it to rise and fall beneath her bare feet. Her breath comes short with the effort of speed and balance . . .

A golden-haired man with eyes like melting amber stands over a map on a table. There is something lionlike about him. He looks up at her and smiles. His Mercenary Badge is dark red and gold. There is something missing. There should be a black line through it. Parno? . . .

Zania holds a blue crystal cylinder between her hands, thick as a man's wrist, as long as Dhulyn's forearm. Shining blue like the deep ice that has trapped the glow of the stars. The Muse Stone. A drop of blood falls from Zania's nose to the Stone. There is movement in the rooms behind her and Dhulyn sees herself, her hair far too short, her Mercenary badge blue and green showing smooth and unscarred, leaping back out of the path of a sword, dashing forward again just as Parno brings up his sword again and running herself full onto his blade . . .

Dashing forward again with her own blade perfectly positioned to pass between his ribs and through his heart . . .

Her Mercenary badge. Blue and green for Dorian the Black Traveler. The black line of partnership running through it . . .

Herself.

An old crone, a young woman with dark hair and a heart-shaped face, a stocky blond man in a Scholar's tunic, and a young boy, thin and round-eyed, and herself. They hold hands in an intricate pattern, ready for the dance. . . .

Herself.
Avylos is standing in the doorway of his workroom, raising his hands to work his magic . . .

A crash, and the workroom door sprang open to reveal Avylos standing in the doorway of his workroom, his hands raised.

Did I not just see that, she thought. No, she realized. She had *Seen* it. Her own hands, she found, were raised, sword pointing straight to the ceiling. The point of Parno's sword rested on the skin above her heart.

"Dhulyn," Parno said. He eased his sword back.

"My soul," Dhulyn answered. Parno grinned back at her, and her heart turned over. He jumped down off the bench. "Zania," he called out to the girl, "Quickly, it's—"

Avylos drew a symbol in light and with a hard gesture flung it toward them. Dhulyn was slammed back, as if a huge wave of water crashed her against the wall, forcing the breath from her body. She slid down, the bench catching her painfully in the small of her back, and tried to get her frozen lungs to pull in a breath of air. Her whole arm would be bruised, if she lived through this, but she had kept hold of her sword. Parno, a shadow on his face like the symbol the Mage had thrown, fell to his knees beside her, and pitched forward, getting his hands out in front of himself just in time to keep from crashing onto his face.

Dhulyn began to cough and choke, her lungs resisting her efforts to breathe. She tried to stand, but her legs were so rubbery they would not support her. Avylos, she saw, had turned to look her way. Could she trick him somehow? She could not draw in sufficient air to speak, but she held out her arms to him, as if begging for his help. Let him just get within reach of her hands . . .

Dhulyn saw a fleeting shadow of doubt fly across his face. Then his blue eyes hardened.

"Wait, my dear," he said, in the language of the Tribes. "I will be but a moment. Kera," he said, turning back to the others. "Get the Stone and bring it to me."

No, don't do it. Still the words would not come, though Dhulyn's breathing was beginning to ease.

Painfully, Dhulyn turned her head enough to see the other end of the room. Zania and Kera were at opposite ends of the worktable. Zania had the Stone and was murmuring under her breath. Ignoring both Kera and the Mage, she was twisting the ends of the Stone as she muttered, but nothing was coming of it.

"Why should I help you?" Kera was looking from the Mage to Zania and back again, her lower lip caught between her teeth. "So you can treat me as you did Edmir?"

"But now *you* will be king, Kera. You will rule. That is what all this is for, everything I have done is to bring you to the throne. All you need do now is bring me the Stone."

"No." Dhulyn coughed. A sound made her turn to Parno. He was still on his knees, holding himself up with his hands. His lips were turning blue, and he did not appear to be breathing. Dhulyn pulled at one of his wrists until she toppled him over. Sucking in as much air as she could, she held his mouth open and breathed into it. His chest moved as his lungs expanded. But not by very much. And not on their own.

Dhulyn looked back to the Mage. And across to the girl holding the Stone. Had Kera answered him?

Zania had stopped trying to manipulate the Stone. Her face was white, and she looked not far from tears. Finally she looked up. "I will give you the Stone for Edmir," she said. Princess Kera gasped, turning abruptly toward the other girl, but shut her mouth on what she would have said.

"It is already too late for that, I'm afraid." The Mage was shaking his head. "Come, give me the Stone, and I will let you at least go free."

Dhulyn forced another breath into Parno and touched his face. "Hold," she said, and levered herself to her feet. She could not see which end of the Stone Zania was trying to turn, but the chants the girl was using were not working. There was only one thing left to try. "Throw *me* the Stone," she said. She cleared her throat, drew in a deeper lungful of air and repeated herself.

"Zania, throw me the Stone."

The young girl's face, still white as snow, hardened. Her grip on the Stone shifted, and she glanced around her quickly, as if she was look-ing for something hard enough to smash it on. Finding nothing, she took a step back, looking between Dhulyn and Avylos.

"Don't let her trick you," Kera said, her voice hoarse with unshed tears. "She heard Parno say your name. How is she better than the Mage?"

Dhulyn breathed in deeply and took two paces closer.

"Listen to me, Zania," she said, and held out her hands. "Pasillon," she said. "Pasillon, Zania. Give me the Stone."

For a moment Zania stood frozen, as if she were turned to stone herself, and Dhulyn's heart sank. If Zania did not believe her . . . Then Dhulyn saw the sudden blaze of understanding and relief ignite across Zania's face, as the girl realized that only the real Dhulyn, the one who remembered, would know that code word. The code word they'd all agreed on. Work as a team. Do not draw the eye of the audience upon yourself. Let others do their work, and have their moments.

Zania gave a quick nod, and tossed Dhulyn the Stone.

While it was still in the air, Avylos flung another symbol of light across the intervening space, but Dhulyn threw herself forward, snatching the Stone out of the air, and rolled with it to the other side of the room.

"Dhulyn, my dear one," Avylos said coming toward her with his hands outstretched.

Parno shifted, slowly, so that his knife was closer to his hand. Dhulyn could not tell whether he had begun to breathe properly, but she forced her attention back to the warm bar of crystal in her hands. She could only hope that what she was going to try would work. She *had* to concentrate, to remember, without the book to refer to. Parno would die if his breathing was not restored, but if she failed in what she was about to try, they were all dead.

"I am not your dear, and never was," she said, turning the Stone over in her hands feeling for the places where her fingers should go. It would have to be the Null Chant again, she would have to hope it worked the same way on both ends of the Stone. Because this time she would not use the end she had tried before, not the symbols of the Marked. The *other* end. The symbol she had seen in the book, the ones she had finally recognized from her Visions.

"Give it to me, my own one, my cousin, my kin. We are the only two, the last. Do not forsake me." He took a step toward her, his voice a charm of music, alluring and pure.

But the music Dhulyn heard was a simple tune, that could be whistled or played on the pipes. The children's song she knew so well.

Perhaps because of the song, or perhaps because she was holding the Stone, running over the chant in her head, Dhulyn had a sudden flash of the Visions she had just Seen, and others she had Seen before. The young Avylos drawing the map in the dirt, consulting with men who were not Espadryni. Those same men running through the camp as her mother told her to hide. Avylos hunted, not—as she now realized—by those who had broken the Tribes, but by two dying Espadryni, who hunted their betrayer with their last breaths.

"We may be the last," she agreed. "And who is to blame?"

Avylos went chalk white, but whether with fear or anger Dhulyn could not tell.

"That was why you kept asking me what I remembered of the Tribes," she said. "That was what you were afraid I knew, what you were afraid I would remember. *You* broke the Tribes. *You* sold us to the Bascani. You."

"No. You are wrong. You said yourself you were too young to remember."

"I have *Seen* it," she said. "Did *you* forget? I bear the Mark of the Seer. Did you not know how the Mark works? I *See* both the future and the past."

Her fingers slid into place on the Stone.

"*Elis elis tanton neel,*" she said to Avylos.

"They kept the power from me," he said. "They told me I was *srusha*, barren, without magic. They did that to me, their own child. Excluded me, shut me out."

"What?" Her voice dripping with disbelief, only Kera, only a princess, would have thought to interrupt Avylos at such a moment. "The whole Tribe in agreement, every man, woman, and child, every new babe taught an elaborate pretense, to trick *you*? Why were *you* so important?"

"Because they would keep from me my rightful rule. Because I was to be stronger than all of them. Because in me the power will be greatest." Avylos was almost spitting.

"Not without the Stone. You are nothing without the Stone," Zania said.

"*Dor la sinquin so la dele,*" Dhulyn said. Let the others keep Avylos occupied. The end of the stone began to turn in her fingers. "*Kos no-forlin sik ek aye.*"

As if he knew how close she was, Avylos threw both hands into the air, fingers flashing symbol after symbol. The furniture in the room trembled, and then jumped into the air, even the worktable, even Parno's sword where he had dropped it. The bench behind Dhulyn rose up and struck her down—only her Mercenary training allowed her to retain her grip of the Stone as she hit the floor. She heard Zania scream, but put it out of her mind as she said the final chant.

"*Kik shon te ounte gesserae.*"

She felt the end of the Stone "click." Felt the power surging like an underground river, felt her own bones begin to tremble. The Stone became a bar of bright light.

Now, she thought. She could wait no longer.

"Avylos," she called. And tossed him the Stone.

"No!" Both girls cried out together, Zania from under the table that held her pinned to the floor, with Kera on her knees beside her. Their faces were stained white with the shock of betrayal.

"Watch. *Watch!*" Dhulyn called out to them, but she was already turning away, crawling to where Parno lay on his side. Did his chest move? From this angle she could not tell. "In Battle," she called to him. Saw his hand move as he opened his fist. *In Death*. Her own breathing eased as she kept crawling. If she was wrong in what she had done, if this was the end, Dhulyn knew where she wanted to be. It was not until she had her hand on Parno's back that she turned once more to watch Avylos herself.

The Mage stood tall, drawn up to his full height. He held the Stone between his hands, his face alight with joy as the blue crystal light washed over him.

Dhulyn's heart sank. She had made a mistake after all. Surely when she had used the Stone herself, it had knocked her out before this much time had passed. But Avylos showed no signs of any adverse effect. On the contrary, his eyes were bright and glowing, his lips split in a huge smile. As she watched, the Mage's head fell back, his eyelids fluttered, his nostrils flared, and a look of blissful contentment crossed his features. But even as Dhulyn gathered her feet under her and reached for Parno's dagger, Avylos' skin paled, his smile became a rigid grin. A wrinkle formed between his brows.

The Mage fell to his knees.

He made a motion as if to drop the Stone, or at least to put it down. His arms curled toward his chest, and began to tremble. The crystal blue light intensified until it seemed to burst from him, from his eyes, his ears, and mouth. Cracks appeared in the skin of his face and head, his shoulders, his elbows, and wrists, and light poured out, filling the room. Suddenly the blue light became crimson, and then a yellow so bright, that Dhulyn shut her eyes and turned away, burying her head in Parno's shoulder.

"Zania." Edmir was so startled by the sound of his own voice that for a moment he was not sure he had actually spoken aloud. "Zania," he said again. Realization brought him to his feet, his hands to the bars of the door. "Valaika," he called out as loudly as he could. "Wait! Valaika, hold on!"

"I assure you, Kedneara the Queen will wish to speak to me." Section Leader Megz Primeau was holding onto her temper by main force of will. She knew the door page was only doing his duty, and that she had to be patient. It was hard, though, considering what was resting on the passing of even minutes.

"Kedneara the Queen has retired for the night," the page was saying. "We cannot disturb her, even for you, Section Leader."

Megz thought quickly. The guard commander had been injured and taken to the infirmary; where would his deputy be? And would she be able to convince him in time? As she was having this thought, noises and a sharp cry from within caused the door page to turn his head. Megz took advantage of this momentary lapse of discipline to push her way past him. Once she was actually in the anteroom, the page made only a token effort to stop her, and settled for preceding her into the inner chamber.

There they found the queen fallen to the floor beside her couch, her chamber pages trying to support her head and shoulders as she coughed and gasped for air. There were horrible wet sounds coming from her lungs, and Megz grimaced. She'd heard just such sounds coming from soldiers whose lungs had been pierced by arrow or blade.

"Sit her up, quickly," she said, striding forward and drawing off her gloves.

"I'll send for the Mage," the door page said.

"No!" Kedneara the Queen coughed more violently after the exertion of speaking that single word. She waved her hand to emphasize her point.

"Whisper, my Queen," Megz said. She lowered herself to her knees, slipped her arm around the queen's waist, and put her own shoulder behind the queen's.

"Edmir. Section Leader, it *was* Edmir." There was blood on the queen's lips. "His hair dyed and rings in his ears, foolish boy. But it was Edmir."

"Yes, my Queen." The three pages looked at one another, mouths agape, fear and confusion on their faces.

"You are my White Sword," rasped Kedneara the Queen.

"I am, my Queen."

"That stinking piece of Red Horse *dung*." More coughing.

"Yes, my Queen." No one could say that Kedneara the Queen was not quick to see the point.

"I must go, Section Leader, I must go in person."

"I know, my Queen, the Black Guards told me." Megz looked up. "You heard her, she must go down to the Black Dungeon."

"But we cannot move her," the young man who was evidently the senior page was shocked, his fear showing in the trembling of his voice.

"We must," Megz said. "Only Kedneara the Queen herself can stop the executions."

"But, Section Leader—"

"Now!" The effort made the queen start coughing again, and Megz gritted her teeth as precious minutes were lost.

"Bring that chair," Megz said, nodding at one of the guest chairs next to the table at which Kedneara the Queen was accustomed to break her fast. The queen's taller, heavier chair would tire them out before they even reached the dungeons. As soon as the chair was close enough, Megz assisted Kedneara to her feet, and settled her in.

"You two." Megz pointed to the two huskier pages. "Pick up the queen and follow me. You, fetch four torches and bring them immediately to the Black Stairs." Megz knew where the torches were kept, ready at all times, and knew that as slowly as they could move, carrying the queen, the third page could quickly catch them up. She would have been better off with guards, even ones unfamiliar with the path to the dungeons, but there was no time. No time.

It was tricky to maneuver the chair on the circular stairs, and only hoarsely whispered orders from the queen herself kept the pages moving. Once at the bottom, another coughing fit forced them to stop completely while the queen recovered. With a whispered apology, Megz placed the first two fingers of her left hand under Kedneara the Queen's jaw, and felt her heart beat, thready and irregular. Megz pulled her lower lip through her teeth. Where did her duty lie strongest, with keeping the queen alive, or with saving Prince Edmir?

"My Queen," she said finally. "I fear you should rest."

"No." The once vibrant voice was whisper thin, but unmistakable in the eerie quiet of the corridor. No one was in any doubt of what Kedneara wanted.

"I will go before you," Megz said. "And light the sconces. The rest of you, bring the queen as quickly as you possibly can." Red splotches in otherwise white faces already showed the pages' unaccustomed exertion. But there was also some curiosity in their rounded eyes.

She raced down the corridor, pausing only to light the sconces as quickly as she could, and reached the door while the sounds of the queen advancing behind her grew faint. She did not wait, however, but tugged fiercely on the bell pull as soon as she reached it.

"Please wait," she said, as soon as the notes of the bell died away. Though she could not see beyond the bars of the gate, Megz knew at least one Black Guard was there. "Kedneara the Queen comes, please proceed no further."

"We cannot stop without word from the queen herself." It was the same soft voice Megz had heard before. "The first of the prisoners is already being bled."

"Will you tell me which it is?"

"It is the woman."

Megz turned and ran back to where the two pages, now red-faced and short of breath, still struggled with the queen's chair.

"My Queen," she said. "They have not begun on the prince, we are in time for him at least, but you must hurry."

Kedneara the Queen signaled that the pages put her down, which they did with relieved grunts.

"I can go faster on my own feet," she said. "There is not so much farther to go. My son." She swallowed. "Give me your shoulder, White Sword." Megz knew she should protest, that she should protect the woman who was the queen from the impulsiveness of the woman who was the mother. But she could not bring herself to argue. They were already too late to save the Jarlkevoso, if they stood here arguing, they would lose their chance to save the prince. And saving Edmir felt like the right thing to do, however much damage it might do to the queen. Though it seemed that at the moment she was not so much the queen, as she was Edmir's mother.

So Megz bent forward, helped the queen put her arms around her neck, and straightened, lifting the other woman to her feet. With one arm around the queen's waist, and the other hand keeping the queen's arm around her own shoulders, Megz set off down the corridor toward the barred door of the Black Dungeon as quickly as she could.

"Shallow breaths, my Queen," Megz murmured as they reached the door.

Kedneara turned to the door, and with an effort that Megz felt tremble through her own body, raised her hand to clutch one of the bars in the door.

"Open for me," she said. "I am Kedneara of Tegrian, and I would have my prisoners back." The queen's voice bubbled unpleasantly, and Megz's stomach chilled.

The door opened without a sound, and a Black Guard stepped back to allow the queen to enter.

"My prisoners," she whispered.

"The younger one is still whole and will be brought immediately, Kedneara the Queen." The Black Guard bowed his head. "But the older prisoner has already been cut."

"Can you stop the bleeding?"

Megz looked sideways at the queen's face, so close to her own. Evidently Kedneara knew exactly what was done here in the Black Dungeon. Then Megz took a closer look. That was not a shadow on the queen's face, but blood dripping from the corner of her mouth.

"A chair for the queen, quickly," Megz said. "And bring more light." But the Black Guard did not move until Kedneara herself waved her hand.

"Look at me, my Queen." Megz dared to give Kedneara a shake. "Stay with us. It won't be much longer."

The arm around Megz's shoulder tightened, and Kedneara the Queen lifted her head. Megz held the queen's gaze with her own. What she saw there made her hiss in her breath.

Edmir could hear footsteps, and a confused murmuring of half-recognized voices. Shadows formed and retreated at the far end of the corridor outside his cell, as lights were struck and carried away. A Black Guard carrying a stool with a low back appeared out of the darkness, and ran down the corridor toward what Edmir judged was the entrance to the dungeons.

"Stop!" he called. "Wait! What is going on? Where is Valaika Jarlkevo?"

Finally a Black Guard came running back to his cell, his feet making no more sound than a cat's. "Come with me, young man," the man said as he unlocked the door.

Edmir tried to dash past, but the Black Guard grabbed his upper arm in both hands and hung on. "Slowly," the man said. "Do not startle her."

Edmir allowed himself to be led, hoping from the Black Guard's words that he was being taken to Valaika. But when they reached the end of the corridor, they turned right, toward the doorway to the upper world.

There, in the light of three candle lanterns, their pierced metal doors wide open, Kedneara of Tegrian sat on a simple stool, held upright by Megz Primeau. Three of her chamber pages stood in the outside passage, gawking through the open doorway. His mother the queen raised her head, and Edmir saw recognition in her eyes.

"Mother," he said, coming to his knees at Kedneara's side. "They have taken Valaika."

A look of inquiry passed over his mother's face, and the Black Guard behind Edmir spoke.

"She is gone, my Queen."

Edmir took his mother's hand and pressed it to his forehead. His shoulders shook, but he said nothing. He felt his mother's hand, light as a breath of wind, stroke his hair. A spot of blood fell on his cheek.

"My son. Oh, my son."

The hand on his hair fell away.

Edmir glanced up, but his mother's eyes were closed now, her breathing stilled. "Caids take you," he said automatically, laying her lifeless hand at her side. He could feel the cold stone under his knees, but nothing else.

Then a hand on his shoulder, Megz's voice above his head.

"What now, my King?"

I'm King, he thought, grinding his teeth together.

Parno turned until he had Dhulyn's face pressed into the curve of his neck, rather than on his shoulder. His chest and throat no longer felt tight, and the air moved smoothly through his lungs. He blinked, trying to clear the afterimages of brightness that still half-blinded him, though he'd had his eyes shut tight. The furniture was back on the floor, much of it broken and tumbled about. At first he thought his ears had been as badly affected as his eyes, but he swallowed, moved his jaw, and slowly he registered the sound of crying.

"Dhulyn, my heart," he said, squeezing her on the shoulder. She pushed herself upright, blinked at him, and, frowning slightly, touched his face with her fingertips. Parno felt himself relax, and despite everything, he smiled. Dhulyn nodded, and turned away, getting to her feet.

Kera was on her knees beside Zania. The player's face was a circle of pain, though it was Kera who was wiping away tears with her free hand. Parno rolled to his feet, ignoring Dhulyn's offer of her hand. So far as he could see, they were alone in the room, except for the girls. There was nothing here large enough for Avylos to hide behind, and the possibility of a trapdoor could wait until they had seen to Zania.

"I can't move the table," Kera said. "She's hurt."

Leaving Dhulyn to check the rest of the room, Parno went directly to the injured girl. The table he lifted off in a moment, and he breathed more easily when he saw that both Zania's legs were straight, and moving. Her arm told another story, however.

"Hold still, little Cat," he told her. "It's just the smaller, outer bone, the best kind of break you could have." He smiled at her. "I've broken my own arm that way several times, and so has Dhulyn Wolfshead. It will hurt to set it properly, but not more than it hurts already. We're not Healers, nor even Knives, but we've done this many times before, and we know what we're doing. All we must do is get the arm straight, and bind it well."

"It *is* Dhulyn Wolfshead, then?" Kera asked.

"Oh, yes, don't doubt it."

"What happened? All I saw was a bright light."

"Time for that soon. We're alive, and that's all we need to know just now. Dhulyn! Can you find something to splint the little Cat's arm? A leg from that stool might do."

Dhulyn bent quickly and picked something off the floor.

"Parno," she said, and something in the quality of her voice made them all turn to look at her.

She held a dull blue cylinder by the very tips of her fingers. It was dirty, and stained along one side, the exposed side, with a pale pink mist, damp and slightly greasy.

But it was the Muse Stone.

"Be careful." The words were out of his mouth before he could stop them. He felt he more than deserved the look Dhulyn gave him. "He must have got past us somehow, got to the door."

"You think he's running about somewhere in Royal House unaware of who he is?" Dhulyn asked. "That's the only way he would have left without it, that's certain." She looked at the Stone again.

"Oh, Sun and the *blooded* Moon." Dhulyn was rubbing the tips of her fingers together, then she lifted her fingers to her nose and sniffed. Her lip wrinkled back to show her teeth in a parody of her wolf's smile. She turned her head and spat on the floor over and over. She looked around her, but finding no cleaner surface, wiped off the Stone on the front of her shirt.

Dawning realization made Parno's stomach churn and his eyebrows crawl up his forehead. Dhulyn had turned away from Avylos, turned her back to him and hidden her face. Her face, and the front of her shirt were clean, but the back of her shirt, much of the floor, and the sides of the girls' faces, their sleeves and hands, were marked by the same residue as the Stone.

"Princess Kera," he said. "Have you an underskirt? Would you remove it please, and use it to wipe off your mouths and faces. Quick as you can."

"What is it?" Kera immediately lifted the skirt of her gown and pulled off her underskirt. Gathering a soft fold of it, she wiped Zania's face before doing the same for herself.

"It's Avylos."

Twenty-seven

"I THINK THAT, IN MY case, the force of the power only pushed me aside." Dhulyn put down the leg of roasted duck she'd been chewing on and picked up a cloth to wipe her hands. She tapped herself on her chest. "*I* was still there, my Visions still came, though I thought they were dreams. And I think that even without my Mercenary Schooling—even without the *Shora*—I would have found my way back, perhaps through the Visions themselves, if no other way."

"And is that what you expected to happen with Avylos?" Edmir spread a coating of nellberry jam on a slice of breast meat, rolled it up and inserted it into his mouth. They were using Avylos' sitting room, the first chance they'd had in days to sit down together. Parno, Dhulyn, and Edmir had kept to the Mage's wing, sorting out his books and devices, in part to learn what they could, in part to make sure nothing remained that could cause any harm. Princess Kera, using Megz Primeau and Zania to help her, had been dealing with the upheaval caused by the sudden death of Kedneara the Queen.

Kedneara's body had been retrieved from the Black Dungeon and was lying in state in the Great Hall as her pyre was being built in the center of the Royal Courtyard. High Noble Houses were coming from all of Tegrian and the subject lands to attend her burning, and the ceremonial burial of the ashes. No one disputed that Kedneara had very obviously died from the same ailment that had plagued her father, brought on by the shock and stress of recent events, and particularly the disappearance of the Blue Mage.

"It's what I hoped would happen, yes," Dhulyn said in answer to

Edmir's question. "I hoped that the wave of power released from the Stone would overwhelm and drown him, as it had done to me."

"And so we'd have a different man entirely to deal with," Kera said, nodding.

"It was a rough chance to take, just the same," Parno said. "If you could find your way back, so could he, and he'd have all that power in him."

"Would he? I don't think so." Dhulyn shook her head. "According to what Zania had told us, Avylos had no power when he first came to her family's group of traveling players. Avylos himself told me that his power had grown little by little, which fit with what Valaika remembered of his first coming to Tegrian. I think he had no magic himself."

Zania was nodding. "That's what I remember my uncle telling us. He did stage magic only when he first joined the troupe, tricks that anyone could do, if they had talent and were taught the method. It was only after he learned about the Stone, and how we used it, that . . . he changed."

"He was *srusha*," Dhulyn said. "In the tongue of the Espadryni it means 'barren,' or 'empty,' though I have never heard it used in connection with people. We surmised that all the men of the Espadryni were Mages, as all the women were Marked with the Sight. But the truth must be that not all had the same degree of power, just as we have all seen different strengths in those who bear a Mark."

"So it would follow that from time to time one would be born with a power greater than others . . ." Edmir said, following the thread of the tale, as Dhulyn had known he would.

"And from time to time, one without power at all," she said. "Oh, he knew the methods—" She drew a symbol in the air. "He'd seen it done hundreds of times, knew what to do and what to say. But until he felt the residual power that the Stone generated even while it slept . . . until then, no magic had ever worked for him. In me, the Stone found a Mark untrained, and so the power it gave me overwhelmed me. But in Avylos it found a broken vessel, cracked and unglazed, which could not hold the power at all."

"And is that why his power did not affect women so well? Because it was borrowed?"

"Can you see the women of the Red Horsemen letting the men have magics which could be used against them? And those women all

Seers? I can't, not if they were anything like Dhulyn Wolfshead."
Parno laughed.

"It seems that some of his magics disappeared with him," Zania
said. "As if, like his powers, they had no permanence."

"Not long-standing magics," Kera said. "There are soldiers that he
magicked who are still whole and healthy, so it seems likely that
Valaika's son will keep *his* health. It does appear, however, that some of
Avylos' most recent magics *have* died with him. His cure of my mother
the queen. His curse on Parno Lionsmane. But other things are still
with us—"

"We've had to prop open the workroom door," Parno said, "otherwise the latch keeps disappearing."

"The ghost eye on my back is still there," Edmir said. He shivered,
and Zania put her hand over his. He smiled at her, but the smile was
strained, and both lowered their eyes as Zania withdrew her hand.

Kera saw this, and her glance went back and forth between the two.
There was something bothering the young princess, Dhulyn thought.
Something she was hesitating to say.

"Will you want the Stone?" Dhulyn asked, when no one else
seemed ready to speak. "It is drained now, but I can finish translating
the book, and . . ."

Zania was shaking her head. "I don't think so. Not after what I've
seen. I'd rather rely on my own talents, and my own powers."

"Then, Lord and Lady Princes, I'd suggest the Stone, and the book
for that matter, should be sent to the Scholars' Library of Valdomar
for study. They know much of the Caids there, and this will be a find
of great importance for them."

"Speaking of powers." Kera sat up straight and turned to Edmir.

Here it comes, Dhulyn thought. *Whatever it is that's been biting the
girl.*

"There's a different power altogether that we have to settle," Kera
said. "Edmir, you have kept yourself in the shadows these last few
days, and I have not argued with you."

The corners of Edmir's mouth tightened, as if he had clenched his
teeth. "I'm sorry, Kera," he said. "I thought it would be less confusing
this way, with everything else that's happened. I'm ready to lift the
burden from your shoulders if you think the time has come."

"Please believe there is no one more loyal to you than I—well, perhaps there is one other," Kera nodded across the table at Zania. "But, Edmir, I have given the events of the past moon much thought, and I believe—whatever *I* might want, whatever *you* might want, you cannot be king."

Edmir sat back in his chair as if he'd been pushed. But the color had come up in his cheeks, his eyes widened. He looked, Dhulyn thought, for all the world like a tired horse seeing the open door of its own stable, but who fears it may be only an illusion.

"Kera." Edmir cleared his throat and started again. "Kera . . . what are you saying? I have not come all this way, they—" He gestured at where Dhulyn and Parno sat next to each other. "—have not done all they have, in order for me not to be king."

"Edmir, please listen. The country believes you are dead. Many who have seen you alive here in the Royal House were told you are an imposter. We know the truth, and those who have known you your whole life will know you and believe, but what about the rest of the country? Ordinary people who have never seen you? With Kedneara dead and Avylos gone, we cannot afford more cause for insecurity and doubt. And as for the subject lands, what will the Noble Houses of Balnia, or Demnion, or—" Kera threw up her hands. "Edmir, I swear to you, if I saw any way for you to keep the throne, safely, and without danger to the country, I would say so."

And it was that last point, Dhulyn saw, that convinced him.

"I will be an excuse for war," Edmir said. "And not just now, but always. Whenever there is discontent, a bad harvest, a long winter, there will be someone ready to challenge my right to the throne," he said. "Someone who will say I am not Edmir, son of Kedneara."

Dhulyn watched. From where she sat, she could see Edmir's hands under the edge of the table, clenching and unclenching. He was not stupid, and his imagination was such that he could always clearly see that all actions and events had a number of possible consequences. Edmir glanced up, and she caught his eye.

"Prepare for what *can* happen," she told him. "That is the Common Rule. I have Seen Visions of you as King, Edmir," she added. He frowned. "But Zania was always with you. I think perhaps you were on a stage, not on this throne. I have Seen you late at night, in a tent, writing. I have also seen your sister, in armor, leading troops into battle, the royal crest of Tegrian on her breastplate."

"Of course," Edmir said. He turned to Kera. "I wanted to be a soldier, like our father. But you were always better at it than I was. It was always you who came up with the plans, the strategies. It was never me, Kera, always you. *You* were the soldier. *You* will be Queen."

Dhulyn folded up the sleeves of her shirt, uncomfortable with being so much covered in the summer heat. She resisted the urge to scratch, for the fifth time, at her wig, but not quickly enough that Parno had not seen the beginnings of the movement.

"We're only a week out of Lesonika," Parno said. "It won't be that much longer. We'll present our documents from Queen Kera to the Senior Brother at our House there, and we won't have to disguise ourselves any longer."

Dhulyn tried to smile without snarling. "It seems that in the last month everyone's lives but ours have been settled. The player Zania Tzadeyeu and her new husband, the soon-to-be famous playwright of *The Solder King*, have left Beolind well laden with gifts from the new Queen of Tegrian, to return to Jarlkevo to collect their caravan."

"And the Stone, and the book, together with your letters, have gone off to Valdomar in the capable hands of Megz Primeau."

"Who, on her return, will also go to Jarlkevo, to become Steward of the House, until Janck Jarlkevoso is old enough to hold the House himself." Dhulyn blew out a short breath.

"As for us, how settled do you want us to be? We're finally back on the road to Delmara after that little detour to earn some money from the Nisveans."

Dhulyn pressed her lips together and shifted in her saddle. Her back was sore, and the muscles in her belly and thighs were cramping.

"Separate beds tonight, my soul," she said, in as pleasant a voice as she could manage. "And *that* means more money spent."

"Ah, but look on the sunny side," Parno said. "Evil Mage destroyed, princes and princesses all where they want to be—and out of our hands, let me point out. As for us, we've got our horses, all our weapons, food for the journey, money for inns. What more could we ask for?"

Despite herself, Dhulyn found the corner of her mouth turning up. Still . . .

"Those Sun-burnt, Moon-drowned Nisveans never paid us."

Parno laughed. "There is one thing you haven't explained, my heart," he said. "It was Avylos who broke the Tribes, or so your Visions tell you . . ."

"But how is it that the women of the Espadryni—Marked Seers as we know them to have been—how is it that they did not See him, and stop it?"

"Exactly."

Dhulyn shook her head. "My mother did not seem surprised, or afraid. She acted as though she were putting into effect long-planned events."

"Do you think we'll ever know?"

Dhulyn put her heels to Bloodbone's sides. "I know we won't make the next inn if we stand about talking."